A Killing Frost

Also by Patricia Wynn

The Blue Satan Mystery Series:
  The Birth of Blue Satan
  The Spider's Touch
  The Motive from the Deed

The Parson's Pleasure

Sophie's Halloo

Lord Tom

Jack on the Box

Mistletoe and Mischief

The Bumblebroth

A Country Affair

The Christmas Spirit

A Pair of Rogues

Capturing Annie

A Killing Frost

Patricia Wynn

PEMBERLEY PRESS

CORONA DEL MAR

PEMBERLEY PRESS
P O Box 1027
Corona del Mar, CA 92625
www.pemberleypress.com

Cover design by Kat & Dog Studios
Cover and endsheet art by permission of Yale Center of British Art
   Unknown artist, formerly attributed to Jan Wyck, ca. 1645-1700
   Repository title: Frost Fair on the Thames, with Old London
   Bridge in the distance
   ca. 1685

Library of Congress Cataloging-in-Publication Data

Wynn, Patricia.
  A killing frost / Patricia Wynn.
      p. cm. -- (Blue Satan mystery series)
   Summary: "Historical mystery set in London in 1716, featuring
the detective duo, the highwayman Blue Satan and Mrs. Kean, with
action centered on the Frost Fair on the Thames"--Provided by pub-
lisher.
   ISBN 978-1-935421-01-6 (alk. paper)
   1. Brigands and robbers--Fiction. 2. Great Britain--History--
George I, 1714-1727--Fiction. 3. London (England)--History--18th
century--Fiction. I. Title.
   PS3573.Y6217K55 2011
   813'.54--dc22
                              2011005201

This book is dedicated to the memory of
my beloved sister

Polly Barnes Coleman

July 3, 1955 – May 17, 2010

Acknowledgements

I am grateful to many scholarly works, too numerous to name on this page, but the following have been especially helpful with this volume: *Ticket to Tyburn* by Kristine Hughes; *Diary of Mary Countess Cowper, Lady of the Bedchamber to the Princess of Wales, 1714–1720; Old and New London* by Walter Thornbury; The Survey of London, now available on the Web; *Social Life in the Reign of Queen Anne* by John Ashton; *Wits, Wenchers and Wantons* by E. J. Burford; *The Jacobite Risings in Britain 1689–1746* by Bruce Lenman; John Strype's 1720 edition of John Stow's *Survey of London & Westminster,* published on CD by MOTCO Enterprises Limited; and of course, *Early English Newspapers* on microfilm at the University of Texas Austin.

Thanks to the Yale Center of British Art for permission to use the image on the cover and the endsheet.

I would also like to thank my daughter Virginia Moore for her invaluable advice and support, my son-in-law Ryan for his enthusiastic prodding, and my husband Tom for allowing me to do the thing I love most.

And, finally, thanks to Marisa Young from Malice Domestic for naming a character central to the plot.

The verses in this book have been taken from *TRIVIA: or The Art of Walking the Streets of London,* by John Gay, which was first advertised for sale in the *Daily Courant* on January 26, 1716, the month in which this story opens.

HISTORICAL BACKGROUND

In 1688, King James II of England and Scotland, a Catholic, was overthrown by his daughter Mary and her husband William of Orange. The King fled to France with his queen and infant son, James, who later came to be known as the Old Pretender. For the next 60 years, both Englishmen and Scots would try to restore James's line to throne. These followers of James were the Jacobites.

William and Mary, the joint monarchs, were succeeded by Mary's sister Anne. Both queens had been raised as Protestants, but when King James took a Catholic as his second wife and raised his only legitimate son as a Catholic, he doomed the Stuart line. By the end of the seventeenth century, England and Scotland were firmly Protestant countries, but Oliver Cromwell's attempt to establish a parliamentary nation had failed. The English had no more taste for Puritanism forced on them by an army than they had had for absolute monarchy. After decades of religious strife, they wished to keep a peaceful balance between King and Parliament, and they feared a Catholic monarch would throw them back into the chaos they had recently escaped.

When Queen Anne's eighteen pregnancies ended with no living heir, Parliament passed the Act of Succession to exclude James Stuart from the throne. It specified that Sophia, Electress of Hanover, the granddaughter of James I and a Protestant, should inherit the Crown of what, by 1714, was Great Britain (England and Scotland having united in 1707). But Sophia died just before her cousin Anne, and the throne passed to her son, George of Hanover.

George assumed his throne in 1714, speaking no English and bringing with him an entourage of Germans, who regarded the English court as a golden opportunity to enrich themselves through bribes and the selling of influence. In this they were no different from other courtiers of the period, but in displacing the English aristocrats, they knocked their noses out of joint, brewing discontent with the new regime.

The establishment of the first political parties, the Tories and the Whigs, late in the seventeenth century, was a natural outgrowth of the conflicts of that era. The Tories supported the royal prerogative; the Whigs championed Parliament as the only true source of government. Naturally, it was the Whigs who courted George in Hanover before he came to England, as he was Parliament's choice. The Tories yearned for the legitimate line, for many believed it was ordained by God. It was this belief, plus the discontent of Catholics who'd been disenfranchised by the establishment of the Church of England, the Catholic Irish who'd supported James II, soldiers from the wars with France decomissioned with no pay, adventurers, younger sons, high churchmen and priests, and people who quite simply enjoyed intrigue, that supplied the Stuarts with their advocates.

In September, 1715, the Earl of Mar, convened the Highlanders and proclaimed James Stuart King of Scotland. Immediately, James's staunchest advocates among the English aristocracy, especially in the North, rallied to his cause. Conspirators in Oxford and the West Country were quickly put down, while attempts for James and his army in France to join the rebels were repeatedly thwarted by the vigilance of English spies. Under the Treaty of Utrecht, ending the War of Spanish Succession, France had agreed to prevent James Stuart from reaching England, had banished him to Lorraine, and had pledged not to supply any invasion undertaken in his cause.

When the Earl of Mar, instead of joining his forces with the English rebels, pulled back to await James's arrival, the English rebels were routed at Preston in Lancashire. Hundreds were imprisoned, and their aristocratic officers were marched to London in irons for trial.

The rebellion appeared to be defeated, but the "Fifteen," as it later came to be known, was not over yet.

O roving Muse, recal that wond'rous Year,
When Winter reign'd in bleak Britannia's *Air;*
When hoary Thames, *with frosted Oziers crown'd,*
Was three long Moons in icy Fetters bound.

The Waterman, forlorn along the Shore,
Pensive reclines upon his useless Oar,
Sees harness'd Steeds desert the stony Town;
And wander Roads unstable, not their own:
Wheels o'er the harden'd Waters smoothly glide,
And rase with whiten'd Tracks the slipp'ry Tide.
Here the fat Cook piles high the blazing Fire,
And scarce the Spit can turn the Steer entire.
Booths sudden hide the Thames, *long Streets appear,*
And num'rous Games proclaim the crouded Fair.

CHAPTER I

January, 1716

On the bank of the River Thames, just south of the tiny village of Lambeth between the Archbishop's Palace and the Manor of Vauxhall, stood a modest property, the secret residence of Gideon Fitzsimmons, the outlawed Viscount St. Mars. Within its wooden palings nestled a neat red-brick house, a barn, a brew house and stables, and a smattering of smaller outbuildings.

This winter morning, a full three hours before dawn, with no church bells near enough to hear and only his countryman's instincts to wake him, St. Mars's groom, Thomas Barnes, rousted himself from his bed in the stables. He put on a pair of thick woolen breeches and a woolen waistcoat over his knee-length shirt, then a pair of leather boots, and hurried to accomplish his work.

A peek at the house across the yard assured him that Katy was stirring. She would barely have slept, as excited about today as he was. For the past few weeks, as they had gone about their duties, tending to the master's horses and keeping his house, tales of the Frost Fair set up on the frozen Thames had tempted them. And, now, St. Mars had given them leave to go.

Tom pitched down hay for the three horses in his charge. Then he saddled Beau, once the favourite mount of St. Mars's father, the late

Earl of Hawkhurst. It was nearly a year, Tom realized, since he had taken the horse from the stable at Rotherham Abbey to rescue St. Mars from his gaolers. Today he had permission to use the big horse, which would have to be exercised in any case. In this inclement weather, with so much snow clogging the highways, he and Katy would never be able to reach London Bridge on foot.

The blacksmith in Lambeth had fashioned them two pairs of ice-creepers to help them walk upon the frozen river—flat strips of iron with spikes bent down at both ends. After bundling himself in a great-coat and woolen scarf, Tom sat on a wooden chest to put his creepers on, sliding them beneath the instep of his boots, and buckling them on with leather straps. As soon as Beau had finished eating, Tom led him out into the bitter cold and crossed the snow-covered yard, pleased to find how well the ice-creepers gripped.

He found Katy in the kitchen, placing extra faggots on the fire. On his entry, she looked up and gave him such a radiant smile that his pulse began to pound.

Fighting a grin so big it strained the muscles in his face, he said, "Best get a move on. Mustn't let Beau get cold."

Katy gave an eager nod and hastened to wrap herself in a woolen cloak and mittens.

"Better wear that scarf the master gave you. We'll be standing on the ice all day." He handed Katy the second pair of ice-creepers and waited, impatient to be off, while she sat to fasten them on.

The master would still be asleep upstairs. Katy had arranged for a local woman to cook and serve him his meals.

Tom had faithfully served St. Mars since he was in leading strings, and had remained with him after he had been accused of a terrible crime. Now, instead of overseeing the vast stables at Hawkhurst House in Piccadilly and Rotherham Abbey in Kent—two of the six estates St. Mars should have inherited from his father—Tom's duties consisted of tending to three horses, while acting as his master's valet, footman, and steward, and carrying out whatever other tasks St. Mars might give him. So far, these had ranged from purchasing a houseful of furniture at auction to helping St. Mars break into a barber-surgeon's shop. Katy, too, had her share of work, from cooking and keeping house for them all to making the master's disguises he wore when venturing into London. The time they had had free this past year had been scant, but now they would have a whole day to divert themselves.

Tom had promised Katy he would not let his worry over St. Mars spoil their outing, even though the master had seemed more restless of late, pacing his room like one of the great beasts in the Tower. It wasn't natural for a young gentleman to have nothing to do, especially a man as hell-bent on action as St. Mars. With no land to oversee, no game to hunt, no friends to meet at the coffee house or the gaming table, he had nothing with which to occupy his time. All he could do was brood over the recent rebellion and the captured rebel lords awaiting trial in the Tower.

Seeing that Katy was ready, Tom put these worrisome thoughts aside, and hustled her outside where Beau was tied. Great puffs of steam issued from the big horse's nostrils. He stood placidly while they mounted. Then, with Katy riding pillion, they took the King's highway to Lambeth, which curved northward along the river.

Tom kept Beau to a walk, letting him pick his own way through the snow. Beneath slippery layers of snow and ice, the road was pitted with deep waggon ruts, and he had no wish to lame his horse.

In the month of November, a brutal frost had descended upon London. With no respite from the cold in fifty days, the River Thames had frozen solid. The tides that carried in ships twice daily from all parts of the world had ceased flowing. The great seaworthy vessels that usually crowded the Custom House dock had escaped to warmer ports. The waterway that bustled daily with upwards of seven thousand boats and seventeen hundred barges, ferrying Londoners from Gravesend to Windsor, had stilled. Then, the snow had come, blanketing every surface in a thick layer of white, and muffling the sounds of life that remained.

The night was black, with no moon or stars to light their way. For days, thick clouds had obscured the sky. Still, the brightness of the snow cast its own sort of glow, revealing objects as darker shades of grey. To their left loomed indistinct structures where houses should be. Rounded mounds marked locations where farmers' carts had been abandoned in the fields. Leafless trees jabbed up like thick, ragged posts, and windmills made slow, ghostly revolutions in the air.

The village of Lambeth soon appeared, confounding their sight. Ice and snow blanketed every object from the graves in the churchyard to the rooftops of houses, which gleamed even in the dark. Mysterious shapes thrust up on both sides, things buried so deeply it would take an astrologer to divine what lay beneath the snow. The glow from the lamps hanging outside the Archbishop's Palace and St. Mary's Church reflected brightly off the white ground, but the light cast everything beyond its reach into deeper gloom.

Tom steered Beau to the west of the palace and let him find his way along Narrow Wall on a trail laid down by other horses. This earthen wall, built to protect the houses from floods, would take them the long way round, but by coming this way, they would avoid the treacherous ice sure to be hidden in Lambeth Marsh.

Along their left lay the small, mean houses of London's watermen, still unlit at this hour to save on candles. With no work now for upwards of seven weeks, the Thames watermen were desperate to feed their families. Behind their houses, Tom could see vague shadows in the snow, the hulls of their overturned boats. To his right in the spring would be acres of neat market gardens with here and there a farmer's house, but as black as the night was, he could make nothing out. The silence, where normally he would hear the snap of sails, the cries of watermen, and the clunk and swish of oars, was eerie. Then, a break appeared between two houses, and he caught his first glimpse of torches bobbing about on the Thames.

For the first time in more than thirty years, the river had frozen hard enough for Londoners to erect booths upon the ice. Vendors of all sorts had set up tents, for the Frost Fair belonged to no one—and to everyone. No royal charter had been required to set it up; no authority had the right to collect fees. Every day, as long as the ice held, revelers from London could make their way down to the river to enjoy the free treat. With river vessels grounded, only coaches and chairmen could carry passengers across the ice, but with the vast amount of snow that had fallen, few carriages were in use. For days, the streets of London had been nearly impassable. Drays and sleds pulled by horses made deliveries to the booths stretched across the ice, and any waterman lucky enough to find work would be hawking food or ale from one of the stands.

As Tom and Katy rounded the river bend, a vista opened up and Katy saw what Tom already had glimpsed. She gasped at the sight of the torches, twinkling like fairy fires, as vendors, holding their flames aloft, bustled about to open their tents. The dancing lights spread from Temple Stairs eastward almost as far as they could see. In her excitement, Katy gave Tom's waist a squeeze, making him chuckle aloud. Startled by the unfamiliar noise, Beau tossed his head, so Tom composed himself before turning into the alley that led to Bull Stairs.

He had arranged to leave Beau with the proprietor of the Bull Tavern, for no other livery stood within reach. At this early hour, the tavern was already humming with custom. They pulled up outside, and a boy ran out to take Beau's reins. When they had dismounted and Tom had repeated his instructions for the horse's care twice, Katy, who had never taken her eyes off the lights, grabbed Tom's hand and gave an impatient tug. Nearly jerked off his feet, he let her pull him down the river bank to the stairs.

Within a few moments, they were both standing on the ice, and Tom was grateful for the foresight that had made him purchase the ice-creepers. Though walking on them was awkward, he could feel the spikes' firm grip. Beneath his boots the surface of the ice was rough from freezing in high wind. The morning was still so dark, he could barely see to put one foot in front of the other. The vendors' torches cast small circles of light near the entrances to the tents, but everything beyond stood in black, the shadows made darker by the contrasting light.

Ahead lay the first row of tents, their pointed outlines faintly visible in the glow from the lanterns hanging in front. Some vendors had hung banners from poles to announce their trade, but there was not yet light enough to read them. As Tom and Katy headed towards Temple Stairs, through the dark they saw the shadowy figures of people moving between the canvas tents. The booths had been set up in two rows, extending south from the bottom of Temple Stairs for forty or fifty yards across the ice before turning to run parallel to the opposite bank to end at London Bridge.

The winter sun might be slow to rise, but money could be exchanged even in the dark. The cries of men and women hawking clothes, plate and earthenware, oranges, meat and brandy, tobacco, and dozens of other goods came drifting to them through the bitter wintry air.

By the time Tom and Katy had reached the farthest of the stalls, the difficult walk had rendered them breathless. They paused to rest and to peer at the banners dangling out from the tents, which gave the makeshift village the look of a London street with its wooden signs. From here, the lanterns flickered across the signs, rendering them almost readable. From somewhere in front, Tom heard a voice crying, "Pancakes!" and his stomach gave a growl. He grabbed Katy's arm and steered her firmly towards the call. But before they could reach the pancake booth, another hawker's cry brought Tom skidding to a halt.

"Strange and bloody news! Printed right 'ere on the ice! Read 'ow the fearsome 'ighwayman Blue Satan chased a foul murderer to 'is death!"

Katy gave a startled cry. Tom hushed her with a squeeze of his hand. He drew her arm through his, before turning in the direction of the chapman's voice.

The sky above their heads was turning grey with the coming dawn. Though the morning was still dark, Tom's eyes had grown accustomed to the gloom. The printer's tent stood in the front row of booths. Tom could see the man, waving sheets of paper back and forth, his cries mingling with the distant voice of an ancient ballad singer selling sheets of music. A steady thump from inside the tent told Tom that the printer was operating the press.

"How much for the chapbook?" Tom asked the old man.

"Naught but a threepenny bit. And, see 'ere, 'ow it's marked, 'Printed on the Thames the Year of Our Lord 1716.' Ye'll not find another'un like it. Thank yer, master," he said, as Tom handed him a coin. "Could I interest yer in the Comical Life and Tragical Death of the Old Woman that was 'ang'd for Drowning 'erself in Ratcliffe 'igh-Way?"

Tom snorted in refusal, while pocketing the octavo he'd purchased. St. Mars would want to see the tale written about him. It was not yet light enough to read the chapbook, but Tom intended to read it, too. It was bad enough that St. Mars had lost all his property and his rights when accused of a crime he had not committed. Now, that people believed a highwayman by the name of Blue Satan was loose in London, terrorizing folk and chasing murderers to their deaths, a second reward had been placed on his young, reckless head.

Tom's stomach gave a louder growl.

"Come along now." Katy had sensed the change in his mood. "You'll feel better once you've got some of those pancakes in you."

His humour had surely not been helped by hunger, so Tom let her lead him to the pancake booth. Inside, they located a bench where they could sit and down coffee and pancakes, while listening to music issuing from another tent.

Tom ate greedily, shoveling down more than a dozen cakes, before a shriek of horror jerked him to his feet. Screams of fright broke over the ice, bringing everything to a halt.

Telling Katy to stay where she was, Tom joined the sudden rush, as people threw off their torpor to fly out of the stall. A commotion was coming from behind this row of booths, to Tom's left near Temple Stairs. On either side, people spewed out of tents, heading for the sounds. Tom was knocked from behind as someone slipped and fell on the ice. The light was better now, the sky a paler shade of grey. The contrasting patches of light and shadow had resolved into shapes. Soon colours would be visible, but the light was bright enough for Tom to see the alarm on people's faces.

A frightening idea gave him pause—maybe the ice had split. Someone might have fallen into the icy water. He thought of Katy left behind alone, but the river beneath his feet felt as solid as before. He took careful steps forward to see what the hubbub was about.

In the second row of tents a wooden hut had been built as a kind of open shelter, in case a group of dignitaries wished to witness one of the races held upon the ice. Behind this structure, which should have stood empty last night, a cluster of onlookers stood gaping and cringing in horror at something just out of his sight.

As Tom craned his neck to see past them, a ghastly image appeared. A man's dead body was leaning against the wooden wall. The corpse must have been placed there after it had frozen, for it was tipped against the wall like a plank. As the glow of dawn illuminated the scene, the strong lines of the corpse's face emerged, etched harshly in death. The light increased, faster now. The agony in the man's expression became visible, making the onlookers gasp. Death had turned the man's flesh blue and stretched it mercilessly over his bones, but some other, more diabolical agent had twisted the muscles of his face into a grotesque mask. Now, the outline of his body was fully revealed. His back was painfully arched like a drawn bow, his hands curled into claws. Then, as Tom stared, mesmerized, something even more alarming emerged in the dawn as the colours of his garments were revealed.

The man was dressed in a coronation suit, his twisted shoulders enveloped in a red velvet robe with a white miniver cape. A sword was belted awkwardly at his hip. His shaven head was topped by a long periwig, which sat it askew, and crowned by a baron's coronet. A sense of horror crept down Tom's spine. His knees began to shake before he forced his gaze away.

A cry was set up to alert the watch, but when someone would have run to fetch a watchman, it was discovered there was no legal authority on the ice. No city ward had jurisdiction over the middle of the Thames. As men huddled in confusion to debate which body to contact, the Thames River Authority or the Mayor himself, Tom turned away from the scene. He could do nothing useful, and it would not help St. Mars for his groom to be questioned about a murder. Still shivering from what he had witnessed, he made his way through the crowd to collect Katy at the pancake stall.

The pancakes he had so recently eaten churned miserably in his stomach. He was not sure he could forget the image of the corpse in the coronation suit long enough to enjoy the fair—not without a strong quart of beer, at least. Something about it, besides the bizarre appearance of the man's clothes, had rattled him. It was a notion that something about that blue, tortured face looked familiar.

ॐ

Back in his house, Tom's master, Gideon Fitzsimmons, the outlaw

Viscount St. Mars, was awakened by an unfamiliar noise inside his bedchamber. He raised himself on one elbow and peered out of the bed curtains to find a strange young woman making up his fire. Then he recalled that he had given Tom and Katy leave to be gone all day, and he suppressed a sigh. He hauled himself to a sitting position to begin what promised to be a long, empty day.

His sudden movement startled the girl. Turning abruptly, she dropped the shovel she'd been using to clean out the hearth. It hit the tiles with a clang, spilling ashes on the tiles, and a cry of dismay escaped her. She winced, then hastened to her feet to curtsy. Two frightened eyes stared back at Gideon from beneath a plain cloth cap. "Oh, pardon, sir! Mistress said as I wasn't to wake you."

"You didn't." Gideon stretched and gave a yawn. "Or if you did, it doesn't matter. I usually rise at this hour. I won't eat you, you know," he added, smiling, as she stayed frozen, as if amazed he could speak.

"No, sir. 'Course not, sir." She bobbed another curtsy. "Would you be wantin' me to go on with yer fire?"

"Indeed I would. It's as cold as a tomb in here. You must be half-frozen yourself."

This won him a shy look. "Oh, no, sir! It was ever so warm in the kitchen when I come in."

"I'm pleased to hear it. Please do go about your work, and don't allow me to disturb you— Margaret, is it? I believe that's what Katy said your name was. As soon as you've finished with the fire, I could take my morning chocolate."

"Yes, sir!"

Another bob, another frightened look, perhaps in contemplation of her next task, and she turned back to the faggots she had stacked upon his hearth. A few embers still burned in the grate. Katy must have replenished the fire herself once during the night. With a few careful puffs from the bellows, the new wood soon caught fire, and a healthy flame reached up the chimney.

Within a short while—much sooner than he had expected, given the inauspicious start—Gideon was sitting up in bed, propped against his satin-covered pillows and warmed by his coverlets, sipping the chocolate Margaret had brought him. When he had finished his breakfast, he kicked off the covers, gave the fire in the grate a few good pokes, and dressed before the fresh burst of heat could ebb. He donned a clean linen shirt and drawers, a thick pair of leather breeches, and a long wool waistcoat and knee-length coat, before settling a brown tie wig on his head. In the meagre morning light he checked in his looking glass to make sure that none of his long yellow hair showed beneath. Then, pulling on a stout pair of boots, a warm felt hat, a pair of riding gloves, and a fur-lined cloak with a high collar and one shoulder cape, he walked down the stairs and outside.

The cold air stung his eyes and burned the tip of his nose. He hunched his shoulders, shuddering as the wind sliced a trail between his shoulder blades. As he set off across the yard, the deep snow crunched beneath his boots. Pausing just a moment, he glanced across the Thames, at the opposite bank. Today his view was of a white palette of snow-covered fields with Peterborough House, the home of his father's friend, looking small in the distance. The horse ferry, which would usually be plying the river from just below the earl's house across to Lambeth Palace, was iced in on the frozen Millbank.

Gideon had taken this house in Surrey to be near to London, but far enough from his family's house in Piccadilly to avoid being recognized by anyone who might choose to reap the reward the Crown had placed upon his head. Here, in the country south of Lambeth, no one knew him as the Viscount St. Mars. To the neighbours he was Mr. Mavors, an eccentric gentleman who dressed in unpredictable ways. They would be shocked to discover that his disguises concealed not only an accused murderer, but also the infamous highwayman Blue Satan.

The winter sun had still not broken over the horizon when Gideon cracked the stable door and slipped inside. As he lit the lantern Tom had left hanging by the door, he was greeted by the rustling sounds of his horses. Looby, the aptly-named gelding, stretched out his long bay neck and shook it like a wet dog, while Penny, his coppery Arabian prize, emitted a series of snorts, jerking her head and stomping, as if indignant that anyone had had the effrontery to set foot inside her domain.

Gideon paused at Looby's stall to offer him a handful of oats, which the horse ate after taking one suspicious sniff. He petted the big gelding's neck and paid him fulsome compliments until Penny became jealous enough to reach her head over the stall door and butt him with her nose. Then, as if he had not purposely teased her, Gideon greeted her with an air of surprise and let her nuzzle at his pockets for the oats he had hidden. As she settled into a state of complaisance, he touched his forehead to hers and scratched behind her ears.

For just a moment he basked in the affection of this sensitive creature. More than anyone else she seemed to understand the perturbation that made it hard for him to sleep at night, but he knew this was just fancy on his part. Nervousness had simply been bred into her bones. It had nothing to do with the question that tormented him. What was he to do with himself now that he had no prospect of regaining his rights?

If he were in France, he could live openly on his own estate, safe from the law. As the *Vicomte de St. Mars,* he would be welcomed at the French court at Versailles or the Palace of Saint Germain-en-Laye, where the followers of James Stuart conspired to restore him to his throne. He could choose to spend his days hunting stag, flying his birds of prey, or overseeing his land. But the last time Gideon had crossed the Channel, he had nearly been discovered by a boarding party searching every vessel for the Pretender. It would be too dangerous to cross it again until the rebellion was over and the freedom of the seas restored. Even if he wished to risk it, no ships could sail now when every northern harbour was locked with ice. He was trapped in England, where on any day a passerby might recognize him and turn him in to claim a reward.

A gust slammed into the stable door and Penny jumped, disrupting their contact. The morning courtesies were over.

Gideon saddled his horse and led her outdoors. Lately, he had formed the habit of riding to Lambeth Butts to read the newssheets at the tavern across from the Dutch pottery. He could always wait for Tom to fetch the papers from the King's Head, but there was nothing else Gideon could do to break the monotony of his current existence, except exercise his horses. The longer nights of winter had been particularly tedious, except that wrapping his face against the cold made it easier to walk about without fear of being identified.

Before heading for the tavern, he rode Penny up and down the snow-covered lanes bordering the market gardens of Lambeth, taking care not to let her slip. Her high spirits made it hard to rein her in, but eventually even she grew tired of fighting the cold, and did not complain when an hour later he stabled her at the White Hart. He paid the ostlers well to see to her comfort, but they were so awed by the privilege of handling such a magnificent mare, he sometimes doubted the need to pay.

In the tavern, seated with his small beer amidst the potters and merchants smoking their long clay pipes, Gideon searched the papers for news. For a few weeks, he had believed the worst news of the rebellion in the North had already reached him. In December, he had watched as the Northumbrian rebels, some his father's friends, had been marched in ignominy to prisons in London. They would be tried in Westminster Hall for treason. The scaffolding for the trial had already been built. Their only chance of a reprieve would be if King George showed them extraordinary mercy. Hundreds of other rebels had been captured and taken to Lancaster, where they had been packed in a room like sheep waiting for slaughter. The rebellion had seemed to be over, even if the Earl of Mar still led a band of Highlanders in Scotland.

Today, Gideon saw that the rumour he had heard and not believed was true. The newssheets reported that on Monday King George had gone before the House of Peers to state that he had grounds to believe the Pretender James Stuart had landed in Scotland.

Monday, also, was the day the rebel lords had been impeached for high treason. James Earl of Derwentwater, William Lord Widdrington, William Earl of Nithsdale, George Earl of Winton, Robert Earl of Carnwath, William Viscount Kenmure, and William Lord Nairn had been brought from the Tower to the House of Commons where the articles against them had been read. The rebellion had been characterized as an attempt to overthrow the Protestant Succession and blamed on Papacy.

Some of the accused lords were Papists, it was true, but among them, also, were devout Protestants. Their fight was not over Papacy, but about the true and lawful succession.

But no matter. They would be tried as villains. And, if James were truly come from France, King George could not afford to be merciful.

The hopes of the Jacobites would be revived, just when the best and most loyal of James's English followers awaited trial. King George would send additional troops into Scotland to capture James. With the Swiss and Dutch soldiers he had summoned from the Continent, the Scots would stand no chance of defeating the Crown's forces. By now, in the dead of winter, there would be nothing for the men to eat, no provisions. And little aid had arrived from France. George's troops were well supplied from the South. The rebellion was doomed to failure, but how many more men would lose their lives before it came to an end?

For a few months Gideon's hopes of recovering his title had rested with the Pretender's cause, but experience had quickly taught him how misguided those hopes were.

Shaking off the gloom the news had brought him, his gaze moved quickly down the advertisements posted in the *Daily Courant*. Few would be of interest. It was unlikely that he would attend the theatre, or require the *Infallible Cure for the Stone and Gravel,* much less the *Vivifying Drops for Barrenness in Women and Imbecility in Men*—at least, he devoutly hoped not.

But there was one announcement he did soon expect to see.

His cousin Harrowby Fitzsimmons, whom Parliament had named Earl of Hawkhurst when declaring Gideon outlaw, was soon to be blessed with an heir. Gideon's friend, Hester Kean, who was both cousin and lady-in-waiting to Isabella, Lady Hawkhurst, had informed him that Isabella was carrying a child. According to Mrs. Kean, the child was to be born in January, so every day Gideon expected to see the notice that he had been displaced even further by the birth of a son.

This news had delivered yet another blow in a year of troubles a man born to such privilege could never have foreseen. It had pained Mrs. Kean to deliver it, too. He had tried for her sake to hide the despair it had caused him, for she was his only friend, his confidante, and he wanted to spare her any heartache on his account.

Today, he did not find the name Hawkhurst among the announcements, but his heart quickened as his eyes were caught by a cryptic message which could only be meant for him.

"If a Gentleman named Mavors, residing near the Village of Smarden, will come to the Bear Tavern, Bear Lane, near Leicester Fields, Tuesday next, at 10 in the Evening, he will learn something to his Advantage."

Once before, Gideon had received a similar message, addressed to the alias he had used to purchase his house on the Thames. Smarden was the village in Kent where he had received mail after fleeing the authorities and finding shelter in a hedge-inn deep in the Weald.

This message could only be from the Duke of Bournemouth, a one-time adversary who, nevertheless, had been useful to him on that occasion. At one time they had been rivals for the favours of Isabella Mayfield, but since her marriage to Gideon's cousin Harrowby, Gideon's illusions about her had been shattered. The Duke, whose intentions had never been honourable, had already seen past her beauty to the shallowness of her soul. But, although Gideon's yearning for her had long since ceased, he had not forgotten the sting of the Duke's scorn for a younger man who fancied himself in love. No encounter with his Grace of Bournemouth was likely to be pleasant, yet Gideon felt eager at the thought of a meeting. At least, he would have something to do besides waiting for the next day's news to arrive.

With King George's blessing, the Duke had married a German princess. He was certain to be a welcome figure at Court. Once upon a time, however, he had secretly flirted with James Stuart's cause. Gideon was one of the only men in possession of this secret, and he had documents to prove it—a list of Jacobites his father had compiled. Gideon had kept the list in the event any of the gentlemen named there sought to excuse themselves by smearing his father's name. The Duke had asked him to burn the papers or hand them over. Perhaps his reason for this meeting was merely to repeat that request. But with James Stuart in Scotland, and the Northumberland rebels in prison, Gideon had a feeling that something more urgent was involved.

In an eager stride he left the tavern and trudged back through the snow to the White Hart to collect his horse. Too engrossed in his thoughts to be cautious, he burst into the stables, and halted in mid-step when he spied two figures standing at the door to Penny's stall.

They both looked up. One was the young hostler he paid to care for his horse. The other was a stranger—and by his looks, a gentleman. He had been leaning over the stall door, studying Penny, but now he straightened and looked Gideon over from head to toe.

"'Ere 'e is, sir," the ostler said, "the gen'leman wot owns 'er."

"Does he, indeed?" The man's eyes narrowed in suspicion. "Why, this is a very fine piece of horseflesh you have here, sir. May I inquire where you bought her?"

Gideon cursed himself for his stupidity. He should never have left Penny in a place where a traveller might see her and wonder how such a splendid horse had found its way into a stable at a common inn. If he had questioned the wisdom of leaving her exposed, however, he would have dismissed the concern with the thought that no one should be travelling the Hampshire road in such deep snow.

Today he had not worn much of a disguise. Fighting an urge to feel if his wig completely covered his fair hair, he strove to calm a quickened pulse. Thinking quickly, he said, "She was a gift from my father, sir, but if you are thinking of making me an offer for her, she is not for sale." He tried to speak with nonchalance, but the muscles in his jaw felt stiff and his words sounded clipped.

The stranger continued to stare, his expression full of mistrust. "Oh, not I, sir. Why, a horse like this must be worth several hundred pounds! I doubt many gentlemen of my acquaintance could afford her."

Gideon judged it best not to respond to this statement, the purpose of which was clearly to elicit information. He nodded pleasantly, and begging the gentleman's pardon, edged past him into Penny's stall. Taking the hint, the hostler hurried to saddle her, and, fortunately, she put up little resistance. Her outing this morning must have tired her, and Gideon had cut short his normal visit to the tavern. All she did, therefore, was toss her head a few times and roll her eyes so the whites showed. Gideon held the noseband of her bridle to keep her still while the boy hastened with his work.

"And do you live hereabouts?" The man was not so easily fobbed off.

Gideon turned a haughty gaze upon him, his noble instincts

roused. "I often pass through, though what business that is of yours I fail to see."

This strategy, though uncalculated, succeeded where a friendlier response might have failed. Faced with hauteur—when his suspicions, if justified, should have provoked fear or guilt—the man began to doubt the notion that had given rise to them. In his uncertain expression, Gideon could see him labouring to revise the scenario he had imagined—undoubtedly one involving a stolen horse. Now he must be wondering if Gideon could be a young nobleman on his way home, or one with a reason, salacious or otherwise, for visiting the White Hart.

Not giving him time to reconsider, Gideon led Penny past him, the hostler running ahead to open the stable door.

Out in the yard, the boy held Penny's head while Gideon mounted. Then, after receiving his usual coin, he tipped his hat to him. Gideon did not turn to see if the stranger still watched him, but he had the unpleasant feeling that the man's eyes were boring into his back long after he had turned out of sight of the White Hart.

Ah, Mulciber! Recall thy nuptial Vows,
Think on the Graces of thy Paphian Spouse,
Think how her Eyes dart inexhausted Charms,
And canst thou leave her Bed for Patty's Arms?

CHAPTER II

In Hawkhurst House in Piccadilly, the London residence of the Earl of Hawkhurst, the tension was close to snapping. For the past month, Isabella, Lady Hawkhurst, had been forced to withdraw from society in anticipation of the birth of the heir. Her mother, Mrs. Mayfield, had insisted on coming from her son's estate in the North to be a comfort to her favourite child, but for two ladies whose every pleasure was derived from Court, isolation had proven to be an intolerable strain. For the past fortnight, at least, they had been at each other's throats, with only the occasional guest to alleviate their boredom. Isabella, who did not enjoy female company, had no choice but to welcome it or suffer her mother's impatient tongue, which usually was directed at her cousin Hester. The gentlemen who habitually flitted in and out of Isabella's chambers, attending her levee and watching while she performed her toilette, could hardly flirt with a lady so big with child she could not decently receive them.

And her condition had led to another change. The doctor's express prohibition of sex had resulted in her husband Harrowby's taking a mistress.

Isabella had accepted the news philosophically when it was relayed to her by Madame Schultz, one of the Hanover ladies of obscure rank.

The Prince of Wales, with generous condescension, often sent Madame Schultz to Hawkhurst House to bear Isabella company.

Today, she had come with Lady Cowper, lady-in-waiting to the Princess of Wales, to inquire after Isabella's health. The tea table had been set up near the fire in the private closet next to Isabella's bedchamber, and the ladies sat around it in high-backed cane chairs. According to rule, it was Isabella's place to make the tea, but not feeling up to the exertion, she had asked Hester to do the honours. A new silver teapot had replaced Hester's favourite, a white porcelain pot with an Imari design, imported from China, its silver mounts added in London.

In spite of Isabella's condition, Madame Schultz reverted to the subject of Lord Hawkhurst's mistress. It was not to be expected that an earl with Harrowby's vast estates would deny himself the pleasures of the flesh when so many tempting creatures offered themselves. Nevertheless, as Hester unlocked the canister and mixed the tea for the pot, Madame Schultz expounded on the evils of such women.

"I do not understand vhy the English ladies tolerate these mistresses," she said, in a heavy German accent. "In Hanover, ve are not accustomed to such indecency in our men. Consideration of one's vife is as important as her honour."

"Well, for my part," Isabella retorted, before stuffing a cake into her mouth, "I see no reason to begrudge Harrowby his amusements, as long as he does not begrudge me mine."

Madame Schultz emitted a scandalized squeak. "My dear lady, if you are not careful, you vill do great harm to your reputation!"

"Pooh!" Isabella had grown tired of Madame Schultz's preaching. The German lady was shocked by the immodesty in English plays and manners, and since she had become something of a fixture at Hawkhurst House, her daily conversation had dwelt on the negative aspects of the English character. Isabella, whose sole object in life was to be entertained, did not appreciate the criticism.

A footman waited at Hester's elbow with the kettle of hot water. She gestured for him to pour it and waited for the tea to steep, while he returned the kettle to a nearby trivet.

"But I assure you," Madame Shultz continued. "Vhy, even Madame Kielmansegge has suffered from such gossip. Only last month, the Prince has spread the vorst tales of her. He said she has intrigued vith all the gentlemen of Hanover, and as a result she said that her acquaintance have abandoned her."

Since Madame Kielmansegge was rumoured to be both the King's half-sister and his mistress, Hester reflected that being suspected of having an affair with every gentleman in Hanover could not be supposed to do her much harm. As the tea was ready now, she poured some for each lady in a delicate porcelain cup, and waited for the footman to hand them to the guests before pouring one for herself.

Lady Cowper took a careful sip from her dish. Then, as soon as the footman had been dismissed, she set the dish down and said firmly, "She complained to the Princess about it, but her Highness assured her that it was not her husband's custom to speak of ladies in that manner. Someone else must have invented the story."

"What did Madame Kielmansegge say to that?" Mrs. Mayfield jumped at the bit of Court gossip like a trout leaping at a fly.

Lady Cowper glanced hesitantly at the ladies encircling the table. After a pregnant moment, she whispered, "Well, I shall tell you, but you must promise not to repeat it." Her expression turned suspiciously bland. "Madame Kielmansegge swore that it was so and pleaded with the Princess to put an end to the story. And to prove her innocence, she showed her Highness a statement Herr Kielmansegge had written, certifying in all the due forms that she has always been a faithful wife to him and that he has no cause to suspect her honour."

The ladies about the table were struck speechless. As Hester caught the twinkle in Lady Cowper's eye, she smiled, but Mrs. Mayfield drew herself up in indignation, "Well! I hope her Highness does not expect English husbands to produce a like certificate!"

"I would not fear it." Lady Cowper said wryly. "I believe it is the first certificate of the kind that ever was given."

Throughout this story, Isabella had been unusually quiet, but of a sudden a sharp cry made them turn their heads her way.

Mrs. Mayfield exclaimed, "What is it, my love?"

Hester took one look at her cousin's face and sprang to her side, as Isabella wailed, "Oh, Hester, my belly hurts!"

✆

At home from the fair that night, Katy busied herself making their supper, while Tom climbed the stairs in search of his master. Though he had managed to forget about the corpse long enough to enjoy the sights, the memory of that twisted blue face still disturbed him.

He was surprised to find St. Mars bent over his writing table, his head propped on one hand and his hawk-like features intent upon the papers he had discovered hidden behind a wall at Rotherham Abbey. This was the first time Tom had seen him reading the papers since he had uncovered his father's killer. And since one sheet contained a list of gentlemen who had contemplated treason against King George, Tom could think of no healthy reason to read it.

St. Mars looked up, and something in his smile put Tom on alert. Something had occurred to distract his young master from the inaction that had depressed him of late. And, as Tom knew well, nothing that any reasonable man would call safe could have done that.

"So, here you are." St. Mars leaned back in his chair and laced his fingers atop his head. "How was the fair?"

"It was just that good, my lord. Katy and me, we thank you for letting us go."

"Did you play at nine pins?"

"We did that, my lord." And what fun that had been, Tom thought, diverted by the recollection. It had been a challenge even though the ice in front of the pins had been scraped as level as possible. Katy had never played the game before, but she had quickly picked up the knack and he had enjoyed watching the delight on her face.

"What else did you get up to?"

Recalled from his wandering, Tom remembered the octavo he'd purchased and dug it from his coat pocket. "I knew you'd want to see this, my lord."

St. Mars took the chapbook written about Blue Satan, and his brow contracted. He looked vexed, but after reading a few pages, he chuckled. "Well, it's clear that Mrs. Kean's brother wastes no time when there's a penny to be made. Perhaps he'll turn out to be a greater success than she expects." He raised his glance. "Did you see any hint of trouble?"

The trouble he referred to would be from Jacobites. Early that morning, Tom had heard a Jacobite ditty or two before the singer had been hushed, but once the sun had come out, no one had dared to utter a treasonous word.

Tom told him about the frozen corpse and watched St. Mars's grin disappear as he leaned forward slowly to rest his elbows on his knees. When Tom had finished describing the way it had been dressed, St. Mars asked, "You say you may have known him?"

Tom reached up to scratch an itch behind his right ear and shrugged. "I couldn't say truly, my lord. Just thought he looked familiar, that's all."

St. Mars seemed relieved. "Well, if you do remember where you saw him, be sure to tell me. It is a queer business. Why anyone would be wearing coronation robes is more than I can fathom, unless he was involved in some strange, macabre rite." He mused for a second, then said, "Well, it has nothing to do with us, so I won't plague myself with it. And neither should you."

He smiled mischievously. "When are these nuptials I've been hearing about supposed to take place?"

Caught off guard, Tom could not suppress his blush. "We thought we'd ask the vicar to read the banns the first time this Sunday, my lord."

"So in a few weeks I'll be able to call you 'Tom, the married man?'"

Tom replied with a nod, but a grin tugged at his lips. He could hardly believe it himself. And he would not believe it, until the vicar had proclaimed Katy his wife.

"We'd be that proud to have you stand up with us, my lord. And if you think she'd come, we'd be pleased to have Mrs. Kean as witness, too."

He was astonished to see a touch of red creep up his master's neck. He had never disconcerted his lord before. His request had taken the young gentleman by surprise—it was easy to see he was gratified—but it had been the mention of Mrs. Kean that had raised the colour in his cheeks.

So, that was the way the wind was blowing, Tom thought.

"I would be honoured to do it, and if you like I shall ask Mrs. Kean if she will. It is not a simple matter for her to escape Hawkhurst House, but I expect she will be pleased."

Then something occurred to him and he frowned. "Wait . . . would the church you spoke of be St. Mary-at-Lambeth?"

Tom nodded, not liking the look on his master's face.

St. Mars shook his head with regret. "I cannot risk being seen by anyone there. A cleric on the Archbishop's staff might know me, and, if one does, he may be too clever to be fooled by a disguise." He thought for a moment, then asked, "Would it matter if you and Katy were married somewhere else?"

"It don't much matter to me," Tom said, before an alarming notion entered his head. "As long as you're not talkin' about the Fleet!" The prison was notorious for the cheap weddings performed in the dozens of marriage-houses in its vicinity, many of them illicit.

St. Mars broke into a laugh. "I would never suggest anything that drastic. But what if we obtained a special license to let you marry outside the parish? There's a church at Newington Butts, another St. Mary's I think. It's a bit farther than Lambeth, but no one would know me there. Why don't you see if you can rouse the parson there?"

"But what should I tell 'im? What reason can I give for not bein' wed in the parish church?"

St. Mars gave him an uncomprehending look. "What business is it of his?" He returned his attention to his papers. "In any event, it is fortunate that the wedding is not to be too soon, for I shall need you to accompany me into town."

Tom felt a familiar lurch inside his stomach. "My lord?"

"Yes . . . it appears our old friend the Duke of Bournemouth has developed a sudden urge to speak to me."

✆

At midnight, Hester rubbed her weary eyes and agreed to the midwife's suggestion that she take advantage of the respite to find some sustenance. Isabella's panicked cries had long since eased to moans, and now, seated in the birthing chair and propped up by a voluminous bolster, she even slept between the spasms. Both the doctor and the midwife had assured Hester that her cousin's confinement was proceeding exceedingly well. At first, Isabella's shrieks had been so terrible that Hester had feared for her life, but after the midwife's repeated soothing, her cousin's terror had abated and the absence of it had seemed to mitigate the labour pains.

Isabella had not been willing to release Hester's hand, however, finding her voice and sympathetic manner preferable to her mother's more strident encouragement or the presence of her friends. Fortunately, after proclaiming herself much too affected by her daughter's suffering to remain in the chamber, Mrs. Mayfield had left the others and gone downstairs to keep Isabella's husband Harrowby company while he awaited the birth of his heir.

Hester wished the gossips, the ladies who had been invited to witness the birth, would take their leave, too. Neither one was here out of a particular fondness for Isabella, or hers for them. Even Hester, who tried not to harbour superstitions, could not believe their presence would be conducive to the health of the child. Madame Schultz had been invited to stay out of fear of offending the Prince of Wales, and Lady Tatham had been called at Harrowby's express wish. They sat on either side of Isabella, exchanging desultory comments, offering unhelpful remarks, and complaining of this or that, while the midwife and two maids had to work around them, heating water, changing and rinsing pieces of linen, and hanging them before the fire to dry. Now, as much as she herself would like to be free of their company, out of consideration for Isabella, she invited the two ladies to accompany her out, and after a weak show of reluctance to leave their friend, they acquiesced.

Walking on tip-toe, Hester led them through Isabella's suite of rooms by the light of a single candle. In the antechamber she stumbled over a dozing footman, who leapt up from the floor to ask if he could bring her refreshments in the saloon. The housekeeper, Mrs. Dixon, had left him instructions to offer Hester the plate she had been keeping warm in the kitchen.

The worst of Hester's hunger pangs had vanished hours ago when she had been trapped at Isabella's side, but she gratefully accepted, aware that it could be several hours before she had another chance to eat. She asked him to bring a light supper for the other ladies, too, before leading them onward.

In the grand saloon overlooking the forecourt, she found Harrowby and Mrs. Mayfield, sitting in cushioned armchairs before a great fire. Facing them was another of the Princess's ladies, Lady Chelmsford, reserved and kind but lately burdened with an air of anxiety, due to the fact that her first cousin had been captured with the Northumbrian rebels and was waiting to be tried. Hester suspected that the countess was here at the behest of his Highness, too, since Isabella and she were scarcely more than acquaintances.

Harrowby caught sight of Hester and leapt unsteadily to his feet. "Mrs. Kean! What news?"

"Nothing yet, my lord," she responded with a sympathetic smile. He had obviously been drinking heavily, but at least he showed concern for his wife.

"Well, sit down, sit down," he said peevishly, collapsing again onto his chair. Spots of brandy stained his indigo waistcoat, and a clocked silk stocking had escaped its garter. He scratched roughly at his shoulder-length peruke, which sorely needed combing. "You can have a bite of supper and answer these ladies' questions for I'm sure I cannot."

Hester and the two ladies who had accompanied her made their curtsies to Lady Chelmsford, before joining the group about the fire. It must have been apparent to her that Madame Schultz had been at Hawkhurst House all afternoon, for both her light brown coiffure and her silk gown were sadly rumpled. Lady Tatham, a tall, thin, woman, the wife of one of Harrowby's friends, still preserved her neat appearance, but wore a habitually discontented mien.

Hester gave measured replies to Lady Chelmsford's polite inquiries after Isabella and Mrs. Mayfield's demands for details. She was no expert on birthing, so the only things she could report were that her cousin was resting between spasms and that on his last visit, her physician, Sir David Hamilton, had expressed satisfaction over her progress.

"Ah, yes." Harrowby spoke from deep in the red velvet chair. "That miserable quack said he'd be back—fairly soon, I should think."

"For shame, my lord!" Mrs. Mayfield leaned playfully towards him and tapped him on the wrist. "Calling him a quack, when you must know that the Countess employs him as her own physician!"

Harrowby turned a browbeaten face to Lady Chelmsford and tried to look apologetic. "No offense, of course. It's just that . . . that fellow said he shouldn't be surprised if the baby was here before midnight. And here the clock struck twelve almost an hour ago, and Mrs. Kean tells me that nothing's happened! Just seems to me he should know his business better, that's all."

Lady Chelmsford excused him with a tired smile. "I can assure you he does, my lord. Sir David took excellent care of her late Majesty, and I believe the Princess has decided to name him her personal physician, too. But, please, do not apologize. I perfectly understand your impatience. You are concerned for your lady, but first children often take twelve hours or more to appear."

"Not so long in Germany, I think," Madame Schultz pronounced. "But our physicians are more learned than yours. And our vomen are stronger."

"I cannot think what is keeping Sir Walter," Lady Tatham dropped into the irked silence that followed Madame Schultz's remark. "I came as soon as I received the news that your lady was confined, and I left him a message saying where I should be. I knew you would wish him here to amuse you, my lord. In these circumstances, there is nothing so welcome as a distraction." Her tone was both ingratiating and fretful.

Harrowby gave her a startled glance and with a strangely harried look quaffed his wine. "Er, quite," he choked out.

His aversion to her husband's proposed visit did not surprise Hester as much as the fact that Harrowby always received Sir Walter Tatham, when it was clear he took no pleasure in the baronet's company. But Mrs. Schultz had whispered to her once that it was Sir Walter who had introduced Harrowby's mistress to him. A well-known courtesan, someone had said.

"Mrs. Kean." Madame Schultz claimed Hester's attention. "Vhen you next speak to your mistress, you must tell her that she vill no longer vant the yellow silk saque that she was vearing today. She vill surely have tired of it, so I vill be happy to receive it."

Mrs. Mayfield huffed. "It is not for Hester to be giving my daughter's clothing away, so if you have any other requests of the sort, madam, you may address them to me! Besides, I doubt she will wish to part with it."

This was a rare occasion when Hester did not resent her aunt's interference. She had grown weary of deflecting Madame Schultz's frequent requests for gifts and doubted she could have responded politely, given her present state of exhaustion. Ignoring Mrs. Mayfield's reproof, Madame Schultz turned and addressed her next comment to Lady Chelmsford, but Hester was still relieved when three footmen entered with trays for her and their guests. She could then remove herself from the group, with the excuse that she must eat quickly and return to Isabella.

Just as she finished the refreshments, Sir David Hamilton was announced. He was an elderly man, with an unquestionable air of authority, having been personal physician to her late Majesty Queen Anne. He made the requisite bows and asked Hester how she had left his patient.

"Well . . . I believe. But I have been resting this past half-hour or so, and I am anxious to return to her. I shall accompany you, if I may."

"And take her mother with you," Harrowby ordered from his chair. "I thought we fetched her here so she could be with her daughter in her time of need," he ended with a bitter snort .

Raising her nose in the air, Mrs. Mayfield stood, contriving to convey to the assembled company that her son-in-law's utterances should not be taken seriously under the current stressful circumstances. She followed Hester and the doctor as they wove their way through a succession of rooms back to Isabella's apartment.

In the bedchamber, they discovered that Isabella's labour had rapidly progressed. The midwife, who sat on a low stool with her hands beneath Isabella's skirts said she could feel the baby's head. Hester's cousin alternated between piteous cries and shrieking at the top of her lungs.

"Now, now, my lady," in bracing Scottish tones, Dr. Hamilton scolded. "There's no need for you to carry on so. You're not the first of my patients to deliver a baby, you know, and I assure you that this is by far one of the easiest confinements I've ever seen."

If Isabella could have lunged for him in that moment, Hester thought, he would have borne the marks of her teeth forever. And, indeed, his words struck Hester as heartless. It was easy for him to disregard a torment he would never feel.

He turned to address Hester, apparently aware that he was unlikely to get a satisfactory response from her cousin. "Has her ladyship decided to feed the infant herself, as I've advised?"

Mrs. Mayfield answered, "No, she will not! My daughter is too important a person at Court to be stuck in the country nursing a child."

The doctor's brows snapped together in an angry frown. "But did I not explain to her ladyship how dangerous it is to put her children out to nurse? Did she fail to understand me?"

Mrs. Mayfield bridled. "I see no cause for concern. Why all my children were put out to nurse, and I never lost a one! The child's wet nurse is a girl from Lord Hawkhurst's own estate. She is here in the house if you wish to examine her."

Dr. Hamilton pursed his lips. "I do not know what mothers are about these days. They refuse to give up their pleasures in London to see to their own bairns." He sighed. "Let me see this girl, then. Perhaps I can put the fear of the Lord into her, if that's the way it is to be."

Hester would have taken him to see the wet nurse, Sarah, if in just that instant Isabella had not cried out for her. She stepped quickly to the bedside to hold Isabella's hand and instructed her maid to conduct the doctor to the young nurse's room. She hoped he would be pleased when he met Sarah, for she seemed an excellent choice. She was calm and placid and clean. Hester had tried to persuade Isabella to nurse the child herself. The stories of infants who died from neglect, disease, or worse, were too common to ignore, but Hester had not been at all surprised when Isabella had refused to take the doctor's advice.

One month of seclusion had been enough to make her despondent. And Harrowby's defection to a mistress would never be healed unless his wife fulfilled her wifely duties. These were, fortunately, never a burden for Isabella, whose appetite for sex was as great as any woman's.

That was another reason why nursing her infant had no appeal. Isabella had engaged in more than one flirtation since being married less than a year ago, and knowing her, Hester could not envision Isabella relinquishing her dalliances. Hester was more afraid that Harrowby's mistress would distract him to the point that her cousin would seek her own pleasure elsewhere.

The next half-hour was so intense that Mrs. Mayfield fled the bedchamber again. Hester, who suffered with every pang of her cousin's, burst into tears the moment the baby sprang from the womb. The midwife bathed the baby boy, cooing over what a fine heir Lord Hawkhurst had sired, while Isabella, exhausted and faint with relief, evinced no eagerness to see him. Briefly, Hester was permitted to take the baby into her arms. She examined his poor little head, shaped by his mother's labour, and his perfect tiny fingers and toes. Then the midwife took him from her, and, while he screamed in protest, she bound his head and legs in a tight swaddling cloth, and forced a foul smelling physick down his throat. Afterwards, she showed the child to Isabella who greeted him wanly.

The maid was sent to fetch Mrs. Mayfield, who came swooping in, grabbed the baby, and shrilled loudly over the fact that her daughter had produced a fine boy for her lord. She called him Rennington, the courtesy title he would be granted out of his father's many honours. It seemed a heavy name for such a little mite, but Hester recalled that it must at one time have been St. Mars's title. The viscounty of St. Mars was still his, having come to him through a French ancestor. She did not know when or how it had come into his possession, but a direct inheritance took precedence over any courtesy title granted by a father.

As soon as little George began to howl, his fond grandmama handed him back to the midwife. She called for Isabella's maid to be fetched, so she could be freshened up to receive her lord.

Exhausted by sympathy and overwhelming emotions, Hester sat in a chair and waited for the proud father's visit.

Propped up in bed, her freshly-brushed blond hair drying in ringlets, the covers about her straightened and smoothed, Isabella greeted her husband with the bathed child in her arms. She looked like a battered angel. No amount of bathing, however, could erase the bruises under her eyes from the effort she had expended. Mrs. Mayfield had tried to conceal them under copious amounts of white paint, but to Hester, this only served to make her cousin look much older than her twenty years.

Harrowby had made a similar effort to tidy himself, she saw, as he entered, followed by the baby's nurse. In the half-hour since he had been sent for, his valet Pierre had done wonders. Harrowby's coat and vest had been changed, a fresh shoulder-length wig set upon his head. His face looked washed, and three new patches had been artfully arranged to draw the gaze away from his bloodshot eyes. The only remaining evidence of his debauch was an unsteady gait. A tremulous smile sat in the place previously occupied by pouting lips.

As he approached Isabella's bed, Mrs. Mayfield could not resist the urge to take credit for her daughter's achievement. "Well, here comes the proud papa! Didn't I tell you, my lord, that my Isabella would produce you an heir? And a fine, stout fellow he is."

The midwife reached round the bed curtains to take the child from Isabella to present to his father, who peeked over the baby's swaddlings to get a better look at his face. Little George's head had been pinched in his travails, and his cheeks bore the abrasions of a traumatic entry into this world.

As the nurse removed some of the wrappings to give his father a better look, Harrowby started, and his eyes went wide. "Egad! What the devil's amiss with his complexion?"

Isabella emitted an indignant squeak, but the midwife and Mrs. Mayfield chuckled indulgently. "Oh, you mustn't mind that, my lord," the latter said. "Little Rennington's skin will clear up completely in just a few days, and his cheeks will be as smooth and plump as little apples!"

But something else had struck Harrowby amiss. His brow contracted in a puzzled frown. "A black little fellow, an't he?"

The room fell silent. In the relief, exhaustion, and triumph that had followed the child's safe delivery, no one—least of all Hester—had noticed the baby's swarthy colouring. But now that it had been pointed out, she knew it was true. The baby's head was covered in black hair. The hue of his flesh did not suggest a child who would grow to be fair. There was no sign of Isabella's glorious golden locks or even Harrowby's light brown hair. To have such pale colouring as an adult, he must once have been a very fair child.

Everyone stared at little George, as if only just seeing him for the first time. Into Hester's mind came the memory of a dark, seductive gentleman, and she felt a chill of horror.

As the meaning of the baby's dark looks sank in, anger flashed in Harrowby's eyes.

Mrs. Mayfield hastened to ease his apprehensions, but her indulgent titters held none of their usual assurance. "Pray, do not be deceived by that dark hair, my lord. Why, that cap will fall out and a new one will grow in its place. Did I forget to tell you that Isabella was born with just such a black mop? And see how yellow her locks are now?"

She went on, reciting all the births she had witnessed in which the baby's early colouring had been misleading. She should have stopped with one, but Mrs. Mayfield had never learned subtlety.

Harrowby listened, his expression still suspicious. He might have believed her if she had sounded remotely convinced herself. Indeed, Hester could see he wanted to believe her very much, but her aunt's clumsy insistence merely served to increase his doubts. Still, he recollected that he and Isabella were not alone. They had an audience in the midwife, Isabella's maid, and the baby's nurse. Whatever else, his pride must be preserved. No matter who the child's natural father was, this boy would be his heir.

Cutting off Mrs. Mayfield's flow of words with a sharp gesture, he straightened. Then, ignoring the infant the midwife was still holding up for his view, he turned to Isabella and said stiffly, "My congratulations, madam, on the safe delivery of your child." He made her a formal bow, then thinking better of it, stepped forward, leaned across the coverlets, and planted a cold kiss upon her cheek. "I shall leave you to your rest," he said stiffly. He did not appear to notice the other women as they curtsied in one body, but departed the room with his dignity wrapped about him like a cloak.

Mrs. Mayfield rounded on the child's nurse and snapped, "If his lordship asks to see the child again, make sure that its hair is covered with a cap! And be ready to leave for Kent, as soon as the snow allows."

In shock, Hester wondered how she could keep St. Mars from learning that the heir to his estate was the by-blow of a villain.

Over the next two days, news of the Pretender's presence in Scotland swept through London and Westminster, frightening the populace, and reminding the aristocracy to take care how their loyalties were expressed. A great many people went to the quarter sessions of the peace at the Guildhall to take the oaths of allegiance, and a like session was scheduled for the following Tuesday. Lady Cowper was said to be very ill, but Hester wondered if her indisposition was founded in distress. Both the chief of her father's family and her cousin Thomas Forster were among the noble prisoners who had been captured and locked in Newgate. And, with the rumour that her husband was to be put down from his post as Lord Chancellor—due to the enmity of Lord Townsend and Mr. Walpole—the poor lady had good reason to feel ill.

Harrowby did not return home until the second day after the birth of his heir. During his absence Mrs. Mayfield kept a careful eye out for his arrival and, as soon as word arrived that he was in the house, she went looking for Hester. She found her in the small parlour with Mrs. Dixon, the housekeeper, going over the menus for the day.

Hester saw her aunt enter and broke off her speech. The purposeful look on Mrs. Mayfield's face boded ill. She dismissed Mrs. Dixon and, as soon as she was gone, took Hester by the elbow and pulled her from her chair.

"Hawkhurst has come. I want you to go see him and discover what his temper may be. If he's settled down at all, then come to me immediately. Isabella's complexion is cleared, and he must see her now that her beauty is restored." She unconsciously patted her own black locks, the colour of which had been enhanced with ministrations from a bottle, as if to indicate whence her daughter's beauty had come.

"But what shall I say?" Hester protested. "What possible excuse can I give for coming in search of him?"

Mrs. Mayfield gave her arm a vicious shake. "How should I know,

· you foolish girl? Now, do you go this instant. I'm certain you'll think of something."

With a sigh she could barely conceal, Hester did as she was told. In truth, she did not wish to see her cousins at odds with each other, but she was not so complacent about her aunt's motives. Mrs. Mayfield was entirely dependent upon her son-in-law's goodwill, both for her own continued residence in town and for the advancement of her numerous, impoverished offspring. It was not to be imagined that her eldest son Dudley would repair the Mayfield family fortunes, not when he had inherited his mother's selfishness and vices. The only chance Isabella's younger sisters and brothers would have to obtain decent marriages and preferments would be if Harrowby funded them.

Never very quick at inventing a lie, Hester went in search of Harrowby without the slightest notion of what she would say. But she need not have worried, for on her way to the saloon, where she hoped to discover him, she was stopped by a footman who was coming to fetch her to his lord.

"He wishes to see me?" she asked, surprised.

"Yes, Mrs. Kean. He desired me to bring you to him directly. He's resting in his bedchamber."

The unusual request spawned a worry in Hester's breast. Harrowby had never commanded her to his chamber before. She feared he intended to question her about the parentage of his heir.

On trembling legs, and with her mouth going dry, Hester followed in the footman's wake to the earl's apartment, where she was greeted at the door of the antechamber by his valet Pierre. The little Frenchman had once been St. Mars's servant, and had more than once come to his assistance.

He bid her formally, *"Entrez, mademoiselle."* She followed him into the dressing room, where an assortment of perfumes and pomades from the jars on the dressing table greeted her nostrils. A large clothes press covered one wall. Wigs in several styles, from high-fronted, full-bottomed ones for Court to bag and tie wigs for riding and hunting, stood arrayed on stands. Pierre rounded on her with an expression that was at once worried and offended. "It is to be hoped that *mademoiselle* will have a greater success than Pierre. Perhaps milord will bring himself to confide in *mademoiselle* what is troubling him. *Normalement,* he has no need for anyone but Pierre, but *évidement* something quite out of the ordinary has molested him, for he is very much upset. Not even his new puce coat, which came from the tailor today, has distracted him."

"Oh, dear." Hester's heart sank. She was convinced she knew what the trouble was. She dreaded the choice between betraying Isabella and lying for her. Fortunately, she could say that she knew nothing at all of her cousin's indiscretions, for although she did have a strong suspicion, she had never been an agent in Isabella's intrigues. She was grateful, at least, to think that Harrowby had not revealed his suspicions to a servant.

"He said nothing to you?"

Pierre shrugged. "Nothing Pierre could comprehend. It appears that he has learned of something very dreadful today, but why he should wish to discuss it with *mademoiselle,* and not Pierre, I do not know."

Hester hastened to reassure him that it must be something very particular indeed for his master not to confide in him. If Harrowby had learned of it today, it was unlikely to be about his wife, unless Isabella had been so indiscreet that the gossips had spread rumours, but perhaps Pierre had not fully understood his master. In the past, news of the Pretender's activities had frightened Harrowby, who, she assumed, had been attending Parliament. She wondered if the King could have expressed some displeasure with him.

"Well, you had best take me to him," she said, taking a deep breath and preparing herself for the worst.

Proud Coaches pass, regardless of the Moan,
Of infant Orphans, and the Widow's Groan . . .

CHAPTER III

Hester followed Pierre into the bedchamber, where he approached the drawn bed curtains and announced her arrival in sepulchral tones. As the curtains opened, Hester was shocked to see a reclining figure, nearly buried amongst the deep coverlets. Surrounded by yards of linen dornick and red wool velvet with gold thread, Harrowby lay prostrate with one limp wrist resting on his brow. A bolster, leaning against a headboard painted with the Hawkhurst coat of arms, seemed to be the only thing holding him up. Pierre had wrapped his master in a gold and scarlet striped banyan and replaced his wig with an exotic turban in yellows, purples and browns. A strong whiff of hartshorn bore witness to his distress.

"Ah, Mrs. Kean," he said feebly, endeavouring to sit with his valet's help. "Thank you for coming."

"Not at all, sir. I am happy to serve you. But I fear you are unwell."

"Not sick," he said. "Not sick, thank God, but I have sustained a shock." He sat up against the pillows Pierre supplied and told the valet to pull up a chair for her.

Pierre drew up an upholstered chair and assisted Hester into it, while Harrowby remained silent, waiting for his servant to retire.

When Pierre did not, but hovered over his master's bed to rearrange his coverlets with military precision, Harrowby snapped, "That will do, Pierre. Leave us alone!"

Hester noted that the Frenchman did not take the same liberties with Harrowby that he habitually took with St. Mars. Instead of insisting that *mademoiselle* should have a chaperon, he retreated in a huff, deepening his master's scowl.

"Damned Frenchy!" Harrowby muttered. "If he weren't such a genius, I'd dismiss him for his insolence."

He sat up straighter, and Hester saw how pale his face was beneath the paint. "The most terrible news, Mrs. Kean. I still cannot quite credit it. I don't suppose my lady or her mother have heard of it yet?"

"What news?" Hester's pulse quickened. What news could rock him to this extent? The Pretender? Surely, it could be nothing about St. Mars? If anything had happened to St. Mars, surely Tom would have told her. But perhaps he had not had time . . . .

"Is it about the Pretender?" she asked hopefully.

"The Pretender!" Harrowby stared as if she had lost her mind. "No, no, it's not about him—though that whole affair is a disgrace!" He put an end to her misery. "It's Sir Walter Tatham. He's been killed."

"Killed? How?" The relief that flooded Hester made her bite her lip in shame. She summoned up what feelings she could for Lady Tatham, who had lost her husband. Neither Sir Walter nor his lady had ever been a favourite with her, but Hester did not need to like a person to feel sympathy for her.

"The authorities insist he was murdered—and under the most vicious of circumstances. They do not precisely know how he was killed, but his body was discovered three days ago. It was frozen solid and leaning against a booth down on the Thames. No one knows how he came to be put there, but it is plain he was killed somewhere else and carried onto the ice. They made a mockery of his corpse, too—dressed it up in coronation robes."

The magnitude of the indignity struck her. A feeling of revulsion brought her upright in her chair. "Why, that is barbaric!"

"Barbaric! Precisely what I should have said, Mrs. Kean, if I had not been so overcome." He cast her a fleeting sideways glance. "I was visiting a friend when a servant came to inform us."

The friend was likely to be his mistress, but Hester did not let on that she knew of that connection. "I wonder why we have not been told. When she hears, Isabella will surely wish me to call upon Lady Tatham."

"Yes!" Harrowby said eagerly. "That is precisely why I called you here. Someone from the family must see if there is anything to be done for the poor lady. But as to why you had not received word, his body was only just identified today."

"But I understood you to say that it was discovered three days ago." A disturbing thought occurred to her. "Now I remember—Lady Tatham wondered aloud what could have become of her husband." She shuddered. "I suppose he was dead even then."

"Yes, undoubtedly. He was found at dawn, the day before my lady delivered her son."

He could not bring himself to say "our" son yet, but at least he could mention the child without too much difficulty. Hester let out a quiet sigh. It seemed she was not going to be examined about the child's parentage.

"If that is all then, I shall go quickly to tell Isabella and say you wish me to visit his widow."

She took hold of her skirts and started to rise, but Harrowby said, ". . . er, wait. That is not quite all, just yet."

"Yes?"

Something else was bothering him. Something of a more desperate nature. But whatever it was, he could not bring himself to be open with her.

He gave an uneasy laugh as if to make light of his own words. "Sir Walter . . . ," he started, then tried again, this time on a different tack. "I cannot imagine who should wish to kill him. Why, how should I? After all, we were the merest of acquaintances. I do not believe he had ever set foot inside this house until a month or so ago."

Harrowby seemed to await her confirmation, so Hester nodded, at sea. She wondered why he should suddenly wish to distance himself from a gentleman with whom he had spent so many hours of late. Then she recalled asking herself why Harrowby tolerated the visits of someone he patently did not enjoy. Still, Sir Walter was dead now, so what difference could it make whether they had been friends or just acquaintances?

"Yes, Cousin?" Hester had never formed the habit of calling Harrowby, "my lord," not when his title truly belonged to St. Mars. She avoided situations in which she must refer to him as Lord Hawkhurst, and did not believe he had noticed. He had sycophants enough to satisfy the vainest of men.

"Is it true it was you who discovered the murderer of that foul man your brother called patron?" he asked without warning. Something in his eyes entreated her.

Hester was astonished to hear him refer to an episode of which, at the time, he had practically forbidden her to speak.

"Yes, I suppose I did," she said, wishing she could tell not just Harrowby, but everyone else, the part his cousin St. Mars had played in that discovery.

He gave a humph, but did not seem displeased. "That is what James Henry told me. And before that there was that terrible business with poor Sir Humphrey. You showed perspicacity on that occasion, too."

Hester gazed down at the hands in her lap. She preferred not to take any credit at all for that discovery, not when she had allowed herself to be so miserably fooled. If St. Mars had not come to her rescue then . . . .

"What I'm getting at, Mrs. Kean, is that you seem to have a knack for making inquiries."

She looked quickly back at him, aghast. "You would like me to make inquiries about Sir Walter's death? Oh, sir, I shouldn't! I barely knew him . . ."

"I don't expect you to go out and arrest the fellow!" Harrowby said, visibly peeved. "I don't even care if you discover him. It's just that there are things Sir Walter . . . that is, things about him . . . . And if I know these things, then maybe there are other people—though God forbid they should know the same about me! And I shouldn't wish them to put two and two together and begin to suspect that I had asked you to inquire discreetly, you see?"

All Hester could see was that Harrowby was working himself into a passion. His voice had taken on a note of panic and his eyes were looking wild. Without knowing what had got him so agitated, over and above the strange manner of Sir Walter's death, she was afraid to ask any more for fear of making him worse. Perhaps, later, he would be able to behave more rationally.

"I should not stay in case I tire you," she said, in a soothing voice. "I shall be more than happy to make a few discreet inquiries when I visit Lady Tatham, and I will do so directly, but I do believe you should rest, sir. May I call Pierre in to you?"

It was her promise to do as he asked, rather than her suggestion to call Pierre that finally calmed him. Nevertheless, he welcomed the thought of his valet's ministrations.

When, after summoning Pierre, Hester left the bedchamber, Harrowby was clutching a bottle of hartshorn to his nose.

She went in search of her aunt, first to tell her that Harrowby was too unwell to visit his wife. At least she could remove Mrs. Mayfield's fears that his absence was a rebuke to Isabella. Thinking over his odd request, she realized suddenly that Harrowby was afraid—sincerely frightened. But of what? Did he think that whoever had killed Sir Walter might try to kill him, too? And, if so, why?

☙

Earlier, on the previous day, Gideon had gone out walking. As far as he had been able to see, from Westminster to the Tower and beyond, snow coated the rooftops of London in thick slabs of white. Watermen's wherries and vendors' carts lay buried beneath piles resembling giant spoonfuls of clotted cream, though soot from all the sea coal fires had begun to lay oily black patterns through them. Not a single ship rode the river with its sails unfurled. The splash of oars and the thud of wood hitting docks, the raised voices of seamen, the squeak of pulleys, the smack of fisticuffs, whistles, laughter, vendors' cries—all had been silenced by the heavy winter blanket. Hardly anyone was stirring out of doors unless he had important business to attend. Only the poorest of Londoners lingered in the streets, huddling three or four to a doorway, begging for a pot of gin.

Now, at nearly ten in the evening, the sky was pitch dark. As Gideon and Tom made their way north, the whole city lay as eerily muffled as it had in the morning. At night it was even harder to negotiate the snow-clogged streets when they could barely see two feet in front of them.

They had walked across the Thames from Gideon's house, the lower part of their faces wrapped in woolen scarves. Despite the cold, it felt good to be outside, to have a sense of purpose, even if it was only to discover what his Grace of Bournemouth had to say. On the other side of the river, as they passed taverns, cookhouses, and coffee houses, Gideon got a sense of the people gathered inside them for warmth. Swearing, laughter, and the occasional sound of an overturned bench or a breaking mug escaped through a drafty window or door. They passed a tavern where Jacobites were singing, emboldened by the news of the Pretender's arrival. Loose handbills littered the streets. When Gideon picked one up and examined it by the light of his torch, he saw it was a copy of the declaration the Pretender had issued months ago, exhorting the British people to rise in his cause. As they turned into St. Martin's Lane, Gideon dropped it, burying his face again in his scarf as they passed the Starr Inn.

All was quiet as they trudged by the darkened church of St. Martin-in-the-Fields. Ahead on their left extended a long row of imposing houses, occupied mostly by the aristocracy and gentry. On their right was an area of smaller, but still respectable houses, filled with doctors and artisans, men unlikely to recognize the Viscount St. Mars. Smoke billowed out of the chimneys on both sides, clogging the air with soot. The smell of sulfur filled Gideon's nose.

Before they reached the part of the street commonly called Cock Lane, Gideon and Tom turned left into Cecil Court and from there crossed into Bear Lane, grateful to see they had at last entered an area where the houses looked narrower and mean.

Gideon hoped that his Grace had given careful thought to their meeting place. He would not wish to be seen speaking with a notorious outlaw. Still, with the dwellings of so many aristocrats within a short distance, Gideon's pulse raced at the thought that someone from his past might see him, until the sign of the Bear emerged in the dark and he saw the nature of the custom it drew.

Inside, the taproom was nearly full. Smoke from dozens of long yellow pipes swirled from between smokers' lips. Low conversations filled the air with a steady rumble. Gideon peered about, squinting at the customers' faces in the feeble lantern light, but the Duke was not yet here. He waited near the door until a party of men vacated the nook nearest the hearth. Then, telling Tom to take up a position near the door, he made himself comfortable beside the fire and settled down to wait.

It was not long before a bustle at the door signaled the arrival of another party. A tall, imposing figure entered, accompanied by a handful of servants. His Grace had taken a few steps to conceal his identity, wearing a felt hat pulled low and cloaking himself in a rough woolen cloak, but beneath the cloak, Gideon spied a flash of black.

He had to laugh at the feebleness of the Duke's disguise. Black was the most difficult, hence the most expensive, colour for a dyer to achieve. It had always been the Duke of Bournemouth's vanity to wear it, and it tickled Gideon that the Duke would not leave it off, even when a black waistcoat was certain to attract the very attention he should be anxious to avoid. Then, Gideon realized that this kind of arrogance reminded him forcibly of his father's, and his amusement faltered. In his father, he had always thought of it as pride.

He had seen no familiar face inside the tavern. So, as Bournemouth scanned the room with the apparent intention of quitting it, should he not see his quarry, Gideon stood and removed his felt hat to reveal his yellow head of hair. The gesture drew his Grace's gaze, and after one searching look, with a flick of his hand he dismissed his footmen to await him outside.

As he neared the table, Gideon bowed. The courtesy was acknowledged with a nod. The two men seated themselves, and the tavern keeper came to ask their pleasure, the depth and frequency of his bows, making it clear he had identified them both as persons of rank. The Duke consented to taste the host's brandy, though a sneer made it plain he doubted it would measure up to the man's boasts. Gideon ordered the same, while Bournemouth peered at him from beneath lowered brows.

When the man had taken himself off, Bournemouth said crisply, "I am surprised you answered my summons. It's been rumoured that you joined the Pretender's cause."

Gideon responded, just as coolly, "Yet, here I am." He did not owe the Duke any explanation of his actions. Nor in these days would it be wise to answer the question implied.

The Duke gave an ironic smile. "It seems you are your father's son, after all."

He did not explain the comment, but Gideon guessed his meaning. His father had refused to commit himself to a Jacobite rising until he was certain it would get enough support from France. That was the practical approach taken by many English Jacobites.

Gideon's own involvement with James's cause had sprung from his situation as an outlaw, and his motive, as well as the result, had been different.

But let the Duke of Bournemouth think what he would. "I assume you did not put that advertisement in the newssheet just to see if I would come."

"No, but the topic is not irrelevant. You will remember that list of names I requested of you?"

Gideon suppressed a sigh of disappointment. So that was all this meeting was to be about. "Yes, but I should tell you that upon reflexion I have decided not to burn it. Do not worry," he said, forestalling the angry protest he could see forming on Bournemouth's lips. "I have good reasons for keeping it which have nothing to do with you. I swear you shall never suffer for its existence."

The promise did not appease his Grace. Still, he shelved his protest for the while. It seemed that, indeed, there was something more pressing on his mind. "There will be a name on that list you may recall when I explain why I asked you to come here. My sister's son, the Honourable Nathan Breed."

He paused when their host returned with their drinks. He set them on the table, and the Duke waved him off.

Gideon recalled seeing the name Breed when he had read his father's papers again. It had caught his attention this time because he had recently seen the name in the newssheets. Nathan Breed had been captured with the Northumbrian rebels and was even now in Newgate awaiting trial for treason.

His interest piqued, Gideon waited for the Duke to proceed.

Now, it was Bournemouth's turn to issue a sigh, though his was tinged with both anger and frustration. "My fool of a nephew has got himself captured," he said. "I tried to stop him, but he would not listen, though I promised to get him a position at Court. He was determined to share James's fate, even when I pointed out that the Pretender himself was unlikely to risk being arrested.

"Nathan has ever been headstrong and wild—wont to spend all his money on women and cards. Now he has learned what recklessness can cost—and learned it in the direst of circumstances."

Agitated, Bournemouth tossed back the brandy their host had brought, forgetting to notice its inferiority. Having drained half his glass, he plunked it back down on the table, and leaning forward, cupped it between his hands.

"You have my sympathy," Gideon said, not knowing what else to say.

The Duke looked him squarely in the eye. "It is not your sympathy I require, but your assistance."

As Gideon raised an inquiring brow, he continued, "I need your help to get my nephew out of Newgate, and out of England."

Gideon started. "Mine?" A laugh of incredulity escaped him. "What makes you believe that I can help? You are much better placed to plead his case with George."

Bournemouth scowled, but there was a deeper emotion than anger in his expression. There was worry as well. "His Majesty" —he pro-nounced the word scathingly— "declines to be moved. Lady Niths-dale's pleas have fallen on deaf ears, and it has been made clear that to beg his Majesty will only raise his ire. Now that the Pretender has actually come, he will be even more obdurate. And I cannot be seen to sympathize simply because Nathan is my kin. The King must make examples of the rebel lords. He fears that leniency will only encourage others to rebel. He knows that he is not loved."

As Bournemouth took another gulp from the glass in front of him,

Gideon frowned. The prospect of his father's friends being brought to trial had robbed him of any thirst.

Bournemouth continued, "Of course, one has to understand his position. In accepting the Crown from Parliament George has tacitly agreed that it is Parliament's gift to grant, not Almighty God's. But he cannot bring himself to believe in such a radical proposition. It threatens the very basis of his existence and the one thing he truly cares about, the Electorship of Hanover. I sincerely believe that, if not for his love of Hanover, he would have refused the English Crown he appears to despise so much. But he believes that England —even Scotland—can be made to serve Hanover."

The Duke's words stung. Gideon did not know whether he hurt more for James or for England. Lust for another's crown was comprehensible, but to despise England—this country that meant so much to them all?

"But this is a distraction," Bournemouth said, waving a slender hand in front of his face. "I cannot permit my sister's son to be hanged. You must know someone who can carry him into France, and you must help me find a way to gain his escape from Newgate."

"But why? Why should I do this?"

"Because I assisted you once, and I shall do so again. Not today, perhaps, but sometime in the future—once German George feels secure on his throne—assuming, of course, there is nothing to link you to the Pretender."

Gideon had not realized it, but throughout the Duke's recital, he had been leaning forward in his seat. Now he reacted so forcefully that his back struck the bench. The Duke had surprised him, first with the preposterous suggestion that Gideon could somehow find a way out of Newgate gaol, then with an inducement he dared not ignore. Gideon was fully aware that it was nothing more than that, an inducement to make him take on an impossible task. But . . . still . . . did it not offer him hope?

"You are saying that if I help your nephew to escape, you will plead my case before the King?"

Bournemouth threw him an uncomfortable glance from under his brows, his lips compressed in a tight, narrow line. Gideon saw he was reluctant to commit himself.

Gideon shook his head, releasing a cynical smile. "I should have known." He tried not to reveal the bitterness that soured his stomach. He did not want Bournemouth to know he had believed in his proposition, if only for a moment. "You say I am my father's son, but at least a Fitzsimmons would never resort to tricks that could lure a man to his death."

"I am not playing you false. I only hesitate to make promises that I may not be able to keep."

"And why should you not? Are you not well-placed in George's affections? You, with your German princess?"

Bournemouth did not wince. He was either an accomplished actor or he did not suffer from a guilty conscience, at least none that concerned his marriage. "All I can engage to do now is to present your case to the King in the best possible light, and only then if he agrees to hear me. You do not know George, but he has not made himself approachable. It may be possible eventually to bribe Madame Schulenburg or Madame Kielmansegge to plea your case, but I cannot tell what the situation will be even a few months from now, much less in the years it may take before the Pretender's business is finished. You must know what havoc his arrival in Scotland has caused. But I could not wait to beg your assistance for my sister's son. His time is short, and the Pretender's presence may shorten it. How can I make promises today when I do not even know for certain how long this war will last?"

What he did not say, but Gideon detected, was that he still entertained fears that his flirtation with the Pretender's cause could come out. Perhaps, after all, there was honour in his hesitation. Perhaps he was unwilling to promise Gideon his assistance in case he got caught, lured into danger by a commitment Bournemouth might find himself powerless to keep.

Somehow, regardless of what the Duke pledged to do for him, Gideon felt a growing desire to help Nathan Breed escape. The spectre of the executions of so many brave men haunted his sleep. He had felt himself drawn repeatedly past Newgate and the Tower, as if in walking past them he could somehow pay homage to the men who had sacrificed everything for James. These gentlemen, the Northumbrian

rebels, were the true believers in James's cause. They believed he had
been anointed in the womb to be their king. James had sycophantic
and opportunistic followers aplenty. Gideon himself could have been
one of those. But the men who had been arrested fighting for him even
before he had set foot in Britain—they had been willing to risk all for
what they believed to be right. That was undoubtedly the reason that
George could not pardon them. Their faith in James's right itself was a
danger to him. It was a faith he not only understood, but shared. He
knew he had no right to sit on Great Britain's throne.

Besides, Gideon thought, reflecting on the decision he realized he
had already made, what else did he have to do with himself? He could
attempt to release Nathan Breed from gaol, or he could waste these
wretchedly cold days in hiding. Hiding not only from the law, but
from himself and his future.

"I will not ask you to promise a favour you may never be able to
deliver." He paused. "All I do ask is that . . . if I manage to free your
nephew, you will use whatever influence you eventually possess to see
my cause put right. You know I am innocent of the charges against
me."

"Yes." It was an admission the Duke had never formally made.
Then, as relief seemed to strike him, his rigid posture relaxed. "I can
promise you one thing, St. Mars. If you manage to save my nephew,
you will be able to count not only on me, but on my sister and her
husband as your friends. I believe I told you once that you had no
friends at Court, but as long as I am in good grace, you will have one
there at least."

Before Gideon could respond, the Duke added with a hesitant air,
"There is one thing . . . I scarcely know what to make of it, but it is
something I believe you should hear. In November, when the prisoners
were being transported, one of the German ladies came to me with an
offer, reportedly from Herr Bernstorff, to . . . that is, if I had a mind
. . . to let Nathan escape upon the road."

Gideon stared, his brow contracted and his mind churning. "And
what response did you make?"

The Duke spread his hands. "As I said, I did not know how to
interpret it. It could have been a trick to obtain an admission of con-

spiracy from me. On the other hand, given the source of the offer, it could just as easily have been an attempt to extract a bribe. Whichever it was, with the potential for peril I judged it best not to bite. But I do not know why, or even if, I was singled out for such an offer. There is hardly a person at Court who is not connected to one of the rebels at least. Forster is cousin to the Lord Chancellor's lady, and Mar himself is brother-in-law to Wortley Montagu, but I have not ascertained if either of them were approached."

"Who is the German lady who conveyed the offer? One of the King's mistresses?"

Bournemouth shook his head. "One would say she is a person of no consequence, a distant connection of Baron Bernstorff." He grimaced with distaste. "She is a venal little creature by the name of Schultz."

❦

Mrs. Mayfield was so relieved to learn that Harrowby nursed no extraordinary ill feelings for her daughter, that she did not object to Hester's plan to visit Lady Tatham. Whatever his lordship desired, she would be eager to grant until she felt him once again securely under her thumb. So she excused Hester from her attendance on Isabella even though she would be needed to help plan the christening of the heir. King George, the Princess of Wales, and Lord Kirkland had been solicited to be godparents and despite the cold and the snow, it would not do to wait too long before securing Lord Rennington's immortal soul.

The King's visit must be prepared for, but there was little Hester could do to that end. Since she did not have the faintest idea what she was supposed to discover with her inquiries, she had no notion how long they would take, but any excuse to escape her aunt was always a blessing.

Before setting out for Lady Tatham's house, she took a moment to pen a letter to St. Mars. She had not seen him in nearly a month, during which time he might have gone away from London, but given the severity of the weather, she could not imagine where he could go. Twice before, he had left for his estate in France, but now, even if so many harbours had not been clogged with ice, the efforts of his Majesty's navy to board and search every vessel for weapons intended for the rebels made a Channel crossing too dangerous to contemplate. The risky prospect had not stopped St. Mars on his previous voyages, but the last time she had seen him, he had stated his intention to stay in England, at least until the rebellion was over. She hoped her letter would find him and that the freedom Harrowby's mission would give her to leave the house might give them an opportunity to meet.

After explaining briefly where she was going, and why, she addressed her letter to Mr. Mavors at the King's Head in Lambeth and sealed it with a wax wafer. As she did, she reflected on what a luxury it was to be able to afford stamps. Harrowby's receiver-general, James Henry, had insisted on paying her a small allowance, so now not only could she afford an occasional purchase, she could send letters without asking Harrowby to frank them.

For once, Harrowby had placed his carriage at her disposal, since neither he nor Isabella planned to go out. It would not be long before Isabella was recovered enough to seek amusement at Court. Already her dressmaker was at work taking in her clothes, and as soon as Isabella had been churched, she would be eager to visit the shops. For now, though, Hester thought, as she climbed into the coach and a footman placed a hot brick at her feet, she would make sure to take advantage of the rare luxury of riding in a private conveyance.

She had not been outside the gates of Hawkhurst House in the past few weeks. When the coach rolled through the gates into Piccadilly, the depth of the snow in the streets amazed her. Where it had not been shoveled, the drifts were so high they reached the girths of riders' saddles. She hunkered down in a corner of the coach, shivering, grateful for the furs covering her lap.

Lady Tatham's house was located in Henrietta Street. A hearse with plumed horses stood stationed at the kerb in front, its horses occasionally stamping their hooves to get warm. After John the footman helped Hester down and saw her safely up the steps, she handed him a penny and her letter to St. Mars with instructions to take it to a receiving-office for the penny post before coming back to collect her.

As she turned to the front door, she saw that the undertakers had been hard at work on Sir Walter's house. The knocker had been wrapped in flannel to muffle the sound, and the windows had been shrouded in black. A mute with downcast eyes opened the door.

Inside, after relinquishing her cloak to a footman, she was conducted through the hall, where Sir Walter's coat of arms had been affixed to the wall with ten-penny nails, then led up the stairs on which other mutes were stationed at intervals. Another one showed her into the withdrawing room, where Sir Walter lay in state, inside an ornate wooden coffin, raised on trellises, concealed by a velvet pall. Silver candlesticks on a sideboard illuminated the room, and a mute with a particularly gloomy face stood by the coffin.

Lady Tatham sat rigidly in a chair, dressed entirely in black from the long lace veil that covered her hair to the bombazine skirt spread over her feet. A stiff black widow's cap framed her face. The undertaker in his sober garb hovered nearby as two old women leaned over the coffin like vultures, picking at a kill. These two would be the crones sent by the parish to verify that the corpse had been wrapped in the woolen stuff dictated by law. Satisfied that Sir Walter's shroud was, indeed, made of woolen flannel and neither linen nor silk, they turned to receive a gratuity from the undertaker, then followed him from the room chatting cheerfully about their next stop.

Throughout the examination, Lady Tatham sat without moving, staring stonily at the far wall. When she persisted in this attitude, Hester stepped over to the coffin to pay her respects to the dead.

Sir Walter's shroud was white with lace at the cuffs. The end was folded about his feet and tied with a piece of woolen thread. A white gathered cap, fastened with a broad chin cloth, hid his shaven scalp. Fine woolen gloves covered his hands, and a woolen cravat enveloped his neck. A faint smell of spices rose from the corpse , but the room was so cold, embalming would scarcely have been needed. Indeed, his face still looked frozen under the white paint and rouge used to soften its appearance. A layer of bran some four inches thick lay at the bottom of the coffin to soften its bed for the corpse. The undertaker had done his best, Hester supposed, but Sir Walter's mouth had been stretched into a grimace she had never seen on his face when he was alive.

She said a brief prayer for his soul, then turned to comfort his widow.

The room was very dark, its curtains drawn and the walls covered with black hangings. Only the tapers on the sideboard cast any light, which Hester blocked with her body when she stooped to take hold of Lady Tatham's hand. Her fingers felt cold even through her gloves, and her hand was clenched tightly like a claw. Unable to see the lady's features, Hester offered the conventional words of comfort she had learned as a clergyman's daughter and conveyed the sympathy of her family as well.

"So they sent you, did they?"

The words, uttered harshly, made Hester start. She stammered, "I'm certain my cousin would have come herself, but she is not recovered from her lying-in."

"And Lord Hawkhurst? Was he not my husband's friend?"

"Indeed, he was! And he was so overcome with shock at the news of Sir Walter's death that he has taken to his bed. It was he who brought the news home and requested me to come in his stead."

A sob shook Lady Tatham. Hester moved to put an arm about her shoulders. "There, there, my lady. I did not mean to upset you with my visit. May I call your maid to you? You should not be sitting here alone."

Only then did Hester discover that the lady's rigidity had been a product not of grief, but of a hard, cold fury.

"Alone?" Lady Tatham spat out, "I have been in this room all day, and you are the first person to enter it to pay her respects. How should I not be alone if no one comes?"

Hester was pricked by a stab of compassion. It was, indeed, strange if none of Sir Walter's acquaintances had come to see the body. But she could not continue stooping over the distraught widow, and she saw no reason for Lady Tatham to remain in the room with the corpse. She insisted gently until Lady Tatham stood and allowed herself to be escorted to her bedchamber, where a footman deposited her in a chair near the fire. The chamber was opulently furnished with fine walnut chairs newly upholstered in green damask, an immense Turkey carpet, and a large collection of expensive China dishes. The room that held them was much simpler, with an old-fashioned wooden ceiling and dark panels on the walls. Hester asked Lady Tatham's maid to bring her mistress some tea.

"I cannot understand it," the lady wailed, pressing a handkerchief to her lips, before anger took hold of her again. She thrust her hands into her lap in a gesture of impotent fury, the white handkerchief gripped tightly between black gloves. "I suppose they were scandalized by the manner of his death and do not wish to be associated with it in any way."

Privately Hester thought the opposite was more likely to be true. The curious usually relished a macabre piece of news they could repeat to gain attention at Court. That made the lack of attendance even odder.

But she said, "It was certainly disturbing, but I cannot believe your husband's friends would be deterred from visiting for that reason. I suspect it is news of the Pretender's arrival that has absorbed them to the exclusion of all else. And although, as I understand, Sir Walter has been dead these three days past, it was only this morning that the news reached us. I came as quickly as I could, as soon as my lord informed me, so I'm certain others will, too, as soon as they are told."

Her words had a soothing effect. Lady Tatham's pursed lips relaxed, as did the hands clasped in her lap. Thinking it might be an advantageous time to change the subject, Hester gently asked, "Have the authorities determined how Sir Walter was killed? I do not mean how he was found," she quickly added. "My lord informed me of the circumstances."

"They . . . they think he was poisoned," Lady Tatham forced out. "There were signs that he had vomited, but also something about the contraction of his spine. More than that they cannot tell me. No one knows how he came to be out on the ice or even dressed in those robes."

"Do they know whose robes they were?" Obviously not Sir Walter's since he was only a baronet, and coronation robes were reserved for peers.

The widow bent forward and shook her head, closing her eyes in a grimace of distaste. "Only that they belong to a baron. There were two rows of sealskin spots on the miniver."

The number of rows indicated the rank of the wearer. But it was inconceivable that the owner of such expensive garments would willingly part with them, even if he did not expect to use them again in his lifetime. Coronation robes were purchased at the investiture of a new peer and handed down from generation to generation. After the peer's investiture, they were only worn at coronations, unlike Parliamentary robes, which were worn at the opening of each session.

"Sooner or later, someone is certain to notice theirs missing, and when they report the theft to the authorities, whoever took them will likely prove to be your husband's murderer."

Lady Tatham gave Hester a dazed look of astonishment. "You think that they were stolen?"

"Surely they must have been! Where else would the murderer have got them? The owner would never have been so foolish as to dress his victim in his own robes."

A visible relaxing of Lady Tatham's shoulders told Hester how much the mystery of the robes had been distressing her. "Of course," she said cheering. "That must be the way of it. Sir Walter need not have been—"

She did not finish, but Hester completed her thought. Evidently, Lady Tatham had been labouring under the fear that Sir Walter had dressed himself in the coronation suit for a reason she could not or did not wish to imagine. What did she know about her husband that would make her conceive of such a possibility?

Lady Tatham's maid returned to the bedchamber with a tray of tea and toast. While she held the tray, a footman brought forward a table. As soon as they retreated, Hester offered to pour the tea, and as she did, she pondered the notion that Sir Walter had dressed himself in the coronation suit.

Certainly there were gentlemen who enjoyed clothing themselves in strange garb, but Hester had never heard that those garments stretched to coronation robes. There was always a first time for everything, but still the question of the ownership of the robes remained. A full set of coronation garments could run to three thousand pounds. And who would dare be careless with such a sum? Between coronations, the robes would normally be locked safely away in a chest until the next rare occasion. The last time they would have been needed was only a year and half ago, for King George's coronation, and given his robust health, there was no reason to think they would be needed again for many years.

Unless . . . . Hester's thoughts flew to the Pretender. What if James Stuart did manage to overthrow King George? Then a new coronation would soon follow. But could he do it? And even if he did eventually succeed, how could Sir Walter or the owner of the robes have known of his arrival in Scotland when even the King, with all his spies and his messengers, had only just been made aware of it? Had Sir Walter been a Jacobite, and was that what Harrowby knew that had made him so fearful?

But, surely, knowing what she did of Harrowby's political leanings, she should be certain that he would never associate with a Jacobite.

None of it made any sense. No, the first notion she had had, that the murderer had stolen the robes, was far more likely. But Lady Tatham's relief on hearing that theory had been interesting, something for Hester to keep in mind.

While these thoughts flew rapidly through her head, she poured the tea into two blue and white China dishes. Lady Tatham's colour had already vastly improved. She took her refreshment with a good appetite, revealing how little genuine grief there was in her distress.

"Have you any children, Lady Tatham?" Hester asked, wondering what kind of companionship the widow could expect.

"Yes, but they are none of them in town. The messages were sent only yesterday, and even if they receive them in good time, they cannot possibly arrive here in under four or five days, not riding as they must with so much snow on the roads. I doubt our eldest daughter will even attempt it. She will soon be confined for the first time. And the second is no horsewoman and often ill. In this weather, she should not come. Our eldest son will come and it is likely that the others will ride with him."

"Then you will soon have their presence to comfort you."

Lady Tatham gave an absent nod, as if their coming meant very little to her. Hester was trying to think of something else she could ask that might help her get to the root of Harrowby's concern, when a second visitor was shown into the bedchamber.

The gentleman was slight and elderly, with an uncomfortable crook in his back. He wore an expensive shoulder-length periwig, a diamond pin on his neckcloth, and many bejeweled rings. He bowed nervously as Lady Tatham presented him to Hester as Mr. Alfred Mistlethwait, a justice of the peace for Westminster. Considering how angry she had been over the lack of visitors, she did not appear very happy to receive this one. Hester was surprised to see a justice of the peace sporting so many gems, but she imagined Mr. Mistlethwait, though merely a mister, must be a man of considerable property, or at least more than the common run of Middlesex magistrates.

He waved away the chair a footman drew up for him. "Won't stay long enough to sit. Came as soon as I heard." He glanced anxiously back and forth between the two ladies. "Couldn't believe the news— that Sir Walter was dead. Just came to make certain of it. Thought I'd better pop round."

Lady Tatham inclined her head, but did not encourage him to sit. Her manner was haughty and cold, making Hester wonder why anyone would visit her if this was the reception they received. Just then, however, a Lady Sichel was announced, and the widow's demeanour underwent a complete transformation. Gratification lit up her features, and she barely managed to recall her grief at the last minute, casting her eyes down and touching her handkerchief to her nose.

This visitor, then, was of sufficient importance to warrant her attention. At last she had the level of company she had desired. Hester did not merit an introduction to Lady Sichel, whom the widow insisted must take her place at the tea table. So, after excusing herself and receiving no more than an absent nod, Hester followed Mr. Mistlethwait, who had also been given an effectual dismissal, and together they descended the stairs.

As they waited in the drafty hall for their cloaks, she made polite conversation, asking if he had known Sir Walter well.

"Well enough," he said curtly. "As I said, couldn't believe he was dead. Had to come and see for myself." There was a hint of relish in his voice.

Uncertain how to respond, Hester opted for silence. Mr. Mistlethwait's manner was ill at ease, however. He fidgeted and played with the rings on his fingers.

"See here," he said, first glancing over his shoulder then turning to grasp her by the elbow. "What do you know about Sir Walter's business affairs? Who's going to see to the settling of them, eh?"

Hester stared at him in astonishment. She pulled against his grip. "I know nothing of his affairs. I am here on an errand for my cousin Lord Hawkhurst."

He immediately loosed her, subdued by her powerful connections. "Hawkhurst, you say?" he said, throwing her a nervous glance. "What does his lordship make of it, eh?"

Hester did not care for Mr. Mistlethwait's manner. She would not discuss her family with a stranger, least of all this man, whose whole bearing seemed untrustworthy. She thought she understood why Lady Tatham had snubbed him.

"What is it you are so eager to discover?"

"That's my business, and no one else's." Then, realizing that she was not likely to be forthcoming with him in his present attitude, he tried a wheedling tone. "It's only that Sir Walter had something of mine, see? And I'm wondering how to get it back."

Before Hester could answer, the footman returned with their cloaks. As she gathered hers about her shoulders, Hester was relieved to recall that the coach was awaiting her outside. She would not be forced to trudge through the snow with this man badgering her.

With Lady Tatham's footman present, she said, "If I were you, I should take this up with Sir Walter's son and heir. Surely he will be the one to settle such matters with his father's friends."

"Friend!" Mr. Mistlethwait snorted angrily. "He'll have to search high and low to find one of those." With that he pulled his own cloak about him and with a lurching step left by the door the footman had opened.

Hester followed him slowly outside, hoping he would not attempt to waylay her, but, seeing his slight figure retreating down the street, she stepped carefully over the frozen ground and took refuge inside the Hawkhurst coach.

As it bounced roughly home, she pondered Mr. Mistlethwait's last remark. So he did not think Sir Walter had many friends? He had seemed to have acquaintances aplenty. He had always spoken of this illustrious person or that, laying claim to their friendship. But if they were not truly his intimates, that could explain the lack of visitors to his widow.

It did raise the question, however, of why so many had pretended to be Sir Walter's friend— Harrowby among them. Hester knew there would always be people with enough force of character to impose their friendship on others weaker than themselves. Some used flattery to accomplish it, others scorn. She tried to recall what Sir Walter had employed, but it was neither of those. His manner towards Harrowby had always been jocular. It had assumed a shared enjoyment in each other's company, or rather a shared joke. But Harrowby had never displayed any genuine pleasure in having Sir Walter about. He had tolerated his jokes and his familiarities, responding only with nervous forbearance. There was no good reason why an earl should endure the company of anyone he did not relish as a friend, not when he had an army of servants to deny access to him.

There must have been a good reason why Harrowby had countenanced Sir Walter's acquaintance. Perhaps because he had procured Harrowby's mistress for him? But would that be enough to gain him permanent favour with an earl? Hester sighed. She could not and would never understand gentlemen. But if that was all there was between Harrowby and Sir Walter, why had he sent her to visit Lady Tatham with such fear?

Then the proud Lady trip'd along the Town,
And tuck'd up Petticoats secur'd her Gown,
Her rosie Cheek with distant Visits glow'd,
And Exercise unartful Charms bestow'd . . .

CHAPTER IV

Gideon received Mrs. Kean's note that evening after Tom fetched his letters from the King's Head. The same post brought the newsletters with the announcement that Lord and Lady Hawkhurst had been blessed with an heir.

On reading this news, Gideon felt for a moment that his heart had stopped. What followed was an intense pain, burning deeply into his chest. If not for the promise the Duke of Bournemouth had made to work for his interest, the pain would have been intolerable. As it was, Gideon crumpled the newssheet and threw it into the fire. He watched it curl into ashes, and thought instead about how he would manage to get Nathan Breed out of Newgate gaol.

The Duke had promised him any money he would need to bribe the guards. The prisons were so corrupt and the guards so venal that each was certain to have his price. The problem would be if the turn-keys were too frightened by the prospect of their own imprisonment for abetting treason to help a traitor to escape.

The task was not impossible, though. The gaol was so old that its walls were crumbling. It might be possible to cut through the bars if Breed had an implement he could use. Something could be smuggled in. But how to do it?

Another problem was how to approach them, when the price on Gideon's head was enough to tempt a saint.

Mrs. Kean's note rested on the table where he had left it. As he picked it up again, a measure of the elation he had felt on reading it returned in the form of comfort. These past few weeks without hearing from her had seemed like months. Now at last it seemed that they would see each other again. The world never looked as dismal when he was with Mrs. Kean.

Her mention of the frozen corpse that Tom had seen on the river had surprised him. He had never met Sir Walter Tatham, but he might have passed him often in town. That could be where Tom had seen his face. Otherwise, he might simply have confused him with someone else, perhaps someone he had seen dressed in coronation robes. The puzzle of Sir Walter's death intrigued Gideon, though. He wondered what Harrowby's connection to the baronet had been.

Well, he would not leave Mrs. Kean waiting. They each had a different mission to pursue, but they always benefitted from each other's counsel. Gideon told Tom to get a messenger to take her a response, indicating that Mr. Mavors would be happy to consult with her at her earliest convenience.

℘

A woman who had delivered a child was supposed to remain in bed for two weeks, not even moving to have the bed linen changed, and to keep to her room a full month until she was ready to be churched. In Isabella's case, there was no need for the gossips to guard her from her husband's sexual appetite, since Harrowby's mistress could answer that purpose. The real difficulty was in keeping Isabella entertained for, since she was not feeding her infant and had no interest in either sewing or reading, she suffered from ennui. She was young and healthy enough, too, that spending two weeks flat on her back was much more than she needed to regain her strength, especially when there were no demands placed upon it. Consequently, within just a few days of her delivery, she sat up in a fit of temper, threw off the bedclothes, and, over the protestations of the dry nurse who had been hired to keep her privities clean with the use of poultices and soothed with herbal washes, declared herself too well to stay in bed.

The restriction to keep to her bedchamber, however, could not be overcome without causing a major scandal. Instead, entertainment must be brought in. The curtains and shutters were opened, and visitors in the form of her hairdresser, her staymaker, and her mantuamaker were admitted, although the staymaker, being a man, should have been banned along with Isabella's husband and other gentlemen. The hairdresser managed to keep her amused for hours, experimenting with the latest styles imported from France. The staymaker, however, was not so fortunate. When he took her measurements, she was convinced he was lying, and it took all the tact he possessed to reassure her that it was much too early to expect her waist to return to its former size. It fell to the mantua-maker to persuade her that her talent with the needle could hide my lady's extra inches until her normal dimensions were regained.

Patience had never been one of Isabella's virtues. She was eager to get back to Court, but she could not be happy until she was convinced that her ability to attract admirers was as powerful as ever. The quickest way to regain her figure would have been to nourish her infant, but when both the dry nurse and Hester reminded her of this, she broke out in tears.

Mrs. Mayfield tried to console her daughter with the news that at present St. James's was not the merriest place. The Court had no sooner gone out of mourning for the Princess of Muscovy, than it had gone back in for the Elector of Triers, to be followed immediately by another period of mourning for the Queen Grandmother of Sweden. It seemed to Isabella that some royal or other would always be dying just to spoil their fun. Since her marriage to Harrowby, she had grown used to indulging her every whim, and she did not like her pleasures to be thwarted. She resisted any suggestion that she would have to restrict her intake of food to regain her girlish figure.

An advertisement in the newspaper over the weekend planted a happier idea. Perhaps it was not her figure, but the antiquated looking glass in her dressing chamber that was at fault. Mr. Arbuthnot, who had kept the great looking glass shop at the corner of Villers Street in the Strand for several years past, had placed the advertisement to advise the public that he was desirous of leaving the trade and was selling all his goods at reasonable prices. Given the bitter weather and Isabella's inability to leave the house, Hester was entrusted with the errand of purchasing a new mirror.

She postponed her errand til Monday in order to have enough time to inform St. Mars that she would be at Mr. Arbuthnot's shop. She did not have use of the carriage, since Harrowby needed it to attend Parliament. A bill had been proposed which would allow the King to arrest persons on suspicion of conspiring against him and to keep them in prison until May. There was strenuous opposition to it in both houses, since it was perceived to be a great danger to the liberties of the English people. Some feared the bill would encourage the laying of malicious information and give a handle to those in power to oppress the innocent, but Mr. Stanhope argued for its necessity in a time of rebellion. Since someone had once made false accusations against Hester's own brother for malicious personal reasons, which had sent him to Newgate, she had worries about the bill. She had communicated her concerns to Harrowby, but doubted he had attended to a word she had said.

She was conveyed to the Strand in a hired vehicle, which had none of the comforts of the Hawkhurst coach. Shivering with cold, she arrived at the great looking glass shop and took refuge inside, where a dazzling display of glass reflected back at her. Shaving mirrors in walnut frames sparkled on the counter, and the walls were lit with mirrors in Italian or French giltwood frames with bird, tulip, and fleur-de-lis motifs. Cupids, twisted foliage, and open foliate surrounds framed the very latest in strikingly clear lead and mercury glass.

The floor of the shop was filled with other furnishings for sale, cabinets both English and Japan, decorated screens and fire-screens, stands, writing desks, bookcases, card tables, tea tables, dressing suits, and chests of drawers either Japan or walnut. Laid on the tables were carved and gilded sconces, and all manner of china, oil pictures and strong-boxes.

In spite of all the riches on offer, the room was not particularly full of customers, shoppers undoubtedly discouraged by the frost, even with the promised reduction in prices. One of Mr. Arbuthnot's clerks greeted her and, when told she was there on behalf of Lady Hawkhurst, conducted her eagerly to see a fine Venetian giltwood looking glass with C scrolls, flower heads, and leaf cartouche. The whole was surmounted by a swagged lambrequins and feathered crest. Hester was certain Isabella would like it, even if it did not make her look any thinner.

A gentleman's voice came from behind her. "My dear, Mrs. Hester! Fancy meeting you here!"

With heart thumping, she whirled to see a foppish gentleman in a scarlet coat and a shoulder-length peruke. His face was made up with white paint, and patches had been placed strategically on his face— one by an eye, another at the corner of his lips, presumably to suggest where he'd prefer to be kissed.

He descended upon her, planting a kiss squarely on her mouth and catching her unawares. As his lips touched hers, she gasped. The moistness of his breath mixed with hers, and a jolt shot through her. Her flustered breathing came in little pants, and she knew she must look flushed. It was more common to greet friends with a kiss than not, but St. Mars and she had never greeted each other as most friends did.

With a firm grip still on her arms, he teased her with a wicked grin, but his colour seemed heightened, too. It was impossible to tell beneath all that white paint, but his voice did sound a little husky when he spoke for the clerk's benefit. "And what brings you here today, my dear?"

He loosed her to let her collect herself. "I've come on an errand for Isabella. She requires a new looking glass."

He raised his brows, which were tinted black, giving him an even more devilish look. "Are the mirrors at Hawkhurst House insufficient to her needs?"

There was a hard note beneath his banter. So he had seen the announcement of the birth, she realized with a sinking feeling. She never betrayed Isabella to him if she could help it, but thought she might make a small exception today. "I'm afraid the looking glass in her dressing room does not show her the reflection she would like to see."

As she had hoped, her honest comment averted his resentment. He laughed, then took her hand and drew it through his arm. He squeezed it, saying, "If you will permit me to advise you, I shall be more than happy to help you select a new looking glass—one that I should wish to see in Hawkhurst House, if it were mine."

Hester thanked him and smothered a smile. She dismissed the clerk, saying she wished to look about.

"Does this mean you do not care for the Italian mirror?" she asked St. Mars, as he led her past a French armoire. "I must tell you that I think Isabella would love it."

"I do not doubt it. I shall find you a better one, however. The one you were looking at is too heavy at the top. It would suit a withdrawing room, but not a lady's chamber." He stopped in front of another mirror, also an arched rectangle in gilt. The divided glass had a mirrored slip surround, delineated by delicate pieces of figured and gilded wood, scrolled shoulders, and a pendant base with trailing foliage and scallop shells. It was the same size as the Italian looking glass, but the effect was much lighter, more delicate, and more pleasing.

"Oh, this is beautiful! I'm certain Isabella would like it."

"Do you?"

Hester turned and gave him a wary look. The last time she had expressed a liking for something, he had purchased it for her. "It does not matter what I think of it. This purchase is for Isabella, not me. What matters more, however, is if *you* like it. If *you* would wish to see it in Hawkhurst House, if it were yours."

He chuckled. "You sound afraid that I will buy it and have it delivered to your bedchamber. You cannot believe I would be so stupid."

"No." She dimpled. "Although you have been known to do outrageous things, I do not suppose you would put me in such an awkward position."

"Of course, I would not. But all thought of your bedchamber aside," he said, intimating with his tone that he still had it firmly in mind, "do you care for this style? It is the very latest thing from France."

"Oh, then we absolutely must have it, for surely there could be nothing more elegant. No, seriously, how could anyone not admire it?

It is too beautiful for words."

"Well, now that the decision has been made, where can we go to talk? We have too much to say to each other to do it in here."

"Do you not wish to see first how much the mirror will cost?"

He waved an airy hand. "Consider it a christening gift. I am not so churlish that I cannot congratulate your cousin on a safe delivery. Besides," he said, before she could express her gratitude for his magnanimity, "I had rather not waste any more of our time."

Mr. Arbuthnot must have been told that the Countess of Hawkhurst had sent Hester to buy one of his looking glasses, for she had seen him hovering in the distance. She beckoned to him and told him to deliver the French looking glass to Hawkhurst House.

With her business concluded, she and St. Mars discussed where they could go to have a conversation in private. Since they were already in the Strand, Hester suggested the church of St. Martin in the Fields, only a few blocks away. St. Mars offered to summon a chair for her, but she turned it down on the grounds that the day was sunny, that she had brought pattens for her shoes, and that, if they walked, they would be able to talk on the way.

Sitting on a chair provided by Mr. Arbuthnot's clerk, Hester affixed her pattens to her shoes, while St. Mars waited. Then he bundled her out the door.

They walked with their arms linked for warmth. Leaning into the frosty wind, St. Mars said, "I begin to think you do not trust me, Mrs. Kean, for you always suggest that we meet in a church."

"If you can think of any other place where we can sit and not freeze to death, I would be amenable to your suggestion." She spoke with a touch of asperity, for it was truly very cold. She was shivering beneath her woolen cloak, which was not fur-lined like his.

He must have noticed that her teeth were chattering because, after glancing sideways at her, he opened one side of his cloak and wrapped her up in it. She laughed, but almost immediately, she felt the warmth of his body radiating through her clothes. It was a bit awkward walking this way at first, but after he stumbled over her foot, he said, "Here— put your arm about my waist and we'll manage better. See . . . that's better, is it not?"

She did see the sense in it, and, as he roughly rubbed her back with the hand he'd thrown about her shoulders, she overcame her shyness. And, then—oh, it did feel wonderful to be pressed against his side. A blast of cold air hit their faces, and he stopped chafing her back to tighten his clasp. She warmed so rapidly then, the blood rushed to her cheeks. Whenever her footing slipped on the snow-covered pavement, his arm cinched about her and she felt his strength.

She had to do something to prevent him from noticing the effect his nearness had on her, so she told him about Harrowby's strange request and her visit to Lady Tatham. As she recounted the even more peculiar behaviour of Mr. Mistlethwait, the justice of the peace, she could feel St. Mars's keen interest in the tautness of his grip.

They trudged up Lancaster Court and reached St. Martin in the Fields just as she concluded her story. They entered the nave through the door on the west side, and the scent of age-old dust met their nostrils. Parts of the church had been standing since medieval days, but over the centuries it had been enlarged and transformed many times, particularly during the Tudors' reigns. The present church, built in the Perpendicular style with the off-center tower at its western end, was covered outside in stone and warm, golden brick. Inside the walls were wainscotted six feet high with ancient oak, which also made up the pulpit and the pews. Corinthian columns topped with gilt cherubim and horns of plenty stood at the entrance to the chancel, above which still hung the arms of Queen Anne.

The old structure had been deemed unsafe. Its walls had been built of rubble, which overtime was spreading, no longer able to support the roof. As Hester looked around, she noted several places where the walls had been shored up with cramps of iron. Having decided that the building could not be saved, the vestry had petitioned the Crown for help in replacing it, but so far no money had been forthcoming. The church was virtually deserted now, except for a few prostitutes who had taken refuge and huddled in the rear pews, their breath visible in the cold air.

An arched window over the door admitted a soft tinted light. St. Mars took Hester's elbow and guided her up one of the aisles past the carved-stone monuments to the dead. A particularly ornate one caught Hester's eye. It belonged to Nell Gwynn, the Protestant mistress of Charles II.

Near the front of the church stood a communion pew. Its existence proved that in the fairly recent past the congregation of St. Martin's had included radical Protestants who refused to kneel for the sacrament.

Choosing this pew, St. Mars ushered Hester inside the railing, and sat at its table beside her on the bench facing the altar. The air inside the church was nearly as cold as it was out of doors, but at least the wind could not reach them here and they could huddle together for warmth. The frigid marble beneath Hester's feet sent up a chill. She had had the good sense not to wear a hooped petticoat to go out in the cold. She wrapped her skirts tightly about her limbs, and stayed where she was when St. Mars slid over to press his leg against hers.

They had not sat this close since the unforgettable night when he had swept her up before him on his horse. Hester knew that she was trembling. She hoped he would think it was from the cold, but the truth was that she was warm enough now. She shook with the excitement of touching him. The chill merely served as a contrast to the warmth that coursed through her. She inhaled his masculine scent of wood smoke, wool, and horse.

He was holding himself rigidly, as if afraid of crushing her. "Let me make certain I understand. You say that when Harrowby sent you to call on Lady Tatham, he would not tell you what you were supposed to discover? If that is the case, then my cousin has reached a new height of imbecility."

Hester could not restrain the giggle that shivered up through her. With teeth nearly chattering, she replied, "I am convinced he was terribly frightened about something, but he could not or would not tell me what it was. It was as if he sent me to her house to see if any danger to him lurked there, in which case, I suppose I should be there to prevent it."

"Hmmph! Very brave of him, I must say. What a credit to the family! And did you perceive any danger?"

Hester tried to convey the sense she'd had of something's being amiss, over and beyond the bizarre manner of Sir Walter's death. Eventually, she shook her head. "I cannot describe it, my lord, but everything about my visit felt strange. It was odd that none of Sir Walter's friends had come to pay their respects. Even if Lady Tatham is not the warmest or the most attractive person, that would not usually be reason enough to shun her under the circumstances. Then, too, there was something queer about the place—so many new and expensive things for a house that one would not expect to be filled with such luxuries. And no expense had been spared on the funerary arrangements when Lady Tatham was the only mourner to be seen—and even she not particularly struck by grief."

St. Mars chuckled, and the tautness in his limbs seemed to ease. As he relaxed, his arm nestled against hers, feeling quite cosy. "If she does not much regret his death, that could be the very reason for the expensive arrangements. She would not wish to be seen to neglect any sign of respect due a husband by his wife. Lady Tatham would not be the first to hide her indifference, or even her relief, at the death of an unloved husband behind an excessive show of mourning."

"True. But she was indignant to the point of fury over the absense of his friends."

"Yes, probably because their neglect mortified her dignity. Could it not have been due to that?"

"Certainly it could. But how do you account for Mr. Mistlethwaite's behaviour?"

"I cannot. Tell me again just what he said."

Hester glanced at St. Mars's face and wished she might see it free of all its patches and paint. It was rare that she got a glimpse of the real man, when he had to disguise himself so thoroughly. Sighing inwardly, she repeated her conversation with the justice of the peace as best as she could recollect it.

"So, in essence, he did the same thing Harrowby did? He tried to discover something from you about Sir Walter's affairs without telling you what that something was?"

Hester pondered a moment, then agreed. "And now that I reflect upon it, there was an element of fear in his bearing, too. Fear that he hid behind anger and aggression. As soon as I mentioned I was sent by your cousin, he released my arm at once, but he seemed very keen to know what your cousin Harrowby would have to say about Sir Walter's affairs. Neither was specific about which of his affairs would interest them, though."

"Hmm . . . and you have no idea? Not the slightest guess?"

"No, and I could not very well put his widow through an inquisition."

St. Mars smiled. "No, I daresay not. Not at this first visit, at least. But you say Harrowby wishes you to see if you can discover who killed his friend?"

"Yes . . . and no. He does wish me to find out what I can about the death, but he no longer claims Sir Walter was his friend."

"Interesting . . . I have never known Harrowby to be fastidious in his friendships, unless someone's tailoring was bad. That could mean either that Sir Walter failed to take Harrowby's sartorial advice or that Harrowby knows something to Sir Walter's discredit and fears to be tainted with it, were it generally known. I'm inclined to think it's the latter."

Hester responded to his ironic tone with an amused glance, before turning her gaze back on the altar. It would be risky to let St. Mars look into her eyes, where he might easily see how completely besotted she was, in spite of his paint. "I'm of a mind to agree with you, sir, though Pierre did allow that his master was so *bouleversé* as to be uninterested in his new puce coat."

"Egads! But it is serious then. I shall obviously have to involve myself before the Fitzsimmons name loses all its luster. How shall I help? Would you like me to see what this Mistlethwait person is up to?"

"That would be useful . . . but there is another matter that perhaps you can advise me on."

"Anything, my dear. I trust you know that by now."

She loosed a chuckle. "Indeed I do, sir! But seriously, it has been puzzling me for some time, even before Sir Walter was found dead. I never had the feeling that your cousin was overjoyed by Sir Walter's friendship—more that he tolerated it out of some painful obligation."

"Was there any obligation you're aware of?"

"Only one. But I shall need you to tell me if it would be sufficient for putting up with a man he did not like. From what Madame Schultz told us, it was Sir Walter who introduced your cousin Har-rowby to his mistress."

"Madame Schultz!"

Hester swiveled to find St. Mars's brow drawn into a frown. She had expected he might react with his characteristic impudence to the news that Harrowby had taken a mistress—that he might find it an occasion to tease her or to poke fun at Isabella—but never that Madame Schultz would interest him. "Yes, do you know her?" she asked.

"No, but I would be curious to know what you know of her."

Hester grimaced and turned to face the bench across from them. "We see her at Hawkhurst House more than either Isabella or I really care to—more even than my aunt, who at first saw her visits as a great personal compliment to Isabella—for you must know it was the Prince of Wales who sent her to amuse Isabella when she could not go to Court. Now, I think he visited her upon us just to be rid of her himself. She is a connection of Herr Bernstorff. His Highness may have thought the King sent her to spy upon him."

St. Mars gave her a curious look.

"Yes. I'm afraid the King and his heir do not get along very well. I've heard it is because the son took his mother's part, which is to his credit, I'm sure, though I cannot say I find him any the more attractive for it. But it is also said that the Prince and Princess of Wales are siding with the Tories, if for no other reason than to annoy his Majesty. They both despise the King's ministers, Herr Bernstorff especially, but also Lord Townsend and Mr. Walpole. They are continually arguing with them over the right to fill Court positions."

"And you have all of this from Harrowby?" He seemed surprised. She was not sure if his surprise was due to Harrowby's relating such information to her or to his having it himself.

"Some of it," she said, "but more lately from the ladies' whispers round the tea table. We have been very confined of late."

When a shadow passed over his features, Hester wanted to kick herself for referring so lightly to the birth of Isabella's child. A silence fell between them, and she started to apologize for her insensitivity, but he forestalled her.

"What is your opinion of Madame Schultz? Is she a truthful person? Would you say she is to be trusted?"

Hester did not like to say unkind things about anyone, particularly if she could not be sure that what she said was true, but as isolated from Court as he was, St. Mars needed her to give him the best answer she could give. "No, I should say not. I do not know the lady perfectly, but from what I have seen her principal business in life is to obtain whatever she can for herself."

His lips twisted beneath the paint. "A genuine courtier, then. Well, I am not surprised." When he felt Hester's questioning gaze linger upon him, he added, "I have recently heard something of her—that is all." He paused, then smiled when her stare persisted. "Very well, if you wish to be involved in a highly treasonous matter, I suppose I shall have to satisfy your curiosity. The Duke of Bournemouth has requested me—very politely, I should add—much more politely than he was wont to deal with me—to help his nephew escape from Newgate and get into France."

Hester felt all the blood drain out of her face. Of a sudden, she felt every bit of the cold.

"Here!" he said, wrapping his arm and his cloak about her. "I did not mean to startle you. And you should know me well enough by now to be certain of my caution."

Hester's jaw fell open in furious protest. She would not be beguiled by that strong arm about her. "Your caution indeed! Why I have seen you—! You always—!"

He threw back his head and gave a delighted laugh. "I always manage to slither out of trouble. You know I do. How can you doubt me? I've half a mind to be offended by this lack of faith in my capabilities."

"Be offended if you like, sir, but do not expect me to rejoice in your foolhardiness . . . my lord!"

"Ah . . . I wondered when you would begin to 'my lord' me again, and here we were having such a nice, warm chat."

"My lord, I beg you—!"

"Your begging will not discourage me, my dear, so let us have no more of this nonsense. I thought I had broke you and Tom of worrying on my account, but if you cannot spare yourself, at least spare me a lecture."

He squeezed her gently on the shoulder and gave her a little shake, but her excitement had flown, and in its place, she felt the welling of a sob. What right did she have, after all, to tell St. Mars what to do? If he only knew how little she would wish to live if anything harmed him. But she knew how much he chafed under the exile from everything he loved. It was that chafing undoubtedly that led him to do such mad things. Surely if not for his discontent, he would settle into a saner life? She tried to imagine him looking over his tenants' farms, perhaps paying a visit to the barn or to the pigs in the sty, and a smile cracked her lips.

"There!" he said, seeing it. "I knew you would be reasonable." He gave her an approving pat before removing his arm from about her shoulders. "Let me tell you what it's all about, and perhaps you can advise me."

He told her how the Duke of Bournemouth had contacted him, about the request he had made, and what he had promised to do for St. Mars in exchange. Hester listened with her fists clenched. She had never much cared for the Duke of Bournemouth, and she never would after he had tempted St. Mars into this venture.

But when St. Mars had finished, she asked only, "Do you think the Duke is to be trusted, my lord?" She knew her voice contained an edge, but it was the best she could manage under the circumstances.

His leery glance told her he had not missed it, but he answered her soberly, "I believe he is. He is more attached to this nephew than he would say—that much was evident. Or perhaps the attachment is to his sister. Whichever it is, I have reason to believe that if I am successful, he will do what he can for me, when the time is right. He did not make any rash promises, you know. He spoke sincerely."

Hester was a bit mollified by his seriousness. At least, he had considered the risk.

"Very well, then. How do you propose to go about it?" She hugged herself for warmth. The chill of his surprise had not left her, but she was still too vexed to nestle against him.

"I plan to smuggle in some implements so Breed can cut himself out, but I shall have to find a way to get them in. His family has paid the gaolers to make him as comfortable as allowed, so his shackles have been removed. He has the use of his hands, and there are other prisoners lodged with him who can help."

Hester recalled what her brother had suffered in Newgate without any money to purchase his comfort, and shuddered at the memory. "Cannot a member of his family take the tools into him?"

St. Mars shrugged. "They must avoid any implication in his escape or risk being charged with treason themselves. That is why Bournemouth solicited me. But they will supply whatever money I need to bribe the guards."

"Well, I certainly hope it is more than the reward that is on your head! Although I suppose an enterprising gaoler could always manage to pocket both."

He grinned at her wryly. "Perhaps we should change the subject."

Hester flushed, but she could not regret the acerbity in her tone, not if it brought him to his senses.

An uncomfortable silence fell between them. Recalling the hour, she knew she should return to Hawkhurst House. She did not like to part with him in this spirit, but the thought of the risk he was taking infuriated her so that she wanted to cry.

Standing up, she said, "Isabella will wonder what has become of me."

He reached for her arm as if to pull her back. Then, thinking better of it, he stood, too. "I shall help you to find a vehicle."

On the way outside, he paused by the prostitutes, who had gathered hopefully near the door, and dug in his pocket to give them each a coin, before catching Hester up outside. The wind chafed her cheeks, but her eyes stung for a different reason.

Ignoring her pique, St. Mars grasped her arm and firmly linked it with his. The gesture reassured her that they were still friends, despite their disagreement.

As they walked in search of a coach or a chair, he said, "Have you been to the Frost Fair?"

Her heart gave a skip. "No, I have been too confined."

"Then make an excuse and meet me there. You must be able to escape Isabella and Mrs. Mayfield one day at least. Say that your brother has summoned you."

A warm feeling suffused her, rising from the tips of her toes to her head. In all the times that they had met, there had always been a reason—a problem to discuss, a need for help—never simply that he wished to have her company. Her resistance melted. "I should dearly love to see it," she said.

"Then, it is agreed." There was no mistaking the pleasure in his voice. "But it must be soon. The weather could change at any moment."

Hester had missed too many treats not to be made anxious by the thought that the ice could melt and rob her of this one. Her mind worked feverishly for an excuse to escape the house. In addition to her usual duties and Harrowby's importunities, the baby's christening loomed. "I will do my best to make it this week. But I shall have to placate your cousin Harrowby. He was not at all satisfied with the report I made, and he wishes me to visit Lady Tatham again."

"Just do not let him keep you from it."

By this time, they had come to the Strand where several chairmen waited. St. Mars questioned a few until he determined on a pair who did not seem too inebriated, and he promised them a special reward if they delivered Hester at Hawkhurst House safe and sound. He pressed a coin into Hester's palm and told her to give it to them only if they did. The fare he gave them in advance assured their cheer on the trip.

"I shall look for your message," he said, when he handed her in. Then, he waved her off, adding, "Pray do not let it be too long."

Summon at once thy Courage, rouze thy Care,
Stand firm, look back, be resolute, beware.

CHAPTER V

G ideon walked home from their meeting, elated by the prospect of taking Mrs. Kean to the fair. He would have been happy for her counsel, but until she accepted his need to perform the Duke's task, he would have to do without. With all the dangers they had encountered together, he had not expected her to be discomfited by another, but he would not let one little disagreement spoil their friendship. He trusted the next time he saw her she would be reconciled to the idea and willing to offer advice. He could not help feeling a bit gratified by her concern. He might have teased her about it, had he not sensed how serious she was.

It was ridiculous, of course. He was not such an idiot that he intended to take any unnecessary risk. She might have trusted him to have some sense, at least, but he had often observed that women could be unreasonable.

Now that she had left, he could think of several things he might have asked her, but it was not at all rare for him to become distracted when they were together. And this particular meeting had posed even more challenges to his concentration than usual. He had held her close to him. He had felt her tremble in his arms, even if her shivering was due to the cold, and as a result his desire to make her quiver with passion was even stronger. Not for the first time, he cursed the fact that his outlaw status forced them to meet in churches, where every like feeling had to be suppressed. He promised himself that once the weather was warm, he would find a place for them to meet that was more conducive to gallantry.

For now, he could do nothing but force his mind onto the problem of how to smuggle a file into Newgate gaol.

It would be imperative to meet Nathan Breed before any attempt could be made. He would need to know exactly where in the prison Breed was lodged and to make arrangements for messages to be sent between them. His Grace of Bournemouth was so concerned that none of his family should be seen to be involved in an act of treason that he had hesitated even to convey to his nephew the information that Gideon would be in charge of his escape. Without some confidence in Breed's compliance with every detail of the plan, Gideon would not be so foolish as to proceed. A preliminary visit to Newgate, then, seemed to be in order.

Back at his house, Gideon stomped the snow off his boots and shook off the frost that had accumulated on his cloak and cravat. Joining Tom and Katy in the kitchen, he seated himself before the fire—something he had never done—while his two servants looked on with consternation. Their stunned, almost shocked, expressions made him break out in a grin.

"There's no reason for you to look so upset. I promise I shall not make a habit of invading your quarters."

Katy flushed and hurried to offer him a dish of heated wine.

Tom, who had known him intimately his whole life, was blunter. "What can your lordship mean by it? That's what I want to know."

"Must I mean anything by it?" Tom deserved to be set in his place, something Gideon's father would have had no hesitation in doing. But he was not his father, and the question emerged in a teasing tone.

Tom's grumbled response was characteristic. "I'm afeared your lordship is up to no good."

Gideon heaved an audible sigh. "On the contrary," he said, "the project I mean to propose to you falls definitely into the category of 'good.' It is quite charitable, in fact." He had not told Tom what the

Duke of Bournemouth had requested him to do.

"I know how your lordship thinks when you use that tone, and it don't mean I have to like it."

"No, but here it is. We're going to save a young gentleman's life. Is there anything to object to in that?"

These words caught Tom's interest, if not his acquiescence. Gideon ordered him to sit across from him, and when Katy brought him his mulled wine, he made her sit there as well. Her soft brown eyes glanced apprehensively back and forth between Gideon's face and Tom's.

"There is a gentleman by the name of Nathan Breed who was captured with the Northumbrian rebels." As Tom's eyes narrowed, Gideon said quickly, "All I propose to do is to smuggle a few tools into Newgate so he can dig his own way out."

As he said the word "Newgate," a little cry escaped from Katy and a hand flew to her mouth. On her raised thumb Gideon saw a shriveled scar in the form of a T, the mark she had received for being the dupe of a thief. A branding was the court's way of showing mercy for a crime that would ordinarily be a capital offense. Gideon had seen Katy's mark before, but having been declared outlaw himself, and occupied by other things, he had never given it any thought. Katy had proved she was no thief, but he had forgotten that her imprisonment could have left scars of another sort.

At her involuntary gasp, Tom scowled and reached a calloused hand to envelope hers. Holding it comfortingly in his lap, he said, "What's this all about, Master Gideon? Why would you want to mix yourself up in this foolishness?"

His manner of address made Gideon wince. Tom only called him "Master Gideon" when he was sorely displeased.

"Nathan Breed is the nephew of the Duke of Bournemouth. If I help his nephew escape, his Grace will repay me by pleading my case before the King." He did not tell them how tenuous the Duke's promise was, not when knowing would surely increase their opposition. He did not mean to involve either of his servants in the greatest risks, but he would need their assistance. If Breed did manage to break out of Newgate, someone would have to wait for him and conduct him to this house. Until Gideon's plan was fully formed, he would not know in what other capacity he would need their help. Distractions could be needed. Provisions certainly would be. Clothes, horses—he did not know what else.

"Don't worry," he said. "I promise not to send you within the keeper's reach. But I shall require your assistance—you, Katy, with disguises, and Tom—whatever else I need."

This last was vague, but he could see that Tom, and to a lesser extent Katy, sympathized with his reason for involving himself in such a venture. They exchanged looks, and some kind of understanding passed between them.

Tom spoke. "All right, my lord. If this will get us back to Rotherham Abbey, we'll do our best, but, mind, I won't have my wife ending up in Newgate."

Gideon smiled at Tom's protective tone. "Nothing could be further from my intention." Then he recalled the promise he had made to Mrs. Kean. "Meanwhile, I have just discovered the identity of the corpse you saw."

Tom grimaced at the memory, but said, "Who was it, my lord?"

St. Mars told him about Sir Walter Tatham and how his cousin Harrowby had asked Mrs. Kean to discover what she could about the murder. "Does his name mean anything to you? You seemed to know his face."

Tom pondered for a while, repeating the name beneath his breath. Then, with a start, "Now I remember 'im, my lord. There was a gen'leman by the name, used to plague your father. He used to come to Hawkhurst House—said he wanted to speak to his lordship on important business. But your father never would see 'im. Told the footman to send 'im away with a flea in his ear."

Sobering, Gideon pursed his lips. "My father never did have any tolerance for fools, but he also could have known something unsavoury about Sir Walter." He thought seriously for a moment before adding, "It could be that my cousin failed to protect himself from Sir Walter's importunities. He could have got caught up in matters over his head. That would not surprise me."

He considered a moment, then said, "I have a job for you, Tom. Mrs. Kean gave me the name of a man who disliked Sir Walter at least as much as my father did. I want you to see what you can learn about a magistrate by the name of Alfred Mistlethwait."

For days, the Hawkhurst household had been in a flutter over the baby's christening. This would be the first occasion for Harrowby to entertain the King, but as much as she might sulk, Isabella could not attend the ceremony. No baptism could wait for the mother to leave her bedchamber without risking that the baby could die before his soul had been admitted into the Church. It was a great honour that King George had agreed to be godfather to their child, and the newly translated Archbishop of Canterbury, Dr. William Wake, was to perform the ceremony for such an important personage as the tiny Viscount Rennington.

The whole of Hawkhurst House braced itself for the visit of his Majesty. The housekeeper, the butler, the clerk of the kitchen, and the chef united to take the event in hand, and Harrowby's receiver-general, James Henry, rode up from Rotherham Abbey to assist. Since neither Harrowby nor Isabella spoke German or French, and the King spoke no English, Hester had expected to be called upon to translate, but Mrs. Mayfield smugly informed her that both the Princess of Wales and Herr Bothmer could perform that service. Instead, Hester was to see that the child was ready and waiting for the celebrants in the withdrawing room. It was clear that her aunt meant this to be a snub, but Hester was secretly relieved not to have to be part of the welcoming party below.

When the great day came, the ladies who had witnessed the baby's birth along with a number of prominent Whigs and their wives assembled in the withdrawing room. Harrowby, Mrs. Mayfield, and a large retinue of servants stood downstairs in the great marble hall with the other godfather, Lord Kirkland, to welcome the King and the Princess of Wales. As soon as the King's carriage was perceived to enter the courtyard, they would all have to go out into the freezing weather to greet the royal visitors. Only Isabella had no role, other than to sit in her bedchamber with just her maid to keep her company.

Both the King and Princess would be accompanied by several members of their households. Protocol would dictate who should remove the royal cloaks, but the Hawkhurst contingent and all the courtiers would have wraps to remove as well. An army of footmen had been assembled to handle the process as speedily as possible. Then, to Harrowby and Mrs. Mayfield would fall the honour of escorting their royal guests up the stairs.

With plenty of time to spare, Hester went to the nursery to accompany the wet nurse and infant as far as the withdrawing room, where Hester would take charge of the baby. By now, his mother should have hired the nurse who would supervise Sarah and raise him, but Mrs. Mayfield had persuaded Isabella that to do so would be a wasted expense until he required more attention than wet-nursing. The process of finding a suitable woman had hardly begun.

When Hester reached the nursery, Sarah was waiting for her with the baby gathered in her arms. He was richly garbed in a long satin gown and swaddled in a bearing cloth of lavishly trimmed silk. His loud breathing— curiously loud for such a little infant—attested that he had fallen into a deep sleep.

Hester had not had much time to visit little George. She saw him only when Sarah brought him to see his mama in a stiffly formal ritual, performed twice daily. Since Hester hoped to see Isabella develop a strong affection for her baby, she had not inserted herself between them during these visits, but she had noted what a bright-eyed, observant child he seemed to be. Her arms itched to hold him, but she knew it would be unwise to become too attached to a child that was not hers and over whom she would never be given the slightest authority.

Seeing him so deeply asleep, she smiled at Sarah. "I see he has been amply fed. I hope the meal will last him until the christening is over."

"Yes, mistress, I did fill'im up. And you're not to worry that he'll wake before parson's done wiv'im."

Hester was bending over the baby, breathing in a sweet mixture of soap and milk, but she paused with her hand on his bearing cloth. She glanced at the nurse, and a sharp note entered her voice. "Why do you say that?" The baby's breathing was unnaturally loud, as if the child were in a stupour.

Sarah shrank, her eyes widening with guilt. "I only did what Mrs. Mayfield tol' me to do, mistress —giv'im some o' that physick she brung me." She gestured at a bottle on the table at her elbow.

With a rush of alarm, Hester hastened to pick up the bottle and unstopped the cork. Taking a whiff, she detected brandy and nothing else.

"My aunt told you to give him this?" When Sarah nodded fearfully, Hester demanded, "How much did you give him?"

"Nobbut a spoonful or two. I woulda giv'im more, but he didn't like it. Kept turnin' his head and spittin' so, I had to hold his little nose. But, after a bit, he quieted down all peaceful, like a good little boy."

Hester closed her eyes, and fought the temptation to slap Sarah's face. When she opened them again, she was shaking. She said, through gritted teeth, "He is quiet because he's drunk. You will be fortunate if he lives to come out of it. But there is nothing that can be done now," she said, as Sarah gasped and clutched her apron to her mouth. "The King will be here soon, and we must not keep him waiting. This is my aunt's doing," she added in a gentler tone, hoping to ward off an ill-timed bout of tears, "which I shall tell my cousins. But if you value your life, Sarah, you must never give him strong spirits again."

Sarah promised, wiping her damp eyes with her apron. Hester's threat was not as empty as it might have seemed, since at the moment she felt quite capable of killing the girl. If Isabella had engaged a proper nurse, this never would have happened.

Gesturing for Sarah to bring the baby, she wove her way out of the nursery suite and went downstairs to the saloon on the first floor. Before they entered the room where the guests were assembled, still trembling with anger and fright, Hester took the infant in her arms and examined him. His mouth was hanging open, and his breathing came in slow rasps. She kissed him on his little forehead and prayed to God that he would be well.

Taking a deep breath, herself, she gave Sarah her final instructions. She was to follow Hester into the room and stand behind her until it was time to carry Georgie back to the nursery. Seeing that the girl had composed herself, Hester turned and nodded to the footman manning the door.

Inside, she found that his Grace, the Lord Archbishop of Canterbury had arrived with his chaplain and archdeacons. He was standing near the door and speaking with James Henry, who, on seeing Hester, gave her a confidential smile. His task had been to escort the newly appointed archbishop and his party up the stairs to join the other guests, who were sitting or standing about in small groups.

His Grace, Dr. William Wake, was an elderly gentleman of scholarly demeanour, who broke off his conversation when Hester entered—a tale about a native boy, a leaf, and an iron pencil—the manner of writing practiced in the East Indies—and allowed James Henry to present her. Her curtsy was somewhat awkward due to the bundle she held.

"And this must be little Lord Rennington." The Archbishop cast a wary look at the infant in her arms. "I shall beg to postpone our acquaintance. It is my experience that babies are much happier if they are introduced to the mysteries of the Church as briefly as possible."

James Henry chuckled, and Hester tried to follow suit, but she would have felt much easier if she had been holding a screaming baby. Then she would know that the brandy had not done poor Georgie any harm. There was an exaggerated rising and falling to his chest that she could not like, and it seemed that nothing would ever wake him.

The archdeacons set a table with the altar cloth, while the chaplain stood by with a small, silver ewer of consecrated water. In every other respect, the room lay in readiness for the ceremony. Despite the bitter cold, the Hawkhurst hot houses had produced an abundance of flowers for the occasion. The carpets had been swept, and a strong scent of beeswax attested to the fact that the furniture had been polished to a high shine. A raging fire threw out warmth from the hearth.

Seated near it was Madame Schulz, who was whispering something into Lady Chelmsford's ear. Only Isabella and Lady Tatham were missing, mourning making it impossible for the latter to attend.

Then, from outside in the courtyard, came the sound of many hoof beats striking the paving stones and signaling the arrival of the King and Princess of Wales with their party of Horse Guards. The guests who were seated got to their feet. Skirts and coats were smoothed as the assembly arranged itself to welcome the King.

Soon, footsteps on the stairs heralded the arrival of the royal party. Hester turned to stand by the Archbishop, as James Henry stepped back to make room for the large number of people who came bursting into the room. First were Harrowby and his Majesty King George, followed closely by Mrs. Mayfield with the Princess of Wales.

As Hester sank into a deep curtsy, she was grateful for the steadying hand James Henry placed beneath her elbow, while managing to execute his own polished bow. They were scarcely noticed, however, as the royal party had first to receive the greetings of the Archbishop and his priests.

While the assembled guests all made their bows, the room continued to fill with his Majesty's attendants, who came scurrying in his wake: his personal servant, the Turk Mehemet, the Hanoverian minister, Herr Bothmer, and the gentlemen of his household, all resplendent in silk and lace and shoulder-length perukes. Her Highness, Princess Caroline, was attended by two of her ladies, the Duchess of Bolton and Mrs. Holland, who trailed the King's party. They had barely reached the room, when the King, with an air of impatience, signaled that the ceremony should begin.

Later, Hester could not have recounted the progress of the rite. Her mind was entirely occupied with fear for the child as he was passed from parent to godparent to priest. She strained to listen for his breathing, her heart stuck solidly in her throat. The ceremony seemed to pass with excruciating slowness, though in reality it could have lasted no more than a few minutes. Georgie slept soundly throughout the prayers, and did not stir, even when his Grace poured what must have been very cold water on his forehead. When the King smiled upon him, the whole party heaved a pleased sigh, but Hester could not feel any relief herself until Mrs. Mayfield passed the baby back to her and she saw his chest was still moving.

The footmen moved forward with glasses of fine French wine for the guests. Hester had to take a glass at the risk of appearing churlish, though under the circumstances she would have found a dish of tea more fortifying. The King, through Herr Bothmer, proposed a toast to his newest godchild. Then his Majesty conferred briefly with Herr Bothmer, who turned to Harrowby and said, "Lord Hawkhurst, his

Majesty congratulates you on the christening of an heir, but begs you will excuse him from taking any more refreshment, for the news from Scotland demands his attention. He desires that you will not abandon the rest of your company to escort him to his horse, but will instead drink a toast to his namesake in his place."

Harrowby bowed and expressed his gratitude for the King's generosity in agreeing to be patron to their child. Mrs. Mayfield curtsied, barely concealing her relief that she would not be obliged to entertain the King.

Before his Majesty quitted the room, Herr Bothmer summoned Sarah with a gesture. In shock, the girl stumbled forward and performed an awkward curtsy before the King, who presented her with a purse filled with coins. Then, with a nod for the whole company, he left, looking very grave.

His departure with the Horse Guards persuaded Princess Caroline to leave, too. With a regal smile, she accepted their bows and curtsies, then turned and swept from the room. Both were followed by their attendants.

James Henry, who had signaled to the footmen to abandon their laden trays and hasten downstairs to provide the parting guests with their cloaks and assist them into their carriages, followed the royal party from the room.

Now everyone else could relax. On James Henry's instructions, one footman had stayed behind, and he hurried about refilling the guests' glasses from the nine dozen bottles stocked for the event. The Archbishop raised his glass to the mother of such a fine infant, and his archdeacons and chaplain concurred by saying "Amen." After the bumper was drunk, as the remaining godfather, Lord Kirkland proposed a toast to George Frederick Richard Fitzsimmons, Viscount Rennington—the baby's second name in honour of the eldest son of the Prince and Princess of Wales. By the time a third glass had been imbibed, the footmen had returned from their duties downstairs and could begin passing dishes of sweetmeats. The Hawkhurst chef had prepared a banquet of delicacies for the King and Princess. He would be disappointed to learn that not one of his carefully concocted treats had ever passed the royal lips, but the other guests were prepared to enjoy them.

In his gentle manner, the Archbishop congratulated Harrowby on the healthy delivery of a child and offered his prayers that their child—and every child in his Majesty's kingdom—would be blessed with God's grace. While Harrowby basked in the congratulations flowing about him, the Archbishop asked if he had taken advantage of this special occasion to make his confession before God.

Harrowby gave a visible start. He reddened and blustered, "I— that's to say, what should I have to confess?"

His Grace smiled patiently. "We are none of us free of sin, my lord. You must not think I mean to imply any particular sin on your part. It is merely that I am a great believer in the efficacy of confession. I have often written that it is one of the few aspects of the Roman faith I wish we had kept."

"Oh! Er . . . yes . . . yes, of course! I quite agree. One can never confess too much, I always say." Rattled, Harrowby took a handkerchief from his pocket and wiped the fine layer of perspiration that had coated his brow. He was spared any further ecclesiastical discourse when James Henry returned to the room to report that the royal party had been sent safely on its way.

"Did anyone give you the latest news from Scotland?" the Archbishop asked.

"Yes, your Grace. It is confirmed that the Pretender landed near Aberdeen and is arrived at Perth. He is accompanied by some officers, in addition to his servants and domestics. It is said he has been very much indisposed since his arrival, which is imputed to the fatigue he suffered at sea, but he is expected to set out for Scone."

Scone was the place where the kings of Scotland were crowned. While the gentlemen and clerics discussed these disturbing developments in quiet voices, Hester set down her barely touched glass in order to attend to the baby, who at last showed signs of stirring. He still did not wake, but his sleep seemed more natural now. He made little moues with his lips, and for the first time since she had fetched him, Hester was able to take a breath of relief. A prick of tears stung her eyes, but she dispelled them with a quivering sigh.

Her aunt was contentedly stuffing herself with sweetmeats. Now would not be the proper time to confront her, and Hester needed to compose herself. She approached Harrowby and interrupted him long enough to obtain his permission for Sarah to return the baby to the nursery. He gave a casual wave of his hand, obviously glad to have the whole affair behind him.

The guests were all deep in talk, Harrowby on his fifth bumper of white wine, so Hester left the room with Sarah unremarked. Reluctant to part with the baby, Hester carried him back to the nursery and laid him in his crib.

Hovering beside her, Sarah darted her a guilty look. "Will you tell 'em what I done now, mistress? Will they be angry with me?"

"I will not until their company has left. You mustn't worry about it, Sarah. You were following Mrs. Mayfield's orders, and so I shall tell my cousins."

Sarah bobbed her a curtsy. "That's the truth of it, mistress. Thank you, mistress. I promise I'll never giv'it to'im again. But what if she tells me to? What shall I do?"

"I hope she never will give such an order again, but if she does, you must come to me at once, and I shall deal with it. Is that understood?"

"Oh, yes, it is. Thank you, mistress." She bobbed two more curtsies, then turned to straighten Georgie's coverlets.

After telling her that she would come upstairs later to make certain his lordship was quite well, Hester returned to the withdrawing room, where she learned that the Archbishop and his attendants had just left. Harrowby, surrounded by so many well-wishers, and more than half drunk, remained in a self-congratulatory mood. Amidst the happy toasts, he seemed to have forgotten his doubts over the parentage of his heir. Mrs. Mayfield's flattery, which worked to greater effect when her son-in-law was in his cups, had gone far towards reconciling him to Isabella.

Hester would be loath to introduce a topic of discord into this newfound harmony, so for the present she would refrain from informing the baby's parents of how her aunt had endangered his life. She knew it was common for poor women to dose their infants with gin to quiet them, but that was in lieu of the services of a nurse. A baby with all the advantages of the Hawkhurst name and fortune should never be subjected to such risks. She foresaw a vicious defense on the part of her aunt, who would argue that she had done it in the interest of pleasing the King by presenting him with a docile baby. And, unfortunately, Hester could not be confident that this argument would not carry with the baby's parents.

The fear she had experienced had left her cold. Feeling alone amongst the company, she moved closer to the fire in search of warmth. Lady Chelmsford, sitting near it, saw Hester and beckoned her to her side. After a brief exchange over the excellence of the refreshments and a polite inquiry after Isabella's health, she asked quietly, "I wonder if you noticed a most interesting item in the newssheets today?"

"Not today. We have been too occupied to read them." It was Hester's custom to read the newssheets to the family, since neither Isabella nor her mother was very literate.

"I thought you must have missed it. There was a most curious item amongst the advertisements, which should shed some light on the strange circumstances of Sir Walter's death—though at the moment I fail to see how. It was offering a reward for a set of coronation robes that have gone missing from a baron's house."

"Indeed? And did they belong to anyone Sir Walter knew?"

"That I could not say, not being well-acquainted with Sir Walter. I mention it in case Lord Hawkhurst would find it of interest."

Hester thanked her and said she would be sure to convey the news to him.

It was not until all the company had left that she could read the item herself. By this time, Harrowby was so overcome by the number of toasts he had drunk that he had fallen asleep in a chair, and Hester was obliged to spend a great many minutes with Isabella, describing everything that had gone on at the "gossips feast," as Mrs. Mayfield called it: what everyone had worn, what the King and Princess had said about little George, and who had flirted with whom. Eventually, she was able to persuade Isabella to order the newssheets to be fetched and to settle down for a reading, but before Hester could locate the item for which she searched, the first pages had to be read.

Today they reported the news Herr Bothmer had already related about the Pretender. While Mrs. Mayfield proclaimed her dread of James Stuart and his men, Hester scanned the paper for the advertisement. She found it and read:

Stolen from Lord Ratby's House in Great Suffolk Street, a coronation Suit. Whoever shall discover the same to his Lordship's Agent, Mr. Dawes, shall have 20 Guineas Reward.

At last, here was the information she had expected to see. It was inconceivable that such a loss would go unreported. Hester hoped this discovery would help alleviate the horror Harrowby felt over the bizarre circumstances of Sir Walter's death. She did not bother relating the advertisement to her cousin and her aunt, since Harrowby had shown no sign of taking them into his confidence. She waited until she could make an excuse for leaving Isabella's bedchamber before going in search of Harrowby, whom she found still sunk in his chair.

As she read the advertisement to him, his expression quickly changed from a look of dazed and drowsy contentment to the haunted mien he had worn of late. Mixed with it was a degree of confusion that Hester found pitiable, as he grasped the front of his wig and gave it a vicious tug.

"Lord Ratby? What the devil would that old court-card have to do with Sir Walter Tatham? You cannot mean to say that he coshed him on the head and trussed him up like a Christmas swan for his Majesty's table? Why, Ratby couldn't lift a frozen pullet without a dozen footmen to assist him!"

Hester explained that the coronation suit had likely been stolen from Lord Ratby, as the advertisement had said, but that whoever had taken it would likely prove to be the murderer.

"If I could discover who took it from Lord Ratby's house, that might resolve the mystery. Is that what you wish me to do?"

Harrowby leaned forward to bury his face in his hands. "I don't know," he said miserably. "I just don't know what good it would do."

"My lord, if you would only tell me . . ."

Her uncompleted sentence brought him to his senses. He raised his head, still avoiding her gaze. "Yes, I suppose you should find out who stole the robes. But do not say you've come on my behalf! Let it be known that I have asked you to assist Lady Tatham in seeking information that could help find her husband's killer. As a widow, she cannot be expected to pursue inquiries herself, so it is only charitable for acquaintances like me to aid her in this respect."

Hester saw that she would get nothing further from him. She left the room not one bit the wiser as to the cause of his distress.

Later, in her room, as she reflected on the day, she recalled the guilty start Harrowby had given when the Archbishop had posed his question about confession. At the time it had struck her that Harrowby's denial of any sins to confess was stronger than the occasion seemed to warrant. Now, as she considered, she wondered what Harrowby could feel guilty about. He was not so devout—nor was society so prudish—that he would consider the taking of a mistress a sin to confess, not when the majority of his fellow peers did the same. If he had reacted with only his mistress in mind, she would have expected his expression to reflect more embarrassment or shame. Instead, she realized now, it had betrayed guilt and fear. Since Hester's visit to Lady Tatham, Harrowby's uneasiness had not abated in the least. She was unable to account for the fear that held him in its grip. Whatever the reason, it had been exacerbated by the Pretender's arrival, but unlike on the previous occasions when news of the Pretender had panicked him, this time she sensed there were other grounds for his fear. Hester, who had been puzzling over a cause for it, now wondered how much guilt played a part.

What had Harrowby done? And what did it have to do with Sir Walter's death?

You'll sometimes meet a Fop, of nicest Tread,
Whose mantling Peruke veils his empty Head,
At ev'ry Step he dreads the Wall to lose,
And risques, to save a Coach, his red'heel'd Shoes . . .

CHAPTER VI

That evening, just before dusk, Gideon walked across the frozen Thames to Black Friars Stairs and made his way to Newgate. The scarlet coat, shoulder-length black periwig, face paint, and patches he often wore to conceal his identity would, he hoped, win his way into the prison to see Nathan Breed.

With a sizeable reward on his own head, he could not be entirely sanguine when approaching the keeper's lodge, but a twinge of fear only enhanced his excitement. For one who had been near despair with boredom, any heightened emotion was welcome. And his risk of discovery was not so great as to cause him serious alarm.

His face was not widely known. As poor as any image of him was likely to be, even if his likeness had been circulated, few people would have the visual acuity to match his painted and patched face with the image. Even the King in a commoner's garb would not be recognized by most of his subjects, since most of them had never seen either him or his portrait. So, Gideon needed only to avoid his former acquaintances, few of whom he expected to meet in Newgate gaol.

By this time, too, he had made use enough of this particular disguise to know how well it obscured any semblance of his real character. He had never indulged in the fashion for paint and patch, except under duress from his valet, and the black wig and the boot blacking he used to dye his brows hid his natural fairness. No one who had known him in his previous life had ever seen him wear such a garish red or affect the manners of a fop. Had she still been living, he might have defied even his own mother to know him.

His real concern, then, was more how the plight of the prisoners would affect him.

In spite of the bitter cold, the streets near the prison were bustling with activity. A crowd had gathered outside the rails of the Old Bailey to witness the trial of James Goodman, alias Footman, who had been arrested for highway robbery a month ago in Buckinghamshire. On being taken by the posse, he had been shot in the nape of the neck. Several small pieces of his skull had been removed from the wound, which was not yet healed, but was sufficiently well for him to stand in the prisoner's dock. The spectators were here to gape not only at an accused highwayman but at the gruesome opening in his head. Gideon hoped the spectacle and the crowd would distract the Newgate turn-keys from his mission.

A different group clustered outside the massive four-tiered gate to the prison. On his rambling strolls, Gideon had seen these same people before, the friends and relatives of the Jacobite prisoners, Whigs and Tories alike. There were clergy, physicians, tradesmen, servants—Gideon wondered how many among them might be disguised rebels themselves. Surrounding them was a party of haranguers, who made jests about warming pans to mock the legitimate birth of James Stuart, rumoured to be another woman's child smuggled into the Queen's bedchamber in a warming pan and foisted on the British people as the legitimate heir. They taunted the prisoners' friends with cries of "Jacks!" and threatened them with the docks and the noose.

After elbowing his way through the unruly crowd, Gideon rang the bell to the keeper's lodge and waited several minutes, stamping his feet and blowing on his gloves to keep warm. When the keeper, Pitt, appeared at the door and demanded to know his business, Gideon affected a hysterical note.

"I insist upon seeing my brother-in-law, do you hear? The Honourable Nathan Breed. And I'll not be deterred, you lout, so you can leave off those insolent glares, or I'll report you to his uncle, the Duke of Bournemouth, who is bosom friend to his Majesty."

The mention of the King forestalled the refusal forming on Pitt's lips, and the wealthy Duke's name made his eyes light up with avarice.

"Mr. Breed, is it? Well, that'll be one o' them rebels. An 'is Majesty's orders are that no one's allowed to see any o' them traitors" —this last was said in such a conciliatory tone that it was plainly a request for a bribe.

Gideon did not give into it immediately, since the garnish Pitt would demand was likely to go up with each visit. He protested that his Majesty could not have meant the prohibition to apply to the nobler prisoners, who were undoubtedly paying for better treatment. He stressed what a favourite of the King's the Duke of Bournemouth was.

The waver in Pitt's gaze revealed that such powerful names gave him pause, so Gideon pressed his advantage. "I've only come at the behest of my poor wife, don't y' know, who's too ill to come herself. But if you will not let me in to see him, I shall simply have to report to his Grace. Truth is, you scoundrel, I've no great wish to grace your foul domain. My nose'll never withstand the assault!" He turned to go, feigning relief at being excused from so unpleasant a duty.

In a hasty voice Pitt called him back. Then, gesturing for Gideon to step into the doorway of his house, where they would not be overheard, he favoured him with a resentful sneer. "I never said you couldn't see 'im. Only as 'ow 'is Majesty's been kinda touchy 'bout them partic'lar prisoners. I could let you in," he said, in a wheedling tone, "but you'd 'aff to pay a little visitin' fee, in case there was trouble later. It's a great favour I'd be doin' ya."

Heaving a sigh, Gideon bargained with the keeper until he lowered the bribe to a Guinea, only contriving to get it this low by promising the same every time he came. Given that Breed, or his family, had already had to pay hundreds of pounds for him to be housed in the Press Yard, this additional charge would be minor in comparison.

As soon as Gideon's coin had left his hand, he was admitted through the great arched gate into Newgate Street and ushered past the grate through which a few prisoners on the debtors' side spoke to their visitors. Already, a hint of the foul odours he would encounter inside wafted towards him—urine, feces, stale beer, vomitus and unwashed bodies. Then, he followed the keeper into the lodge, where the full force of the Newgate stench hit him.

Gideon covered his nose with a large handkerchief and tried breathing through his mouth, but still his stomach rose in protest. Taking a few seconds to control it, he reflected how much worse the stench would be in the heat of summer. Inside the lodge, he glimpsed two new prisoners being received. A turnkey was weighing both men down with a collection of handcuffs, fetters, and chains. The more iron he applied, the more the prisoners would have to pay to have them removed. The two men looked stunned as they shrank from the cold, heavy metal. Pity tore at Gideon's heart, but he forced himself to ignore these men. He was not there to save every prisoner, some of whom might even deserve punishment—though none probably as harsh as they would get. He forced his thoughts back to Nathan Breed, and peered about to learn the disposition of Newgate gaol.

From the lodge, he could see into the Gigger where the debtor prisoners clustered at the grate to speak to their visitors. Sounds of clinking mugs and drunken voices floated up from the taproom in the cellar, where the prisoners with liberty could purchase spirits. In the Hall Ward next to the lodge, more debtors huddled about the fire.

Pitt handed Gideon off to a turnkey who led him upstairs and through the wards where felons were housed to the Press Yard, or Governor's House, where he had been told he would find Nathan Breed. Every hold or ward they passed was crammed with prisoners, the arrest of so many rebels awaiting trial having packed the gaol to its limit. Men were layered on stacked bunks, their eating, sleeping and relieving quarters compressed into one crowded space. Several wards had ceilings so low, no prisoner could stand erect.

In the Governor's House, the ceiling soared again to ten feet. It was even possible to breathe, though the stench from the other wards was still powerful. This ward looked out over a narrow, stone-paved passage where prisoners who could pay for the privilege were given a little space to exercise their legs. On entering the room known as the

Press Yard, Gideon spied several young men in gentlemen's clothing, sitting at a table before a blazing hearth, drinking, joking, and smoking long clay pipes. Wigless, they were engaged in wagering and playing at cards. This, and their apparent jollity, made Gideon feel as if he had entered a tavern, save that the walls and floor of the room were made of thick, crumbling stone, crude charcoal drawings marred its walls, and it was crowded with narrow pallets.

The appearance of a visitor caused the gentlemen to break off their game. As they turned to face him, Gideon recognized Lord Derwentwater's wild younger brother, Charles Radcliffe, and Tom Forster, a distant cousin of the Radcliffes, who had been appointed the Jacobites' "General."

The rest were strangers to him, including a man in clerical garb seated next to Forster. Gideon did not think Tom Forster would see through his disguise, for they had met only once. But neither would he, he realized, be able to identify Nathan Breed.

Fortunately, he had reckoned without the services of the turnkey, who, holding out his hand for a coin, announced him loudly, "A gen'leman to see ye, Mr. Breed."

The youngest of the seated gentlemen, whom Gideon's entrance had caught in the middle of a laugh, leapt to his feet and came forward, an eager, puzzled expression upon his sensitive face. With mincing steps Gideon hastened to meet him, threw his arms about the fair young man, and kissed him on both cheeks, saying, "My dear brother-in-law, how good it is to see you! Your sister sends her tenderest regards." With his mouth near Breed's ear, he whispered, "Bournemouth sent me."

If Breed had been on the point of denying his acquaintance, he betrayed no sign but quickly entered into the masquerade, expressing joy and surprise to see his brother-in-law. Then, he took Gideon aback by embracing him ecstatically again. Gideon heard a low voice in his ear. "Take care. Spies amongst us."

"Naturally, dear boy," Gideon said, pulling back. He gave a simpering smile for the benefit of their audience, but a jab of caution recalled him to his own vulnerability. "Of course I'll carry your affectionate reassurances to my wife. Her distress at the thought of you in here has been most affecting. It will be a relief to her to know you are bearing up so well."

The gentlemen who had risen with Breed were waiting for introductions. First, however, the turnkey must be appeased. With a show of fastidious disgust Gideon dug into his pocket and hauled out another coin. As he had hoped, this bought the turnkey's willingness to leave him alone with the prisoners. He retreated, saying Gideon had only to call out when he wished to be released.

If not for Breed's warning, Gideon might have dispensed with his foppish manner. Since he did not know which men were to be trusted, he judged it best to maintain his guise. He had provided himself with a name, and this he offered to the company with an elegant bow. "Robert Johnstone, gentlemen, at your service."

In turn, Breed presented each of the gentlemen who shared his ward. Gideon caught just a few of their names while he pondered how to speak privately with Breed.

One of the prisoners said, "I did not know you had a sister, Breed."

Nathan answered gaily, "Oh, half a dozen at least. Radcliffe, you'll remember Mathilda, my elder sister but one. A kind girl, but given to nervous complaints."

Only twenty-two himself, Radcliffe nodded. "Ah, yes. Mathilda. So you are her husband," he said to Gideon. "Pray give her my regards.

Tom Forster clapped Gideon upon the back and sent his greetings along as well. He spoke of having met Mathilda once at Court.

Gideon, who did not know if a Mathilda Breed even existed, shook his head regretfully. "Yes, but that would have been years ago. She never leaves home now. Says she can't abide the movement of a carriage and don't have the strength to ride.

"But that is neither here nor there," he said, as if recollecting the purpose of his errand. "Tell me how your cases are faring. What have you heard?"

Nathan said, "We know James Stuart has landed in Scotland." His tone was cautious, but beneath it Gideon detected suppressed elation, as if Breed believed the Pretender would manage to come to their aid.

Indeed, this must have been what the prisoners believed, else Charles Radcliffe should be despondent over his brother's imminent trial.

In Newgate, they could not drink to the Pretender's health or call James "his Majesty"—not without running the risk of being sent up on another charge of treason. At least they had the sense not to add to their current difficulties.

Breed invited Gideon to join them in a glass of wine, then called for one of the servants—for the wealthier gentlemen had their personal servants in prison with them—to bring Gideon a fresh glass from the cellar. Apparently, this served as a signal to Radcliffe and Forster, who returned with the others to the gaming table.

Breed held Gideon back with a light grasp of the elbow, until the volume of jokes and laughter from the others increased enough to cover his voice.

"Who are you?" he said, beneath the noise.

Gideon matched his whisper to Breed's. "My name is Mavors. Your uncle sent me to help you escape."

A startled look came over the younger man's face. "But James—"

"His chances are poor. And George has resisted any pleas for mercy. The trials are moving forward. Seven of the captured peers are to go before the bar of the House tomorrow."

He did not wait for Breed's reaction, before continuing, "If I can get tools to you, can you cut your way out?"

Breed nodded, but Gideon's news had upset him. It took some effort for him to concentrate. "The iron bars are rusty, and the walls are crumbling. The others will help."

"I will come as often as possible and attempt to bribe the guards. I'll need to know of your progress, so I can be ready to take you to safety when you break through."

The others' voices died down, giving them no further opportunity to speak. The servant returned from the taproom with a new round of glasses, and Tom Forster proposed a toast to Mathilda Johnstone, to which Gideon drank with a professed sense of honour at the condescension of the illustrious company.

He saw no reason to linger and, in truth, the gentlemen's gaiety oppressed him. He could not tell if they were blissfully ignorant of the cruel death they faced or if they merely bolstered one another's spirits by ignoring it. Whichever it was, he could not join them, knowing the fate that was likely to be theirs.

He made his goodbyes and promised to visit again soon. The turnkey, who had accompanied the servant back in, had waited, and now he prepared to show Gideon out. As Breed embraced Gideon again, he reached beneath his cloak and grasped the iron file he had concealed in a deep, hidden pocket. He worked it inside Breed's coat, pressing it to the other man's side. Breed gave a start, then shifted his hand to cover it before Gideon released his hold.

"I'll bring you a concoction from our new chef," he promised. "The Frenchie's a genius with a cooking pot."

He waved to the others, then followed the turnkey back through the crowded gaol. Once again, the intolerable stench of the lesser wards nearly overcame him. He was glad for the foppish disguise which made it inevitable he should cover his nostrils with a perfumed handkerchief.

Before he left the turnkey, with feigned tears Gideon told him how grateful he would be for any kindness shown to his wife's poor brother, and reinforced these words with a generous gratuity. The turnkey, who gave his name as Fell, accepted the money with a cagey look, suggesting he would be receptive to Gideon's bribes. It was too early to secure his services, but even if only his negligence could be bought, that would assist the introduction of tools into the gaol.

As Gideon was exiting through the gate, a startled roar came from down the street. The crowd outside the gaol turned as one body and rushed towards the Session House from whence the sound had come. It split in two as four turnkeys ran from the prison and pushed their way through the throng. Gideon let himself be carried along by the mob, until the reason for the excitement floated back to him in shouts.

The accused highwayman, James Goodman—in spite of his gruesome injury and the irons that weighed him down—had managed to leap over the spikes of the bail dock of the Session House into the Old Bailey. Plunging into the crowd outside the court, who stood there agape, he had escaped and vanished into the streets. With a mixture of horror and awe, Gideon left, wondering what, if anything, this dramatic escape would augur for Nathan Breed.

∅

The advertisement about the stolen robes had requested anyone with pertinent information to seek Lord Ratby's agent at his lordship's house. Accordingly, the following afternoon, Hester, accompanied by a footman in the Hawkhurst livery, walked the short distance to Great Suffolk Street where, after making a few inquiries, she was soon directed to his lordship's house. Nervously, she presented herself at the door and was shown into a narrow hall to wait while his lordship's servant carried her message to his agent.

Within a few minutes she was taken upstairs to Lord Ratby's bedchamber, a dark paneled room with a carved wood ceiling and thick velvet curtains pulled over the windows, the space lighted entirely by tapers. There she found a small company of men assembled about a high curtained bed, set off from the rest of the room by an ornate wooden railing, where Lord Ratby lay wrapped in layers of wool, in visible agitation. Two of the attendants she recognized as his valet and his physician. The third she imagined could be the agent referred to in the advertisement.

Before anyone could greet her, Lord Ratby perceived her, and starting up from his pillows, pointed an accusing finger at her and said, in quavering tones, "You there! What do you know about this scandalous business? What have you to do with my coronation robes?"

"Now, now, your lordship," his physician, a vigorous man with a cheerful countenance, spoke in a loud, bracing voice. "What did we just say? It will do you no good to carry on in this way. You must think of your heart."

Hester swallowed. She wished Harrowby had not sent her on this errand. She determined it best to wait for his lordship's attendants to soothe him before she attempted an answer. The valet—his nerves very sorely tried—dabbed at his master's forehead with a damp piece of linen, but was roughly shoved aside. The doctor tried to persuade his lordship to take a dose of laudanum to ease his palpitations.

The third man, lean with a dark, narrow face, quietly left his master's side to approach her. His voice was low and somber when he presented himself as Mr. Dawes, his lordship's man of business. He asked her what information she had come to give.

It was plain that Lord Ratby had been gravely disturbed by the theft of his garments. Hester hoped it would be in her power to ease his agitation, but she had come to receive information, not to give it. Mr. Dawes told her that Lord Ratby had just suffered a very distressing visit from a local constable, who had informed his lordship that his missing robes had been discovered on the dead, frozen body of Sir Walter Tatham.

It did not surprise Hester that such terrible news would act powerfully on the spirits of an invalid. She doubted the humanity of her visit now. She whispered her fears to Mr. Dawes who, she could see, was inclined to agree, but feared his lord's temper if he were to let her go. The furious sounds coming from the bed seemed to have abated, and, as they both turned to peer in that direction, Hester saw that Lord Ratby had allowed himself to be soothed. He had refused the laudanum, but lay back against his pillows. His blue-tinged face no longer wore an angry mask. Fury had exhausted him. He had barely strength enough to raise a hand.

With great tact, Mr. Dawes approached him and, speaking in a soft, low voice, explained that Hester had come on behalf of Sir Walter Tatham's widow, but that she did not wish to alarm him if he was not up to receiving her. Lord Ratby turned his gaze upon her again, this time with a listlessness she found more distressing than his previous outburst. He said nothing, but with his eyes managed to indicate that he would see her now.

Hester stepped inside the railing and moved to the bedside, where she encountered the smell of the baron's decaying breath. She refused the chair Mr. Dawes would have pulled up for her, not wishing for Lord Ratby to have to strain his neck to see her. She had not yet had time to reveal her connection to Harrowby, but now, in the gentle manner she had perfected at many invalids' bedsides, she told his lordship that she was cousin to the Earl of Hawkhurst, who had taken it upon himself to assist Lady Tatham with her inquiries into this tragic business. She could tell by his expression that this connection did her no disservice, though her mention of Sir Walter's widow caused more agitated movement of his hands.

When he spoke, his voice was weak. "How did he come by my robes? I don't even know the fellow."

Disappointed to find that his ignorance of the affair was as great as hers, Hester shook her head. "I am afraid Lady Tatham is as much in the dark as you are on that point, my lord. In fact, I came hoping you would have some notion of who might have stolen them."

The colour rose abruptly in his cheeks. She was afraid she had set him off again.

"But, of course," she amended hastily, "if they were stolen from you, I see that you would not. I wish I could be helpful to you, my lord, but indeed, we are as puzzled as you by this whole affair."

"What the devil's Hawkhurst got to do with it, eh? Not interested in the widow, is he? Not with that tasty armful of his."

Hester bit her tongue in order not to reveal her offence at this reference to Isabella. "No, my lord. Sir Walter was . . . an acquaintance of Lord Hawkhurst's. But my cousin was often in his company of late, and the death was so sudden, he was moved to take an interest in the affair."

"Humph! Got to be more to it than that. Don't try to bamboozle me, girl! I may be ill, but that don't mean I'm a fool. I know a humbug when I hear it."

"Indeed, Lord Ratby, you are mistaken. My cousin simply wishes to help Lady Tatham unravel the bizarre set of circumstances."

"Then why don't he come here himself, eh? Why send a girl to do a man's job?" He peered at her with a gimlet eye. "I know him, ye see. He don't care a fig for anybody but himself. I'll be a Dutchman if he don't have some interest in this."

Hester could say with convincing truth, "If he does, my lord, he did not entrust his reasons to me." She was ready to give up on Lord Ratby. Clearly he knew nothing about how his robes had been stolen, and if she sat here much longer, suffering his insults, she would be tempted to forget he was an invalid.

Before she could withdraw, a bustle at the door announced an arrival. A voice off to her right languidly said, "My dearest uncle, what is all this fiddle-faddle? I came as soon as I could!" She turned to see an elegant young gentleman poised just inside the door of the chamber. He was dressed in the very height of fashion, with a powdered wig tied in a queue with a black velvet ribbon. The hair was brushed back from his forehead over a pad in the toupet style and dressed over the temples with pigeon's wings. His coat and his stockings were of the finest silk, and generously embroidered. Jewels twinkled on his fingers and his chest. On his narrow face he wore a great deal of white paint and patches, and he affected a listless air.

"My dear boy!"

Hester turned to see that Lord Ratby's eyes had lit up and his cheeks looked flushed. He reached out both hands to the visitor, who came mincing forward on ruby-covered heels and took them in his clasp. The "dear boy" then bowed with an exaggerated degree of respect and kissed Lord Ratby's knuckles.

"I came as soon as I heard the dreadful news," the vision declared. "What a shock to you it must have been! And now I hear that a gentleman was murdered while wearing your robes. My dearest uncle, whatever can the world be coming to?"

"It's an impertinence! The grossest sort of impertinence!"

The young gentleman looked up when he had finished his remark, which he had offered rhetorically. Only then, it seemed, did he espy Hester. "But I interrupt, my dear uncle. Who is this charming creature who has come to see you?" He took out a quizzing glass and peered closely at Hester, allowing his gaze to travel insolently from her head to her toes. There was an insolent note in his voice, too, when he drawled, "I hope you do not mean to marry her, for I assure you I should be devastated to think anyone had replaced me in your affections."

"More like, replaced you in my will!" The older man cackled, clearly flattered by his nephew's suggestion. "Don't be a simpleton, Horace. You know my petticoat days are over. This is Mrs. Kean. She's come on the part of her cousin, Lord Hawkhurst. Make your leg to her, you impudent dog! I doubt not, you'll be more to her taste than an old codger like me."

This long speech provoked a coughing spell, which the younger man ignored.

"Mrs. Kean, your servant." Lord Ratby's nephew dismissed her with a careless bow and a smile that was more of a sneer. Then he demanded to know how his uncle's coronation robes had found their way onto a body in the middle of the frozen Thames.

Lord Ratby's choler surged as he repeated that he had not the slightest idea. His physician, who had greeted the young man's arrival with evident disapproval, came over to the bed to take his patient's pulse. "I beg you will be careful now, Mr. Gayet, or you'll have his lordship in a temper again."

"I'll be in a temper if I wish!" Lord Ratby's volume increased as he shoved his doctor off. "Don't tell me what I may or may not do, or I'll turn you off, you miserable leech!"

Mr. Gayet laughed. "That is telling him, uncle. By gad! I hope I have one-tenth of your fire when I'm half your age."

"I said careful, sir, and I meant it," the doctor warned, "or your uncle will be carried off!"

"Indeed, sir!" The valet stretched an arm across the bed to mop his master's brow.

Lord Ratby fumed and fussed until his breathing came in gasps, and he fell back spent upon his bolster.

Mr. Gayet gave a chuckle. "Ah, very well, very well. You had better calm down, uncle, or they will all of them pitch me out. But I don't see how you tolerate the lot of them. Nothing but a bunch of old maids!"

Hester, who had not moved during this scene because she was hemmed in by his lordship's servants, thought that now would be a good time to withdraw. Mr. Gayet seemed determined to provoke his uncle into a fit. Lord Ratby was clearly devoted to nephew, but she could see why his physician did not approve of the younger man's visits.

"If you will excuse me, Lord Ratby, I shall leave you to your rest." She curtsied to him and inclined her head to the other men present.

Mr. Dawes offered to escort her out. She welcomed the chance to speak to him more privately.

"How long has your lord been in this invalidish state?" she asked him quietly, as her footman met them at the door and followed them down the dark, paneled stairs.

"He's been indisposed for quite some time—nearly five years—but only an invalid this past one. As you can see, he chafes against restraint, but his medical man insists that his heart will give out if he is not careful."

"I do not doubt it. You can see it in his colour." They had reached the bottom of the stairs now, and Hester turned to face him. "Mr. Dawes, have you truly no notion of who might have stolen the coronation robes?" After he shook his head, she added, "Where were they stored?"

"They were kept here, in a chest in Lord Ratby's dressing chamber. The chest was locked, but since it also contains my lord's parliamentary robes, the key is always kept nearby. I suppose any visitor to Lord Ratby's bedchamber could have taken them."

He added hesitantly, "My lord does not recall meeting Sir Walter, but his memory is not as good as it once was. Is there any chance Sir Walter could have called here and . . . and borrowed them?"

"I do not believe that is likely. Have you questioned the servants? Surely no one could have visited this house without their knowing."

He seemed disappointed. "I have, and they all assure me that no one has come that they do not know well. I live in Leicestershire, you see. That is where my lord's seat is located. So, I am not as familiar with his London acquaintances."

A strong idea had taken hold of Hester, but she did not know how to advance it. She said, "Lord Ratby appears to be very fond of his nephew."

"Yes, he is always happy to see Mr. Gayet. My lord has no children, so Mr. Gayet is his heir. He is very attentive, particularly since his uncle has been bedridden." Mr. Dawes delivered this information in an expressionless tone, but Hester thought she detected a certain edge.

"I see," she said, leaving his statement at that. Even if it had been proper to voice her suspicions, she was convinced it would be useless. If Lord Ratby were to die and Mr. Gayet to inherit, he would become Mr. Dawes's new master.

She thanked Mr. Dawes for showing her to the door and gratefully climbed into a hackney the footman had secured for her.

Harrowby was likely to be upset when he learned that her questions to Lord Ratby had not turned up any answers, and she could not tell him of her suspicions just yet. It seemed she had reached the limit of her ability to investigate. If St. Mars would help her, she might learn more about Mr. Horace Gayet. She did not like the way he had provoked his uncle. The question was what connection, if any, did he have with Sir Walter?

When the hackney drove up to Hawkhurst House and let Hester down outside the gates, she was approached by a short but lean, grizzled man with long, muscular arms and a pipe clenched between his teeth. His beard was encrusted with ice, giving the impression of a gnome who had fallen asleep in the snow and been awakened by magic.

After assuring himself that she was indeed Mrs. Kean, he reached inside his heavy woolen cloak and pressed a letter into her palm. Seeing St. Mars's handwriting, Hester quickly concealed it in the pocket of her skirt and thanked his messenger with a two-penny piece. The old man accepted this as no more than his due, then with an impudent wink, said, "Nate, waterman, at yer service," and took himself off. Hester gazed after him, wondering how such a character had come to be in St. Mars's employ.

Upstairs, alone in her bedchamber, she drew out the letter and read, "Mr. Mavors would be honoured by the presence of Mrs. Hester Kean at a celebration in honour of the birthday of Prince Frederick, at the Frost Fair on Thursday, 19 January, where two oxen will be roasted upon the ice. A carriage will be waiting for her outside the gate to Hawkhurst House at any hour she appoints."

Hester's nerves tingled with excitement, and her heart beat fast with joy. Then, just as quickly, her spirits sank. How could she ever hope to escape Isabella and Mrs. Mayfield?

The lashing Whip resounds, the Horses strain,
And Blood in Anguish bursts the swelling Vain.
O barb'rous Men, your cruel Breasts asswage,
Why vent ye on the gen'rous Steed your Rage?

CHAPTER VII

Hester found her cousin in her bedchamber, standing before her new French looking glass and trying on a gown, while her mother supervised the woman who knelt on the floor pinning the hem.

"So there you are Hester," her aunt said, her tone implying that Hester had been shirking her duties. Hester had hoped for a private audience with her cousin, but lately could never catch her alone.

Ignoring her mother's remark, Isabella asked, "Oh, Hester, what do you think of my new embroidered silk? Does the colour suit me?"

Hester could answer truthfully, "You know it does. Yellow always becomes you. It is much your most flattering colour."

Isabella primped and swiveled before the mirror, making it hard for the dressmaker, still on her knees, to hold onto the hem. With brown eyes agleam and golden locks bouncing, Isabella did present a charming picture. It had been months since Hester had seen her in such good health, and she wondered what had happened to raise the bloom in her cousin's cheeks.

The reason soon became apparent. "You will need to get your best dress hung out, for at last we are returning to Court!"

Hester was taken aback. She wondered that her cousin could be enthused over something that would not happen for another fortnight.

"That is wonderful news, Bella. When shall you go?"

"Tomorrow. There's to be a celebration in honour of Prince Frederick's birthday, and his Highness has invited us to his chambers. There will be music and cards! No dancing, since his Majesty is determined to keep the Court in mourning. But I am so happy. Everything has been so tedious, but now we may be merry again!"

"But . . ." Hester's mouth fell open. "Isabella . . . you have not been churched."

Her cousin gave a giggle. "That is the very best part of it. His Highness sent Madame Schultz to tell me that as long as I feel well enough, I needn't wait any longer. He will send his own chaplain here tomorrow, and I can be churched at home in time for the evening!"

Shocked, Hester stifled a protest while struggling to make sense of the news. She had to assume that if the chaplain performed the ceremony, it would be in order. Thinking about the rite, she realized there was no absolute waiting period prescribed in the *Book of Common Prayer*. Certainly, something on the order of thirty or forty days was the custom, as was performing the ceremony in church, but her own father had performed it more than once in his patron's private home. The rite had been banned for years under the Puritans, and strict Non-Conformists still refused to participate in what they considered to be a test of conformity to ecclesiastical discipline, but anyone who preferred their loyalty not to be questioned should be careful to observe it.

Mrs. Mayfield had observed her stunned countenance, and now she spoke with a mixture of smugness and viciousness. "It is not for you to disapprove of what his Highness allows!"

"No!" Hester hastened to defend herself. "I was merely surprised, that is all. And you do feel completely well, Bella? I trust that everyone at Court will be informed that the rite has been observed?"

"They shall, Miss Prune Face," Mrs. Mayfield asserted, "for I shall be there to tell them." She would be proud to spread the news of his Highness's favour.

"And this will be tomorrow, you say?" Tomorrow, she thought, as Isabella nodded. That would be the day St. Mars had invited her to the fair.

She had felt Mrs. Mayfield bristle at Isabella's suggestion that her cousin be included in their party. Hester was often caught between Isabella's enthusiasm for a large number of companions and her aunt's desire to exclude her so she would be cognizant of her place. Now, Hester's stomach quivered, as if she were about to step out on a slack-rope, like a rope-dancer at Southwark Fair.

If she could manage to get Mrs. Mayfield to prevail without provoking Isabella to champion her, and without her aunt realizing how much, for once, their desires conformed . . . .

"That sounds delightful, Isabella," she said. "I had been about to ask you if I might go see my brother that day, but if you desire my presence at Court, of course, I shall be happy to go."

"I should think you would be!" Her aunt snorted. "But I do not see any use in your going. The play will be very high—much too high for you! And I do not know how you will occupy yourself while the rest of us are at cards."

"But you cannot wish to visit Jeremy when you might go to Court!" Isabella could not conceive of a more preferable pleasure. "There will be music, and I know you love that."

"Indeed." Hester hesitated. "But I have not seen my brother this month or more, and he did particularly wish for me to come. I do not like to slight him by giving into a greater temptation."

"And indeed you should not! What would my poor dead brother think if you neglected your family?"

Since Mrs. Mayfield had given no thought to her clergyman brother, Hester's father, in months, other than to use his daughter as an unpaid servant, Hester was not fooled by this appeal.

"Pooh!" Isabella affected no such sentiments. "You can see Jeremy any day. You will and you shall go to Court! I will not have you working in that bookstall with him when the rest of us are having fun."

This was turning into one of those rare occasions when Hester wished her cousin were not so fond. "There was some talk of going to the Frost Fair," she said. "I have not seen it yet, and it cannot last much longer."

"But won't it be very rough? No one in polite society goes to fairs now."

Hester could feel her aunt's stare. She tried not to tense as she gave a regretful smile. "As much as I love Jeremy, Isabella, I cannot claim that he is a member of polite society."

"Humph!" Mrs. Mayfield looked disgusted. "I should say he is not. But Hester is right, my dear, that she should not slight him. One should never be above one's relations, I always say." As condescending as her speech was, her expression betrayed delight that Hester would find herself joining the ranks of impolite society, where no doubt Mrs. Mayfield believed she belonged.

"Very well. Do as you wish." The tone of Isabella's voice suggested that the subject had grown tedious. Turning back to her mirror, she tilted her head left and right to examine the angles of her face. "Have you completed that business for my lord?"

Hester realized she had not reported to Harrowby since her visit to Lord Ratby. She sighed. ""No, I fear it is scarcely begun."

"You are mighty secretive," Mrs. Mayfield said, giving her niece a suspicious look. "I wonder what sort of intrigue you can be getting up to."

Hester squarely met her gaze. "If you wish to know about it, you have only to ask my lord."

Mrs. Mayfield did not dare question her son-in-law. She turned away, muttering how surely it could not be of any consequence or her lord would have confided it in his wife. Though plainly annoyed, she seemed reassured by Hester's complete lack of embarrassment. Since Hester still had no notion why Harrowby had been so upset by Sir Walter's death, she had nothing embarrassing to hide.

Presently taking her leave, Hester waited until she was well clear of Isabella's chambers before giving vent to the exultation she had been holding in check. Her smile stretched so wide, her face almost hurt. Tomorrow she would go to the Frost Fair with St. Mars, and neither Isabella nor her mother had managed to take the treat away. She could have laughed, but she was sufficiently cautious not to tempt fate. As she walked through the long gallery on her way to Harrowby's apartment, she wondered what gown she should wear, or whether it would make any difference when her dress would certainly be covered by her cloak.

She was thus happily employed when she encountered James Henry coming towards her.

"So, there are you, Mrs. Kean."

Hester chuckled, thinking how different the words sounded when uttered by him. There was no accusation in James Henry's voice, just a hint of pleasant surprise.

He gave a puzzled smile. "Have I said something amusing?"

"No, nothing. Forgive me. I was reflecting on how disagreeable those very words sounded when they were recently spoken by my aunt."

At the mention of Mrs. Mayfield, his smile disappeared. He said with a hint of wryness, "I am glad she has given you something to be merry about. Were you coming in search of my lord?"

"Yes. Is he able to receive me, do you know?"

"Not if what you have to say is of a private nature." He looked a question at her. "His barber is with him."

Hester's smile was noncommittal. "Then I shall return later." She gratefully turned around, eager to seek her own chamber and bask in the anticipation of her treat.

"Mrs. Kean?" A tentative voice called her back.

Hester turned to find him standing with an uncharacteristic tilt to his shoulders. His figure was usually so confidently erect, his manner so steady. "Yes?"

"Might I have a word?" He paused. "It is not often that I get up to town, and I should like to . . . have some conversation with you."

There was something strange in his manner, which put Hester on her guard. Nevertheless, she smiled and acquiesced. They were near one end of the gallery with no servants in sight. James Henry gestured to suggest they should stroll the gallery together. Hester turned and matched her pace to his.

Glancing at his profile, she was struck, as she always was, by his resemblance to St. Mars in the aquiline cast of his features, the same forceful Hawkhurst nose and brow. It amused her to search for their similarities, as well as their many differences. Last year, St. Mars had revealed to her that James Henry was his half-brother, the bastard son of the former Lord Hawkhurst and a Huguenot woman he had rescued from persecution in France. Though never acknowledged by his father, James Henry had been raised to fill the trusted post of receiver-general for his father's estates, had been paid a generous allowance, and had been given a house of his own in Kent. Hester did not know if Harrowby knew of their relationship or whether he even suspected it, but James Henry's service and judgement were indispensable to him.

Several of the portraits that gazed down from the gallery walls bore a likeness to the man at Hester's side, reminding her that they were his ancestors, as well as St. Mars's and Harrowby's.

After they had taken a few paces, James Henry said, "I have not had a chance to speak to you since the christening. There was something about you that day . . . I thought you seemed out of sorts."

Hester sighed. "Oh, yes. That." She told him what her aunt had done, and how frightened she had been for the infant.

As he listened, his jaw tightened, and when she had finished, he said, "Thank God no harm was done! Does my lord know of this?"

"I have not told him yet. It was my intention to tell him and Isabella, but . . . I am ashamed to say it . . . I cannot be certain that either of them will regard it in the same light as I did. My aunt administered the spirits so the child would be docile for the King, and as long as Georgie was not harmed, I'm afraid they might even approve of what she did. I've given the nurse firm orders never to dose the baby with spirits again and to come to me instantly if my aunt ever suggests it."

"That was well done." He nodded. "For a moment, I thought that might be why my lord has seemed distracted, but you say he knows nothing of it?"

"I am certain he does not."

"Then it must be something else." His sideways gaze begged her for information, but Hester did not feel able to betray Harrowby's confidence. It was clear that whatever he had asked her to undertake was to be kept between them.

"The child . . . my lord was pleased?"

Ah, Hester thought, *so he has noticed.* She temporized. "Naturally, he was relieved that Isabella survived her confinement. The wait was very long, though Dr. Hamilton assured us there were no complications. Then, the news that he had been blessed with an heir was most welcome."

"I do not get the sense that he visits, or indeed, that he even thinks of the child." James Henry's concern was palpable.

"It is not every gentleman who takes a close interest in his off-spring, I believe."

"Mrs. Kean—" he halted beneath a portrait of the first Earl of Hawkhurst, painted by Van Dyck—"I hope you do not think it odd for me to speak to you of these matters. I only have the family's inter-est at heart."

Hester turned to face him, and said hastily, "I know it. That is as clear to my cousins as it is to me. Let me assure you, however, that all is well between them. I believe there is something else preying on my cousin's mind, though I do not know what it is. He has been very distracted since Sir Walter Tatham was discovered dead."

He frowned, bemused. "That must, indeed, have been a shock, but I did not know that Sir Walter and my lord were such good friends."

"They had been rather often in each other's company, at least since I returned from my brother's house in December."

"I see." James Henry's tone suggested that he was even more con-fused than before. As they resumed their stroll, he glanced sideways at her again, and his smile indicated a change of subject. "It has occurred to me that you and I share . . . that is to say, we occupy similar places in this household. I hope my saying that does not offend you."

"No, indeed." How could it? Though he was unaware, she knew their positions were almost identical. She was cousin to Isabella, and he to Harrowby. They both were dependents, though her relationship to the family was openly acknowledged, and James Henry's father had provided for his security.

She wished she could tell him that she knew about his birth, but since St. Mars had been the source of her information, she could not without betraying their friendship.

"My duties are confidential and . . . rather solitary," he said, glanc-ing her way again. "There is no one I can speak to about them . . . no one I dare trust when something arises that . . . . In short, I should like to think that I can speak to you about matters which concern the family. You, too, seem to have their best interests at heart."

He was asking her to be his confidante. Hester's heart leapt into her throat at the honour he had paid her, although she could not ask the same of him. She could not refuse, but neither could she ever be perfectly open with him. She did have the family's interest at heart, but second always to St. Mars's, and James Henry had never been his brother's ally. It pained her that the two men, both of whom were honourable, should be suspicious of each other. She was sure those feelings stemmed from jealousy and from St. Mars's not having known of their kinship until after his father's death. Her first loyalty would always be to St. Mars, but she could not be happy about deceiving his brother.

"I will always be honoured by anything you wish to discuss. And I shall do my best to respect any confidence."

He was pleased with her answer. "Thank you. I shall value your discretion. " He laughed self-consciously. "My work can be lonely at times."

"I do not doubt it. Mine can, too," She could not return his laughter. A lump had lodged in her throat from the compliment he had paid her. Would she ever be expected to keep a secret from St. Mars? And if she were, how would she act? She had kept Isabella's secrets from him, but only those that betrayed her cousin's foibles. What sort of confidence would James Henry expect her to keep?

"Do you return to Rotherham Abbey at once?" she asked, wishing to change the subject.

"Yes, I leave in the morning. And there are errands I should make."

They had reached the end of the long line of portraits, and he halted as if their paths would diverge here. "I should speak to my lord again before I go." He took Hester's hand and surprised her by kissing it. A flush came over his cheeks. "Until I see you again, then?"

"Yes." Feeling suddenly very awkward, she curtsied and wished him a safe journey, before seeking her bedchamber to pen a message to St. Mars.

On Thursday, near noon, as soon as Isabella and her mother left for the Palace, Hester wrapped herself in her warmest cloak and followed them out of the house. She crossed the forecourt and passed through the gilded iron gate leading out into Piccadilly. A hackney carriage stood in the road. As she hesitantly approached it, its door was thrown open by someone inside. The driver sprang down from the box and let down the steps.

Expecting to find St. Mars inside, Hester hurried to mount them, not wishing to risk his being seen from the house, but instead she found Katy seated on the bench.

After greeting her with a respectful bob of her head, Katy handed her a pink loo-mask. "The master said you should wear this. He said it would be best."

A thrill of trepidation grazed Hester's spine, as a recalled conversation around Isabella's tea table sprang into her mind. One of the ladies had said that wearing masks, except to masquerade balls, was become so associated with the demi-monde, that she had vowed she would never wear one in public again, "for it invites the most impertinent behaviour!" Certainly, the ability to hide one's identity gave a lady much more room for license, and the corollary was that it invited license, too.

The wearing of vizard-masks at the theatre had been banned by Queen Anne years ago for just that reason in the hope the measure would cut down on vice by exposing women of ill-repute. The rule had never been much enforced, but the Society for the Reformation of Manners had its spies everywhere, and they would pursue a warrant against any woman they believed to be a whore. Hester doubted that Isabella would leave off wearing masks unless it became completely unfashionable, but a countess had no reason to fear an association formed by mere lawyers and merchants. Hester, when not under her cousin's protection, had to be more circumspect, but surely the wearing of a mask at the Frost Fair could be justified when vizard-masks were often worn to protect the face from wind. Wearing a full-mask, however, would make it impossible to converse, as they had to be held on with the teeth.

St. Mars would have to wear something to hide his identity. She trusted he would protect her from abuse, whether from impertinent men or the morality police.

"I assume my lord will be masked, too? Are you here to take me to him?"

"Yes, mistress. He'll be waiting for you at Temple Stairs." Katy made Hester turn round and tied on her mask.

Hester was glad St. Mars had not risked coming for her himself. He was not always so prudent. Then, a thought occurred to her—perhaps he had meant to protect her rather than himself. Her reputation would certainly be damaged if anyone saw her riding in a closed carriage with an unknown gentleman. But that was ridiculous, she recalled, for if anyone recognized him, her reputation would be the least of their worries. A more reasonable explanation was that he wished to insure he was not spotted by anyone in the family or one of his former servants.

It did not take their hackney long to arrive at Temple Bar. The driver set them down in the crowded street. Then, as they wove their way through the Temple buildings towards the river stairs, Katy said, "Mrs. Kean, you know that Tom and me, we'll be getting married soon, and we would be very proud if you would witness our vows."

Hester smiled with unfeigned pleasure. "I shall be very happy to see you wed. You will have to tell me where and when to come, and I will do everything in my power to be there."

Katy beamed. "Thank you, mistress."

That was the last word they exchanged, for they had to mind their steps. Hester's pattens were not made to walk upon ice, and she had to place each foot down carefully to avoid slipping. The Temple streets were teeming with people on their way to the Frost Fair. As Hester made her way across the terrace, through a parting in the crowd she caught a glimpse of the village constructed on the ice. Booths were arranged into formal streets, some like an extension of the Temple streets themselves.

The words of an old ballad came to her:

> *I'll tell you a story as true as 'tis rare,*
> *Of a river turned into a Bartlemy Fair.*

Then someone tall and lean strode up to her. He wore a tricorn hat and a greatcoat with many shoulder capes. The upper half of his face was covered in a black mask. But she recognized the blue eyes shining through it, and the fair hair tied into a queue with a black ribbon.

He swept off his hat to make her a bow, but all the time his sapphire eyes were dancing. Hester curtsied and turned to thank Katy, but St. Mars's servant had melted into the crowd, leaving Hester alone with St. Mars.

He took her gloved hand and pulled it through his arm. As they turned to walk towards the stairs, he said, "Do you realize, my dear, this is the first occasion we have met for no other reason but pleasure? I am determined that not a word regarding corpses or treason or mysteries shall be uttered by either of us today."

Hester chuckled. "Do you think us capable of that, my lord? I am not at all certain that I can make conversation without them."

"Nonsense! Do you mean those are the sort of things you discuss over the tea table or in the withdrawing room at Hawkhurst House?"

She laughed. "If I did, your cousin would have turned me out long ago."

"And with reason. But we shall endeavour to forget them today."

Hester did not wish to spoil their outing, but her conscience forced her to say, "I will be happy to forget them, but I do have much to tell you, my lord."

"And I you, but nothing so urgent that we cannot first have a bit of fun, I hope?"

"No, nothing so urgent."

"Good, then, let's go."

They had reached the steps leading down to the river bank. St. Mars took a firm hold of her hand and cautioned her to mind her footing. Then at the bottom of the stairs they stepped out onto the ice, and with a thrill, Hester realized that she was standing solidly on her own two feet upon the River Thames.

Directly ahead stretched an avenue of booths made of tents, no less crowded than Fleet Street at Temple Bar. Customers pushed into every tent. Between them salesmen hawked wares, from orange peddlers and ballad sellers to a man crying out, "Buttons and buckles!" Urchins ran around the tents, hurling snowballs at one another.

They were not the only people masked in the crowd. Hester spied other gentlemen with masked ladies on their arms, deserting the Court's formality for a vulgar sort of pleasure. The women might be other gentlemen's wives, of course, or, perhaps, the men's mistresses.

A shiver ran through her—excitement she thought—before she sensed the icy cold pressing up through her shoes. St. Mars noticed her shaking and pulled her closer as they braved their way through the crowd.

"The oxen are being roasted between here and London Bridge, but there is much to see before."

Indeed, a milliner's tent had just caught Hester's eye, but she pretended not to notice it for fear St. Mars would insist on buying her a hat. Forgetting to be careful, she moved away from it too fast and her foot slipped. St. Mars caught her before she fell and set her slowly back on her feet.

"I do not see how you are able to keep your footing so well," she complained, embarrassed.

He grinned and raised one boot to reveal an ice-creeper, explaining that Tom had had them made.

"It's a pity you did not think to procure a pair for me, along with the mask."

"Oh, but I did—think of it, that is. Then I realized that without them you would be obliged to hold on to me."

Hester's mouth flew open in surprise. She tried hard not to dimple. "I would never have suspected you of being so unchivalrous!"

"Not at all! I promise to lay my life down to keep you from falling."

"It will serve you right if I do fall on top of you and crush you!"

"I doubt you could, but please feel free to try."

Seeing that he was completely shameless, she could do nothing but laugh. She did, however, accept the arm he offered, as they continued their stroll.

A toyshop stood just beyond the milliner's tent, and they paused to see what it contained. The crowd about it consisted mostly of women to whom the owner was extolling the benefits of a rare blacking for the hair, guaranteed to remain black, even if wet. Hester had no desire to turn her light brown hair black for fear of looking like her aunt, whose tint was so unrelievedly black as to resemble a crow's.

Instead, she moved towards the end of the row where a sign proclaimed, "Ye Rowling Press Printers."

"Here," St. Mars said, snatching up a page that had dried. "You must have one of these." While he produced his coin for the printer, Hester read the poem, which said it had been *Printed on the Ice on the Thames, at the Maidenhead, Second Booth, at Old Swan Stairs, Jan. 19, 1715-6.*

Upon the Frost in the Year 1715-6

Behold the Liquid Thames now frozen or'e,
That lately Ships of mighty Burthen bore.
The Watermen for want of Rowing Boats,
Make use of Booths, to get their Pence and Groats.
Here you may see Beef Roasted on the Spit,
And for your Money you may taste a bit.
There you may print your Name, tho' cannot write,
'Cause num'd with Cold: 'Tis done with great Delight.
And lay it by, that Ages yet to come,
May see what Things upon the Ice were done.

From the Printing-house, Bow-Church-Yard

Hester thanked St. Mars, professing great pleasure to have the remembrance. She knew he would not let her go without a gift, and this one seemed as sensible and inexpensive as she was likely to escape with. It was not so dear that she could not pretend to have bought it herself. And in spite of the crudity of the poem, the last two lines resonated with her thoughts.

She wondered if in ages to come people would be impressed by the things done on the frozen river, or if frost fairs would become so commonplace that no one would regard this one at all. For her, she was certain it would remain the most glorious fair in her memory.

"Come, look here!" Instead of turning left to follow the next "street" of booths that ended beneath London Bridge, St. Mars drew her to an open space behind the printer's tent, where she spotted an engine of a kind she had never seen. From a scaffold, a large ring had been suspended, and along this ring sat five miniature coaches, each with a child riding inside. Hester watched as the children flew round and round, squealing with delight.

She turned to question St. Mars with a smile.

"They are called flying coaches. Like the new stage coaches that go to York and the Bath."

"Oh, yes! I've heard of them, but never seen one."

"Then it is clear I shall have to escort you to more fairs. Heaven knows what else you may have missed!"

She laughed with pure joy to think that they might have other excursions like this. Then, as if her mind refused to permit such bliss, she wondered how long she would be forced to meet St. Mars in secret. It was a year since he had been declared outlaw. How many more years would he be content to live in the shadows before he gave up England for good to live in freedom abroad? And when he made that choice, as surely he should, would she then spend the rest of her days as Isabella's servant without his friendship to brighten her days?

Hiding these dismal thoughts from him, she turned to gaze towards the bridge. Beyond the flying coaches, she saw gaming tables and men bowling at pins. A kneeling woman was selling drinks of some kind, her mugs and a pitcher placed directly before her on the ice. Since no charter from the Crown had been required for this fair, the offerings were more varied and spirits seemed even lighter.

After watching the men play at nine pins for a while, Hester and St. Mars returned to the booths to see what the next street offered. Here a few goldsmiths had opened shop, as well as turners, and among the latter was a seller of Tunbridge ware. Hester paused to see the wooden toys and admired a miniature tea set in yew wood. She bought a painted box for Isabella and a spinning top for Georgie. On their stroll towards London Bridge, they passed more printers and toyshops.

By the time they reached the bridge, the sun had nearly set and Hester felt thoroughly frozen. Icy cold had seeped through her shoes and had mounted relentlessly through her flesh and bones. Until now, only excitement had kept her warm, she realized, as an uncontrollable shiver passed through her.

St. Mars put an arm about her shoulders. "We should get you warm. Something to eat will help."

The shopkeepers were lighting lanterns to hang outside their booths. Tired and cold pedestrians were making their way home, but the majority were staying for a slice of the promised beef. St. Mars ushered her behind the row of tents to an open area on the ice where two large fires had been lit and upon which two oxen were roasting on spits. This was a treat offered by the King to celebrate the birthday of Prince Frederick, a child of nine who was next in line to his father the Prince of Wales. Hardly any Briton had seen him, since he lived in Hanover, but all were willing to celebrate his birth.

The fires, almost as much as the beef, had attracted spectators, for indeed it seemed a miracle that the ice did not melt beneath the flames. Hester and St. Mars made their way closer to the burning spits, which threw out a comforting warmth. As they waited for the meat to be carved, St. Mars took hold of Hester's hands and blew heat into them, sending tingles down her spine. She smiled up at him, shyly . . . expectantly . . . and thought she heard a sudden intake of breath. His hands slid to her elbows. He pulled her to him. Then his hands were at her waist.

With his blue eyes casting a spell, Hester parted her lips.

A scream jerked them apart. People shoved and scattered, terrified, as a group of horsemen plowed into the crowd. St. Mars pulled Hester to safety, as she caught sight of a half-dozen drunkards, spurring their mounts and laying about them with their whips.

They were dressed in gentlemen's clothing with fashionable wigs. Masks covered the upper half of their faces, but the rings on their fingers and the threads of silver and gold woven into their coats sparkled in the light from the vendors' torches. As they whipped their horses into a frenzy, they hooted, shouting out insults to the people they were trampling.

St. Mars swiftly drew the sword from his hip. "Stay here," he commanded. Anger sharpened his voice. His teeth and his fists were clenched.

"My lord, don't! Please!" Hester grasped his arm. He made as if to shake her off, but she said, "There are six of them, my lord! And they are mounted!"

He hesitated, his rage increased by the sense in her words. He did not pull away, but every angle in his face betrayed frustration. Beneath her fingers, the muscles in his arm twitched.

All about them people were shouting, some crying out in pain. The horsemen were out of St. Mars's reach, but their mischief had not yet ended. As Hester and St. Mars watched their retreating backs, they saw what the next target would be. The horseman in the lead was heading for the tent nearest Temple Stairs as if he meant to ride it down.

A cry of "Mohowks!" flew over the ice. Several men gathered in pursuit. Hester could say nothing then when St. Mars lifted her hand from his sleeve, and said, "I must go now!"

She let him, but as he hastened away, she started to follow. One glance behind her revealed the path of destruction. The drunken riders had swept out from the riverbank near London Bridge and had cut a swath over the ice. Their plan, if they had one, seemed to be to mow down some of the booths near the Temple and escape to the bank beyond. Their assault had been timed so the cloak of dusk would hide their features, and the hour was too early for any watchmen to be on duty. No watchman would have been there to witness in any case, Hester realized. There was no watch house in the middle of the Thames.

She stooped to help an old woman who had struggled to her knees. When she next looked up, she spied the last of the riders laying a whip into his mount. Harried and scared, the horse slipped on the ice. With a terrified neigh, it tumbled, sending its rider sliding across the surface. As his comrades thundered towards the distant bank, he quickly picked himself up and stumbled towards his fallen mount.

The pursuing mob gave an eager, vicious cry and surged towards him. In a frenzy now, the fallen man strove to right his horse, but the animal was screaming in pain and flailing its legs. The painful cries made Hester cringe, but the thrown rider merely cursed. Waving his whip, he called after his friends and ran slipping and sliding after them, pursued by the angry mob. The last of the other horsemen glanced over his shoulder. Seeing what had occurred, he halted then hesitated, before turning his mount to go back. He reached the fallen man and bent in the saddle to give him an arm up. His own horse stumbled under the new burden before finding its footing. Then, in response to both riders' kicks, it bolted just ahead of the furious crowd.

By this time, the other three horsemen had reached the bank, avoiding the tents in their haste to escape, but St. Mars's quick stride had outpaced the crowd. As the horse with the two riders regained its legs, he leapt forward to unseat them. A whip struck within an inch of his face. Hester gasped as he ducked, just managing to avoid the hit. Then, as the pair galloped away, he was forced to halt, his shoulders heaving with exertion.

The man who had fallen gazed back, and for an instant the light from a torch illuminated his face. A glimmer of recognition flickered in Hester's brain, but the face was too far away and the impression was quickly gone.

The crowd roared its frustration with growls and shouted oaths. As St. Mars turned back to examine the injured horse, Hester went to meet him. He waved her back and joined the group of men who'd formed a ring around the writhing animal.

Unable to watch what must inevitably come, Hester turned away. Distressed, she first assured herself that there were no injured people still needing help. Then she went to wait between two of the tents in the row leading to Temple Stairs.

How long it took to put the poor horse out of its misery, she later was never able to tell. The coming of dark, the dancing light from the lanterns and torches, and above all the screams of the injured beast gave what remained of the day the quality of a nightmare. At one point, St. Mars found her and urged her to go home, but she insisted she would not leave until his gruesome business was over. One look at the pallor in his face convinced her that it would be unfair to leave him to suffer through his charge alone. He did persuade her to sit inside a booth where she could drink some hot rum punch, and, nearly frozen by this time, she agreed.

The warm spices in the punch comforted her. The spirits dulled her senses. Still she could think of little else but what would be transpiring on the ice. The horse's suffering had cast a pall over the fair, which did not begin to lift until the animal's painful shrieks had ceased. When, soon afterwards, St. Mars joined her, he sat down silently beside her and beckoned to the waiter to bring them more punch. His attempt at a smile was so weak as to wring her heart.

When the punch arrived, he took hold of the bowl with both hands and gulped down the steaming brew. The rum restored a bit of colour to his face. He set the bowl down and wiped his mouth on his sleeve. After a few moments, he spoke in a soft, regretful voice. "That was a very fine piece of horseflesh. Whoever treated it that way should be hanged." Anger emanated from him. His clenched jaw twitched. Hester could see what pains he was taking to restrain his temper.

"I am sure he will receive the judgement he deserves, my lord," she ventured.

"Are you? Are you so certain that justice prevails?"

Hester could not blame him for his bitterness, not when he had been treated so unfairly himself. "If not in this world, then surely in the next." Even had she not been a clergyman's daughter, she would have believed that. It was what all Christians believed, be they Papists or Puritans.

With a despairing laugh, he buried his face in his hands. Then, after a moment, he rubbed it vigorously and sat up. "I am very sorry, Mrs. Kean. It appears that my attempt to entertain you has been spoiled."

"I am sorry, too, but I shall try to remember only the happy part of the day."

That won her a hint of his usual grin. "An excellent philosophy. I wish I could practice it, but I can't help thinking that from now on, a good many of my thoughts will be devoted to figuring how to avenge the death of that horse."

"I know I needn't quote you the appropriate passage of scripture on revenge, my lord."

"Indeed, I hope you will spare me that."

"Besides, it would be useless. I cannot think of any way to discover who those young men were."

He considered a moment and gave a shrug. "You are probably right. They were clearly Mohowks, and not content with merely breaking windows, ripping off door knockers, and slitting people's noses, they decided to trample a few people. My father always said the Mohocks were the spoiled sons of Whig aristocrats. If he was right, that should considerably narrow the list."

"Surely, you do not mean to discover them!"

Reluctantly, he shook his head. "No, I have enough to occupy me at the moment."

Hester recalled what he had said about helping one of the prisoners to escape, and she questioned him with a look.

His answering gaze told her that he had let slip something he had not meant to divulge. He hastily changed the subject. "But you must be cold! I should return you to Hawkhurst House."

She could not insist to know his business, and it was true that she was extremely chilled. The sun was long gone. Together they stood and made their way back to Temple Stairs and on into Fleet Street, where St. Mars procured a hackney for her and paid the driver to take her home.

Before he handed her in, he held on to her hand and kissed her fingertips. "I shall not be discouraged by this. I promise we shall have our day of fun."

Hester smiled. It was not until later, when she was alone her room, that she allowed some tears to fall.

Winter my Theme confines; whose nitry Wind
Shall crust the slabby Mire, and Kennels bind;
She bids the Snow descend in flaky Sheets,
And in her hoary Mantle cloath the Streets.
Let not the Virgin tread these slipp'ry Roads,
The gath'ring Fleece the hollow Patten loads;
But if thy Footsteps slide with clotted Frost,
Strike off the breaking Balls against the Post.

CHAPTER VIII

The next day, due to increasing lawlessness at the fair, all the booths were forced to close down. The great Frost Fair of 1715–1716 was at an end. In the days following, King George came to the House of Peers and gave his assent to the bill that empowered him to secure and detain any suspected persons until late in May. Since it was now certain that the Pretender had come into Scotland to lead the rebellion, he asked the Commons to fund an immediate defense to discourage any foreign power from coming to the Pretender's aid.

In both Europe and Britain, the weather turned harsher. Reports from as far away as Grenoble stated that so much snow had fallen over the past fortnight that the roads were completely blocked. The desperate conditions in the mountains had driven wolves down into the plains, where they had invaded villages and devoured the inhabitants. The same conditions prevailed in the Highlands of Scotland, where Robert Roy was believed to command the rebels near Faulkland. Their numbers, however, were said to be not as great as formerly reported. The roads were so deep in snow that neither man nor horse could get through.

In London the winds blew in such a gale that a ship full of prisoners was forced to turn back to sea. A French ship with money, arms, and ammunition for the rebels was driven ashore and stranded near St. Andrew's. Its cargo and men were all saved and carried off to Dundee. The Pretender was reported to be in Scone where his coronation was planned, but in spite of the rescue of the ship of provisions, the brutal weather could only spell the eventual defeat of the rebels.

Still angry over the incident with the Mohocks, Gideon fought the temptation to brood and, instead, threw himself into a flurry of activity. Over the next ten days, he made several visits to Newgate to see Nathan Breed, each time taking with him the head of a pick or a blade. He could not conceal a whole tool beneath his coat, but what was needed most were sharp points to chip a hole through the prison's ancient, crumbling walls. Breed and his friends seemed so confident of their ability to dig out that Gideon had not yet tried to bribe the turnkey, though he curried favour with Fell by means of generous gratuities. After a few of these visits, it appeared that Fell might easily be persuaded to look the other way when the prisoners were ready to make their escape.

Back at home, alone in his bedchamber, Gideon pondered the difficulties of his plan. His intrusion into the kitchen of his house had not been met with pleasure, so he had resolved never to invade it again. The trouble, he realized, was that this house was simply too small. If his servants were to have any privacy, then they must have a space kept apart from his.

It felt strange to come to this realization. Gideon had been raised to consider his dependents not precisely as his property, but certainly as subject to his every whim. In his current circumstances, however, they were bound to him only by fidelity and affection. Even his father had known that servants should be treated fairly and with respect, and he had taught this to Gideon by example if not in words. Lately, with no other society available to him, and no reason he could see to insist on the ceremony associated with the status he had lost, he had reached out to Tom and Katy for companionship. It was hard for him to discover that although Tom and Katy were part of his household, he was not necessarily a welcome part of theirs.

Over the next several days, determinedly pushing such melancholy feelings aside, he tried to refine his plan for getting Nathan Breed out of England. Until the ports were open and the weather had improved, there would be no way to smuggle him out of the country and into France. He would have to be lodged in a safe place where the authorities would not find him. He could spend a few nights here in Gideon's house and eventually be moved to the inn deep in the Weald where Gideon maintained rooms, but now the weather was changing. The river was starting to thaw, and the problem of how to get Breed across the Thames had become nearly as great a challenge as the escape from Newgate itself.

Usually, there were only three ways to cross the Thames: by London Bridge, by the horse ferry on the Mill Bank, or by boat. There was still too much ice in the river to make the latter two feasible, and surely, as soon as the authorities were aware of an escape, they would send soldiers to watch the bridge, along with the major roads leading out of the City. If the escape were immediately discovered, then Gideon would need a place to house Breed nearby until the search was given up.

He was puzzling over this dilemma when he heard Tom's boots upon the stairs and glanced up. In spite of the brutal weather, Tom had spent the past few days trying to learn something about the justice of the peace, Mr. Mistlethwait. Now, as he paused in the doorway, his square, stolid face looked eager.

"You've discovered something." For the first time in days, Gideon felt a lift in his mood. "Stand over by the fire, and tell me what you've found."

Tom moved gratefully across to the hearth. He had taken off his wet coat and boots downstairs, but his ruddy cheeks revealed that he was fresh from his horse. With the Thames starting to thaw, he had been forced to ride across London Bridge. It could be several days before the horse ferry was operating again, which meant every foray into town required a much longer trip and more hours out in the cold.

"I learned that Mr. Mistlethwait is no better than the men he sends up, my lord." His shoulders hunched, Tom rubbed his palms together and held them out to the blaze.

"Oh? In what way would that be?"

"He's just as crooked as they are, that's what. They say he takes money from them that can pay to get 'im to look the other way—from thieves and such. Heard he's made himself quite a tidy little fortune doin' it, too."

Gideon raised his brows. "This is very interesting, Tom. How did you learn it?"

Tom answered with a touch of pride, "I went to his house and got to talkin' to his servants—pretended I'd come on a neighbour's business, see? But the neighbour weren't at home, so I got to chatting with one of 'em. This footman, my lord—he didn't have nothin' nice to say about 'is master. Said he was clutch-fisted with his servants and his wife. But he's rich as a Dutchman, as any man could see. I saw 'im leavin' his house, and you shoulda seen the jewels he was sportin', my lord! Bigger and brighter than any JP should have, for sure, so I says somethink about it to his man. The way he cocked 'is head at me made me wonder more about it. Then I caught sight of how many of those people who were brought before 'im were walkin' out, free as birds, so I waited round the corner and spoke to a few of 'em.

"Took me a day or two to figure out how to go about it, but when I did, they more or less said the same thing. Said you could buy your way off, s'long as you had money enough to do it."

Gideon sighed and shook his head. "In short, a sterling example of the English judiciary. Sometimes, Tom, I fear the country is lost. But excellent work. The question, now, is what business Sir Walter Tatham had with an unsavoury magistrate like Mr. Mistlethwait."

Tom shrugged. "As to that, I couldn't say, my lord."

"No. We must discover that some other way. Perhaps Blue Satan could pay an evening call on Mr. Mistlethwait." In his present humour, Gideon found the prospect of some action very appealing.

His groom's expression turned mutinous. "Now, you won't go doing nothing foolish, my lord! From what I saw, his house is locked up, tight as a castle. And he's got a goodly number of footmen. It wouldn't surprise me if some of 'em weren't gaolbirds he's pressed into workin' for 'im in exchange for not sending 'em up. And when I saw 'im, he had a pair of 'em taggin' right along of 'im, so don't be thinkin' you could stop him on the street."

"Hmmm." Disappointed, Gideon sighed, "You may be right. Very well, I shall have to think of some other way. Meanwhile, I should consult with Mrs. Kean. Perhaps by now she's discovered what my idiot cousin's problem is."

Tom picked up the poker and prodded the coal fire in the grate. With his head turned away, he said casually, "Has your lordship thought any more about gettin' that special license you talked of? Me and Katy are ready to get wed as soon as can be. Then, mayhap, you could ask Mrs. Kean what day she could come and we could fix it with parson?"

A sense of guilt made Gideon frown. He had forgotten his promise. With his mind focused on freeing Nathan Breed, he had little patience for dealing with domestic matters. He sympathized with Tom's eagerness to marry, but not with his Puritanical reticence to bed his fiancée. Katy was no virgin, so it seemed incomprehensible to him that Tom still slept in the stables. Whatever his reasons, however, they were none of Gideon's affair, and Tom would need his assistance to get the license.

As Gideon recalled, the Faculty Office, where the Archbishop's registrar dispensed permission to be wed without banns, was in Little Carter Lane, close by Paul's Bakehouse. As long as the Thames had been frozen, the shortest way to cross into town had been on foot, which meant that on his recent trips to Newgate, the office had lain out of his way. Now, however, until the horse ferry resumed operation, he would have to cross by London Bridge, a different situation, which made him leave off the refusal he had been about to give. "We can get it tomorrow on the way to Newgate. The license will be good for any place and any time. But until Breed is freed, I cannot plan to attend a wedding. Till then, I'm afraid you and Katy will just have to wait."

❦

The cruel winds had kept everyone in Hester's family confined to Hawkhurst House, where the weather had preyed upon their spirits. Even Hester was unable to overcome the gloom, since her mind would dwell on the ruin of her outing with St. Mars. The day that had promised so much happiness had been cruelly spoiled by the act of a few dissolute men. Among the injuries they had inflicted—for no other reason than their own amusement—was the prevention of something Hester had long wished for. Now, with the violent images of the day persisting in her mind, she could not recapture the moment when St. Mars had faced her, and it had seemed that he might kiss her, not in the spirit of friendship or in teasing as he done before, but with desire. Now, she had to question whether she had imagined the heat in his eyes and that insistent tug upon her waist. More distressingly, she wondered what the future could possibly offer them when she could not even see him without constructing a labyrinth of subterfuge.

She had told herself that it would be enough to have him regard her as a trusted friend, but as the months had passed, the time when she was not with him had fed her unhappiness. She reminded herself that anyone should be grateful to have the position she occupied at Hawkhurst House—and she was—but she could not help yearning to have her own life with a man she found compatible. That was a vain wish for anyone in her impoverished situation, she knew. Surely, only a fraction of the human race would ever be that fortunate. It was her duty to accept her life as it was and to thank God for the roof over her head and the food she received.

Besides, even if St. Mars were to regain his title, how could she know whether their friendship would remain as strong as it was now? If he could choose the people with whom he spent his time—if his choice were infinite, as it would be if he were the earl—who could say whether he would still select her? It was not that she thought him fickle. He was too honourable for fickleness. But peers had more to consider when choosing their friends, and especially their wives, than an outlaw who must take comfort wherever he could find it.

If he was condemned to remain an outlaw, would he ever think of her fondly enough to ask her to share that life with him?

Such notions were not only idle, they were useless. Hester determinedly turned her thoughts to something more productive. In the chaos at the fair, she had forgotten to tell St. Mars about Lord Ratby and Mr. Gayet. He had suggested he had something to impart to her, too, but now she would have to wait until their next meeting to hear it.

Harrowby was not so patient. On the very next morning after the celebration of Prince Frederick's birthday, he had summoned her to his bedchamber to hear what she had learned. Hester had followed the footman to his apartment and waited while an army of footmen and Harrowby's valet made way for her to sit at their master's bedside, then exited with curious looks.

Harrowby was sitting up in bed, drinking his morning chocolate. He wore a bright silk turban to keep his shaven head warm, and the thick coverlets were pulled up to his chin. Even with a large fire burning in the hearth, the room was exceptionally cold as the wind pounded the house and rattled the windowpanes. Seated in her chair next to his bed, Hester gathered her wool shawl about her shoulders and tucked her skirts tightly about her legs to keep them warm.

She told him about her visit to Lord Ratby's house, and asked him if he was acquainted with Lord Ratby's heir.

"Mr. Gayet? Of course I know him. He's very fashionable. Has excellent taste. Wish I knew who his tailor was."

Hester stifled an impatient sigh. As yet, she had no proof to support her suspicions, so she decided to tread lightly with her qualms about Mr. Gayet. She knew that Harrowby often mistook the quality of a person's dress for an assessment of his character. "I met him when he came to see his uncle. Someone must have stolen the robes from Lord Ratby's dressing chamber, and it seems that few, if any outsiders would have had a chance to take them."

"It was one of the servants, then. I daresay old Ratby has got himself a new valet. Best if you look into that."

"On the contrary, my lord. Lord Ratby's valet has been in his employ for many years and appears entirely devoted to him. His master's health is in a very precarious state. Any excitement could send him into a fit from which he would be unlikely to recover. I gather Mr. Gayet, who is much indulged by his uncle, has a tendency to over-stimulate him."

She hoped that Harrowby would put two and two together and come to the same conclusion she had reached, but the calculation was too much for him. "Then, if it is not the valet, I suspect it was a footman. But I fail to see what good this issue of valets and footmen is doing, Mrs. Kean! What I want you to discover is who among Sir Walter's acquaintances might know something about his affairs! You should focus on that! I doubt Sir Walter ever spoke more than two words to either Lord Ratby or Mr. Gayet. I certainly never saw either gentleman in his company, nor did I ever hear him mention their names. This business of the robes is pure distraction."

"If you consider it as such, sir, then of course so must I." In spite of her conviction that Mr. Gayet had had something to do with the murder, it was at least important to know that he had not been a friend of Sir Walter's. There had to be some connection between them, but whatever it was, it must not have been widely known.

"I'll tell you what you should do," Harrowby said. "Go visit Lady Tatham again, and tell her the next time a good piece of beef is sent up from the estate, that I shall send her a haunch."

As this was as good an excuse for a visit as she could think of herself, Hester was content to agree.

"And then make certain it is sent, of course. What else have you learned?" Harrowby demanded.

Hester gave him a helpless look. "I have not had much luck yet. But if it is Sir Walter's business affairs that interest you, I shall have to apply to his son. Lady Tatham said that he would be coming to London to look into them."

In the middle of taking a sip, Harrowby jerked, spilling his chocolate on his bedcovers. "How soon will he be coming?" he gasped, and coughed. The china cup clattered when he set it in its saucer.

"As soon as possible, I suppose, but as the roads are said to be impassible, I can only assume he will be detained."

"Detained?" His eyes were wide and wild. "For how long?"

Hester offered an apologetic smile. She tried to soothe him gently with reason. "Sir, I can hardly be expected to predict the weather."

He made a visible effort to collect himself. "No—of course you can't! You take me much too literally, Mrs. Kean! I never said that you could! But what sort of business would this son of his undertake?"

Hester could no more be expected to know that than she could be to guess the weather. But Harrowby's insistence had reminded her of something. Avoiding his question, she said, "There was a gentleman who called at Lady Tatham's, a Mr. Mistlethwait, who asked me much the same thing. Lady Tatham said he was a justice of the peace."

If anything, this news upset Harrowby even further. Turning a milky white, he gasped out, "A justice of the peace? Did he say what he was after? Did he say anything about me?"

"No, nothing about you, but he also seemed very anxious to know who would be handling Sir Walter's affairs." Hester stared at her cousin to see how this news affected him, but it seemed merely to confuse him.

He jerked up straighter in the bed, and knitted his brows. "Nothing about me, you say? But he wanted to know the disposition of Sir Walter's affairs? Curious . . . very curious." He caught her studying him, and swiftly lightened his expression. "Well, of course, he could have no reason to ask about me. If he had, it would have been the grossest impertinence! But I can't help wondering what his connection to Sir Walter was. You should look into that, Mrs. Kean."

"I will be happy to, sir, as far as I am able. Does that mean you wish me to devote more time to my inquiries?"

"Yes, yes! Take all the time you need."

"Shall I tell Isabella and my aunt that I have your permission to be absent? They are not used to my not being at their disposal."

Harrowby assumed an outraged posture. "I am the master of this house, am I not? If I want your assistance, I shall have it, and no questions asked! If they give you any trouble, just send them to me."

"Willingly, sir." Hester gave him her brightest smile and assured him that she would pursue her inquiries until he was satisfied, no matter how many days they might take her from Hawkhurst House.

She left him, feeling more cheerful herself. Now with Harrowby's leave, she would have the freedom to come and go as she pleased.

She would have to produce something for him, of course, and in truth, her curiosity was sorely piqued. She would see if St. Mars had learned anything about Mr. Mistlethwait. It did seem odd that both he and Harrowby shared a concern about Sir Walter's business affairs, particularly when neither would be explicit about what those interests were.

She was not deterred from her suspicion of Mr. Gayet, however, for he was still the most likely person to have stolen Lord Ratby's robes.

Two days later, her suspicions of him were deepened when she noticed a familiar name in the *Daily Courant.* One of the advertisements read, *Stolen or strayed out of the Stables of Lord Willimott in Duke Street on Thursday, a black Gelding, 5 Years old, about 15 Hands high, white Boots and white Blaze. Whosoever shall bring any Tidings (so as it may be had again) to Mr. Dawes at Lord Ratby's House in Great Suffolk Street or to Lord Willimott aforesaid, shall have a 2 Guineas Reward, and reasonable Charges.*

Hester's breath caught in her throat. The description was exactly that of the horse that had been so brutally mistreated at the Frost Fair. It took no more than a second for her mind to supply the connection between the horse and Mr. Dawes.

Her first inclination was to inform St. Mars instantly of this news. But then she recalled the murderous expression on his face after the horse had been put out of its misery. She did not wish to encourage St. Mars to commit violence while his temper was still aroused. And, besides, the advertisement had said the horse had disappeared from Lord Willimott's house, so it was possible that someone else had been the horseman. She supposed it was even possible that the rider had stolen the horse and there was no actual connection to Mr. Gayet, but this she did not truly believe. Still, she thought it best to question Mr. Dawes before she got St. Mars involved.

At last, more than a week after her conversation with Harrowby, the weather that had gripped London for most of two months began to ease. The harsh wind was succeeded by weather so warm, the servants reported that the Thames had started to thaw. Harrowby eagerly escaped the house, but before he did, he found the ladies in Isabella's closet, where they were plying their needles, and told his wife and her mother in no uncertain terms that Hester would be engaged on important business for him and that she was not to be hindered in any way. Isabella, who was just as eager to return to Court, accepted this with no resentment and scarcely any interest.

Her mother was not so easily appeased.

Unable to restrain her jealousy, when it appeared that Harrowby was favouring her niece, she tossed her coal black hair, and said, "I am sure it makes no difference to me what Hester does, my lord. Only I do not see why you would prefer to take her into your confidence instead of your wife. I am sure that Isabella and me would be very happy to assist you, if only you would tell us what your business is."

As he heard this speech, Harrowby turned red, then purple with rage. "If I wish you to know my business, madam, then I shall inform you of it! And, if I do employ Mrs. Kean, it could be because she don't ask impertinent questions about matters that don't concern her, unlike some people I know." He glared.

Then a sly look came over his face. "The weather should be warming up very nicely in a week or so. I daresay the roads will soon be passable. Maybe you would like to return to your son's house to see how your other children are faring?"

Mrs. Mayfield had no wish to be exiled to the country, and as Harrowby well knew, it could be months before the road to the North was passable by anything but a mule. So, she swallowed the retort Hester could see forming on her lips, and waggled her finger at him, showing her teeth in a brittle smile. "You will have your little jests, my lord. I was just saying to Isabella how wonderful it would be to see you back in good humour, and now I see that you are."

For once, Harrowby was not fooled by her flattery. All he said was, "Hmmph!" as he turned on his heel and stormed out.

Mrs. Mayfield rounded instantly on Hester. "Don't you think I cannot see what you are about, miss. You are trying to drive a wedge between my Isabella and her husband."

Hester was nearly provoked to respond, but nothing could be gained by challenging her aunt when she was in such a vicious mood. As soon as Harrowby's interest—whatever it was—was resolved, she would be once more at her aunt's disposal, and this particular resentment would pass. Her aunt might even enjoy a sense of triumph when she realized that Hester was no longer of any use to her lord. She would be pleased to gloat. Meanwhile, she could do nothing serious to harm Hester, so it was best to let Harrowby speak for them both.

Hester did feel she ought to say something to Isabella, however, so she turned to her now. "I hope my absences will not inconvenience you, Bella. I assure you that your husband has not taken me into his confidence. In fact, you would find the errands on which he is sending me to be quite tedious. He has just asked me to convey a haunch of beef to Lady Tatham."

Isabella widened her eyes and shook her head. "Poor Hester," she said, putting her needlework aside. "Thank God, the miserable weather has broken, and today I can go to Court again. You can ride with me in the carriage if you like and the coachman will take you on to her house."

From her chair Mrs. Mayfield issued a sniff, but even she could not be envious of Hester's errand.

Hester thanked her cousin and asked when she expected to go.

"I shall be ready in an hour, but first I must dress." She stood from her chair, and Hester did also. "I cannot wait to hear what His Highness—"

Her thought was interrupted when Lord Rennington's nurse entered with the baby in her arms.

"Oh, bother!" Isabella said with a pout. "I forgot. It's time for the visit. Well, bring him here," she said sulkily, "so I can see him."

Young, and thoroughly intimidated by her mistress, Sarah approached her, holding out the baby as if she knew he was nothing but an inconvenience to his mother. When Hester saw that Isabella meant to do nothing more than glance at him, she decided there must be a change.

Crossing the floor in a few steps, she held out her arms and said to Sarah, "Give his lordship to me." Then she took him and, cooing and cuddling him, smiled down into his sleeping face. "See how beautiful and soft he is, Bella. How fortunate you are to have such a healthy, handsome baby." Hester gently pulled the blanket away from his face. Then she took Isabella's fingers and lightly rubbed the back of them across his cheek. At that moment, he opened his eyes, gave a little squint, then with a little sucking motion of his mouth, drifted back off to sleep.

Looking down at him, Isabella gave a giggle. "He is a bit like a kitten, isn't he?"

"Yes, and he smells like sweet clover. Here, take a whiff." She held him up to her cousin's nose.

The baby must have recently been nursed, for it was true that his breath smelled sweet. Isabella's face broke out in a smile, and she said, "Ohh . . . how dear my little Georgie is!"

"Would you like to hold him before you get dressed?"

Isabella appeared to consider it, but then the clock in the small withdrawing room next to her closet struck. She glanced towards the door, and the spell was broken.

"Lud! Look what the hour is! If I do not hurry, his Highness's table might be formed before we arrive. Take Georgie away. I can hold him tomorrow."

Trying not to show her disappointment, Hester returned Lord Rennington to his nurse. At least, her cousin had taken a new interest in her infant. And she had learned something pleasant about him. Isabella was such a sensual person, Hester was convinced she would enjoy fondling the baby, if she would only give it a chance. It would not be many weeks before he was sent to live in the country, where she might not see him again for months. Hester knew in her heart that he would be a strong, handsome child—how could he fail to be with two such well-featured parents? He would be clever, too if he took after his father, but if his character was to be admirable, he would need to be taught better than either of his parents had been. Both Isabella and the lover who had sired little George had been raised to be selfish, but Hester had seen the goodness in both. Surely if they had been taught to think of others, they might have learned?

And, even if selflessness was not something that Isabella could teach her son, if she could only learn to love him, Hester believed her cousin might grow a little less selfish herself.

Resolving to be present at as many of the baby's visits as she could before he was sent down to Rotherham Abbey, she left Isabella's apartments and went to call not only upon Lady Tatham, but upon Mr. Dawes as well.

'Tis She who nightly strowls with sauntr'ing Pace,
No stubborn Stays her yielding Shape embrace;
Beneath the Lamp her tawdry Ribbons glare,
The new-scower'd Manteau, and the slattern Air;
High-draggled Petticoats her Travels show,
And hollow Cheeks with artful Blushes glow;
With flatt'ring Sounds she sooths the cred'lous Ear,
My noble Captain! Charmer! Love! my Dear!

CHAPTER IX

Hester paid the second visit to Mr. Dawes at his master's house. On this occasion, when she asked for him at the door in Great Suffolk Street, she was shown into his office, a dark paneled room situated on the ground floor at the rear of the house.

Mr. Dawes was surprised to see her, but greeted her courteously enough. After he seated her comfortably across his desk, he resumed his own chair and asked, "Does your appearance here this morning mean you have uncovered some new information with respect to Lord Ratby's robes?"

Hester had given a great deal of thought about how to broach the subject of the missing horse, and had decided not to reveal her suspicions immediately. She doubted Lord Ratby would believe anything she said that reflected negatively on his nephew. More importantly, she worried that the shock of learning that his heir might be a Mohock could cause him to fall into a fit from which he might not recover. She could not prove her suspicions, but she herself was persuaded. She recalled her feeling for a brief second that there was something familiar in the horseman's figure. She could not put it into words, but when she recalled his profile, she was convinced it could have belonged to Mr. Gayet.

"Actually, no," she said now to Mr. Dawes. "I have come upon another business entirely. I noticed your advertisement in the *Daily Courant.*"

He frowned, clearly puzzled. "Do you refer to the advertisement concerning the horse?"

"Yes, I believe I saw a horse of that description last Thursday week, but I cannot be certain. Was the animal from Lord Ratby's stable?"

"Yes, it is one he keeps for Mr. Gayet's use. His lordship can no longer leave the house, but his nephew is quite the dedicated horseman, as Lord Ratby was in his day. It pleases my lord still to keep his stable, and he makes certain that Mr. Gayet is well mounted. It is a matter of pride to him, as Mr. Gayet is his heir."

She nodded. "I see. Yet, the newssheet said it was lost from Lord Willimott's stable?"

Mr. Dawes imperfectly restrained a sigh. "Yes, according to my master's nephew, he had stabled the horse at Lord Willimott's house, but when he went to retrieve it, the animal was gone. My lord was naturally very upset to hear the news. Added to the fact that the horse itself was valuable, the news came hard on the heels of the theft of his coronation robes. He fears that Jacobites had something to do with it."

Hester searched for a hint of humour on Mr. Dawes's face, but discovered none. Lord Ratby's agent was too adept at his job to suggest that his employer could be indulging in a flight of fancy. Still, she imagined he thought it.

"But," he said, remembering, "you said, you might have seen the horse?"

"Yes . . . ." Hester paused, wondering still how much she ought to divulge. She liked Mr. Dawes and sympathized with his difficult position. Deciding she could leave it to him to determine how much to tell his master, she continued, "It was on the Thames. At the Frost Fair. A group of young men rode through the crowd, and one of the horses slipped on the ice."

A look of foreboding was forming on Mr. Dawes face.

"The animal had to be destroyed. Its leg was broken."

"The rider . . . ?"

"I'm afraid he did not stop. The crowd was very upset by the incident. The young men were all wearing masks. No one could be certain of their identities."

Visibly shaken, Mr. Dawes, nevertheless, revealed a measure of relief. "Did you recognize him, Mrs. Kean?"

She wanted to say that she was certain, but she could not. "I was not afforded a sufficient look. When his mount fell, he was at a considerable distance from me."

He inhaled a deep trembling breath. "Then he could have been whoever removed the horse from Lord Willimott's stable." He stated it as a fact, but his expression begged her to confirm it.

Hester was forced in all honesty to agree, but she did not hide her skepticism. "That is possible, certainly."

"Mrs. Kean—" his tone implored her—"without any certainty on your part or other witnesses . . ."

"Pray do not concern yourself, Mr. Dawes. As you say, there is nothing that either I or anyone else can prove. I leave it to your judgment whether or not to inform Lord Ratby of the incident. One cannot even be certain that it was his lordship's horse."

Relief issued from him in a sigh. "To be certain, there is that. It would pain his lordship greatly to believe such a fine animal had to be destroyed." He said nothing about the suspicions she obviously entertained, and Hester had to be content with the knowledge that he shared them. She knew he was correct. Nothing would be served by taking them to his lord, especially when his death, which might result, would only lead to Mr. Gayet's being rewarded by an earlier receipt of his inheritance.

She stood to go, and Mr. Dawes sprang up to hasten her departure. They parted in perfect understanding, his features bathed in nervous gratitude.

As Hester left Lord Ratby's house a second time, she recalled a detail about something Mr. Dawes had said, which made her realize he had had his doubts even before she had made her statement. When he had spoken of the horse being taken from Lord Willimott's stable, he had used the word "removed" not "stolen."

On Gideon's next visit to Nathan Breed, he was grateful to find the young gentleman alone in his cell. His friends had gone to take a turn in the yard, leaving him behind to write a letter. When Gideon entered with the guard, he was bent over a piece of paper with ink, sand, and sealing wax to hand.

Putting down his quill, he stood and greeted Gideon with the effusion of a brother. Then, as soon as Fell had left them alone, he said in a low whisper, "I believe we shall break through one of the exterior walls within a few days. And when we are successful, what then?"

Gideon, too, kept his voice low, even though a constant din from the other cells—shouts, the clanking of irons, and clattering of plate, and the occasional sob or raucous cough— should keep them from being overheard. "That is precisely what I have come to ask. Now that the Thames has begun to thaw, it's imperative that we find a place for you to hide on this side of the river until we can get you safely across."

Breed looked alarmed, as if he'd believed all the details had been arranged.

Gideon explained, "My own house is at Lambeth, where you are welcome to stay as soon as we can shift you. And I know a safe place where you can be hidden for a while in Kent. But, for reasons I cannot give, there is no one I can ask to hide you on this side of the Thames, nor can your own family do so, for fear of arrest."

Hurt, mixed with shame, suffused the young man's face. "Of course. No one else should be made to suffer for my decisions. I hadn't . . . that is, I should have thought . . ."

"The first place the authorities will search for you will be amongst your family. You must think of someone else you can trust, someone whose friendship with you is not well known."

As he had hoped, this explanation restored the younger man's pride, if not his confidence. His hurt look disappeared, and he considered seriously for a moment before a mischievous smile brightened his features.

"I do know someone, but we'll have to pay her to do it. She'll not take the risk for free."

"Is she to be trusted?"

Breed gave a rueful shrug. "I believe she is, as long as we offer her more money than the reward she would get for turning me in."

Gideon frowned. "I doubt you should put your faith in a friend of that kind, Mr. Breed."

Breed grinned. "Oh, I think she has enough affection left for me not to wish to see my head hanging on London Bridge. She was my mistress, and we only parted company because I could no longer afford to keep her. I played too deeply—the luck was never with me. Nancy was too clever to tie herself to a man who had to borrow funds from her to bide until rent day, and she was much too beautiful to waste herself on a younger son."

Gideon considered his proposal seriously, then agreed. "Money should be no object, for your uncle will pay her whatever it takes. And, if she is ambitious, she will not wish to risk alienating a duke. In fact, your uncle's rank and favour at Court could be details I can use to persuade her. When did you part?"

"Not more than ten months ago." Breed winked. "I doubt she will have forgotten me just yet."

Gideon was disturbed by the younger man's flippancy. They were both risking their lives in this venture. Since Breed's was already forfeit, perhaps he had taken the attitude that nothing more could harm him. "My concern is that by now it is likely she has found a new protector, in which case she may not wish to risk crossing him. And if she confides in him, he could betray you."

This recalled the younger man to the danger in his situation. As he reflected on Gideon's words, the true toll of his captivity registered briefly on his face. The carefree mask slipped, revealing a frightened youth underneath. Breed licked his dry lips, then met Gideon's searching look with a brave smile. "Nancy is the only person I can think of. If she will not do it . . ." He did not finish, but his look was a plea.

"Give me her direction. I will see how easily she can be persuaded."

"Her name is Anne Cole, but she is better known as Nancy. You can ask for her at the Piazza Tavern in the Hummums. That is where we had rooms." The Hummums were the Turkish baths in Covent Garden, the area where most courtesans were to be found.

Nodding, Gideon started to leave, but Breed clutched at his sleeve to ask, "What news do you have of his Majesty?"

Already, Gideon's mood was sober. Now, a grimmer feeling passed through him, as he said, "I only know what I read in the newssheets. They say his troops have been forced to retreat from Perth. They have orders to burn everything behind them, so the Government troops will find nothing to provision themselves with, but I fear, that is a plan which can only fail."

Breed's brows narrowed in confusion. "Why, when it is a well-acknowledged military strategy?"

"That is when the retreating party has other resources at its back, but in this case, there can be little to feed them in the Highlands at this time of year. I fear it will only lead to the disaffection of the local populace when James needs every friend he can make. And it will not stop King George, who can supply his own troops from the south. The burning may delay them, but it will not defeat them."

He saw that Breed wished to argue the point, but a glance about them recalled him to his current situation, and he smothered the words he had been about to say. Releasing Gideon's sleeve, he left him to call the guard.

The trial of the rebel lords was scheduled to take place within the fortnight. Gideon feared that once the principal conspirators had been condemned, the Crown would turn its attention to Nathan Breed and his friends in Newgate. Without a moment to lose, therefore, on the very evening of his visit to the gaol, Gideon went in search of Nancy Cole.

He went still dressed as a fop, his features disguised by a thick layer of white paint and a great number of patches, his yellow hair concealed by the enormous black periwig. In the dens of Covent Garden, where men of every stripe sought pleasure in vice, he was certain to encounter gentlemen from Court.

He knew many of these dens himself. When he had first come on the town, at about the same age as Nathan Breed, like most other young aristocrats he had explored the illicit pleasures the great City had to offer. He had indulged in drinking, whoring, and gambling in the accepted style, but it had not taken him long to realize that happiness would never be found in these pursuits. There was a tediousness to them that could not occupy his active mind, and an emptiness, too, that would never satisfy his heart.

At the base of this indulgence had been the unshakable belief that his future was determined, that no matter what foolishness he might engage in, he could always find fulfillment in his heritage. He had assumed, not unnaturally, that his rank and his possessions would always be there, that he could, at any moment, turn his mind to the more satisfying pursuits of family and estate. Even then, when he was indulging his wilder tastes, he had never been able to understand the men who gambled away their patrimony or engaged in indiscriminate sex. In his mind had been the certainty that frivolous, sinful pursuits were not ends in themselves, but only a childish set of rites through which he must pass into adulthood unscathed. Now that he had lost everything—home, family, and respect—he found he had no taste for vice at all. While some men in his situation might turn to it as an escape from their losses, he found its sameness more intolerable and its emptiness more productive of pain than either abstinence or sobriety.

He was reflecting on how greatly his life had changed since he had indulged in the vices of Covent Garden as he made his way up Catherine Street, where harlots called out lures to him. Ignoring their cries, he walked down York Street past its well-built houses, and entered the Little Piazza by way of narrow Tavistock Court. The Piazza Tavern stood on the corner leading to the newly built Tavistock Row, erected where the old wall of Bedford House had stood. The humble sheds that had once leaned against it had grown in number and size as the local herb market had expanded. Across from the last of these stalls, at the south end of the arcade, passed a constant stream of revelers, from pickpockets, whores, and actresses to City merchants and aristocratic rakes.

The doorway to the stairs leading down to the bagnios was filled with dissolute men and wanton women, the separation of male and female bathing days having long since been abandoned. Prostitution had always been illegal, but the authorities could get no one to testify against the traders in human flesh. Gideon ignored the pressing invitation of a diseased-looking harlot and, careful to guard against pickpockets, pushed his way through the throng to the tavern on the ground floor.

This was not a business he had ever patronized. Still, he knew by repute that it was kept by a William Luffingham, a man whose connection with the stage helped him arrange liaisons between actresses whose income from their trade was insufficient for their support and the gentlemen who would pay for their undivided attentions. He was aided in this by a woman whose history would not pass the mildest form of scrutiny.

It was the woman, Mary Furness, who greeted him in the smoke-filled taproom and, after serving him a mug of beer, asked if he would like to take himself upstairs and see what other pleasures he might find.

When he asked to speak to Nancy Cole, her unctuous smile vanished and the hardness of her life crystallized into a stony glare.

"Now, what d'ye want with 'er, me charmer, when there's bolder and prettier girls right upstairs? Come along now, and I'll fix ye up wiv one ov'em. Just see if I don't."

"Thank you, but my business is with Mrs. Cole."

"That priggin' doxy! You'd best be advised by me, my dear, and have naught to do with the likes of 'er! Why, she'll take ye for all yer worth and stab ye in the back to boot. Now, I've got a pretty little virgin upstairs, not more'n fifteen if she's a day—I swear on m' mother's grave—and she's got some tricks'll make ye ferget about that other'n sooner'n ye can speak 'er name."

Far from tempted by the image she had conjured—even if he had believed it—Gideon perceived that he would get nowhere with the procuress. In addition to not wishing to lose his business, she seemed to be nursing a grievance against Nancy Cole. He wondered if Luffingham would be any more forthcoming.

"Will you tell me, at least, if Nancy Cole is still living in this house?"

She seemed to think she had found another way to persuade him, for she assumed a sympathetic tone. "Ah, now, me dear, that's just it, don't ye see? She's up and gone off with a gentry-cove, and she's 'is doxy now. I misdoubt he'll want to share'er. Now, 'adn't you better stay 'ere wiv' me?"

"She has a protector?"

From the furious look she gave him, he could see that Mrs. Furness was not the kind of procuress who rejoiced in her former girls' good fortune. Such private arrangements robbed her of her share of their income.

Only money would loosen her tongue. Gideon chastised himself for not tumbling to this sooner, but his previous dealings with such women had always been straightforward. He reached into his pocket and brought out a golden Guinea. The way her eyes fixed on it told him how best to proceed.

"If you tell me where to find Mrs. Nancy Cole, this coin will be yours, and you need not share it, either with Luffingham or with any of the girls upstairs."

At the mention of her employer, the old slut threw a guilty look over her shoulder. And when Gideon started to hold the coin up higher where all might see it, she snatched it from his hand and shoved it through the pocket slit in her skirt.

"She's in James Street, just beyond Mr. Clay's 'ouse," she said, in an ungracious whisper. "Now, either take yerself upstairs or get out."

Gideon gratefully left the tavern and elbowed his way again through the bathers—a group of cursing, laughing revelers, reeking of spirits and smoke. As he headed towards James Street, he wondered if he risked running into Nancy's protector by visiting her tonight. But his target was so close, and the trip from his house to Covent Garden so long and cold, he could not persuade himself to wait. He decided to make the attempt and deal with whatever consequences he met.

Tonight was only slightly less cold than the nights had been during the great frost, but in spite of this, the streets about Covent Garden were filled with men, warmed by wine or gin and lust. Keeping his head down, Gideon crossed the smooth gravel of the square and, passing between a pair of posts, entered James Street, which cut north between the two arcades of the Great Piazza. He strode past the larger, more elegant houses, before entering the narrower stretch leading to Long Acre, along which Mr. Clay's establishment could be found.

Clay's house was a well-known curiosity, for through its front window pedestrians could watch a handful of French women who sat all day, chewing paper for their employer's creations in *papier maché*.

A few questions to people on the street pointed Gideon to the house where Nancy Cole lived. When he knocked on the door of the tidy brick house, it was opened by a burly manservant with a bald pate and a cauliflower ear who asked him roughly what he wanted. Adopting an authoritative tone, Gideon stated that his business was with Mrs. Cole, and Mrs. Cole alone.

The man informed him that his mistress was not at home. Looming over Gideon with a threatening glare, he added that she was not in the habit of receiving visits from strangers. But when Gideon intimated that he had some news to impart which could be to Mrs. Cole's advantage, the man's attitude changed. He advised Gideon to call back during the day between the hours of ten and noon when her "cully" would not be with her.

There was nothing Gideon could do but return on the morrow. Frustrated, he turned his steps towards the livery stable to retrieve his horse, telling himself that his effort had met with a certain degree of success. He had learned when he could speak with Nancy Cole without encountering her protector.

The next morning, dressed again in his fop's costume, Gideon stabled his horse in one of the livery stables lining Hart Street and made his way on foot to James Street. Covent Garden presented a very different aspect by day. Fruit and vegetable sellers pushed their wares from the market stalls, and in the open area of the piazza men from the neighbouring shops had come together for an impromptu game of football, undeterred by the melting snow in the streets.

Passing in front of Mr. Clay's house at this hour, he had to dodge the crowd of passersby who had stopped to peer into the window, where the French women sat munching and spitting out paper, like so many cows chewing their cud. Exclamations of amazement and loud guffaws from the spectators followed Gideon as he tripped past them in his high-heeled, diamond-buckled shoes and knocked on Mrs. Cole's door.

The same manservant answered the door and showed Gideon into a narrow hall with two straight-backed chairs perched against the wall. Instructing him to wait there, the servant disappeared up a clean flight of stairs.

Gideon was not left waiting long before the man returned with the news that Mrs. Cole would be happy to receive him in her parlour.

He was shown into a pretty sitting room with all the appearance of a recently furnished love-nest, with velvet-upholstered chairs and red curtains to match. Besides a settee for two, there were four cushioned chairs with a table for playing cards. Against the wall stood another small table on which were placed a tray with a carafe of wine and two glasses, as well as two small tea caskets with locks. Everything bespoke the comfort a gentleman might wish to enjoy on his visits to his mistress.

Nancy was not in evidence. Her manservant told Gideon to sit, adding that his mistress would soon join him. Gideon settled himself on one of the straight-backed chairs and tried to stifle his impatience. He waited a quarter of an hour before the door to the inner chamber opened and a lady appeared.

She was dressed *en déshabillé,* in a flowing mantua of pale yellow silk, its neck open to reveal not only the soft mounds of her breasts, but the pink tips of her nipples. Her dark brown hair was brushed to a lustrous shine and hung down her back in ringlets, with a few curls trained alluringly over her right shoulder. When she paused in the doorway, the smile she bestowed upon Gideon was both inquiring and seductive.

He sprang to his feet and made a bow, astonished to find that his breeches were growing tight. It had been too long since his physical urges had been satisfied, and he was far from immune to feminine beauty. With his thoughts immersed in Nathan Breed's escape, he had not bothered to speculate on Nancy's appearance. If he had tried to guess, he would have expected a coarser woman, perhaps. Seldom had he beheld a courtesan with such striking physical beauty. Her features were small and even—nothing too remarkable—but there was elegance and grace in her carriage, and an air of something he could only describe as intelligence.

"May I help you, sir?" Breaking his trance, she moved into the room with a swish of silk, giving the impression of a floating cloud. Even her voice revealed a better background than the street. She extended her hand for him to kiss, then sank gracefully onto the settee across from his chair.

Gideon tried not to envy the man who had the right to sit beside her. He tried not to think of how soft her skin would feel, or how well her breasts would fill his hands. The frustration he had felt with Mrs. Kean came rushing back to stir his pulse and cloud his brain. The futility of any nearer relationship with her suddenly oppressed him, but he could not think about that now.

Clearing his throat, which had suddenly grown thick, he resumed his chair and forced his brain to his purpose.

"I was sent here by Nathan Breed," he began.

A slight stiffening in her posture told him that his news came as an unwelcome surprise. She said nothing, however, but waited for him to go on.

"He was taken up with the rebels at Preston and is awaiting trial in Newgate."

She shook her head sadly. "I heard that he was. What a tragedy that he decided to take up arms against our good King George."

The glint in her eyes belied the sadness in her voice. She obviously knew not to let him trap her in a treasonous expression, if that had been Gideon's intention.

"I have spoken to him. He said you once had a fondness for him."

A burst of musical laughter dissolved the tension between them. "Dear Nathan! Indeed, I did once have a tendre for him, but when he foolishly gambled away his allowance, I had to break off our intimacy. I hope he harbours no ill feelings?"

"None at all. He blames himself entirely. In fact, he still looks upon you as a trusted friend."

A new wariness entered her eyes. She had not missed his choice of adjective, and indeed he had hoped she would not.

She regarded him silently for a moment. Then, tilting her head, she smiled, and a dimple appeared in both cheeks. "How is it that I get the feeling you are here to ask a favour for him?"

Gideon chuckled. He could hardly blame her for being reluctant to get involved with a man accused of treason, and the manner in which she revealed her caution showed she had a sense of humour.

"I confess, madam, that I am. Will you please hear my request?"

Still dimpling, she nodded, and after leaning forward once to smooth her skirts, settled down comfortably on her settee as if to hear a good tale. If her move was calculated to seduce—which perhaps it was—it could not have been more effective, as warm as Gideon felt. The graceful motion of her shoulders bending towards him, the further exposure of her breasts, the suggestion of intimacy between them—all conveyed with one accomplished sweep.

Gideon could not help imagining the pleasures of being entertained by such an attractive woman. He even wondered briefly how willing she would be to forsake her current protector for another gentleman—one who lived a secret life.

He had a critical reason for speaking to her, however, so he suppressed his errant thoughts, relegating them to future consideration. First, he swore her to secrecy, wondering how much a courtesan's oath could be believed, but reflecting that Breed had trusted her. Then, he told her of the possibility that Nathan Breed could escape and, if he did, of his need for a place to hide for a few days until he could be moved to a safer haven.

Throughout Gideon's brief tale, she listened seriously with no alteration in her expression, and when he stopped, she did not instantly respond. She waited as if to see what other words might accompany his request.

Though Gideon was prepared to offer money for the risk she would take, he knew better than to offer it before she asked. Finally, she broke her silence by saying, "I should like to help Mr. Breed, of course, but I must tell you that this is not my house. I inhabit it through the generosity of a friend."

Now he was "Mr." Breed, Gideon noted. With one subtle change, she had made it clear that no past relationship between them would secure her willingness to help him.

She had not refused him outright, though. It seemed the time for negotiating was here.

"If you will forgive me, Mrs. Cole, I had guessed as much," he said, with reference to the house.

"Nancy, please," she said, bestowing on him one of her warmest smiles. "All my friends call me Nancy. And you, sir? I do not believe you gave me your name."

Gideon did not know why, but he hesitated over which alias to give her. "It is Johnstone," he finally said, "but, if I am to call you Nancy, then you must call me Robert."

Again she smiled, conveying the feeling that something much more tender had passed between them. "Not Sir Robert?"

He chuckled. "No, I fear not. Why? Would it matter?"

Grinning coyly, she shook her head. "Not at all. There is merely something about you, sir. I feel a title must be in your future."

"I shall not refuse one if it comes my way, but that has nothing to do with today's business. Will you help Mr. Breed or will you not?"

"I should like to be of service to him, but it will not be easy. I fear my friend would not forgive me, if he were ever to find out. He is a courtier, you see, and very loyal to the Crown. He would not wish for his loyalty to be tainted."

"Is there no room in this house that would be free from his scrutiny? A servant's perhaps?"

She appeared to consider this idea. "There is Alfred's apartment."

"The servant who admitted me?"

"Yes. And he is very loyal to me. But his loyalty comes at a price. I could not ask him to risk his neck unless I was prepared to pay him for the risk." She gazed limpidly at Gideon, but the implication was clear.

"Nor would Mr. Breed expect you to risk yours without compensation."

She did not blush. Instead, her smile rewarded him for being clever enough to follow her drift.

"Then, yes, I believe I could hide Nathan here safely for a few days, but I shall first have to consider the costs, not only for Alfred and myself, of course, but to prepare a space and to keep him comfortable. He will require food and drink. And, perhaps, some clothes?"

"I will take care of the last, but he will certainly need to be fed. How much would you require?"

She considered, appearing to give his question serious thought. If she had tried to read his face before deciding on a sum, Gideon would not have been surprised. He was shocked, therefore, when, appearing to come to a sudden decision, she announced, "One thousand pounds."

For a moment, he was speechless. Such a sum was preposterous, but when he searched her face for any sign of humour, what he found instead was a firm stare.

"You seem astonished, my dear Robert, but surely I must think of what I should lose if the secret were to escape. What if my protector were to learn what I'd done?" With a sweeping gesture, she indicated the room and its furnishings, the whole of the house implied. "All of this could be lost to me. And the loss would be that much graver if Nathan were discovered here. I should be lucky to escape with my life. The sum I have indicated would get me to the Continent and help me to start a new life."

Gideon could not argue with her logic. He was in no position to barter for Nathan Breed's life. He temporized. "I shall have to obtain his consent."

"And I shall have to consult with Alfred, who may have objections I have not addressed." She smiled coolly at him, as a man of business might in the midst of unconcluded negotiations. Then she dismissed him suddenly, holding out her hand and saying, "I shall look forward to hearing from you again. And when you call, I hope you will come at this same hour for we shall then be assured of all the privacy we desire."

Did he imagine it, or was there a promise of something else in her voice? Something for him, apart from their business? Desire could be confounding his hearing, or perhaps her voice was simply so sensual that it always held promises she did not mean. Feeling his throat constrict and his pulse race feverishly, Gideon took a long time over his bow, doing his best not to appear flustered. He did not wish to leave her with the impression that she had only to promise him sex and he would forget his duty to Nathan Breed.

Once outside, he was grateful for the cold, sharp air that greeted him. His heart was still pounding, and still his breeches were tight. In all his life, he had never met a woman so blessed with allure. His earlier imaginings, however, about taking her for his own mistress had suffered a rude check. This was a woman who would always put her own interest before anyone else. What might not such a woman do if she discovered his true identity? And Gideon was not at all certain that he might not let it slip in a moment of passion and trust.

Nancy Cole had lain repeatedly with Nathan Breed as his mistress. They had shared the most intimate of relationships, some would say even more intimate than that of husband and wife. Certainly in the world he had come from, this was typically so. Yet, she clearly was prepared to see him hang, to be drawn and quartered, if her price was not met.

He thought suddenly of Mrs. Kean and was struck with a burning need to see her. The tightening in his groin did not go away, but instead intensified. The idea that flew through his head now was impossible, he knew, but for a moment he could not restrain his imagination. He had to stop in his tracks, take a few deep breaths and recall where he was, in order to resume his walk.

A burst of mental clarity had come to his assistance. He could not doubt that if he were in the same situation as Nathan Breed, Mrs. Kean would risk her livelihood, her home, and even her own safety to help him get free. And, she would do it for no money, even without the history that Breed and Nancy had shared. Of course, she had never lived the desperate life Nancy Cole must have lived. She had not had to give up virtue to put food into her mouth or a roof over her head. Perhaps it was not fair to compare them.

Still, the contrast remained firmly in his mind as he turned his steps towards Newgate to confer again with Nathan Breed.

Contemplate, Mortal, on thy fleeting Years;
See, with black Train the Funeral Pomp appears!
Whether some Heir attends in sable State,
And mourns with outward Grief a Parent's Fate;
Or the fair Virgin, nipt in Beauty's Bloom,
A Croud of Lovers follow to her Tomb.
Why is the Herse with 'Scutcheons blazon'd round,
And with the nodding Plume of Ostrich crown'd?
No: The Dead know it not, nor Profit gain;
It only serves to prove the Living vain.
How short is Life! how frail is human Trust!
Is all this Pomp for laying Dust to Dust?

CHAPTER X

The timing of Isabella's return to Court had turned out providential, for she was in the full stream of activities when the real social season began. In spite of everyone's anxiety over the rebels' trials and the war in Scotland, the Duke of Montagu decided to launch the annual round of amusements with a masquerade ball. He gave two hundred tickets to the Prince and Princess of Wales and asked them to invite whomever they wished. His Highness promised Isabella six of them, but the clamour for tickets among the courtiers was so great that in the end, Isabella received only four. That meant that her party would be limited to herself, Harrowby, Mrs. Mayfield, and Lord Kirkland, who had reinstituted himself as her principal admirer.

After the three weeks that his body lay in state, Sir Walter Tatham's funeral was to take place three days before the ball. Harrowby conjured several contradictory excuses why he could not attend, but he insisted that his wife could not ignore an obligation to a lady who had sat up most of one night to witness the birth of her child. On the evening of the funeral, therefore, Isabella and Hester went to sit with Lady Tatham while Sir Walter's son and a small group of friends attended the rite.

The widow Isabella and Hester encountered was once again not so much a grieving spouse as an aggrieved and injured party. As the funeral cortège left the house, solemnly falling into place behind the carriage with its black plumed horses, it was impossible not to notice how small the gathering of mourners was. This evening, however, Lady Tatham was gratified to have the Countess of Hawkhurst to bear her company, and she did everything she could to put a good face on the number of mourners, recounting all the urgent circumstances that had prevented Sir Walter's friends from attending.

In an attempt to conceal her shame, she ignored the other ladies who were sitting with her to entertain Isabella, who was too absorbed in thinking about the ball to notice much of anything else. With Lady Tatham were one of her daughters and a pair of maiden cousins, who had relinquished their chairs to the countess and Hester and retired to the far side of the room.

Prepared for the dearth of company by her first visit to the house, Hester was too adept to betray her awareness of it. With the object of sparing her hostess painful thoughts of the obsequies that were then taking place, she tried to make conversation, raising a topic that had greatly exercised the Court over the past two weeks: the question of who the author of *Town Talk* might be.

"They say it must be Sir Richard Steele—" Isabella repeated the rumour she had heard— "but for the life of me, I cannot see how anyone would know."

When Lady Tatham agreed and had nothing more to add, Hester volunteered, "I suspect it has something to do with the subject and the style of his writing." When her two listeners stared blankly at her, she added, "Whoever has read *The Spectator* must have noticed a similarity."

Her comment elicited no response. If anything, it extinguished the conversation. She was forced to conclude that Lady Tatham was no greater a reader than Isabella.

As a widow in mourning, she naturally would not be attending the Duke of Montagu's ball, even if she had been so fortunate as to receive a ticket, which she had not. But she was quite happy to hear Isabella's plans for her costume and the lavish entertainment she expected from the second duke, who in addition to a taste for extravagance of every sort enjoyed playing practical jokes.

"Is it true that he once gave a dinner for people who stuttered, and a second one for gentlemen with squints?" Lady Tatham asked, with wide eyes.

"Indeed it is so!" Isabella said, giggling. "How I would have laughed had I been in attendance!"

"Perhaps you would not," Hester said, "for to be in attendance, you would have had to have one of those infirmities yourself, in which case you might not have found it so amusing."

"Pooh! I should still have thought it vastly droll, I assure you. I cannot wait to see what sort of entertainment he has devised for us."

Privately Hester considered that as much as she would like to attend a masquerade ball, she might fear becoming the butt of one of his Grace's jokes.

"Will the Dowager Duchess attend?" Lady Tatham's ingenuous look could not fool Hester, who saw the prurient interest behind her question.

"La! I sincerely hope not," Isabella laughed. "I should hardly know where to look if anyone should address her as the Empress of China, which I am sure someone would."

The poor duchess was as mad as a hatter and spent her life in seclusion at Newcastle House, her brother-in-law, the Duke of Newcastle having more charity apparently than the step-son who had inherited her fortune. Having run through his own money, the first Duke of Montagu, on the death of his first wife, had courted the mad Dowager Duchess of Albemarle, presenting himself to her in costume as the Emperor of China. Since their marriage, she had been kept in a deluded state, with all the pomp and ceremony owed to her imperial title of empress, while her considerable fortune had passed into her husband's hands. On the duke's death, she had been transferred to the guardianship of her brother-in-law.

Finding gossip about such a pitiable figure little to her taste, Hester changed the subject. "What shall you do, Lady Tatham, when your son inherits this house?" She was prepared to react with sympathy, for it could not be pleasant to lose one's house, but she was not prepared for the offense with which the widow answered her.

"If you think I shall be sorry to leave this place, you are mistaken, Mrs. Kean, for I have wanted to leave it these several years past. Since the herb market was expanded, all sorts of disagreeable persons have moved in. Why, there is hardly a gentleman's house left on the street! They are most of them tradesmen now, but my son says it will not be long before it has nothing but taverns and victuallers on it. I shall be glad to retire to my son's house in the country, where he has assured me I shall be most welcome. And, of course," she added, with a gracious nod at Isabella, "I will always be very happy to visit my particular friends here in town."

The invitation she sought was not forthcoming, as her hint was too broad for Isabella, who smiled absently, her mind clearly on the upcoming ball and the flirting she would engage in there. But Lady Tatham took her smile as proof of future pleasures to be met and was satisfied for the moment. Hester wondered how long she would languish in the country before realizing that the Earl and Countess of Hawkhurst had no real friendship for her.

Hoping to soften her disappointment, Hester said, "With the uncertain weather we're having, may we hope it will be a few months at least before the country can claim you?"

Flattered, Lady Tatham gave a trill of fake laughter. "Oh, lud! Yes, of course. I shall not think of departing till May, though I shall not feel obliged to wait until his Majesty's birthday. As a new widow, I cannot be expected to participate in the festivities, I hope."

Hester doubted the King would miss Lady Tatham either, but she was willing to allow Sir Walter's widow the fantasy of being regretted by King George. Reverting to something that had interested her more, she said, "So, you have wanted to leave this house. Was Sir Walter not easily persuaded?"

Lady Tatham snorted, forgetting to show a proper respect for her departed spouse. "Nothing I could say would budge him. He said this house was too convenient to his business affairs, but what business he had besides lounging all day with his friends, I do not know." Realizing then how her remarks must have sounded to the countess—if Isabella had been paying attention—she assumed a mournful look, "But such is the consideration we wives often receive, even from the best of husbands, as I'm sure your ladyship will agree."

Isabella gave another absent smile.

Hester suppressed a sigh at the thought of the long evening ahead, but she persevered to keep a conversation going. Before too long, as she had expected, Isabella's toleration for female company reached its limit and she spoke of her need to go.

"I know how pressed you are for time," Hester said, to ease her cousin's way out the door. "Why do you not go home and let me take a hackney later? I am more than happy to remain until the gentlemen return."

With Isabella present, she had not been able to ask Lady Tatham any questions without revealing Harrowby's private concerns. Now that her cousin was leaving, she could try to elicit more information from her.

Lady Tatham released her noble visitor with great reluctance, but Isabella was impervious to anyone's needs but her own. She did not even attempt to match her hostess's regretful tone when she escaped the house—not to return to Hawkhurst House, Hester knew, but to go to the Palace where she could still attend the Princess's drawing room.

With her departure went nearly all of Lady Tatham's pretensions. She was barely civil to Hester, until Hester said, "I hope you do not think my questions impertinent, but Lord Hawkhurst has particularly requested me to do everything within my abilities to assist you in sorting out the mystery of your husband's death. He has been more distressed by it than anyone can imagine, and he will not be satisfied until the perpetrator is brought to justice."

This latter comment was not strictly true, but still in ignorance of Harrowby's real motive, Hester believed it the most politic thing to say. She did think that, perhaps, finding the killer would solve whatever problem Harrowby had.

Her remark, which conveyed evidence of the earl's particular friendship, did provoke Lady Tatham to treat her with greater openness.

"Dear Lord Hawkhurst!" she exclaimed. "But how I wish he would speak with me himself."

"He would, I am certain, but he is greatly worn down by affairs of state, as you know—the Pretender, the trials—it's a wonder he has a mind for anything else." Hester felt like biting her tongue for telling such falsehoods, but Lady Tatham's self-importance must be satisfied.

"Of course! I should hate to be the cause of more worry. You must tell him I forbid him to lose sleep over me."

With her fingers crossed beneath a fold in her skirt, Hester solemnly promised to deliver the message and hastened to take advantage of the opening Lady Tatham had given her.

"I know my cousin will wish to hear if the authorities have told you anything new about Sir Walter's death. Have you discovered anything more about it?"

"My son did make inquiries. He was told that Sir Walter must have been given poison nut. And as common as that is, it is unlikely we shall ever know who administered it. He was even asked if we kept it in this house."

"Do you keep it . . . to poison rats, I mean?"

"Not here, for we have never been troubled with rats in this house. If we have any at all, it will be at our country house, but every other house in London may have it for all I know, so there is no help there."

"Lady Tatham, did you read the item in the newssheet, about the loss of Lord Ratby's coronation robes?"

"I did not see it, but his lordship's agent, Mr. Dawes, came round to ask me if I had any idea how my husband had come to be dressed in his master's robes! Of course, I told him I did not, and I sent him away with a flea in his ear! Of all the impudence, to ask me a question like that!"

"It must have been very distressing."

"Indeed it was! As if I should be party to anything like it! 'I am a lady,' I said to him, 'and whatever business your master and Sir Walter got up to together is no affair of mine!'"

Surprised, Hester asked, "Did your husband know Lord Ratby? Or Lord Ratby's heir, Mr. Gayet?"

"Not to my knowledge," Lady Tatham said. Then she added bitterly, "I suppose Sir Walter had many friends he never made known to me. Why, as bosom friends as he was with Lord Hawkhurst, I am sure his lordship never set foot in my house. They were always off on gentlemen's business, he told me."

"Do you have any idea what that business was?"

But here Lady Tatham's confidences came to an end. She gave Hester a worried glance, which seemed to contain ignorance and resentment, as much as fear. Then, with an uncertain laugh, she said, "Oh, la! Who knows what nonsense these gentlemen get up to? I daresay, as a maid, you may have no notion of what married men are like, but I assure you, they do not confide everything in their wives, nor would we wish them to."

Hester knew she would get no more out of the widow, but there was one further question she had to ask. "I daresay that must be, for I have heard it expressed by other wives. But as far as concerns Sir Walter's business affairs, was there anything he left—among his papers, perhaps—that makes any reference to my lord?"

Lady Tatham looked astonished. "Papers? Concerning Lord Hawkhurst? What sort of papers would those be?"

"I'm afraid I've expressed myself very badly," Hester apologized. "I thought my lord made some reference to some business or other he had with Sir Walter—something that was not yet resolved—but I may have misunderstood. If you were to discover anything regarding my Lord Hawkhurst, however, I am certain he would wish to be notified of it."

"Of course."

Hester made further efforts to gloss over her interest in Sir Walter's affairs, repeating gossip that Lady Tatham might have missed while secluded by her mourning. She did not normally repeat rumours, but the ones she chose were harmless enough, and gossip seemed to be the only entertainment Lady Tatham enjoyed.

After what seemed a very long time, the gentlemen returned and Hester could take her leave. Making her way home to Hawkhurst House in a hackney coach, she felt completely at a loss. Whatever Harrowby's concerns about Sir Walter's affairs might be, she had failed to uncover them. Lady Tatham was unaware of any matter involving Harrowby—of that, Hester felt certain. Indeed, the lady implied that her husband had no real business affairs at all. Surely by now, also, Sir Walter's son and his executor would have gone through Sir Walter's papers. If there had been anything in them mentioning Harrowby, they should have discovered it by now, and unless they wanted to keep his widow in the dark, she would have had some hint of it. If there were anything that could injure Harrowby, the damage by now would certainly have been done.

Hester had no sooner reached this conclusion than a different one came to her. Harrowby's panic had resulted from Sir Walter's murder. That there had been some uneasiness between them before, she was now convinced, but it was only on the discovery of Sir Walter's body that Harrowby had become ill.

If she could uncover the murderer, perhaps the reason for his panic would become clear. That led her to another idea. What if the murderer knew what the reason was? Then whatever had terrified Harrowby could still threaten him. The matter could be anything, but it could also have something to do with the murder itself. She would have to solve the murder if she was ever to learn what frightened Harrowby.

Arriving at Hawkhurst House, Hester found her suspicions had been correct—Isabella had gone out. Hester went to her bedchamber and was taking off her wrap, when a footman brought word that Mrs. Schultz had called and was waiting for her in the saloon.

Stifling a grimace, Hester instructed him to say that she would be with the visitor in a minute. After combing her hair and making her way to the great room, she found Mrs. Schultz inspecting the bottom of a porcelain Chinese bowl. She showed not the slightest trace of embarrassment at being discovered in snooping. Indeed, her gaze lingered over the collection of China plates, as she made a slight curtsy to Hester.

Happily for Hester, Mrs. Schultz refused the refreshment she offered, saying, "I have not come to wisit, but only to bring two tickets to the Duke of Montagu's ball. Her Highness has obtained them from Lord Vinchester, and as his Highness the Prince had promised more to Lady Hawkhurst, he has asked me to convey them to her here."

"Did you not see my cousin at Court? I was certain she had gone there."

"Perhaps, it is so. But I have come from the Duke of Nottingham's house, vhere his Highness has been entertained."

"I will see that she gets them. You must thank their Highnesses for their kindness."

"Of course, but his Highness vill also be wery happy to receive Lady's Hawkhurst's personal expression of gratitude."

This reference to his obvious desire for Isabella made Hester uncomfortable, even as she acknowledged that neither Isabella nor her husband were likely to be offended by it. Such were the ways of Court. And if Isabella succumbed to the Prince, it would not be out of gratitude for a pair of tickets to a ball, but for her own pleasure and the thrill of having made a conquest of a prince. At least, her financial situation was such that she was not obliged to give into him for money.

"When your mistress comes home, vill you tell her for me that I should like to have her pearl necklace to vear to the ball? I have not so many jewels of my own and she vill surely have no need for them."

"I shall ask her, but I believe her intention is to wear them in her hair." Hester did not know if this was true, but she would not encourage Madame Schultz's impertinence.

She was glad when the unwelcome visitor took her leave, and she could return to her bedchamber, the tickets to the ball burning a strange hole in her pocket.

In the morning, Mrs. Mayfield summoned Hester to her room and gave her an errand to fill. Earlier, Hester had read to her an advertisement about the highly esteemed styptic to fasten loose teeth, and now, with the ball approaching, her aunt was desperate to try it. The styptic promised to fix teeth in their sockets like nails to a board, "whether they be rotten or sound, or your money shall be return'd." The tooth in question was not yet so painful as to require pulling, but it was situated in a flaccid spot on her gums and its roots would no longer take a firm hold.

Hester wished she had enough time to write to St. Mars to arrange a rendezvous, but Mrs. Mayfield would not let her put off her errand until the morrow. Sighing, she left her aunt's room and went to collect her cloak and gloves. The snow was melting in the streets, and the kennels would be filled with water, so she fetched her pattens, too.

She had just sat down in a chair in the hall to put them on when Harrowby descended the stairs, attended by three of his footmen.

"Ah, Mrs. Kean!" he said, seeing her, "I am glad to have caught you." Instructing his servants to await him in the hall, he impatiently beckoned her to follow him into the offices on the west side of the house. Normally, these were the province of James Henry, but he was not in town, so the rooms were empty today.

Harrowby closed the first door behind them, and not bothering to sit, asked her what she had managed to discover from Lady Tatham.

"Nothing, I fear, that will satisfy you, Cousin. The one thing that appears certain is that Lady Tatham is ignorant of any of her husband's business. And, unless his heir and his executor have discovered something amongst his papers, of which she has no current knowledge, there is nothing in that house that regards you."

At the mention of Sir Walter's heir, Harrowby looked alarmed, but by the time Hester finished her speech, he seemed reassured. "You are certain his lady knows nothing about me?"

"I could swear to it, sir. She looked confused when I mentioned his papers. Indeed, from her reaction one would assume he had no papers to leave. I doubt that any have been found."

He walked to a window and stood, frowning out of it and chewing on his lower lip. When, after a few minutes, he still did not speak, Hester offered, "If I may make a suggestion, perhaps if I discovered who murdered Sir Walter, and why, your worries could be laid to rest."

On the contrary, this notion seemed to agitate him further. He did not say why, merely, "I fail to see what Sir Walter's death could possibly have to do with me! What I need to know is who he might have taken into his confidence. You are certain Lady Tatham and her son know nothing about his affairs?"

His continued refusal to be forthcoming with her made Hester speak sharply, "No, I cannot be certain of that, any more than you can be, sir. But, if they are aware of any matter that concerns you, they will soon make it known to you, surely."

At this, he blanched and looked so pale, she thought for a moment that he might faint. "Sir!"

She put out a hand to support him, but, pulling himself together, he waved it away, saying, "'Tis nothing. A momentary weakness. Something I ate, no doubt. But, yes . . . yes . . . ," he went on, as if speaking to himself, "if Sir Walter's son does know, he could turn up here at any moment. If he does, then I shall refuse to see him. Yes, that's it! You must instruct all the servants to deny me."

Hester was more confused now than ever before. Harrowby's fear began to alarm her. "I can certainly tell them to do that, Cousin, but is Sir Walter's son a violent man? Is he likely to attack you?"

He looked at her as if she had lost her senses. "Attack me? Violent? Do not be ridiculous! Whatever could have given you that impression?"

Speechless, Hester could only gape. Harrowby's fear waxed and waned more frequently than the tides. "I cannot imagine, sir," she admitted in a weak voice.

"Then I suggest you keep your hysterics to yourself! Indeed, Mrs. Kean, I had thought you more level-headed than most females. I wonder whether you are suited to handling this matter, after all."

"Indeed, sir, I begin to wonder, too. Perhaps you should put James Henry upon it."

His eyes grew round, and he grasped her arm. "No, you mustn't breathe a word of this to James Henry, or to anyone else. Is that clear?"

Taken aback, Hester shrank from him, but nodded. "I promise I shall not mention it to anyone in the house."

"Good girl." Barely aware of what he did, he released her. "Then, you may go about your inquiry. I must go. There is someone I must visit."

Frustrated, Hester would not let him leave her until he had at least answered one question. "Sir, to your knowledge, did Mr. Gayet know Sir Walter? Could he have been in Sir Walter's confidence?"

"Now it's Mr. Gayet again! I do not know why you persist in mentioning him."

"If you are going to entrust me with this matter, sir, you will have to accept my conclusions. I am convinced Mr. Gayet knew something of Sir Walter." She would not elaborate until she knew what part he had played in Sir Walter's death, and how to prove it still remained a mystery.

Harrowby sighed. "Very well, then. No, I know of no connection between them. And Mr. Gayet's a very fashionable sort of fellow, as I've told you. One may meet him anywhere. Why, I saw him myself at the St. James Coffee House only yesterday and we exchanged a very pleasant few words. Capital suit he had on! A delightful shade of puce. He'll be at his Grace of Montagu's ball. If he knew anything he shouldn't know about me, he gave no sign of it, I assure you, and I do not wish you to go putting notions about me into his head, Mrs. Kean."

At the mention of the ball, Hester thought of the two new tickets upstairs in her room, and the skin between her shoulder blades prickled. She had not mentioned Madame Schultz's visit to Isabella, who was still abed. "I will not do that, sir, but . . . if there were a way I could satisfy myself as to his ignorance concerning you and Sir Walter—without alerting his curiosity—would you object if I pursued it? I would promise to be very prudent."

Impatience made him grimace. Their discussion had clearly gone on longer than he could stand. With a wave of his hand, he turned and left the room, saying, "Do whatever you wish, whatever you judge best. Just pray remember what I said."

Hester stood where he had left her, her heart setting up a wild beat. Did she have the nerve to carry out the notion that had just occurred to her? She was almost certain she would be able to recognize Mr. Gayet in a mask. She had seen him masked before, and even at that considerable distance, his profile had struck her as familiar. She had not been looking for him on that occasion, so, presumably, he would be easier to find if she was, but she could not accost him by herself.

If she called upon St. Mars for assistance, he would not hesitate. He would argue that the safest place for an outlaw would be at a masquerade ball. All the guests would be in disguise, so what better place for an outlaw to mingle?

She knew him well by now. No risk of discovery or arrest would deter him. If there were to be a cautious voice, it would have to be hers.

She could barely think for the choice she faced. It would be wrong and foolish to make it with her mind in such turmoil, so taking her pattens back into the hall, she buckled them on, deciding to wait for a moment of reflection to decide.

The styptic to fix the teeth had been advertised for sale at two locations, at Mrs. Maws's perfumery at the entrance to the west-walk of the Royal Exchange and at the Seven Stars Toyshop up against St. Dunstan's Church in the West. The latter location was not only closer, it would afford her a chance to see her brother Jeremy and the woman he would marry as soon as she came out of her widow's weeds. Jeremy's beloved, Sally, had inherited a bookstall against St. Dunstan's under the sign of the Scroll and Bible.

Rufus, the gatekeeper of Hawkhurst House, helped Hester into a hackney coach, which set her down in Fleet Street near St. Dunstan's within a quarter of an hour. She discharged her errand first, to be better able to judge how much time remained for a visit.

She had bought the bottle of styptic and was leaving the Seven Stars Toyshop, when a familiar figure wearing a red coat, a fur-lined cloak with a shoulder cape, and a black, full-bottomed wig waylaid her outside the door.

It was all Hester could do to stop herself from greeting St. Mars by name. In her surprise, she uttered a garbled greeting, which made him laugh as he turned to fall into step beside her.

"I was visiting my banker across the street," he explained, "when I saw you set down."

"Your banker! Does he know . . . ?"

". . . who I am? No, he merely receives instructions from my estate in France to pay a certain Mr. Mavors of Lambeth. When I saw you, I thought you must be on a visit to your brother, so I waited to catch you when you left the bookstall."

"I was on my way there next, but neither Jeremy nor Sally is expecting me, and you and I should talk."

He gave her a teasing nod. "Agreed. Besides, I have news I've been meaning to give you for days."

"Then I'll postpone my visit. This is a very lucky meeting," she added, wondering with a sinking feeling if, indeed, that were true.

Hester believed in providence, but she was the first to say it was impossible for mere mortals to distinguish providence from chance. Did she dare think this encounter with St. Mars was a sign she should tell him of her perilous idea?

"If you think it warm enough, we could stroll on the Temple terrace. I know how you like to meet in churches and huddle in pews, but surely we've offended enough worshippers by now and should leave them in peace?"

When Hester chuckled, he offered her his arm. Taking it, she felt her heart give a skip. She still could not decide on the wisdom of sharing her notion with St. Mars, but the combination of fortuitous circumstances was beginning to exert a strong influence on her—first the delivery of the two tickets and now the meeting with him in time to prepare for the ball—when she was sure she would never have mustered the courage to summon him herself.

The Temple streets were crowded with bewigged attorneys and berobed students, intent on their own business. As St. Mars steered a pathway through them, Hester was grateful she had no acquaintances in the Temple. She could feel reasonably free of the worry that someone would spot her on the arm of a strange gentleman and report it to her aunt.

The weather was still cold, but a weak sun greeted them on the pavement. A handful of strollers were there, hoping to soak up a few feeble rays. This was the first time Hester had glimpsed the Thames since the day they had visited the Frost Fair. Every sign of the celebration had vanished. There was nothing left to remind her of the crowds or the booths, except for a few patches of snow in shady spots on the terrace where the sun could not reach. The river was stirring with a hint of its normal business. A few small boats had ventured out on the water, despite the floating blocks of ice, and wherries once again crowded the steps. Along both banks, burly men unloaded crates and baskets. The breeze carried a slight scent of fish and a hint of spring to come.

St. Mars directed her to a spot where they could look out over the river. Giving a glance over his shoulder to make sure they could not be overheard, he said, "Now, what is it you wish to tell me? I shall let you go first, but we must not part this time till we've managed to deliver all our news."

"Very well." Hester took a deep breath. She would tell him this much and see his reaction. "I know the identity of the horseman who disrupted the Frost Fair."

Her announcement took him aback. His smile vanished and he stiffened. "Tell me how you know."

She recalled that she had never had the opportunity to tell him about Lord Ratby and Mr. Gayet. "I shall have to start by telling you where I first encountered him." She proceeded to do so, describing her visit to Lord Ratby to discover how his coronation robes had ended up on Sir Walter's corpse. She told him of her unfavourable impression of Mr. Gayet, and of her belief that his antics were designed to gain his inheritance by hastening Lord Ratby's death, repeating all she had learned from Mr. Dawes. "Then, a few days after our excursion to the Frost Fair, I saw an advertisement describing a lost horse and instructing anyone with information to give it to Lord Ratby's agent. Mr. Dawes had need to be circumspect, but he did confirm that the horse was kept by Lord Ratby for Mr. Gayet's use." She explained why Mr. Dawes could not tell his employer about her suspicions.

She went on, "As soon as I read Mr. Dawes's name in the news-sheet, I realized why the horseman's profile had seemed familiar. I am certain it was Mr. Gayet, my lord."

St. Mars's brow was furrowed in a forbidding expression. "We do not need his confirmation to know your suspicions are correct. I did not see that day's newssheets, though if I had, I should not have known who Mr. Dawes was." He chewed the inside of his mouth. "I don't mind telling you, I would like to have a few minutes alone with Mr. Gayet."

"That may be accomplished—" she bit her tongue to keep from blurting out her idea— "but as much as you would like to have words with him about the horse, I should also like to know what his part was in Sir Walter's death. I believe he is the key to that mystery, my lord."

His face showed nothing but eagerness now, as she had suspected it would. "How? How can I see him? I promise to get whatever information you wish, even a signed confession to Sir Walter's murder if you like. I would like to see the fellow hang. Any man who would treat a beautiful animal like that deserves such a fate."

"Before I say anything more, I should like to know what you have to tell me."

He nodded. "Yes, before I forget . . . You recall mentioning the magistrate who behaved strangely at Sir Walter's house? Mistlethwaite was the name."

Hester opened her eyes widely. "I had almost forgotten him, but yes, I do recall. Have you discovered anything about him?"

"Not I, but Tom. And, someday, when we have time, I will tell you how he went about it. I had not thought him capable of such guile. In brief, it appears that your Mr. Mistlethwait enriches himself by selling acquittals. That is to say, when someone is brought before him charged with a crime, he lets them go free, provided they pay him enough."

Hester frowned, trying to figure how this fact could be relevant. "I do not see how his being corrupt could have any relation to your cousin Harrowby, yet both seem very concerned to know who will take over Sir Walter's business. Lady Tatham maintains her husband had no particular business, yet both men are worried that some piece of information about them, or a matter of business they had with Sir Walter, might end up in his wife's or his heir's hands."

"It may be something too unsavoury for a woman's ears. Is Harrowby still worried, then?"

"Indeed, he is. When I told him Sir Walter's son and executor must by now have come across any papers that could concern him, he turned an ashen grey. But he would not tell me anything else. I suggested that if I found out who killed Sir Walter, his mind might be relieved, but he insisted his concern had nothing whatsoever to do with the murder. Instead, he wished me to discover who was in Sir Walter's confidence, and I cannot fathom why. There is something he does not wish anyone to know, including me."

St. Mars looked annoyed. "Was there ever a greater fool than my cousin Harrowby? I only hope he has done nothing to bring disgrace upon the family." As she waited for him to continue, his lips twitched and he shot her a sideways glance. "Unlike my own disgrace, of course."

"But yours was not of your own making! And if Harrowby were in trouble, it probably would be his own fault."

"I am glad you agree with me on that point. It is a vital distinction." He turned to lean against the stone railing. "But joking aside, what makes you think that discovering Sir Walter's killer will put Harrowby at ease?"

Hester gave a helpless shrug. "I don't know that it will, but surely there must be some connection. Whatever it is that frightens him must be of great significance. Someone else hated Sir Walter sufficiently to murder him, and I cannot believe there would be two completely different motives for that strong an emotion. And since your cousin will not tell me what it is that frightens him, perhaps understanding the murder will give me some idea, at least."

He gave a nod. "Very well. Now tell me how I am to go about waylaying Mr. Gayet."

When suffocating Mists obscure the Morn,
Let thy worst Wig, long used to Storms, be worn,
This knows the powder'd Footman, and with Care,
Beneath his flapping Hat, secures his Hair.

CHAPTER XI

A half-hour later, Hester left the Temple in a whirl of emotions, not least among them regret. She could not imagine what had possessed her to be so foolish. But St. Mars had coaxed the idea out of her and convinced her that the plan would work, giving all the reasons in support of it that she had expected him to give.

He had also proposed a solution to the problem she had not yet considered: where to get a costume for the ball. With Katy's talents with a needle, he had no worries about his own disguise. But there was not enough time for Katy to concoct a costume for Hester, too. In her place, St. Mars suggested the services of his former valet Pierre.

It was Pierre who had dressed him in the blue satin cape to disguise him from his cousin, and for nearly a year he had managed to keep the secret that the caped and masked figure known as the highwayman Blue Satan was really St. Mars. Hester had no maid of her own, but all she needed, St. Mars said, was to put herself in the hands of his capable valet.

Unfortunately, the moment she arrived at Hawkhurst House and delivered the styptic to her aunt, Mrs. Mayfield insisted she was needed to assist her preparations for the ball, giving Hester no opportunity to consult the Frenchman. She was kept running errands between Mrs.

Mayfield's and Isabella's chambers, working with their seamstresses on their costumes, and searching for fringes, mislaid ribbons, and pieces of lace to provide the finishing touches to both.

Even when she did manage to find a free moment, she did not dare speak with Pierre, for in the afternoon Harrowby was closeted in his chambers. Finally, in the evening he took himself off to the Theatre Royal in Drury Lane, where *The What d'ye Call It,* "a tragi-comi-pastoral-farce" was playing. Pleased with his design for his own costume, which he swore to keep secret, he so far forgot his troubles as to hum a little tune as he left the house.

Isabella went separately to the play, in the company of Lord Kirkland and two of his friends. She could not be gayer than as the focus of a party of gentlemen. Hester supposed that Harrowby would conduct his mistress to the play, and she wondered if Isabella would bother to cast a curious glance at the woman who had secured her husband's affections. Though there appeared to be no animosity between husband and wife, Harrowby had not resumed his place in her bed.

Mrs. Mayfield did not go out, but invited a few friends to play at cards. Hester's aunt was so committed a gamester, Hester had no doubt the play would be deep. She sighed for the charge on the Hawkhurst estate, but at least she would not be expected to play. She had to greet the guests, make sure they were settled comfortably round the table, and see that everyone was served with drink. Soon, however, she was able to plead a headache—a plea that nobody noticed—and retire quietly from the room.

As quickly as she could, she went in search of Pierre and found him pressing the coat his master had worn that day. He greeted her with a surprised lift of one brow.

Hester wasted no time before telling him what she needed, assuring him that her objective in attending the ball was to discover something about the affair troubling his lord. "I still have no notion what it is that disturbs him," she said, in response to his pursed lips, "but he has asked me to make inquiries about Sir Walter Tatham. He does not know what I intend to do, but if he were to find me at the ball, I have no fear of his being angry with either me or you. He has given me permission to question one of the Duke of Montagu's guests, but says I must do so discreetly.

"It is my cousin Isabella and her mother that concern me. If either were to recognize me, it would provoke their questions, and Harrowby would not be pleased."

While he completed his ironing, Pierre listened skeptically to her account. When he had finished placing the coat in the clothes press, he turned to her with a jaundiced eye. "I 'ope *mademoiselle* does not take Pierre for a fool. It is not like *mademoiselle* to engage in such intrigue. Would mi'lord St. Mars 'ave anything to do with this *folle entreprise?*"

Hester had hoped to keep St. Mars's name out of her account. It was not that she questioned Pierre's loyalty to his former master, but she reckoned the less he knew of the matter, the better it would be if she were ever found out. She had forgotten the little Frenchman's vanity. He wished to be nothing less than omniscient.

"Yes," she admitted, "but I assure you, Pierre, in this instance, his lordship has his cousin's welfare at heart. He is greatly concerned to preserve the family name, and if Harrowby is threatened, the whole Fitzsimmons family could be at risk."

"*Mademoiselle* should have trusted Pierre. If I am not to be trusted—"

"I give you my word, Pierre, your loyalty has never been doubted! Why, it was my Lord St. Mars who instructed me to come to you. He relies on you greatly. It was only my wish to spare you from involvement with the one detail in this affair that your present master must not know that prompted me to omit his name. For you know that Harrowby must never discover that my Lord St. Mars is hiding in London. If he did, it could mean your master's head."

Pierre tossed his head, as if to say there was nothing she could tell him that he did not already know. "*Ah bon,*" he said, "so I must prepare for *mademoiselle une belle costume.* Then, I shall 'ave to take *mademoiselle's* measures." He eyed her figure, and Hester tried not to blush when his gaze traveled to her face and he frowned.

"What is it?" she asked. "Is anything wrong?"

He gave his Gallic shrug. "*Mais non.* There is nothing wrong, *bien sûr. Mademoiselle* is possessed of a very graceful physique."

Hester could not be embarrassed by his compliment, since he gave it the way another man might comment on the finer points of a horse.

"It is simply, I do not at once see how *mademoiselle* can be completely disguised. It would be easier if she were a man, for then one might use a wig. But it is much too late to try to find a lady's silk wig. I 'ad better reflect upon this *un peu, mademoiselle*."

"Yes, please do. It is most important that I not be recognized, not only to avoid my cousin and aunt, but in case the gentleman I wish to question turns out to be Sir Walter's murderer." And, if she were discovered, she would certainly be asked who the gentleman was who had accompanied her to the ball. Whatever else occurred, St. Mars must not be exposed.

The next day passed in a whirl of excitement. Mrs. Mayfield was so pleased to be going to the ball that she occasionally forgot her perpetual resentment of her niece. Isabella was in alt, and repeatedly expressed her curiosity to know what entertainments his Grace of Montagu had devised for their pleasure.

In the afternoon, just as the ladies were settling down to the tea table, Harrowby paid a visit to his wife's chambers. Instead of heading to the coffee house or to see his mistress, he agreed to join the ladies for a dish of tea.

His smiles were explained when he challenged them all to discover what costume he would be wearing that evening. Patently pleased with himself, he laughed gaily at every incorrect answer.

After a few unsuccessful rounds, Isabella cried, "A running footman!"

"Now, my dear," Harrowby said, shaking his head in reproof, "didn't your mother propose that just a few moments ago?"

"Oh, pooh! So she did. Well, you shall just have to tell us, Harrykins."

He clapped his hands and giggled. "No, I shall not. What fun would it be, an' I did?"

"The King of Egypt!" Hester offered, not expecting to guess correctly, only pleased to see her cousins enjoying each other for the first time since Isabella's confinement.

Then she recalled that she had sent word for Sarah to bring Georgie to see his mother in the afternoon. Afraid that the appearance of his heir could destroy their newfound harmony, she almost left the tea table to intercept Sarah, but an instant's reflection convinced her to stay. Right now, Harrowby was in a jubilant humour. It might be months before she could catch him in another. Better to see how he reacted to the baby today.

As if she had conjured him with her thoughts, just then the little viscount made his entry in the arms of his nurse. Sarah perceived her lord too late to make a hasty retreat. Her start, however, on seeing Harrowby, told Hester that Sarah had not forgotten Mrs. Mayfield's strictures about keeping the baby out of his sight.

Mrs. Mayfield glared daggers at her, but tried to cover the blunder with a laugh as she stood to chase Sarah away. "Shame on you, Sarah, for disturbing his lordship when he is trying to enjoy his tea."

If anything could have been calculated to spoil the moment, her aunt's behaviour was it, Hester thought as Harrowby blanched. Hester stood, too, in hopes of smoothing over the incident.

"Nonsense!" she said. "What better place for a father to see his infant than in this happy gathering." Swooping down on Sarah and taking the baby from her arms, Hester turned and presented him to Harrowby, saying, "See how your son has grown, my lord? Will he not turn out to be a fine, handsome lad?"

Indeed, Georgie was in splendid looks, with smooth, pink, healthy cheeks, a far cry from the red, wrinkled thing Harrowby had seen. Sarah had obeyed one of Mrs. Mayfield's rules in keeping the baby's black hair hidden beneath a linen cap. The fearful glance with which Harrowby first greeted Hester's sally noticeably eased as he caught sight of his undeniably pretty child.

He raised an astonished eyebrow. "Well . . . by gad! He is improved, an't he? I haven't seen such perfect skin since my mother died. She never had a blemish in her life, I swear it."

"Ah, perhaps that's where Rennington got his." Mrs. Mayfield was quick to seize the moment. "Did I not tell you his skin would clear up, Hawkhurst? But new fathers are always horrified by the way their newborns look."

Hester had been holding up the baby so his father could see him. Now, she unwrapped enough of his swaddling to free one of his little hands, which immediately latched onto her finger. She offered his hand to Harrowby, who was considering his mother-in-law's remarks as if he might even believe them.

"Feel here, how strong his grip is. It won't be long before you'll be teaching him how to take hold of the reins."

She could tell by Harrowby's expression that such an activity had never occurred to him. His eyes widened. "Teach him to sit his pony, d'you mean?"

"If you like. Or you could just take him up before you on your saddle and let your groom do the teaching. Not immediately, of course, but childhood passes so quickly. By the time you have made a few trips to Rotherham Abbey to see him, I daresay he'll be ready to ride."

Just then, Georgie did something that not even the master of revelry at Versailles could have planned. He waved his fist, and as it connected with Harrowby's finger, he grabbed it and held on.

Harrowby's resistance melted in an instant. "Look there!" he said. "I do believe he knows his papa!"

"Well, of course, he does!" Mrs. Mayfield exclaimed. "Who else should he know?"

While her phrasing was not the most elegant, it found favour with her son-in-law, who raised and lowered his finger instinctively, shaking the baby's hand, smiling down on him, and making foolish noises.

Hester released her breath, only then realizing how long she had been holding it. The ice had finally been broken. The worst was over. Whether Harrowby believed he was the father of his heir or not, he clearly wished to accept the child. He might choose to reject him later if Georgie gave him trouble, but with a little management to keep their interactions as pleasant as possible—a task Hester would share with his nurse and her aunt—no gross breach was ever likely to occur.

Careful not to stretch this first meeting so long that the child would start to fret, Hester gently pulled him away with the excuse that his mama must be given the opportunity to kiss him before Sarah took him away. Isabella, by now, was pleasantly accustomed to these brief visits, so Harrowby could be treated to the sight of his beautiful wife bending over her baby in a relaxed, motherly pose. Indeed, Isabella now quite enjoyed these opportunities to rub her lips against the baby's soft cheeks. As Hester had predicted, the sweetness of a baby had won Isabella's sensual heart. As long as she was spared any of the unpleasant duties of caring for an infant, she was quite prepared to love her child.

Hester sent the baby away with a conspiratorial nod of approval for Sarah, who curtsied and left, visibly relieved. The tea party briefly resumed, until Harrowby extracted a promise from his wife and his mother-in-law not to leave that evening until they had seen his dress for the ball.

"And what shall you go as, my dear?" he asked, when standing to go, remembering at last that it would be polite to reciprocate her questions.

"I do not think I should tell you," Isabella said, pouting, "though I daresay you may have guessed. I shall be a shepherdess again. Everyone says I shall be the prettiest one there."

"I do not doubt it," her husband said, with a gallant bow. "And I shall be the envy of every gentleman present."

Isabella dimpled at the compliment, and Harrowby took himself off, humming the tune of a country-dance.

Mrs. Mayfield let out sigh and gave Hester a rare look of approval. Then, lest her niece think she deserved better treatment in future, she preened and said, "I knew my lord would come to admire his son. It only needed for him to see how adorable our little Rennington is. But do not be forcing the child on him too often, Hester. Gentlemen do not wish to be bothered with their children."

"No, Aunt." It would be a waste of breath to point out that the reconciliation they had just experienced had been due to her efforts. Hester was so accustomed to her aunt's unfairness, that it no longer warranted so much as a sigh.

Only one incident occurred to disturb their pleasure that day. Just before the ladies retired to their rooms to dress for the ball, a footman

came to inform them that Sir David Hamilton had called and was
waiting in the antechamber off the hall. When it appeared that neither
Isabella nor her mother had sent for the physician, Hester told the
footman that she could receive him in the saloon, but the footman
said that Sir David had expressed a desire to speak only with Lord
Hawkhurst.

This seemed a bit strange, but the ladies' minds were too consumed
by thoughts of the ball to give it more than passing consideration. Isabella and Mrs. Mayfield each went to their rooms and Hester ran back
and forth between them, lending their maids a hand, until the sound
of Harrowby's raised voice below in the hall drew her to the stairs.

Peering over the balustrade, she was just in time to see him starting
up, vexation in his gait. The sound of the front door being shut suggested that whoever had earned his ire had just taken his departure.

Fuming and muttering to himself, Harrowby reached the first
floor, spied Hester, and immediately launched into a diatribe. "Can
you believe the impertinence of that quack? Asking me to intercede
on behalf of his kinsman, Lord Carnwath, as if anything I said would
sway the King! If I were so foolish, it would more likely land me in the
Tower, too. And so I said!"

Hester shook her head in commiseration, but her sympathy was
for Sir David, not Harrowby. "I know it must have annoyed you, but
think how desperate all the prisoners' relations must be."

"Serves them right for having traitors in the family!"

"I don't suppose they are happy about it. Most people do have
some connection to a rebel, even if it is a distant one." She was trying
to calm him down. "Perhaps he believed he would find a sympathetic
ear in you."

He looked horrified. "Sympathetic to the rebellion, d'you mean?"

"No, no, not at all!" Hester amended hastily. "I simply meant that
you are so congenial, he might have thought you would listen to his
kinsman's case."

Relieved, Harrowby allowed himself to be mollified. Still, he said,
"Well, I would not. Told him to bend the Princess's ear, if he's as much
in her favour as he claims. Now there's somebody the King might
listen to."

"Excellent advice. So, you see, Cousin, Sir David was not entirely wrong in coming to you."

Taken aback, but not so dense that he did not comprehend the compliment, he mused a moment, before saying, "Dare say he wasn't. That don't mean I want the pack of 'em coming here just the same. If any more traitors' relations come looking for me, tell them I am out."

That evening, when the ladies assembled in the withdrawing room to await Lord Kirkland's arrival, they were reminded by John the footman, that his lordship did not wish them to leave until they had seen his costume. Thoroughly bored by the subject by now, Isabella fretted that he would keep them waiting when she was eager to leave for the ball. She looked the ideal of rural seductiveness in her snug-fitting gown with a white, lacey apron beneath a very low-cut bodice, her golden curls trained loosely over her shoulders. Mrs. Mayfield looked imposing as the Egyptian queen Cleopatra, with a band of golden cloth cutting a swath round her forehead. It did not take Hester's knowledge of her aunt's habits to perceive that the colour of her hair had been obtained from a bottle, for no one's hair was naturally that black.

Lord Kirkland arrived, dressed as a harlequin from a light comedy. The ladies had no sooner exhausted their laughs and comments on his garb when the door opened again and Harrowby swept into the room.

Hester gasped, and Isabella uttered a shriek before she recognized her spouse, who stood proudly before them in a black half mask and a blue satin cape.

"There!" he said. "Did I not say I should surprise you? Bet you thought it was the scoundrel himself."

"Indeed, I did, Harrykins! You gave me quite a fright, you naughty man. Shame on you!" Isabella said, trying to pout, but not really angry at all. As Lord Kirkland exclaimed, "Bravo! Well done, Hawkhurst!" a flurry of giggles escaped her.

Now that Hester had a moment to recover from her shock, she was at considerable pains not to laugh. With his full-bottomed wig, and his pear-like physique, Harrowby did not resemble Blue Satan so much as he did a buffoon at the opera. She recalled how much he had envied Blue Satan his satin cape, and now it seemed he had commissioned one for himself. Pierre had designed both garments, of course, but apparently had taken the precaution of making this one different from the first, which as far as Harrowby knew, Pierre had never seen.

Something diplomatic must be said, though, so Hester volunteered, "It is a very elegant costume, Cousin."

"An't it? I don't know if you'll remember the highwayman's cape exactly, but I've added a few improvements of my own. I thought an extra shoulder cape and these gold buttons at the throat would give it a nobler look. After all, mustn't go round dressed no better than a damned criminal. Not really the thing for an earl to do. Ought to look a touch better at least."

Mrs. Mayfield issued a trill of fake laughter and profusely complimented him on his successful surprise. When he had had enough of her effusions, he interrupted her flow of speech, saying, "Well, that's enough now. Time to be off, or we shall miss one of his Grace's famous jokes, and I for one could use a little cheering up." He darted an impatient glance Hester's way, as if to say he had expected something more helpful from her by now.

As the two gentlemen and ladies made their way out of the room and down the stairs, Hester hoped that, after tonight, she would have something significant to report to him.

She waited until she was certain they were all gone, and no one was likely to return for a dropped glove or a forgotten fan before, with her heart lodged in her throat, she went to Harrowby's apartments in search of Pierre.

Although it had felt awkward to let him take her measurements, it was not very different from her staymaker's doing it. Although women did the actual sewing of the whalebones into the fabric, it was the staymaker himself who took his customer's measurements. Mr. Paine, who made Isabella's, and therefore, Hester's, was so used to running his tape round ladies' waists and breasts, that he knew instinctively how to put them at ease. Pierre had displayed the same indifference to his task. Hester might have been a chair being measured by an upholsterer for all the interest Pierre had shown.

She had been too busy all day to wonder what disguise he had concocted, but as she knocked on the door to Harrowby's dressing room and was ushered inside, she wondered fleetingly whether her costume would be even half as pretty as Isabella's.

She was stunned, therefore, when Pierre turned to the clothes press and with a flourish presented her with a suit that looked very much like a footman's livery.

Feeling as if the ground had fallen away beneath her, Hester breathlessly asked, "What is that?"

"But it is *mademoiselle's* costume, of course!"

"But those are breeches!"

Pierre shrugged. "*Mademoiselle* said she does not wish to be recognized. And who, I ask you, would ever suspect that *Mademoiselle* Hester would go about in a man's garments?

"See here," he explained enthusiastically, holding up a pair of blue stockings with brown garters. "I have taken one of the footmen's costumes and in the place of the gold stripes, I have sewn this charming blue satin. Milady Hawkhust will never recognize this costume as coming from a Hawkhurst servant."

"But what about shoes?"

Pierre gave an impatient shake of his head. "Did *monseigneur* not say that Pierre would think of everything? I have borrowed a pair of Alfred's. His foot is only slightly longer than *mademoiselle's.*"

It was true that he had altered the livery beyond all recognition. The Hawkhurst livery was brown with gold satin stripes at the seams. Replacing the stripes with blue completely changed it. Hester took a closer look at the stripes and realized they had come from the scraps from Harrowby's costume.

Pierre eyed his handiwork critically. "A paler blue would have been more beautiful, but there was not enough time to visit the mercer."

"And my hair? How can that be disguised?"

"I shall dress it myself. Never fear."

Hester tried to swallow, but her throat had narrowed. Was it too late, she wondered, to call the whole thing off?

Just then, the clock in Harrowby's bedchamber struck the hour of eleven. St. Mars would already be waiting for her outside in Piccadilly. If he was willing to risk exposure, should she be so faint-hearted?

"Very well," she said, taking a deep breath. "Tell me what I should put on first."

Pierre produced one of his master's fine lawn shirts with ruffles at the collar and wrists, instructing her to tuck it well into the breeches. He laid out the stockings and garters as if he were laying out the clothes for his master. Then he discreetly retired from the room, telling her to advise him when she was ready for him to sew her in.

Hester had never felt so exposed as when she removed her hooped petticoat in Harrowby's closet. Moving as quickly as she could, she donned the shirt and took comfort from the great length of its back. The breeches were entirely a different matter, however, as she had never worn drawers of any sort. The fabric chafed between her legs. Before she admitted Pierre, she sat and pulled on the blue stockings, which only reached half-way up her leg. It felt strange to tie the brown garters below her knees, but when she peered in the long glass, she had to admit that she presented a nice trim figure of a footman. She'd left on her chemise so the two layers of linen helped to hide her breasts, but the lack of lacings gave her a terrifying sense of freedom.

Summoned, Pierre quickly and efficiently sewed up the seam he had left open in back. Then he helped her into the matching jacket. Its masculine cut did more to hide her curves, and Pierre skillfully applied his needle to the areas that were too big. He gave her one of Harrowby's linen neckcloths and tied it for her. Then he bent and held Albert's buckled shoes so she could slip them on.

"Now," he said, looking critically over her, "*le maquillage* and *mademoiselle's* hair." He set her at Harrowby's dressing table, removed the pins holding her hair, and ruthlessly brushed out the curls she had meticulously arranged. Since for years most gentlemen had worn full-bottomed perukes, their heads were generally shaved, but a few sported their own hair. Few servants, on the other hand, wore wigs, for to supply them would be an extravagance. Hester's hair was longer than most men's, but when Pierre tied it back with a blue satin ribbon, she agreed that it would pass.

Then, because she was supposed to be a courtier and not a true running footman, Pierre applied a thick layer of white paint to her face and placed two patches, one at the corner of her mouth and the other high on the opposite cheek. He studied her for a minute longer, then stepped aside and said, "Voila!"

When he moved away from the mirror and Hester saw her reflection, she was amazed by how different she looked. Even with careful scrutiny she would never have recognized herself. She slowly came to her feet and turned this way and that.

"You are a genius, Pierre."

He took the compliment as his due, smiling with a gracious air. "It would be better if *mademoiselle* carried a snuffbox," he said, "but milord 'Arrowby would be certain to recognize his. Without a snuffbox, a fan would suffice."

"Oh, but I have one!" Hester exclaimed, glad to have thought of one thing, at least. "It's in the pocket of my skirt. I have never carried it, but I thought I might tonight as no one in the family has ever seen it." The fan was a generous gift from St. Mars, which she had rarely unwrapped, and then just to remind herself of the day he had purchased it for her. She had told him she would never dare display it for fear of provoking her aunt's demands to know who had given it to her, but St. Mars had been in a curious mood that day, and to refuse his kindness would have been churlish, especially when she had cherished his gift.

Pierre fetched her pile of clothing, and extracted the long tape with a pocket on each end, which she wore beneath her skirt, tied about her waist. He handed the pockets to her, saying, "You will not be able to wear this with your breeches, n'est ce pas? But the jacket of your suit has pockets sewn in."

"I shan't need much from it, just a handkerchief, the tickets to the ball, and the fan."

While she was transferring the handkerchief and tickets to her suit pockets, he said, "If *mademoiselle* will condescend to wear them, I would be honoured to lend her my cloak and my gloves." Pierre made this offer with a proud bow.

Hester was taken aback. She had forgotten that her own garments would not do. "You are too generous, Pierre, but yes, I should be very grateful to wear them." Her throat narrowed and she found it hard to swallow. She had been playing at dressing up, but she truly was about to go out into the town, clothed as man.

If she had been at all concerned that the quality of Pierre's garments could give her away, she was soon disabused of the worry, as Pierre again visited his closet and retrieved a very elegant cloak and a fine pair of gloves. She should have known better than to question his judgement or his taste. Indeed, foreigners often commented that with the freedoms the English enjoyed, it was impossible to tell master from servant. Every tradesman and milkmaid sought to imitate their betters in their dress. It was no wonder that a valet would have invested so much in his.

"I know that *mademoiselle* will be careful not to soil them," Pierre said, with the only hint of anxiety he had shown over the evening's events.

Hester promised to take good care of his belongings.

For the finishing touches, he produced a blue satin half-mask and a tricorn hat, which, though a bit snug, would sit atop her head. Then they discussed how she might best re-enter the house and reclaim her own clothing.

"If *mademoiselle* could contrive to come in by the kitchen gardens on the stable side," Pierre said, "I shall wait for you there."

"I am sure my Lord St. Mars will help me to do it. What time do you expect your master to arrive? I should return before he does, for you could be waiting on him."

Pierre gave a prim little nod. "That is something I cannot say with any certainty, for milord may choose to remain out. But I shall wait up for him, just the same."

Hester supposed he meant that Harrowby might spend the rest of the night with his mistress. She thanked him for all the inconvenience she had caused him. Then, as the clock struck the half-hour, she said that she must go, for St. Mars would be waiting.

Pierre preceded her down the stairs. Hester stayed out of sight, around the turn in the steps, while Pierre sent the only footman in the hall to the laundry to see if their master's shirt was dry. The two engaged in a bit of wrangling before Will, the footman, conceded to Pierre's superior position. Even then, Hester suspected he did it only because Pierre railed at him French. In a moment, she heard the little valet's loud whisper telling her to hurry, and she tripped as lightly as she could down the stairs.

Before he permitted her to exit the house, Pierre touched her chin and reminded her to carry herself with arrogance, for nobody, he said, would recognize her then. Trembling with nervousness, Hester thanked him with a wavering smile, before nearly running from the house. As she crossed the courtyard in her borrowed clothes, she felt like a different person—freer, in spite of the fear she felt.

Gideon had been sitting in a hackney coach in Piccadilly for the better part of an hour. He had witnessed his cousin's departure, and watched as Isabella, her mother, and their escort took a second carriage. That had been the signal for him to settle down to wait, as he guessed that Hester would not be able to put on her own costume until after the others were gone.

The driver of the hackney grumbled that his horses were getting cold, but Gideon understood that he was principally worried about being cheated out of his fare. Gideon promised him an extra half-crown for waiting, which silenced the man for a while. After three quarters of an hour had passed, Gideon wondered whether Mrs. Kean had succumbed to second thoughts. If she had, he supposed he should not blame her for being prudent, for if discovered, she would have much to lose. He even entertained doubts himself, not for his own risk, but for the danger of involving her in his kind of recklessness. He wondered how much longer he should wait before giving her up, but reminded himself that she might have become distracted by domestic business.

Eventually, it was not a lady who appeared at the gate, but a man he did not know. As Rufus, the old gatekeeper, opened the tall iron gate to Hawkhurst House, he touched his forelock to the man, who, strangely, appeared to be a servant himself. For a moment, Rufus's lantern threw light up onto the stranger's face, and Gideon was astonished to see that it was painted and patched, until he realized that the footman's livery must be a costume for the ball, and the gentleman a guest of his cousin's.

As the young man looked up and down the street, Gideon did

wonder mildly why Harrowby's guest had been left to make his way to the ball alone. Then he sat up and braced himself as the figure came hesitantly towards him, no doubt to engage the services of his coach.

Instead of speaking to the driver, however, the young man approached his window and peered inside. "My lord, is it you?" he said, in a voice that was almost certainly Mrs. Kean's.

Gideon's jaw flew open. He hastened to open the door. "My dear," he said, "can that be you?"

A nervous laugh answered him before the figure climbed rather awkwardly inside. Recovering slowly from his daze, Gideon extended both hands to assist her.

"Are ye ready t'go now?" the driver called down roughly, then added an angry comment under his breath. Gideon thought he heard a reference to "Mollies," and laughed, before he gave his assent and reached across Mrs. Kean to shut the door.

"My dear Mrs. Kean," he said, careful to speak her name softly, "I confess, I am dumbfounded." Once enclosed in the small space, he would have known her, even if she had not spoken. He would know her scent anywhere, even with the traces of others' on the clothes she wore.

"I do not wonder at your amazement, my lord," she said in a breathless voice. "I was astonished myself when I saw the costume Pierre had prepared for me."

"I do not doubt it, but I commend your courage for wearing it. What was he thinking of?"

"Is it too scandalous? If it is, please let us turn around at once! I know he chose it so I should never be recognized, but if it shocks you, my lord, please do let us turn back!"

"Shocks me? No, indeed. I hope I did not give that impression. I am simply in awe. And we must not waste all your splendid efforts. I daresay Pierre was right. It would be very difficult to conceal your identity otherwise."

"The disguise has worked so far, for Rufus did not know me. He gave me a curious glance, no doubt because he did not recall letting a gentleman in, but Pierre told me to walk arrogantly, so I raised my nose in the air, and it was plain he did not even think of challenging me."

"I cannot see you in the dark. Tell me where he got all your clothes."

She was turned towards him, and he could see her outline in the dim light. He reached over and touched the hat on her head, then worked his hands down to her hair.

"The hat is Alfred's, I think," she said, "and it feels a bit too small."

"That is probably for the best, for it won't fall off." Her hair felt like silk beneath his fingers, and he was tempted to stroke it. "He did not give you a wig?"

"No, there wasn't time. What with everyone else's preparations, I had very little time to consult Pierre."

He felt the ribbon that confined her queue. "I'm sure this will suffice. I've never seen you with your hair done this way."

She chuckled. "Well, I should hope not."

Finding it difficult to swallow, he dropped his hands to her shoulders. He was feeling carefully, when she said, huskily, "The cloak is Pierre's, and I must say it is very fine. The rest is a Hawkhurst livery, but he has altered the colour of the stripe. What is your costume, my lord?"

If her question had not stopped him, he might have continued exploring. This was a game he would gladly play as long as she tolerated it. "See if you can guess," he said, capturing both her hands and placing them on either side of his hat.

"I can make out your tricorn now," she said, a hint of laughter in her voice. Her hands moved lightly down the sides of his head. When she did not encounter a wig, but instead felt the hood that covered him to the shoulders, she said, "A domino! I should have thought of that myself. No one will know you at all! That will give me one less thing to worry about." She pulled back, asking, "Is that all?"

The loss of her touch was painful, as if an elixir had suddenly been withdrawn. "Not quite," he said, "but you shall soon see for we are almost there."

He let down the window and told the driver to stop, then turned back to Mrs. Kean. "We can walk from here. I doubt many of his

Grace's guests will be arriving in a hackney."

He leapt down first, then turned to assist her, but refusing to take his hand, she gave a neat little jump and landed at his side. She whispered, "You must not treat me like a female, my lord, or everyone will know that is what I am."

The driver had set them down on the corner of Duke and Russell Streets in front of the Nag's Head Inn. A lantern was hanging beneath its sign, and it threw some light their way. Now, he could make out the white paint on her face, and the trimness of her figure. There was also light enough that she must have finally seen the cape he was wearing.

She gave a quick gasp. But then she astonished him by laughing.

"What?" he said. "No scolding? I was certain I should receive the edge of your tongue. Tom treated me to quite a lashing before I escaped the house. You do not object to my costume?"

She shook her head. "Perhaps, I should have reacted like Tom, if I had not— But no, you must see for yourself."

"You intrigue me . . . but there is nothing very new in that. Very well, where you lead, I shall follow."

He saw that he had disconcerted her, but she would not admit how uncomfortable she was in the role of leader in this sort of enterprise.

"Should we not have a plan first?" she asked.

"I thought the plan was to find Mr. Gayet and try to question him."

"It is, of course. But when we find him—if we find him, I suppose I should say—then how shall we go about getting him alone?"

Gideon smiled at the tentative note in her voice. He did delight in teasing her. "It is my humble opinion—and I offer this, having discovered myself in rather intricate situations more than once—that it is sometimes best to have no plan. As soon as we decided upon one, we would be certain to have to abandon it. Better to compose our actions on the spur of the moment, depending on the circumstances we find."

She heaved a sigh. "I see. Then, I suppose we should go in."

She turned to lead him, but he caught hold of her arm. "It is perfectly permissible for two gentlemen to walk arm in arm. But I do advise you to walk with your head up. You might even strut a bit."

She bit back a laugh, but she did take his arm as any gentleman might do, and once they were walking, she threw back her shoulders. "Like this, my lord?"

"Yes, my dearest friend. Just like that."

Now is the Time that Rakes their Revells keep;
Kindlers of Riot, Enemies of Sleep.
His scatter'd Pence the flying Nicker flings,
And with the Copper Show'r the Casement rings.
Who has not heard the Scowrer's Midnight Fame?
Who has not trembled at the Mohock's Name?

But when the Bully, with assuming Pace,
Cocks his broad Hat, edg'd round with tarnished Lace,
Yield not the Way; defie his strutting Pride,
And thrust him to the muddy Kennel's side . . .

CHAPTER XII

Like Hawkhurst House, Montagu House had been built as a country mansion beyond the edge of the city, but situated conveniently for visits to Court. The trade generated by such a large household had drawn people to settle just outside it, in a community known as Bloomsbury, in the same way that villages had developed on the outskirts of castles. The Great Fire had hastened the building of more houses, so that now, the City of London stretched through Bloomsbury to the Duke's front gate, while beyond it lay open countryside, a popular place for duelists.

The mansion itself stood quite a distance back from Great Russell Street, its deep forecourt set behind a long imposing wall with one turret-like structure on either end and a pedimented gateway in the centre. Few guests were arriving at this late hour, but the servant who checked their tickets at the gate found nothing strange in two gentlemen electing to come on foot. With Southampton House just to the east, and noblemen's lodgings nearby in Duke Street, it was not surprising that two gentlemen would stroll to the ball, even in the cold.

Waiting carriages with their attendant coachmen and footmen filled the forecourt. As Hester and St. Mars moved past them on their way to the door, St. Mars said in a low voice, "Remember to hold your head up and never lower your eyes, unless in a deep bow. In fact, you would do better to stare, no matter how rude it may seem. Too much modesty in a gentleman is certain to attract notice."

Hester straightened her shoulders, vowing to act as if a rod had been bolted to her spine. Without the confinement of her stays, she could breathe with greater freedom than she ever had. It gave her an unaccustomed sense of strength, an alarming degree of liberty.

The house they approached was a double-pile, a single rectangular block, two rooms deep, with a central dome and projecting end pavilions in the French style. Wings of offices flanked the forecourt on both sides. At the main portico, a large single door with a pediment, a second servant took their tickets and admitted them to the entrance hall, where their ears were immediately assailed by a roar of merriment. Two hundred voices raised in greetings, gossip, and laughter came at them from every direction. The splendour of the house, the glittering light from hundreds of candles, and the sight of so many people in masquerade confused Hester's senses. She was glad for the feel of St. Mars's steadying grip on her arm, as her eyes made sense of the overwhelming details.

The entrance hall was a splendid room, built in stone and decorated with exuberant paintings of flowers, pairs of Ionic columns spaced around the walls, and a ceiling painted with allegorical figures. The two halls behind it were crowded with arriving guests, their waiting pages and footmen in an array of liveries. Somehow, in the midst of the *mêlée,* one of his Grace's footmen found them and relieved them of their cloaks. As Hester and St. Mars worked their way through the crowd to the staircase, she tried to make out the identities of the people she passed. In all that gathering, however, she was sure of only one, the Duchess of Bolton, and then only when she heard the lady complain of the pain in her feet. She was amazed at how well the addition of a simple mask could conceal one's features. This discovery gave her more confidence in her own disguise, but it made her wonder how difficult it would be for them to find Mr. Gayet among such a crowd.

St. Mars led her up the great staircase filled with guests—its vast walls painted in fanciful scenes of classical battles and pastoral idylls, its unusual railing of wrought iron—to the vestibule, which gave entry to the saloon on the north side of the house. Here, overlooking the garden, the majority of guests were assembled. Almost immediately, Hester heard the distinct, barking laughter of the Prince of Wales, and turned to see him dressed in the habit of a Dutch boor. He was surrounded by a group of gentlemen and a lady shepherdess, who she thought must be Mrs. Holland, his favourite. There were several others in the room dressed like countrymen, shepherds and milkmaids, farmers, and yokels of all kinds. Hester was only one out of dozens of running footmen. It seemed the aristocracy took great fun in imitating their servants.

The saloon was a magnificent room, painted with beautiful landscapes, including floral swags and Corinthian columns, covering even the doors—so well concealing them, in fact, that it was difficult to spot them. Hundreds of candles glistened from the ceiling and in sconces. The notes of a minuet came faintly from a small orchestra at the end of the saloon, while couples moved gracefully through the space in formal steps. The acoustics of the room were such that voices assailed them from all sides.

St. Mars leaned to whisper in Hester's ear, "I suppose you elected to wear that costume simply to avoid dancing with me."

She laughed and shook her head. But in her heart she sincerely bemoaned the breeches she wore. Whenever she had released her guard enough to imagine attending a ball with St. Mars, dancing had always figured in her fantasy. That she was condemned never to have that pleasure was something she had learned to accept, but the realization of it never failed to sadden her. Now, she firmly put such a notion out of her head and said, "Perhaps we should stroll about and see if I cannot spot Mr. Gayet."

Together they made their way around the floor, dodging gesticulating guests and inclining their heads as various ladies and gentlemen ventured tentative greetings, trying to place the two newcomers. They were half-way round the floor when, before she could stop him, St. Mars ran into a familiar back, clothed in a blue satin cape.

Harrowby turned in the middle of a laugh, and started at the sight of a costume so like his own. "Good gad! Wherever did you get the notion of coming as Blue Satan, sir? I was certain of being the only one to think of it. If my valet spilled my secret to you, I shall have his hide!"

St. Mars scarcely hesitated as he raked his cousin from head to toe. While Hester watched tensely, she glimpsed the flicker of a smile at his lips as he spoke. "Indeed, sir—" St. Mars made a reverent bow, so deep it bore a hint of insolence—"if I had known that you intended this masquerade, I should have endeavoured to think of something more original."

If Hester had worried that his voice would be recognized, she was relieved by the haughty inflection he employed. It was so unlike his customary tone.

"Eh? Well, no matter, what? All in fun, don't ye know?" Harrowby looked as if he feared this tall, slim gentleman in the black domino might call him out. "I like the cut of yours better," he confessed. "Much more like the real scoundrel's, eh? And I should know, for I was the first gentleman he had the impudence to hold up. You've got the mask all wrong, though," he added, with belated triumph.

St. Mars made another haughty bow, and Hester did her best to imitate his movement. Harrowby was forced to reciprocate or risk offending the strangers he confronted, but it was clear that a great deal of his pleasure had been curtailed by the sight of a similar costume.

Hester did not wish to be trapped into speaking to him. She was not at all sure she could hide her sex with a deeper voice. Surreptitiously, she tugged on St. Mars's coattail, then again, harder this time, until he backed away from his cousin and turned to follow her back the way they had come.

A sigh escaped her, as he moved to walk beside her. "So that is why you laughed when you saw my costume," he whispered.

"Yes. I did not worry about your choice once I had seen Harrowby's. I hope you admired the gold buttons. They were an improvement of his."

St. Mars gave an appreciative nod. "Now we know how he would dress if he were forced to turn outlaw."

Hester bit her lips to avoid smiling and turned her attention to the guests. Raucous laughter was coming from an inner room, so she bent her steps that way. In the doorway, she paused, astonished by the sight of two very long tables, one set with more than two hundred dishes, the other with a variety of rich wines. The commotion they had heard was coming from the second, where one of the guests was pretending to be a tavern keeper selling drams. A group of gentlemen surrounded him, encouraging him in his joke by buying more and more to drink.

As Hester and St. Mars drew near, they saw that one gentleman in particular had over-indulged, urged on by his drunken friends. Turning suddenly away from the table, he cast up his accounts all over the floor. The company scattered with shrieks and oaths.

Next to Hester, St. Mars expressed his disgust with an oath. He took her arm and had started to pull her away, when catching a glimpse of the gentleman who had been encouraging the drinker most, she uttered a cry. "There he is, my lord!" she whispered, nodding in his direction. "There is Mr. Gayet."

The hand about her arm tightened. "Which one?" he said, a hard cast tightening his jaw.

"There, the running footman in the red and gold livery. That is his uncle's—Lord Ratby's livery." Hester was certain this was her quarry, for he also wore the distinctive tie-wig with the pigeon's wings she had seen Mr. Gayet wear.

The group of drinkers had turned their backs on their sick friend. Now, they stood about, looking bored, as if without a person to taunt or to urge to misbehaviour, all their fun had come to an end. After a few minutes more, Mr. Gayet jerked his head towards the door, and the rest followed him out.

"A proper little flock of sheep, aren't they?" St. Mars said grimly, as he took Hester's elbow and led her after them.

The men did not pause in the saloon, but made their way directly to the vestibule, jostling people roughly as they went. A snigger from the last one, as one of the guests spilled his wine over the front of a lady's skirt, made it clear that this had been his intention.

They headed down the stairs. Before following them, St. Mars pulled Hester aside, out of the flow of guests descending and ascending, and said in a voice only she could hear, "You should not be present when I confront him. If you stay, a footman will find you a hackney."

"No," she said. "I wish to come with you."

He hesitated. "I fear things could become unpleasant." His body seemed to thrum with the need to fight.

If I come with you, perhaps I can stop you from taking dangerous risks, Hester thought, but she did not make the remark aloud. Instead, she said, "It was I who got you into this, my lord. If it should appear unwise to accost Mr. Gayet, I should be there to decide whether it is worth the risk." She could see his reluctance in his frown and the way his gaze moved repeatedly from her face to the turn in the stairs where Mr. Gayet and his friends had just disappeared. That his reticence was due to concern for her safety, she had no doubt. St. Mars would never do anything to put her in jeopardy.

With a sigh of resignation, he said, "Then, shall we?" and turned to follow the departing men.

Below them in the hall, Mr. Gayet and his party stood about, waiting for their cloaks. As St. Mars and Hester took the last step onto the ground floor, a footman offered to fetch theirs, so they soon were able to exit Montagu House, hard on the heels of the Mohocks.

For that was who they were, Hester realized with a tremor, as the word sprang into her head. She had no doubt that these young gentlemen were little better than thugs, urging one another on to harm strangers for no better reason than that they found it amusing. But did their notion of fun extend to murdering a man? And, if so, was not poison a very odd choice of weapon for youths with a taste for violence?

The Mohocks crossed the bustling forecourt and exited onto Great Russell Street on foot, hooting and careening, and clapping one another on the back, as if to rouse their animal spirits. It was long after one in the morning, yet they obviously had no intention of retiring. On the contrary, they had the air of a pack of vicious dogs, setting out on the prowl.

As St. Mars and Hester reached the gate, they paused to see where the men were headed and saw them turning down Queen Street towards Drury Lane.

"Let's stay behind them," St. Mars said. "If we're lucky, they'll separate and we'll be able to get Gayet alone."

Falling into step beside him, Hester nodded, though privately, she thought their chance of catching him alone would be very slight, at least for the next few hours. Once out with their friends, gentlemen the age of Mr. Gayet tended to remain out all night, and she would not be able to risk returning to Hawkhurst House after three or four o'clock. Isabella, Harrowby, and her aunt were quite capable of seeing the last of his Grace of Montagu's guests out the door, but she would not dare stay out until dawn.

When they reached Queen Street, St. Mars let loose her arm, and shifted his hand to his sword hilt. Ahead, in the dark night, they heard the rowdy voices of the Mohocks. Their bodies moved like shadows down the centre of the street. As they progressed, occasionally they paused in front of a house while one would run up to the door to bang the knocker. Then all would run skipping on to the next bit of mischief.

They continued on into Peter Street, but then paused in High Holborn, where a dispute arose. When Hester and St. Mars drew near, he took her hand and pulled her into the shadows, from which they could overhear the men's argument. A light from the White Hart on the corner illuminated their masked faces, and Hester easily picked out Mr. Gayet among them.

It seemed that a few of the men wished to turn left into Holborn to terrorize the watch. A watch house stood no more than a quarter of a mile up the street, she knew, and from their pleas she learned that no greater fun could be had than tipping one over, except perhaps to catch an old watchman inside and roll him over and over.

A few, including Mr. Gayet, expressed the tediousness of doing this yet again. They preferred to head down Drury Lane in search of a different kind of sport. Finally, given the intransigence of the leaders of each faction, the decision was made to divide into two parties. Only two of the Mohowks stayed with Mr. Gayet as he turned into Drury Lane.

"Our odds have just improved," St. Mars whispered, as they waited for the Holborn contingent to walk out of sight. "Are you still with me?" He squeezed her hand, and she squeezed his back.

Taking this as her answer, he said, "Then, I have a plan, but we must make haste."

Pulling her with him, he led her after the three men, but at a much faster pace. Moving from shadow to shadow along the street, they were close to overtaking the three Mohocks when the men stopped to trade barbs with a cluster of prostitutes. Here they were not far from Covent Garden, where every vice could be found and no one would bear witness to the crimes. The prostitutes gathered about the gentlemen, begging for their business, before they discovered that the men they had accosted would rather steal their pleasures than pay. In the scuffle that ensued, St. Mars grabbed Hester's elbow and led her farther down the street.

"My lord," she said, in a breathless whisper, "I fear those poor women are being abused!"

"I know," he said in a tight voice. "But they are not outnumbered, and they will fight back."

The sound of curses emanating from the men behind them, amidst the women's shrieks, gave Hester some comfort. From the sounds that came to them through the dark, Hester imagined that the women had made good use of their teeth and fingernails. There had been some half-dozen women to the three men, so she hoped the greater numbers would prevail. They were not the only ones in the street, she realized, as other shadows moved past them, but how many gentlemen would come to the rescue of whores?

Still distressed, she was about to ask St. Mars what they could possibly do, when he led her beyond Long Acre and into the first alley they reached. There, out of sight of Mr. Gayet and his friends, he placed her behind him, while he stood at the entrance and peered out.

The alley was extremely narrow. It had no exit except a narrow passage at the back, which turned left behind some houses, presumably leading into another alley or court. From between two close-standing brick walls, where they had concealed themselves, it was impossible for Hester to see or hear the result of the scene they had witnessed.

"Are they still fighting?" she asked, dismayed to hear the quiver in her voice.

Fortunately, St. Mars did not appear to notice it as he strained to hear what was happening up the street. "I believe our friends have been routed, and none too gently, as I'd hoped. That should dampen their courage."

Turning towards her, he grasped both of her hands and said, "I believe this will be our best opportunity to question Mr. Gayet. Will you trust me to manage it?"

Without the slightest notion of what he meant to do, still she did not hesitate. "Of course. But what should I do?"

"Just stay behind me, and when I give an instruction, obey it instantly."

Hester promised she would, and he turned back immediately to take up his watch.

There were no lamps in the alley, just lighter areas at the openings at either end. Hester's eyes had become so accustomed to the dark that the opening onto the street looked like a grey curtain, against which St. Mars's silhouette was strongly etched. He barely seemed to breathe, he stood so still, and Hester did her best not to make any noise. Soon, she thought she heard men's voices coming nearer, raised in anger and recriminations.

Before she could reflect with any satisfaction on their misery, three male figures walked past the alley, their shoulders slumped. Then, quicker than she could attempt to discern Mr. Gayet's outline, St. Mars stepped silently out, grabbed the hindmost man with one hand over his mouth, and dragged him into their hiding place.

His attempt to muffle the Mohock's voice was only partially successful, but the man's outraged cry sounded a great deal like the complaints they had all been making. With what seemed like one motion, St. Mars pushed him up against a wall and pulled his weapon from his sheath. In an instant, the man felt the tip of a sword pressed into his cheek, and heard a voice in his ear, whispering gruffly, "If you cry out for your friends, I shall have no choice but to run you through. Do you understand?"

The whites of the Mohock's eyes shone out, even in the dark. His head gave a jerk.

"Take his sword," St. Mars ordered Hester. Then, as she hurried to obey him, he asked the man, "Are you Gayet?"

A surprised pause, then the man violently shook his head.

Hester could make out enough of his form to confirm this denial, but she thought she heard footsteps and voices returning. In as low a voice as she could manage, she said urgently, "This is not Gayet, and the others are coming!"

With no hesitation, St. Mars grabbed the Mohock by his neck-cloth, still with his sword in the man's face. Then, swinging him around with his back to the entrance just as the other two rushed into the alley, he shoved him roughly into them. One of the others fell with him, but one stepped aside and managed to stay on his feet in the narrow space.

Hester pulled back deeper into the alley to give St. Mars room to retreat as this man lunged forward, but St. Mars was too quick, and succeeded in wounding his arm. Dropping to the ground, the Mohock let out a cry that held more than a hint of fear, while his two friends, again on their feet, approached St. Mars cautiously, only one of them still armed.

For a moment, Hester thought she might be killed right there in an alley off Drury Lane, dressed in the costume of a running footman, and she wondered what sense her family would make of her demise. But as the men groped towards them, she realized something that St. Mars must already have known. The alley the Mohocks faced was so black, they could see nothing in front of them, while their forms, slightly illuminated by the lamps on Drury Lane, were visible to her and St. Mars. For a few moments, at least, while their eyes adjusted to greater darkness, even a woman with no skill with a sword would have an incomparable advantage.

The wounded man was scurrying backwards, calling out to his friends, "Help me! Get them! There are two of them!" As he crawled, he frantically rummaged about on the ground.

Realizing he must have dropped his sword when he'd been wounded, Hester quickly swept the space with the first man's weapon and encountered something that moved. Careful not to come close to him, she bent and located the blade. That was two without weapons, she thought, tightly grasping the sword's hilt.

The first Mohock who had been disarmed held back as his friend blindly swept the air with his sword. St. Mars let him advance into the alley a few steps, then called out pleasantly, "We simply wish to exchange a few words with Mr. Gayet. The rest of you may go, unless you prefer to fight it out."

As the advancing Mohock paused, the man at his feet cried, "Don't you dare leave me, you miserable cowards!"

Armed now with the answer he had sought, St. Mars gave a devilish laugh and lightly pinked the sword hand of the advancing man, who cried out in pain.

"It's you they want!" Gayet's second friend cried out. "This has nothing to do with us."

"Cowards! I'll kill you for this!" Gayet shouted after them, as the two pulled backwards out of the alley and turned to vanish into the night.

St. Mars had already stooped to raise Mr. Gayet by his neck cloth. When he struggled to free himself, he felt the tip of St. Mars's sword on his chest and stilled.

St. Mars's voice held a frightening mixture of anger and cheer when he said, "My friend here is holding the weapons your two . . . associates, shall we call them? I really should hesitate to call them friends . . . the swords they so obligingly have dropped. And, unlike me, he's adept with both hands. So I advise you to stop squirming, before we enjoy the pleasure of running you through."

Gayet must have made some kind of movement, for St. Mars added quickly, "I would also advise you not to call for the watch. They would be most interested to hear of your activities with respect to their watch houses."

"What do you want?" There was fear in Gayet's sullen tone, but Hester was determined to ignore it. She reminded herself of Sir Walter's corpse and the horse Mr. Gayet had so brutally treated.

"We wish to ask you about the murder of Sir Walter Tatham."

There came a shocked silence, then Gayet asked, "Why? What has his death to do with me?"

"Oh, come now! You cannot believe this assumption of innocence will fool us. Not when we know you stole the coronation robes from your uncle's apartment. Why don't you tell us why you poisoned Sir Walter and dressed him up?"

"I didn't poison him! I didn't even know him. Not really. I certainly didn't recognize his corpse. None of us did."

In the darkness, St. Mars's pause seemed pronounced. Hester guessed he must be reacting to the note of truth in his captive's voice.

"What do you mean you did not recognize him?"

"When we found him . . . dead. It was dark . . . too dark to see. At first we thought he was just a sot passed out from drink. We . . . tried to rouse him, but then, we smelled the stench—he'd been sick—and we thought he must have choked on his vomit. And his body was stiff . . . frozen."

"Then what?"

"I hardly know. We'd been drinking pretty deeply. I suppose we amused ourselves for a while, saying what we could do with a frozen corpse. We decided it would be a great joke to leave it somewhere where someone would find it . . . and be . . . startled by it. Then . . . one of us got the idea of dressing it up."

"I imagine that someone was you," St. Mars said, not hiding the contempt he felt. "Only you could have obtained your uncle's robes."

"So what if it was me? We didn't mean any harm by it. It was all just in fun."

"You have a strange notion of fun, as many, I fear, have witnessed. But let us return to Sir Walter. Where did you find his body?"

"Somewhere near Covent Garden . . . in King Street I think. I cannot tell you exactly. As I said, we were more than three sheets to the wind ourselves."

"Why did you take it onto the river?"

"I don't know." Gayet was getting impatient. "It was an amusing notion at the time."

"You couldn't agree on whom to scare with your corpse? So you decided to frighten as many people as possible?"

"Something like that. What does it matter? I didn't kill him. And why shouldn't we amuse ourselves? We've precious little else to do."

"'Little else to do,' while you wait for your uncle to die? Did I mention we also know how hard you are trying to hasten that event?"

Gayet's voice grew smug. "My uncle would never believe you. I'm his golden boy."

"And how hurt would he be to find out? But no, that might kill him off, and then you would benefit. It would be much fairer if you were the one to die. He would be disappointed, true . . . he might even go off in a fit of apoplexy, but at least you would not benefit from his death."

Gayet struggled, but there was no way to escape the strangling grip at his throat or the point at his chest. "Don't kill me," he finally begged. "I've told you all I know."

"You cannot conceive how tempting it is to put an end to your worthless life. I should do what you did to that horse—break your leg and leave you for a stranger to put down."

Between gasps, Gayet whimpered, "I didn't intend for him to break his leg. He slipped on the ice." A note of wonder entered his voice. "Is there nothing you do not know?"

"I'm afraid we know more about you than anyone could wish." The venom in St. Mars's voice sent a shiver down Hester's spine. "You enjoy hurting people. You think only of yourself. If I hear you have caused your uncle to have an attack or that you have abused another horse, I promise to find you, and it will not go as well for you next time.

"Have you noticed," he added, in a purring voice, "that your friends have not bothered to return with reinforcements. Perhaps, they would like me to kill you."

"But you won't?" Gayet was pleading again. "I promise to do as you say. I'll even go into the country for a spell."

"The sooner you get out of London, the better off everyone shall be." And with that, still holding him by the throat, St. Mars roughly dragged him out into Drury Lane and pushed him into the kennel, which was running with melted snow and refuse. Hester followed, brandishing a sword in each hand. When Gayet saw her, he gave an involuntary cry, then scrambled up from the ground and took off running like a hare.

St. Mars turned to look at her and doubled up with laughter. "Here," he said eventually, taking both swords from her and tossing them back into the alley, "it would be prudent for us to vanish, too, although I do not think his friends will return. They've been humiliated, and obviously lack courage. Your true bullies usually do."

"My lord," Hester exclaimed, "that was magnificent! If I had not been here, I should never have believed you could subdue three armed men by yourself!"

"But I was not by myself. I had my two-handed second to watch my back. That was very clever of you to find the other villain's sword. But, come along. We mustn't stand about and trade compliments here."

For a while they said nothing as St. Mars hurried her away from the scene. Mr. Gayet had fled south, so they headed back to Long Acre and turned left towards Piccadilly and Hawkhurst House. In a few minutes, when St. Mars spoke again, his voice was low.

"If we keep to the shadows, we should spot anyone who comes after us before we are seen. Shall I find you a hackney carriage? Are you tired?"

"Not at all."

Indeed, as Hester skipped to keep up with St. Mars's longer strides, she felt invigorated. In her entire life, she had never felt such freedom as she had tonight, running with him through the streets in the dark, with no skirts or stays to hamper her movements. "We can walk all the way back if you do not mind." She leapt lightly over a piece of rubbish the melting torrent had deposited in their path.

He laughed.

"What? What do you find so amusing?"

"I was just wondering what Tom would say if he could see us. He would be gravely shocked."

"I suspect he would, but his shock would be as nothing compared to the scandal that would have arisen if I had been discovered dead in an alley dressed like this."

He stopped and pulled her to him, then kissed the hand gripped in his. "You don't think I would have let anything happen to you?"

Her heart leapt in her breast. "No, I know you would not. It is just that I had no idea . . ." How could she tell him that even she, as much as she admired him, had never imagined how graceful and skillful he could be. She wondered what he might do if she lingered, but just then, the bells of St. Paul's in Covent Garden struck three and she knew she must go. "Let us just say that I shall be much less worried about your future escapades after seeing the cleverness you employed tonight."

"Well, that is one benefit of this evening's entertainment I had not foreseen. But now that we are speaking of it, did you get all you wished to learn from Gayet? I would have asked you while we had him, but I did not want him to hear your voice. The terror he felt was due in part to thinking he had two armed men to fight."

"Yes, I did. And I even believed him. The senselessness of what he did fits everything I have observed in him. And, earlier tonight, I started to wonder if poisoning would be the manner he would choose of ridding himself of an enemy."

"Good point," St. Mars agreed, pulling her arm through his to resume a more leisurely walk. "Now that you know the role Gayet and his friends played in Sir Walter's death, what shall you do? Will you tell Harrowby?"

"I hardly know. I suppose I shall have to in order to find out if it was the dressing up of Sir Walter's corpse that upset him. But truly, I fear it was not. He has repeatedly told me to forget Sir Walter's murderer and concentrate instead on his business dealings."

"Then, we should learn what those were, and if his widow is ignorant of them, then perhaps Mr. Mistlethwait will be our source."

"I shall have to think about how to approach him."

"Perhaps we can waylay him the way we did Mr. Gayet . . . you in the shadows with a sword in each hand and me . . ."

Her laughter cut him off. "I do not think we can make a regular practice of this, but—" she sighed— "we did perform rather well together, I thought."

"My dear Mrs. Kean, we always work magnificently together. There is no news in that."

In a few moments, far too soon for Hester, they reached Piccadilly and circled round through the streets of new houses to the back of Hawkhurst House. There, on Glasshouse Street outside the fence to the deep garden, the neighbouring houses were dark. The only light that reached them came from a half moon and a few large stars.

When Hawkhurst House had been built, during the reign of Charles II, there was nothing beyond it to the north but countryside. The garden fence, which ran along the back of the estate, though tall and solid as a wall, was made only of wood. Years later, an espalier had been planted along the inside, and the shrubs had grown thick, providing a deeper barrier.

When Hester and St. Mars reached the fence, St. Mars asked, "Are you certain Pierre will be at the door?"

"He has never failed us yet. And if he is not, he will have to explain how I came by this costume. Besides, he will be anxious to learn what's become of his cloak."

His chuckle came softly to her through the dark. "Your logic, as usual, is perfect. Then I shall not keep you. But what about the stable dogs?"

"They will awaken, but they know me. They should settle down before anyone comes out to see what is wrong."

"I could come with you. They know me, too."

Hester bit her lip, hating what she had to say. "I'm afraid there are a few new ones who do not."

"Ah." Sadness tinged his voice, though he tried to hide it. "Of course, there would be. Then, I had best help you over before the others get home."

The espalier was daunting, but St. Mars told her the shrubs were thinner near the corner post where she could safely place a foot. "I often climbed over it as a boy. Take hold of my shoulders," he commanded, as he put both hands at her waist. "When I throw you up, lift your foot over the plank and feel for the post behind it."

He paused with his hands on her waist. The black domino covered his features. In the dark she could not see his eyes. The moment lengthened, and her pulse beat a faster tempo. She felt a flush spreading up from her toes. Then, before she could speak, he bent and with a powerful thrust lifted her up over his head. She flailed her legs in surprise before locating the plank with the outside of her foot. She followed it to the other side where the thick post met it. As she shifted her weight to rest upon the post, St. Mars's grip slid from her waist down her arms to her hands. He held onto them tightly while she gained her balance, then guided them to the top of the plank, so she could brace herself. Hester felt with one leg behind her and found a little space between two shrubs. From here, it should have been fairly easy to lower herself to the ground, except for the fact that she had not climbed trees since her childhood. She landed clumsily, scraping herself on a branch on the way down.

"Ouch!" She fell backwards past another branch, landing on her bottom with a thud.

As she hastily picked herself up and dusted off her hands, St. Mars's whisper came from between the planks, "My dear, are you hurt?"

"No, but I'm glad you did not witness my descent. It was far from graceful."

She heard him laugh, but the sound of a bark, and then another cut short any goodbyes they might have made.

"Best hurry," he called softly. "I'll soon be in touch."

Hester turned and ran lightly up the long garden walk to the house. The mixed group of dogs, who slept outside the stables in the courtyard in front, came running around the house and met her before she was halfway up the path, whimpering with pleasure as soon as they recognized a friend. Hester usually appreciated their greetings, but she resented the interruption they had caused between her and St. Mars. As their tails beat soundly against her legs, she hushed them impatiently. Then, she covered the remaining hundred yards to the garden door, where Pierre said he would be.

His welcome was more discreet than the dogs', but only slightly less frenzied. *"Vîtes! Vîtes! Mademoiselle* must hurry! Just as Pierre 'eard the dogs, I also 'eard the coach of milord arrive. I must run to 'is chamber to receive 'im."

He sped her through the house and up a back stairwell, racing ahead to make certain there was no one to see her. Reaching her chamber door, he turned to relieve her of his cloak and begged her to bring the other garments to him in the morning before her cousins were awake. Then, he fled towards Harrowby's apartment, leaving Hester alone to catch her breath.

She closed the door, grateful to be spared Pierre's questions, so she could savour the night's events. Reliving every moment of their adventure, she was struck by the way St. Mars and she had worked together, as if words were not essential for their communication. She wondered if he felt about it as she did, or if he was so used to skirting danger that the night had seemed nothing out of the usual. She could have wished for more time, especially when they had stood in the relative safety of Glasshouse Street. No one would have seen them there, if he had clasped her to his chest in her man's clothes. But such wishes were futile.

That did not stop her from concocting two or three more satisfying scenarios while she undressed. Then, as she snuggled for warmth under her covers, it dawned on her that if St. Mars had wished, he might have kissed her. Tonight, outside the pales, before the dogs had barked, he might have taken some of the liberties he'd hinted at. Certainly, tonight he had not flirted with her as much as he often had of late.

He must have been teasing when he had complained of their always meeting in churches. If he truly had those kinds of feelings for her, if he found her at all attractive, surely there had been time enough for at least one kiss.

He might have taken any number of kisses before he'd thrown her over the fence, but with all the circumstances in favour of intmacy, even with his hands about her waist, he had not. He had not been tempted enough. It seemed they were friends and nothing more, after all, and she had been stupid to think otherwise, even for a second.

The thrill that had elated her all evening seeped out of her like air from a bladder. Her chest felt crushed. Her eyes filled and, for a moment, she could not swallow. Then her innate good sense reasserted itself. She allowed that she was tired, that the wee hours of the morning could often bring sadness. She had never expected St. Mars's love and was happy to have his friendship.

But she must be on guard never to let her imagination run away with her again.

Who would of Watling-street *the Dangers share,*
When the broad Pavement of Cheap-side *is near?*
Or who that rugged Street would traverse o'er,
That stretches, O Fleet-ditch, *from that black Shore*
To the Tow'rs *moated Walls? Here Steams ascend*
That, in mix'd Fumes, the wrinkled Nose offend.
Where Chandlers Cauldrons boil; where fishy Prey
Hide the wet Stall, long absent from the Sea;
And where the Cleaver chops the Heifer's Spoil,
And where huge Hogsheads sweat with trainy Oil . . .

CHAPTER XIII

It had taken all of Gideon's restraint not to give in to the urges he had felt. For one insane moment, he had been tempted to take Hester somewhere they could be alone and make love to her. But where he could take her, he did not know. The thought of his estate in France had flashed into his brain, but no sooner had he thought of it than he had remembered how dangerous the passage would be. Then a dozen questions had pressed into his head. Would she wish to go? And what would it mean if she did?

The notion that they might marry gave him an immediate thrill, but it came too suddenly for him to act. To ask Hester, or any woman, to share his exile—would it be merely a selfish whim? Surely a sane man would reflect before risking his greatest friendship on a desperate act of loneliness?

In the end it was not his doubt about the answer she would give or even prudent thoughts about his Majesty's ships in the Channel that prevented him from seizing her, but the promise he had made to Nathan Breed.

He had not told Hester that all his plans for the escape were in place. There was not a moment to waste. The six impeached lords, who had pleaded guilty to the charges, would soon be brought from the Tower to Westminster Hall to receive judgement from the court erected there for that purpose.

After that, it could not be long before the prisoners in Newgate would be brought to trial.

Two days before the Duke of Montagu's ball, Gideon had sent a message to the Duke of Bournemouth, who had immediately approved the money Nancy Cole had demanded to hide his nephew. When Gideon reported this to Nathan Breed, it was evident the young man was both shocked and hurt by the sum she'd demanded. He said that for that kind of extortion, she ought to be willing to lodge the Pretender himself, but with her assistance given purely as a matter of business, at least he trusted she would uphold her side of the bargain.

The exact hour of his escape could not be set—all depended on the vigilance of the guards—but the second night after the Duke of Montagu's ball was the date appointed for the first attempt. Gideon would wait with Tom in the alley that led to Black and White Court, a narrow passage not far from Newgate that opened into Fleet Lane. Gideon would carry a disguise for Breed, which he hoped would fool the prison guards if the escape was noticed. The success of their plan would all hinge on Breed, as he would have to leap onto the nearest house, clamber across a series of roofs, then somehow let himself down to the street in the dark.

At ten o'clock on the appointed night, under the cloak of a light drizzle, Gideon and Tom silently made their way to the Old Bailey to wait for Breed. After weeks of bitter cold, the Thames at last had thawed. They could be rowed across by Nate, the shrewd and grizzled waterman in Gideon's employ, who, happy to be back on the river, pulled with long, enthusiastic strokes. They left Nate at the bottom of Playhouse Stairs outside the City wall, where he was to await their return. If Breed's escape went as planned, they could be rowed back across to Gideon's house, with no need for Nancy's help. If, on the other hand, a hue and cry prevented them from reaching the dock, they would carve a circuitous route to Covent Garden to hide Breed with her until he could be safely moved across the Thames.

As they made their way past Bridewell and set foot on Fleet Bridge, the odours from Fleet Ditch rose to meet them like the stench from a rotting corpse. No matter how many times the City had tried to clean up the Fleet, it was still as muddy and foul as it had ever been, the receptacle of the offal and animal dung from the butchers' yards near Smithfield and the waste from mills in Turnmill Street, along with the common sewage all the way from Caen Wood and Highgate down to the Thames. To the north, near the Old Bailey, east of the Fleet Prison, lay a maze of wretched streets dating back more than five hundred years, even if the buildings themselves had been rebuilt after the Great Fire. The nearby presence of the ancient debtors' prison meant that the alleys and courts of this part of the ward were the province of thieftakers, hawkers, and hucksters, many in the illegal marriage trade. Even at this hour of the night, tavern and alehouse keepers stood on the watch for couples seeking a clandestine marriage, to be officiated by one of the drunken or degraded parsons living in the Fleet. As Gideon and Tom approached, enterprising men and women darted closer to them ready to offer them the cheapest wedding. When they realized the figures were both men, they faded back into the rain to huddle on the thresholds of their houses.

It was Gideon's hope that the constant movement of people on these streets would make it easier to evade capture. The beggars that lingered in doorways, the vendors plying their wares, and the coming and going of patrons at the taverns should make it hard for the watch to spot any illicit activity. It should be impossible to tell who was up to no good, when every other doorway led to an establishment selling wine or gin.

The street Gideon had chosen as the place to meet Breed had the advantage of a second entrance, in case he was spotted crossing the Old Bailey. Otherwise, its proximity to the Sessions House could only be regarded as a foolhardy choice. As Gideon and Tom took refuge between the walls leading into Black and White Court, Tom gave a shudder, which had nothing to do with the rain that was filling the kennels with water and dripping from the brims of their hats.

They huddled against the brick wall of a building, attempting to stay dry, as the rain fell in rivulets from its eaves. Nervously, and to reassure himself it was still there, Gideon patted the bag with the frayed stable boy's cloak and hat he had brought along for Breed. There was nothing else he could do to pass the time but keep watch for Breed's arrival and avoid the notice of the passersby. Many, on perceiving them, gave a startled glance then darted past with wary glances over their shoulders, fearing they might be footpads on the lurk for victims.

Gideon settled down to wait, his legs thrumming with the need for action. Restless and frustrated he had barely slept the night before. His mind had kept returning to the moment when his hands had enveloped Hester's waist, and how tempted he had been to feel more. He shook his head to stay focused. Here, in the darkness of the street, with the minutes passing with excruciating sloth, it was hard not to think of her and to ponder his intentions.

The clock at St. Sepulchre's tolled eleven o'clock. Breed's escape should be well underway. It was impossible to guess how long it would take him to climb to the roof. The rain would make his leap to the adjoining roofs more treacherous. Gideon never once doubted the attempt would be made, however, for to remain in Newgate would mean facing death. With that fate at his heels, Breed should not hesitate.

When midnight struck, it was clear that something had gone wrong. Gideon was about to send Tom to the nearest tavern for news when he heard two men passing in the street. Bits of their conversation reached his ears, the words, "prisoners" and "escape" made his innards spin like the flying coaches at the fair. A soft cry from Tom meant that he had heard them, too.

Gideon gripped his arm. "Run see what you can discover in the taproom at the Fleet. You won't have to linger, if what I fear has happened."

As Tom left to do his bidding, Gideon rubbed anxiously at his face. If the prisoners' attempt to dig through their wall had been discovered, the talk in the taproom would be of nothing else.

His fears were confirmed before long. Hasty steps alerted Gideon to Tom's return.

"I didn't need to go into the Fleet," Tom said, gasping for breath. "A man from the Hand and Pen was talking to a couple in the street. This morning, one of the turnkeys spotted the bars that were cut. The prisoners were searched and their tools were took. They've been moved to new apartments and double-ironed."

Gideon's heart plummeted. The failure of their plan could mean death to Nathan Breed and his friends. It was even possible their trial would be hastened now.

There must be another way to save them, but he would not be able to concoct it here. With a gesture to Tom, he led him away from Black and White Court, scarcely noticing the heavy rain soaking through his cloak.

⌀

The morning after the ball, Hester awoke early to return the footman's costume to Pierre. She took her breakfast in the small parlour, with the intention of writing his Highness the Prince of Wales a note to thank him for the tickets to the Duke of Montagu's ball. The note would come from Isabella, of course, but as she never penned a letter of her own, she would never question Hester about it. The risk of Hester's duplicity being discovered was very slight, for it was likely that her cousin and the Prince both would be too taken up with new entertainments in the offing to give but passing thoughts to a ball which had already taken place. She ruefully reflected that if the Prince had hoped in sending the tickets to gain any extraordinary favour with Isabella, he hardly needed to have bothered, for she was so predisposed to please him it was unlikely she would ever deny him. If he ever were so tactless as to mention the gift, it was equally improbable that Isabella would recall from whence she had received the tickets she had used.

Finished with her morning chocolate, Hester was sitting at the writing desk and had just sealed her note to the Prince, when James Henry entered the room. A guilty conscience made her start. She had not been aware that James Henry was in town. His demeanour today was even soberer than usual, making her wonder whether her escapade of last night had been discovered.

When she asked him when he had arrived, however, he responded with no hint of reproach, just a show of mild concern.

"I came in last night. My lord and my lady had left for the ball. I asked for you, but the servants told me you had retired early. I hope you were not unwell?"

Hester gave a small, guilty laugh. "No— No, indeed! It is simply rare that I have the opportunity of an early rest. What brings you to town?" she asked, hoping to redirect his thoughts.

"My lord asked me to come. He has a sudden additional need for money, and I must make arrangements with his bankers." A furrow in his brow revealed that something worrisome was on his mind.

Hester peered anxiously at him. "Not for my aunt's gambling debts, I hope?"

James Henry would never be so indelicate as to roll his eyes, but the sideways look with which he responded was wry enough. "No, and thanks be to God for that. But I am a bit troubled, and there is little I can say to my lord about it."

When Hester kept staring at him, he cleared his throat. "The bulk of the money, as I understand it, is to go towards the purchase of a coach."

Surprised, she straightened in her chair. "Now, that is curious. Neither he nor Isabella has said anything to me about purchasing a new carriage."

James Henry shifted uneasily on his heels. His cleared his throat. "I gather the coach in question is not for the family, but for . . . a friend."

It took Hester no more than a few seconds to fill in what he had left unsaid. When she did, she saw the reason for his disquiet. For what "friend" would a gentleman buy a coach if not his mistress? And a mistress bold enough to ask for and to receive such an expensive present could end up costing the estate a great deal.

James Henry must fear that Harrowby could be foolish enough to let his paramour ruin him. Hester thought of St. Mars, banished from his home, and felt indignant on his behalf. She did not need to hide her emotion for, if James Henry detected it, he would think her pique was all on Isabella's account—and, in truth, a portion of it was. Not that her cousin had a right to any of St. Mars's money, but spending that kind of sum on a mistress was an insult to any wife—even if the wife neither demanded nor merited her husband's faithfulness.

She did not pretend to misunderstand. "Oh . . . I see why you are concerned. Have there been any other . . . extraordinary expenses?"

"Yes, I am afraid there have."

Hester winced at the gravity on his face, but she did not ask what the expenses were.

"When I speak to my lord, I'm afraid I shall have to point out that if he continues to deplete his inheritance at this pace, the result will be a severe tax on the estate."

"Oh, I am certain he will listen to you," Hester said. "He always does. He has a great respect for your management."

"I shall hope he does. But," James Henry added with a rueful look, "in such cases as this, gentlemen are not always reasonable."

That afternoon, Isabella wished to go to Court to hear the gossip about the ball. Mindful of her deception over the tickets, Hester decided it would be prudent to accompany her to be able to divert the conversation should the Prince of Wales mention his gift.

Fortunately, his Highness was not at St. James's, but the Princess was. When she received them in the room the King had built for her last year, Isabella thanked her prettily for the tickets she had received. Then, as the conversation turned to the ball the Duke of Newcastle would give the next week, and the latest news from Scotland, the moment of danger passed. Messengers had arrived at Court with the report that the Pretender's troops had retreated from Perth. In haste to escape from the King's forces, they had been forced to abandon their iron cannons and wall guns.

In the course of the afternoon, gaming tables were set up, and Isabella went halves with Lady Chelmsford at hazard, dice being the only sort of game she enjoyed, as she was not adept at cards.

Hester stood and watched the play, but finding it tedious, she took a stroll around the room, slowly weaving a way through the groups of chatting courtiers. On her second turn, as she dodged a pair of gossips, she encountered Lady Cowper, standing near a window and gazing out onto a courtyard, still patched with snow. When the lady, who was not in waiting this week, acknowledged Hester with a smile, she stopped to speak.

"Do you not play today?" Hester asked.

Lady Cowper gave a weary laugh. "You cannot know me, Mrs. Kean, if you think I am capable of venturing two hundred Guineas at play—for I assure you that none sit down to the table with less."

Hester assured her of a similar unwillingness to wager. Then she added, "I am happy to find you recovered. I heard you were not well."

"It is my lord who concerns me." The lady sighed. "We have had much to worry us of late." She hesitated, then gave Hester a confiding look. "You have heard that my lord was appointed Lord High Steward for the trials?"

At Hester's nod, she continued, "As they say, 'tis a 'grinning honour' at best. Of course, my lord is always grateful for his Majesty's trust, but the post is a considerable burden. Not only must he condemn the rebel lords to death—a terrible task!—but there is not one farthing's allowance for all the expense. The servants must all have new liveries—ten footmen, four coaches with two horses, and one with six! I was told it was customary to make fine liveries upon this occasion, but I had them all made plain. I think it very wrong to make a parade upon so dismal an occasion as that of putting to death one's fellow creatures, nor can I go to the trial to see them receive their sentences, having a relation among them—my Lord Widdrington. What a pity that such cruelties should be necessary!"

Hester listened in sympathy. The Stuart cause had attracted so many followers that hardly a noble family would escape unscathed. The rebel lords' guilt had been decided even before their trials. She wondered if a similar fate lay in store for the prisoners in Newgate.

For the next several days, the Court was busy entertaining the Prince of Anhalt, the Princess's cousin. On the masquerading day, there was a drawing room held for the King, but he did not appear. The entertainment was magnificent and, according to Harrowby, could not have cost less than five or six hundred pounds. Monsieur d'Iberville, the Envoy Extraordinaire from France, was there, and was heard to spread the rumour that the Pretender's retreat from Perth was nothing but a feint, concocted in France to delay battle until the Regent of France could send him more aid.

The next evening, as Isabella's guest, Hester attended the play, a farce, *The Cobbler of Preston*. The news that the Pretender had been forced from Perth had a visible effect on the audience, who greeted every loyal statement with enthusiastic acclaim.

The following day, 9 February, the members of both houses of Parliament stood on temporary scaffolding in Westminster Hall, with both the King and the Prince of Wales in attendance, while Lord Cowper asked the prisoners if they had anything to plead in arrest of judgement. The rebel lords answered severally that they had not, upon which the sentence of death was pronounced and they were remanded back to the Tower.

At Court the next day, it was said that the Prince of Wales had been much touched with compassion. Several people of rank made solicitations to the King for mercy for the condemned lords—who had been advised to plead guilty as the best means to soften his Majesty's heart—but their requests merely served to steel his resolve. The executions would proceed.

☙

By the time Gideon was permitted to visit Nathan Breed again, his family had paid for his new fetters to be removed. He had been placed in a different room in the Press Yard, his severe punishment abated by the deposit of yet another five hundred pounds, plus twenty guineas key fee, and rent of twenty-two shillings per week.

The men who shared his space now were strangers to Gideon, but each one of them must have been very wealthy to afford one of the most expensive rooms in London.

When Gideon entered, one gentleman was enduring a tearful visit from his wife. While the two conversed in low, anxious tones, the lady's maid, her only escort, waited at the door.

Breed was lying upon his bed, staring up at the ceiling. The leap in his eyes when he spied Gideon spoke volumes. He must have wondered if his failure to escape would put an end to Gideon's help. His greeting was more somber than before, though he tried to assume a brave face. An unshaven chin, rumpled clothes, and empty bottles on the floor gave witness to his despair.

Gideon barely had the heart to face him after the news he had read that day. On seeing it, he had cursed James Stuart and the Earl of Mar until he had given himself a headache. Now, he would have to relay it to the young gentleman who had risked his life for the cause.

According to the day's newssheets, more than ten days ago, on the fifth of February, on advice that the King's army was advancing and no more than eight miles away, James had ordered the clans to be ready to march at night towards Aberdeen. When the hour of the march had arrived, he had ordered his horse as if to go with them. Then he had left by foot, accompanied by only one of his domestics. He had gone to the Earl of Mar's lodging and from there to the waterside where a boat had carried him and Lord Mar on board a French ship, the Maria Teresa. Two other boats had carried the Earl of Melfort and Lord Drummond, with General Sheldon and ten other gentlemen to the same vessel. The Lord Tinmouth and the Earls Marshal and Southesk had been left to shift for themselves. The clans had dispersed and run for the hills.

Breed took in the news with little perceptible emotion. He seemed already to have accepted that the cause was lost. He stood and rubbed a hand over his face. Then, the two walked to the window overlooking the yard and gazed down at the narrow space paved in Purbeck stone, where a few privileged prisoners turned their faces up to try to catch a bit of sun. Gideon wasted no time reviewing the plan that had failed, but immediately started plotting a new strategy. A searching glance had revealed that the walls in this portion of the gaol were sturdier than those upstairs, rendering another attempt to dig out unfeasible. He asked Breed if he had thought of any new means of escape, ending his question with, "There has to be some other weakness we can exploit. Is there anything you've observed that we can use to trick the guards?"

"Nothing." Breed hung his head and gave it a shake. "They are particularly keen on watching us now. With so many wealthy prisoners in here, I doubt they have ever had such an opportunity to enrich themselves."

Gideon mused. That would be true, but the alternative—being

placed in a cell with fewer liberties—would not necessarily offer more chances for escape. And the unhealthy conditions too often spelled a different sort of death. He doubted Breed would want to give up the meagre comforts he had. At least in the Press Yard, he could receive visitors. If he had a wife or mistress, she might even choose to move in here with him, though he doubted many gentlemen would demand such a sacrifice of anyone they loved. Just now, the lady visiting her husband was preparing to leave. She covered her hair with her riding hood, and her maid did the same. Gideon heard the lady promise to come again in the evening.

He turned his attention back to Breed. "There may be nothing for it. We shall have to bribe the guards. And do it handsomely to replace the sum they would have if they kept you in here for months. I'll need you to prepare a list of all the guards and turnkeys. I'll need a total sum before I ask your uncle for the money."

When Breed agreed, patently ashamed to beg his uncle for more money, Gideon dug in his pocket and extracted a few coins. "In the meantime, it would be a good idea to treat them regularly to a glass. I trust there are no abstainers among them?"

Breed snorted. "This lot? Not a night goes by that they don't get roaring drunk. It was pure chance that they spotted us, for by midnight they are usually all three sheets to the wind. That doesn't mean they wouldn't notice if one of us tried to walk out, but they don't often come up to the Press Yard at night. Unfortunately, one of them did, and now I'm in this room where the walls are thicker."

Gideon felt he had gained all the information he could to begin working on a new scheme. Pledging to come again soon, he followed the lady and her maid out of the Press Yard. He was surprised at how little notice the two women attracted, until he stopped to speak to the turnkey Fell, who told him that the women came every evening. Gideon pressed a gold coin into Fell's hand, earning a leering thanks before following the women through the lodge and out into the street.

As the two women passed through the crowded lodge, he noted again that the guards barely raised their heads. He drew much more attention himself.

This observation sparked a sudden idea. Perhaps the Duke's money could be better spent than on bribing the guards.

❧

Since his successful introduction to his infant heir, Harrowby had spent more time at home, often joining the ladies at their tea table before going out for the evening. These were pleasant occasions, as Sarah always brought the baby to his parents when he was replete with milk. Hester had noticed before that infant boys tended to respond well to men, and Georgie was no exception. A steady bond of affection was developing between the earl and his heir.

One afternoon, Harrowby joined Hester in the small parlour before going to his coffee house. Isabella and her mother had gone to call upon the Countess of Berkeley, who had recently been delivered of a son, leaving Hester to preside over the teapot, while Harrowby jiggled his son in his arms and made silly sounds that were like music to her ears.

In the past week or so, he seemed to have forgotten whatever fear had haunted him since the discovery of Sir Walter's body. His conversation now turned exclusively on the rebel prisoners and happenings at Court, and Hester did not like to resurrect a topic that had so distressed him. She almost thought it would be prudent to halt her inquiries if they reminded him of his fears, especially now that he and Isabella appeared to be reconciled. From hints that Isabella and her mother had thrown out, it seemed that Harrowby had resumed his rights as lord and master of his wife. No doubt he was thinking of another little being to keep Georgie company in the nursery.

It was a shock, therefore, when a footman entered the parlour to announce the visit of Sir John Tatham, and Harrowby, emitting a strangled cry, nearly dropped the baby. "Sir Walter's son? Ye gods!"

As he stammered a refusal to see Sir John, Hester sprang from her chair and went to take Georgie from his arms. "Cousin?" she said. "Whatever is the matter?"

"What can he want?" Harrowby looked wildly about as if searching for a place to hide. "What can he mean by pursuing me here?"

"Pursuing you, my lord? I was not aware that you had met. Do you mean he followed you from his house?"

"Followed me? Of course, the blackguard didn't follow me! I've never set foot near his house. I'm quite astonished by you, Mrs. Kean. This is no time for nonsense. I asked you to discover if he might call on me, and here he has come, and it's all your fault!"

Hester's mouth fell open. She would have denied his statement, but he was clearly so panicked that it would do no good. Perceiving that the footman was still waiting to be told what to say to Sir John, she told him to ask Sir John to await her in his lord's antechamber, but first to send in Sarah to take Lord Rennington back to the nursery.

"But I told you! I refuse to see the scoundrel," Harrowby was saying. "He should be tossed out of the house on his ear!"

"My lord," Hester spoke soothingly, "if we do that, there is sure to be a scandal. You would not want people to ask questions, now would you?" Sir John might easily wonder himself why he had been so treated when as far as Hester knew, he had never set eyes upon Harrowby. "Shall I tell him you are not available to speak to him right now and try to discover what his business might be?"

Sarah entered the parlour, made a brief curtsy, and reached for the baby. As Hester placed him in his nurse's arms, Harrowby, who had started pacing the room and muttering to himself, gave her a fearful look, but said, "I suppose you are right. I should not have him thrown out. But I shall not see him under any circumstances, no matter what he's come for. If he makes any demands, you may tell him so, and then bring his demands to me."

Hester knew better than to ask what sort of demands Sir John might make. She would be more likely to find that out from Sir John himself. Surely, he would not be as secretive and panicked as Harrowby was.

"Very good, my lord. I shall see what he wants and return to you here?"

He nodded, waving her off before collapsing into a chair. When she glanced back from the door she saw that he had buried his face in his hands.

It seemed that whatever Harrowby had been fearing could soon take place. As Hester made her way downstairs to the antechamber where Harrowby's unexpected visitors were taken to wait for an audience with his lordship, she wiped her hands, which had suddenly grown moist, on her skirts. At the base of the staircase, she gathered herself, taking a deep breath before she walked into the antechamber.

Inside, the only waiting visitor, a young gentleman in a shoulder-length wig of light auburn hair and a suit of light brown silk, was seated nervously on a chair. As soon he saw her, Sir John leapt to his feet, a relieved expression on his face.

"Sir John? I am Hester Kean, Lady Hawkhurst's cousin. I made your acquaintance on the evening of your father's obsequies."

"Yes, Mrs. Kean. I perfectly recall that visit. You and Lady Hawkhurst were so kind as to sit with my mother." His tone was cordial, his manners much more pleasing than she would expect from either his father or his mother. It was hard to picture this pleasant young man as the bringer of doom.

But it would not do to delay the discovery of his errand. "You wished to see my lord?" she said.

"Yes." To her surprise, he answered with a blush. "I hope his lordship will not think it presumptuous of me to call, but before returning to the country, I wished to thank him for his many generosities to my mother during her period of affliction."

Hester paused. There was nothing in his manner to suggest his visit had any other purpose. When a few seconds had gone by, and he had added nothing else, she felt obliged to respond, "I am certain Lord Hawkhurst will be happy to receive your message. Unfortunately, he is unable to receive you at the moment, but I shall relay it to him as soon as possible."

If anything, he seemed relieved to be absolved from delivering it himself. His nervousness vanished, and he smiled like a young man who has been spared a frightening ordeal. He stammered, "I—if you would, that would be most generous. I am on my way home, you see, else I would come again. But if you think it a sufficient proof of my gratitude, then I shall be glad—that is, I shall not trespass on his lordship's time."

Hester assured him that his message would be thanks enough, but could not help asking, "Do you make your residence in the country, then?"

"Oh, yes. My mother and my father have always preferred Court life, but I find it does not suit me. I had rather occupy myself with the family estate."

"For which your mother must be very grateful." As Sir John received this with another blush, Hester bade him a safe journey, accepted his bow with a curtsy, and watched him depart with no little sense of relief.

Aware that Harrowby must be cowering behind a settee, she hurried to deliver Sir John's message. When she walked through the parlour door, she found him standing behind a chair, gripping its back with both hands as if he might use it as a shield. His eyes were wide with fright, but all he said was, "Well?"

"I believe everything is quite well, my lord," Hester said. "Sir John came only to thank you for your kindness to his mother."

He looked as if he would like to believe her, but couldn't. "Did you send him away? And did he say when he's coming back?"

"I am certain he has no intention of coming again, Cousin. He spoke most clearly on that point. He said he was returning to the country immediately and only wished to pay his respects on his way out of town. He appears to be a shy young gentleman, not addicted to City life, quite different from either of his parents."

"If he's shy, then he must be a changeling! There is nothing timid about Sir Walter or his wife."

"Perhaps he is, sir. A most open and pleasant young gentleman. I doubt you have anything to fear from that quarter."

He had gradually relaxed his grip upon the chair, and now he stepped around it and took a seat, wiping his forehead with a handkerchief. "Well, suppose you are correct?" He took a deep, grateful breath. "Perhaps it is over then."

"Over, sir?"

If Hester had expected he would confide in her now, she was soon disabused of the notion. He glared at her from beneath his lowered brows. "There is no reason for you to refer to this business again," he said. "'Tis a thing of the past. 'Much ado about nothing,' eh? You may run along now, Mrs. Kean." He stood and straightened himself. "I am going to the coffee house. I'm certain you have many things with which to occupy yourself."

Considering all she had undertaken for him in "this business", his dismissal was insulting, but Hester could see that he was eager to recover his dignity. Whatever danger had passed, she was certain it had been something that reflected poorly on his character.

As she pondered his change in behaviour en route to her bed-chamber, she became even more convinced that Harrowby's relief was due to some punishment he had managed to avoid. Something so dire that it could have ruined him. He might wish her to forget his anxiety and Sir Walter's murder, but what if he had done something to put her family at risk? Or worse, the title and inheritance that rightfully belonged to St. Mars.

She wondered what St. Mars would have to say about this strange new development.

. . . resign the Way,
To shun the surly Butcher's greasy Tray,
Butchers, whose Hands are dy'd with Blood's foul Stain,
And always foremost in the Hangman's Train.

CHAPTER XIV

Several petitions requesting mercy for the condemned lords were submitted to the House of Commons, but they gained no support. A motion by the Duke of St. Albans in the House of Lords to address the King with a request to reprieve the prisoners passed by a slim margin. When the Duke of Bolton presented the request to the King at the Palace, his Majesty sent a response that he would do what he believed most consistent with the dignity of his crown and the safety of his people.

The executions were set for Friday on Tower Hill. In Parliament, the Earl of Nottingham gave a speech, saying he hoped the King would pardon the prisoners whether or not they had confessed. The King and their royal Highnesses were said to be so furious over Lord Nottingham's speech that it was expected he would be removed from his position as President of the Council, but upwards of three hundred prisoners in Lancaster did receive mercy, upon their humble petition, on condition they transport themselves to the colonies.

The night before the executions, Lord Nithsdale escaped from the Tower. A reward of a thousand pounds was offered for his capture.

Gideon heard this piece of good news when he stood in the crowd on Friday morning and watched Lord Derwentwater walk between the black-draped rails from the Transport Office to the scaffold on Tower Hill. After spending some time in prayer, the young lord—at twenty-five, just a year younger than Gideon—read a speech in which he affirmed his loyalty to James III, his rightful and lawful sovereign, and said that he would die a Roman Catholic. He died bravely, his head severed with one blow.

Then Lord Kenmure mounted the scaffold, accompanied by two divines of the Church of England. He submitted to the block without making a speech.

No coffins had been provided by their friends, so their bodies were wrapped in black baize and put into a coach. Some in the crowd said sneeringly that this was done to incite pity. Lord Kenmure's body would be carried in a hearse to the water and put on board a ship to Scotland for burial. Lord Derwentwater's would be taken to Dilston in Northumberland to be interred amongst his ancestors.

For a long while, Gideon stood frozen to the spot where he had witnessed the beheadings until a jostle from the crowd awoke him to the need to move. Numbly, he made for Thames Street and the key at Fishmongers' Hall where Nate awaited him in his wherry.

Gideon tried to erase the violent images from his brain, afraid it would be weeks, if not years, before he could close his eyes and not see them. Beneath his pity for the men, whose only sin had been loyalty and whose only error had been faith, was a strong awareness that it could have been he who stood on that scaffold. If he had sought redemption for his father's death by joining the cause his father had believed in or if he had let himself be tempted by James's empty promises, he could have been one of the headless corpses bundled into that carriage.

He shivered in the cold. Though the worst of the frost had ended, it was still winter. Down at the river, Nate huddled inside his boat, puffing on his long clay pipe. Seeing Gideon arrive, he uncurled himself and took a grip on both oars. As soon as Gideon was aboard, he wordlessly started the long trip back, pulling with a strong, steady rhythm.

Gideon was grateful for Nate's silence. There was comfort in the clunking of the oars and the lapping of the water. He closed his eyes, but a vision of Derwentwater's lifeless head made him jerk them open again. There would be no relief in thought. It was action he required.

The morning was scarcely over. There might be time enough to pursue the idea that had struck him on leaving the prison.

He instructed Nate to deposit him at York Stairs and told him to wait. From there he made his way to Covent Garden and James Street on his way to speak to Nancy Cole.

This morning, he had dressed in a new green coat. If he was going to pose as a fop, he had realized, he would need more than one fine coat. He still wore the long black peruke and hid his face behind patches and white paint.

If Alfred was surprised by the visit, he gave no sign, but admitted Gideon after a careful look up and down the street. In response to Gideon's request to see Nancy, he allowed that his mistress was alone. Gideon waited below for permission to climb the stairs, but on this occasion he was not left to cool his heels for long. Instead, he was shown into Nancy's bedchamber where she was seated at her dressing table, putting the finishing touches to her toilette.

Her clothes on this occasion were, if possible, even more revealing, in spite of the cold in the room. No more than a thin layer of silk hid her curves from his eyes. Gideon supposed she must have schooled herself to be impervious to the cold to be able to dress with such abandon, but this time he had girded himself against her allure. As beautiful as her physical self was, he would not be deceived into thinking her character matched it. This knowledge could not stop him from feeling a strong yearning for sex, however. He knew it would be hard to keep his mind on his purpose.

She greeted him with coyness. "My dear Robert! I had not expected the pleasure of seeing you again," she said, dusting her cheeks lightly with powder and glancing at him in her looking glass.

Her cheerful tone took him aback. "You must have heard that the gaolers discovered the prisoners' attempt to escape."

"Indeed, I did. So I ask myself what possibly could have brought you here this morning." She met his gaze in the mirror. "Dare I hope it was merely to see me?"

His pulse started to quicken. He fought the temptation her words had provoked. "And if it was? I thought you were the exclusive property of another gentleman?"

She gave a charming pout. "If you mean to be disagreeable, I wonder that you should have come. It is true I owe my current circumstances to my protector, and there is nothing I would do to disappoint him. But I trust that does not mean we cannot be friends?"

In other words, she would keep her options open. She was wise, he decided, to keep a few admirers in the wings. Anything could happen to rob her of her protector—death, disease, loss of fortune—or else, he might simply lose his taste for her, though at the moment that was impossible for Gideon to imagine. In spite of his caution, he felt himself responding to her playfulness. Then it occurred to him that she might have greeted him in this way merely to cloud his judgement.

He bowed to concede her point, but the smile he returned her was stiff. "Nevertheless, I apologize for coming so late in the morning. I shall not take up much of your time."

A flicker of interest lit her eyes before she assumed a guileless look. "Oh? You have something new to ask of me?"

"Yes. I am still determined to help Breed escape, but our chances are more limited now." He took a deep breath and continued, "The last time I visited Newgate, I noted that the guards and turnkeys scarcely glance at the lady visitors when they leave. If these ladies come every day with their maids, I wonder if the guards would notice a prisoner who left dressed in a woman's cloak?"

Nancy cocked her eyebrows at him. "And you have come to me because . . . ?"

"I wonder if you would undertake to visit Breed on several occasions, and on one of these carry him a gown and a hooded cloak?"

Her eyes grew round, and she gave an incredulous laugh. "My dear Robert! You want me to pose as Breed's wife and visit him in Newgate . . . regularly?"

"No . . . as my wife, Breed's sister. Naturally, I would not expect you to do it without compensation."

Her smile turned ironic. "Well. That is certainly a relief. But do you find me so unremarkable as to be indistinguishable from Nathan in a woman's clothes?"

Gideon had to laugh. "Of course not. It's not you he would imitate, but your maid."

She cast a droll eye about the bedchamber, saying, "It may have escaped your notice, my dear Robert, but I do not employ a maid."

Her statement sobered him. This was the part of his proposal he dreaded most. "No, it has not escaped me, but I know a woman who can fill the role. And I hope you will not be offended if I say that your qualities should be a great asset to this plan, for in your presence, who would notice any other woman's features?"

"I fear that flattery will get you nowhere in this case, no matter how beautifully expressed. I have a great fondness for Nathan, but I cannot risk my life to assist him. And who's to say I shouldn't be called up for treason if I helped him to escape?"

He frowned. "You would be using an assumed name. And if you like, I can arrange a disguise for you. A wig of a different colour, a little paint, and a man who saw you only by candlelight would have a hard time discovering your identity. By the time the authorities noticed Breed was absent, you would be back in your house with no one the wiser."

Her attention was caught. She stared at his face, but he could not read the direction of her thoughts. Then, the moment gone, she shook her head. "No, it would never work. I could not be away from home as many times as it would take to lull the guards. Not without alerting my protector, and as you can see—" her eyes wandered over her apartment again—"he is very generous. I cannot afford to lose him."

"The Duke of Bournemouth could make it worth your while. He might even wish to thank you in person. The Duke is a connoisseur of feminine beauty."

This bait did give her pause. He could almost see the possibilities swirling through her brain, as she speculated on whether she could ensnare a powerful duke and imagined what his wealth and position could bring her. He had the impression that Nancy's ambition was boundless. She might next set her sights on the King himself. Then she could aspire to a title. Charles II had turned his many mistresses into countesses and duchesses, and already King George had asked the government to name Madame Schulenberg Duchess of Kendal.

She asked warily, "How much do you think he would promise, if I do as you ask?"

Gideon shrugged. "I should hate to venture a guess before speaking to his Grace. But if you will consider it, I shall offer myself as go-between until the negotiations are complete. But they mustn't take too long. I fear it will not be long before Breed is brought to trial."

She gave a dismissive gesture, her mind clearly consumed by how much she should demand. Absently she said, "The executions for my Lords Widdrington, Nairn, and Carnwath have been postponed until the seventh of March. I doubt the courts will proceed until their fates are determined. And I hear the Princess of Wales has taken a personal interest in their cases and is using her influence to save them."

Gideon was dumbfounded. Nancy knew more Court gossip than he did. But of course, she would coax that information from her protector. And how would he know anything, outlaw that he was?

"Be that as it may, I would not wish to hesitate, and neither will his Grace."

"Then you may start by telling him that I shall do it for ten thousand pounds—and a visit from his Grace, of course. I trust you will tell him that he will not be disappointed?"

Gideon scarcely winced at the amount. By now, he had learned the kind of prices she demanded for her loyalty. If there were anyone else in London he could ask to do this, he would, but there was not. As it was, he dreaded having to ask Katy to play the role of maid.

With no more than token resistance to her demand, therefore, he left for his house to compose a letter to the Duke.

As Gideon had foreseen, the most difficult aspect of his scheme to help Nathan Breed escape was the need for Katy to accompany Nancy on her visits to Newgate. When he called her and Tom to his room to tell them of the part he required her to play, the terror on her face and the anger on Tom's made him wince.

Neither would dare express their emotions forcefully. He was, after all, their master. But as he watched the fear and anger playing over their features, he became keenly aware that they served him of their own free will. For the first time since he had escaped from being hanged, he believed Tom might exercise that will and desert him.

Before it could come to that, however, he asked them to hear what else he had to say.

"I would not ask Katy to do this if I thought there would be the least danger to her. There is no law against visiting a prisoner in Newgate. Women—even ladies—do it every day. And there is nothing illegal in taking clothes to a prisoner.

"Besides, I shall accompany her and Nancy on the first occasion, and if you like, Tom, you can go with them on other visits. All Katy needs to do is to pretend to be Nancy's maid, to wait in a corner while she visits Breed, and to come out each time with the hood of her cloak pulled up to hide her face. Then, when the guards are accustomed to seeing you," he said, addressing Katy directly, "you will leave the prison alone, trying not to attract any notice. Nancy will leave with Breed dressed in a gown and cloak similar to yours. So you see, there will be no moment when you are compromised."

He had seen Tom's face thaw slightly at the promise that he might escort her into the prison. Katy's eyes, however, were just as large. Her lips trembled when she asked, "What if they see the branding on my thumb? What if they think I'm trying to escape myself? Won't they take me back?"

Gideon suffered a pang of remorse. He had not realized that her fears ran so deep. But the way to overcome them, as Tom himself had taught him, was to face them head on.

"It's still cold," he reminded her gently. "You will have your mittens on. And there is nothing about you to suggest that you have been in gaol before. If Tom is with you, acting as Nancy's groom, will you not feel safe?"

A look he knew had come into Tom's eyes. It was not impatience, so much as resolve. Gideon had seen it whenever he had been reluctant to get back on a horse that had thrown him. Tom must have realized that Katy's fright was much worse than the danger she faced, and although he might not recognize his own irrational fears, he was quick to spot them in others. This timid woman was not the Katy with whom he had fallen in love.

He met her turned-up gaze with an expression of firm encouragement.

She took a shaky breath and smiled, as if she felt a bit foolish. "Very well, my lord," she said, turning to Gideon. "I'll do it."

"Good girl! For that, I'll promise you a new gown for your wedding gift. And if he escapes, Mr. Breed will be undyingly grateful. Now, I must convince his uncle to support the plan. And, in the meantime, we will need another gown like one of yours, but big enough to cover Nathan Breed, and a hooded cloak, too."

The answer from the Duke came quickly, and the next night found Gideon and his Grace seated at a table in the Bear Tavern again. After Gideon explained his plan, he asked the Duke if he would agree to Nancy's terms.

The look he received on naming her price of ten thousand pounds would have caused many a man to quake in his boots, but Gideon knew how desperately the Duke wished to save his nephew.

"Is this whore the only woman you can trust?" he complained. "Why not simply engage an actress to play the part?"

"Because we cannot be certain that an actress—someone completely unknown to your nephew—will not decide to go to the authorities and demand a reward for information. Your nephew knows Nancy Cole well enough to believe that she will fulfill her pledge."

"I should hope so! For that sum, she could raise an army and take possession of the gaol." The Duke sighed, bending over to pinch the bridge of his nose. "Are you certain this woman is clever enough to succeed?"

"That is something you will be able to judge for yourself. But, yes, I have no doubt she is resourceful enough. A clever woman, indeed. There is nothing common about her, and dressed a bit more modestly, she might pass for a countess . . . if not a duchess."

The Duke scowled. "I suppose I should go see her before I give my consent. A sum of that size is not immediately available. I shall likely have to borrow some portion of it.

"Give me her direction," he said wearily. "I shall call on her tomorrow."

Gideon gave him the information. Then he said, "Just a word or two of caution. Visit her mid-morning, if you do not wish to run into her protector. And I should advise you not to negotiate terms when you see her, but leave that to me. If you do, you are likely to come away having promised her more than ten thousand pounds."

The Duke raised an eyebrow. "That alluring, is she? Well, I doubt I shall be taken in. My head is a good bit tougher than yours."

Gideon inclined his head, but he could not help giving the Duke a knowing smile.

The next afternoon, he received a message from the Duke of Bournemouth, stating briefly that the plan could go forward, and that his bankers would be at Gideon's disposal. Gideon would have liked to have seen the effect Nancy had had on him but knew that thought was unworthy.

After checking with Katy, he sent a note to Nancy appointing Monday for their first visit to Newgate. Unfortunately, their first visits would have to be made in the morning to avoid annoying Nancy's protector, but he had already made it clear to her that soon they must be made in the evening, too. It would be up to her to concoct excuses to satisfy her protector, but as dim as the light in Newgate was during the day, it would still be imperative that the ruse be conducted at night. Not only would the dark make it easier to disguise Nathan Breed, but the guards were more likely to be drunk. And while Nancy and Katy were getting them used to their visits, Breed would be bribing them further and further with drink.

Nancy responded to Gideon's message that she would see him Monday morning, reminding him that she expected to be paid five hundred pounds in advance of every visit, with the remainder being paid upon Nathan Breed's escape.

Gideon swallowed his irritation and went to draw on the Duke's bankers.

☙

Hester hesitated to ask St. Mars to meet her again. She had not recovered from her realization that his flirting had been merely a diversion. Afraid she might have revealed more of her feelings on the night of the ball than was wise, she was uncertain how to behave when seeing him next, but she believed Harrowby's behaviour should be a matter for his concern. How urgent it was for St. Mars to learn of it was something she did not know, however, so she waited to see if he would send for her first.

When several days went by and still she had not heard from him, her suspicions seemed confirmed, but she also knew that the news she had read in the newssheets—the discovery of the prisoners' attempt to escape and the rebels' executions—would have sorely affected his spirits. When the prisoners' attempt was discovered, she combed the newssheets to see if St. Mars had been involved or captured. Her heart had nearly stopped beating until by reading every word she had assured herself that he had not. But recalling his plan to free the Duke of Bournemouth's nephew, she realized how small her concerns were relative to his.

She could not help worrying about his safety when he undertook such a mission, but, after seeing him in action, she wondered if, instead of disapproving, she ought rather to have offered her assistance. It had been weeks since he'd told her of his intention to free Nathan Breed, and in all that time she had not once asked how his plans were progressing. She had been so caught up with Harrowby's problems and, in truth, in flirting with St. Mars, that she had forgotten to be a true friend. Her disapproval had been so clear, it was no wonder he had not taken her into his confidence.

By the time she had reasoned this out, more than a fortnight had passed, but that was enough time to adjust to her disappointment. Although her heart was gravely bruised, she would find the resolution to accept St. Mars's friendship on whatever terms he wished. She had made that resolution many times before, but this time, she vowed, she would keep it.

It was harder to arrange to see him, for she could no longer use Harrowby's errands as an excuse. As soon as he made it clear that he wanted her to forget about Sir Walter, Mrs. Mayfield reasserted her control. Hester could only hope to be sent on errands for Isabella or to slip out of the house when everyone was occupied, but this hope was all but crushed one afternoon at the dinner table.

It was the day before James Henry was due to return to Rotherham Abbey, so Harrowby and he had been closeted with business. Only the family and James Henry were present at dinner. They had just enjoyed a first course of a gravy soup remove of chicken and bacon, followed by roast beef with horseradish and pickles, Scotch collops, a giblet pie, and a fine boiled pudding, and were on to the next course of turkey, three woodcocks, a hare with savory pudding, and hot buttered apple pie, when Harrowby, with great good humour, announced his intention to host a masquerade ball.

Isabella and her mother nearly flew out of their chairs in transports, while Hester looked to James Henry to see how he would feel about this latest extravagance. The indulgent smile on his face astonished her when he had so recently expressed his worry over the sum Harrowby's mistress was costing. He caught the question in her gaze and managed to indicate with a motion of his head that he would explain something to her later when they were alone.

The others were busy deciding on a date for the ball. Harrowby thought it would be wise to hold it before the King left for Newmarket races, the first week of April. "There is talk that now the Pretender's been routed, his Majesty will go to Hanover for the summer, so if we wish for him to come, we must hold it soon. It's not certain he will, of course, but he did attend the Duke of Newcastle's ball."

Isabella was so happy, she did not even pout at the thought of entertaining the King, for as she said, "We shall invite enough people that we needn't be bothered too much with him. And he was no trouble at his Grace's ball for all the Germans were there."

This ingenuous statement drew another smile from James Henry, and he glanced at Hester as if to see whether she shared his amusement.

Normally, such honesty would have prompted a smile, but Hester could not help feeling anxious about the preparations that would be required.

"Do you think a month is long enough to prepare for such a large event?"

Mrs. Mayfield rounded on her. "A month indeed! Why, that is all the time in the world, so do not think we will let you spoil this just because you envision a bit of work. Just because your duties have been lighter of late doesn't mean they will always stay that way."

Hester knew it was best to keep silent when her aunt was in this mood, but she was a bit surprised, and hurt, when Harrowby failed to intercede in her defense. She imagined he was so eager to put his recent fears to rest that he was grateful to his mother-in-law for taking her back in hand. Hester lowered her eyes to her plate, holding her tongue, and the lively conversation resumed.

Harrowby and Isabella were both accustomed to hearing Mrs. Mayfield speak to her in that manner, but James Henry was not. When Hester ventured a peek at him, a grim look was on his face. She knew he had no love for her aunt.

A number of tasks were raised, everyone of which Mrs. Mayfield declared could be handled by Hester, from the invitations, which must be individually written, to the supervision of the menu and the flowers. An orchestra must be engaged, and that, too, was left for Hester to undertake, though she had not the slightest experience in hiring musicians. It would all be manageable, of course, but with all there was to do, she would have to abandon any thought of uncovering Sir Walter's killer and discovering what mischief Harrowby had got himself into.

By the time the meal was over, she had a list of jobs so long as to fill her days and nights for weeks. The baby's christening was nothing in comparison.

Mrs. Mayfield plainly relished the resumption of her authority over her niece. As she pushed back from the table, she told Hester to instruct the cook to make a gruel of lentils for Sarah to increase her milk. Then, with an admonishment not to be too long in joining her to receive more orders, she swept from the room.

Hester stood more slowly, embarrassed by her aunt's treatment, but mortified even more by James Henry's angry gaze. She knew Mrs. Mayfield's bullying would soon subside and become more tolerable. She had learned when to assert herself and when it was best to submit.

James Henry, however, would not allow her aunt's behaviour to go unremarked. As he made his way to her side, he said quietly, "I fear this ball will put an uncomfortable burden on you."

She tried to steer his attention to another subject. "It will be a considerable challenge to get everything done in time, but I confess, I was surprised not to see any protest forming in your eyes. I thought you were worried by the sum of Harrowby's expenditures."

"Oh . . . as to that, I managed to persuade my lord that a carriage was more costly a gift than was reasonable. He has decided to cancel the order. In truth, I believe he was relieved to receive my opinion, so he must have had reservations about it all along. The ball will be a lesser charge, and he might have decided to give it anyway. Such things are expected of a gentleman with his wealth, and they can only curry favour with the King and the Court.

"But I had not thought of what it would mean for you. And your aunt!" His jaw twitched in fury. "She should not be permitted to speak to you in that manner."

Hester gave him an ironic smile. "It is a small price to pay for dependence."

"Nevertheless, I cannot stand by and allow it to continue. I flatter myself I have some influence with my lord, and I shall speak to him about it directly."

"I pray you will not! I should hate to see you become her enemy. If she ever feels threatened by you, she will try to have you dismissed—possibly with the thought of putting one of her younger sons in your place. And, sadly, if she becomes determined, I cannot count on Harrowby's standing up to her. She can be very shrewd in her dealings with him." Hester hoped her cousins would never be so foolish as to let James Henry go, for without his careful management, the Hawkhurst fortune could soon be dissipated. It should definitely not be entrusted to anyone Mrs. Mayfield recommended. Besides which, the thought that James Henry could lose the position his father had intended for him was simply unfair.

They had been standing near the dining table. Now, to Hester's deep concern, he started pacing the room with a strange, nervous air. She had never seen him so agitated.

"I beg you will not distress yourself on my account," she said, trying to soothe him with a lighter tone. "I promise, she is not always like this. She is worse at the moment because her authority was thwarted for so many weeks. But whenever she's tried to cut me out of Isabella's affections, Isabella has always supported me. She has sufficient fondness for me to be my protection."

"But it is wrong!" James Henry astonished her by stopping before her and taking her hands in his. "I had not intended to rush this, but her cruelty brings me to the point."

As she stared at him in consternation, he continued, "You recall what I said, that you and I occupy similar positions in this household?" He paused to see her nod, then continued, "I have given both our situations a great deal of thought, and have come to a decision which I hope will benefit you as much as it will myself."

He looked down, as if it was difficult to meet her eyes. "My job is rather a lonely one, as you must have seen. I visit each of his lordship's estates at least four times per year, and Rotherham Abbey more often. With so much time on the road, I have not formed any attachment that could lead to my domestic felicity, but I am as desirous of having a wife and sons as the next man—perhaps even more than most, knowing that I have a respectable estate to pass on."

As he spoke, a glimmer of his purpose came to her, but she was too stunned to stop him. His kindness and consideration rendered her speechless.

"This will seem sudden—" he raised his gaze, and she witnessed his determination—"but as I said, I have reflected upon it before, and now I see that the sooner I ask you to be my wife, the sooner I can remove you from this intolerable situation."

Hester gasped. Even suspecting his intention did not lessen the shock. She had never received an offer of marriage and had convinced herself she never would.

Her immediate inclination was to say no. No matter how practical she tried to be, her heart still yearned for a union based on love. And as much as she admired James Henry's many excellent qualities, she was not in love with him.

She was in love with St. Mars. But how many times had she warned herself to expect nothing from him? Had she not just been reminded that he did not feel the same attraction to her? Certainly not enough to overcome the difference in fortune between them, for even if he was an outlaw in this country, in France he was a viscount with all the freedom and privileges of the nobility. There he could expect to find a bride who would add to his fortune.

James Henry awaited her reaction with a somber air. There was nothing of the lover in his proposal. Rather, she detected a combination of duty, respect, and—yes, the loneliness to which he had just confessed. Prudence made her hesitate to throw away an opportunity which might never come her way again, but she was determined to be fair to him.

"Yes, this is sudden," she said, "too much a surprise, I'm afraid, for me to know my own mind. But you do me great honour, sir, and in fairness, I must tell you that I have no portion at all."

He smiled gently. "I am fully aware of your situation, and I assure you that it is of no consequence to me. I have not set my sites on an heiress. But—" turning somber again—"perhaps, you consider my birth too obscure for an alliance with your family? That is a point to which your relatives may take exception. I do not know how my lord would take the news."

"No, of course not!" Hester hastened to say, anxious not to hurt his pride. "Indeed, the honour would be all mine, and if I accepted your proposal, my family's objections would only influence me with respect to their future treatment of you. But—"

The issue was too important. She was too flustered, too upset, to evaluate her options clearly. "As grateful as I am for your offer, Mr. Henry, I must have some time to reflect. You have taken me by surprise. I cannot make such a decision when my spirits are overcome."

He did not seem offended. Indeed, his proposal had been made with no eagerness, but with the practicality and sense she often proudly claimed for herself. Clearly, he had given a great deal of thought to the notion of his marriage and, ready to settle down, had decided she would make him a worthy wife.

A few awkward moments passed before he bowed and informed her that he would wait to hear her answer when he returned from Rotherham Abbey in a month. Hester curtsied and they parted—he to his horse, and she to gather her wits before dealing with her aunt.

James Henry had offered her what could be the perfect solution to the dependency she feared might choke the very life from her, body and soul. She would be a fool to refuse it. He was a fine man. An honourable, considerate, competent man. His heritage was more noble than her own, even if it came from the wrong side of the blanket. She had often remarked the ways in which he resembled his legitimate half-brother St. Mars, as often as she had observed their differences. Surely, she would grow to love him, as wives often did in arranged marriages. And knowing him already, she knew she had less reason to fear ill-treatment or even infidelity—a far better prospect, in fact, than most aristocratic brides would have.

So, why was there such a painful lump in her throat?

✆

Everything Gideon could do to free Nathan Breed was set. He had escorted Nancy and Katy to Newgate and presented them to Breed as his beloved sister and her maid. As he had expected, Nancy played her role as if she had been born to the stage. If Katy, at first, appeared nervous, it seemed only natural, and it gave her an air of innocence and timidity not ill-suited to the situation. After a few minutes in the Press Yard room, far superior to the common felon quarters she must have occupied in gaol, she visibly relaxed.

Gideon had procured a large basket for the food and wine the women would bring with them each time they visited. Ultimately, it would be used to transport the maid's clothes that Breed would wear for his escape.

For now, Gideon's plan was to accustom the guards to seeing the women arrive alone, or on occasion with Tom. Katy had assured him that she was no longer afraid, which had gone a long way towards repairing Tom's feelings.

With nothing to do for the next few weeks but allow the plot to develop at its appointed pace, Gideon was finally at liberty to see Mrs. Kean. Not that she had ever been far from his thoughts, but Breed's escape was a matter of life and death. Gideon had not dared allow himself a moment's indulgence.

Now, he recalled his pledge to investigate Mr. Mistlethwait. But, in case something had occurred in the interim to make this unnecessary, he decided to consult with her first. It was a bit odd that she had not contacted him these past few weeks, herself. The realization made him a bit uneasy.

He sent Nate around with a note, instructing him to see that she received it alone and to say, in case anyone asked, that it came from her brother, Mr. Jeremy Kean. Jeremy should be planning his own nuptials sometime this year, depending on how long his sweetheart Sally decided to mourn her dead husband. As her marriage had not been based on affection, nothing longer that a brief period of respect was required, but Sally would wish to maintain the appearance of decorum.

Nate was able to give him Mrs. Kean's reply. She said she was overwhelmed with planning for a ball at Hawkhurst House, but that she could meet him the next morning briefly outside the Rose in St. Paul's Churchyard.

Disappointment dampened the excitement Gideon had felt on the prospect of seeing her again. St. Paul's Churchyard was clearly not the private spot he had wished for their rendezvous. Although he knew Mrs. Kean's time was never her own, he had hoped she had taken his hints, which in his opinion had been pointed enough, and would wish to be alone with him, too. It had only been by keeping his focus on the tightest rein that he had been able to resist seeing her immediately. The tension of planning Nathan Breed's escape had built his nervous energy to a bursting point and nothing would give him greater relief than indulging all the fantasies about Mrs. Kean that he had postponed on the night of the ball.

But, perhaps, he had only imagined she had felt it, too. Women were said to have a much greater sexual appetite than men, but if they did, he thought with great frustration, then they must be blessed with greater self-control, too. He could not believe that anyone had stronger urges than he had himself, or surely they would go mad.

But, if St. Paul's Churchyard it was to be, then to St. Paul's Churchyard he would go.

See yon' bright Chariot on its Harness swing,
With Flanders Mares, and on an arched Spring,
That Wretch, to gain an Equipage and Place,
Betray'd his Sister to a lewd Embrace.
This Coach, that with the blazon'd 'Scutcheon glows,
Vain of his unknown Race, the Coxcomb shows.
Here the brib'd Lawyer, sunk in Velvet, sleeps;
The starving Orphan, as he passes, weeps;
There flames a Fool, begirt with tinsilled Slaves,
Who wastes the Wealth of a whole Race of Knaves.

CHAPTER XV

In the morning Gideon told Nate to deposit him at Puddle Dock stairs. From there he made his way up the hill, past St. Andrew's Church and the Dean's House to St. Paul's Cathedral Yard where, pausing amongst the busy shoppers, churchgoers, beggars, and street vendors, he took a moment to admire the recently completed dome, designed by Sir Christopher Wren. It was an architectural achievement beyond anything most Londoners had ever seen. Gideon, who had made the Grand Tour of the Continent, had seen its like in Florence and Rome, but he was proud that there was now such a great dome here.

He circled the cathedral clockwise and soon located the sign of the Rose over a stationer's shop in the northwest corner of the churchyard, not far from Stationers' Hall. He was heading for its door when he spied one of the Hawkhurst footmen standing outside of the shop, a lanky, red-haired fellow by the name of Will. Seeing one of his former servants here took Gideon up short. He was puzzled and annoyed to find that Mrs. Kean had brought an escort, but until he could speak to her, he would not know why she had done it. He did not wish to give Will a chance to study his face, for in spite of the wig, paint, and patches he wore, Gideon would not put it past a sharp lad like Will to penetrate his disguise. Footmen often aspired to loftier positions, and an ambitious fellow who wished to become a valet would be sure to observe gentlemen closely to learn the secrets of their toilettes.

Far beyond frustration now, Gideon strolled past the stationer's shop, pretending to look into the different booths and stalls, and wondering if Mrs. Kean would be able to spot him. He was wearing his new green coat, not the scarlet one she knew. He made a tour of the nearby windows, then seeing her emerge from the stationer's, strolled past her and made a pretence of jostling her while his attention was diverted.

"Your pardon, milady," he said, touching the brim of his hat and blocking her passage until she glanced up into his face.

As she excused him, she looked rather pale, but her gaze met his long enough to beg his patience. She turned to her footman, and Gideon heard her say, "Will, I find that this errand will take a bit longer than I anticipated. Please go to the chandler's and carry him this request. I shall be there by the time he's filled it."

She handed him a sheet of paper and pretended to return to the stationer's shop while Will crossed to the other side of St. Paul's. Then, as soon as he was out of sight, she turned back to Gideon, and said, "I am sorry to have so little time, but if we take a quick turn in Stationers' Hall Court, even if Will comes back, he will not see us."

As she headed briskly in that direction, Gideon followed her, asking, "What's the reason for all this haste?"

She did not stop, but answered him over her shoulder, "Your cousin Harrowby has decided to host a masquerade ball at the end of March, and since my aunt has decided that I can oversee all the preparations, I do not have any time to waste."

"Shall I attend it?" he called out teasingly, hoping to raise a smile.

A hitch in her step was the only reaction he got. "I pray you will not think of it, my lord."

"Not even for a dance with you—when you might reasonably be expected to wear a skirt?"

The smile she gave him over her shoulder looked wistful. "You will have your joke, my lord."

A note he had never heard in her voice made him falter in his stride. Either Mrs. Kean was very sorely tried by the work Mrs. May-field had imposed on her, or something else was wrong. She would not even wait to take his arm. He had to hurry to keep pace with her as she reached the end of Cock Alley and entered the court.

A new red brick Stationers' Hall had been built to replace Abergavenny House, purchased in the last century by the guild but destroyed in the Great Fire. To the left of the hall was an open space, the garden of the former house, where there was room to stroll.

When Mrs. Kean did not slow her pace, Gideon complained, "I shall find it very hard to speak to you, if I only see the back of your head."

She gave him an embarrassed, agitated look. "Please excuse me, my lord."

"I will, if you will take my arm. . . . There, that's much better now, isn't it? Now, we can talk like friends."

The timid smile on her face vanished, and she blinked.

He felt as if something was making her leery of him. But before he could determine what it might be, she surprised him by saying, in a cautious voice, "I read of the prisoners' failed escape. Has this put an end to your involvement, my lord?"

Perhaps that's it, he thought. She had never been happy with his plan to help Nathan Breed escape.

"No," he said, masking his impatience. "Although it was a setback, I have thought of another way to free him."

Instead of scolding him, as he expected, she said, "I am very occupied, as I said, but if there is anything I can do to help you, I hope you will ask."

Her offer brought a smile to his lips. "So, you have more confidence in me since our midnight escapade?"

She gave a shy nod. "Indeed, I cannot doubt your abilities. But I also realize how remiss I was as your friend not to offer my help, especially when you have been so generous with yours."

"That is precisely why I am here, my dear Mrs. Kean. I had almost forgotten my promise to investigate Mr. Mistlethwait, but I thought I should speak to you first to see if you still wished it."

Her brows drew together. "That raises something else we should discuss. For some mysterious reason your cousin no longer wants me to look into Sir Walter's business. Yet, I cannot feel easy about it. I'm certain he is hiding something."

She told him about the fright Sir John Tatham's visit had occasioned, and about Harrowby's abrupt change in manner the moment he felt the danger had passed.

"His relief was so complete—and so sudden—I began to suspect that he had escaped being discovered in some crime. Before Sir John was announced, he was acting as if his earlier fears had been unwarranted. Then, when Sir John's name was sent up, it was as if all the furies of Hell had been sent to punish him. He even spoke of pursuit. Then, later, when I assured him that Sir John had no other purpose to his visit than to pay his respects, it seemed all risk of danger had passed."

Gideon heard her story with a growing sense of disgust. "It does, indeed, appear that my cousin is benighted. I wonder what shame he has brought upon himself. Do you think it is something that involves this fellow Mistlethwait?"

"I do not, for the simple reason that the mention of Mr. Mistlethwait's name had no effect on him. Instead, it seemed that whatever concern Harrowby had was shared by Mr. Mistlethwait. Both expressed worry about Sir Walter's business affairs and about who would be in charge of them after his death."

"It sounds as if they both did something reprehensible that Sir Walter knew about. Perhaps he was using the information against them, using his power over them to get something he wanted."

"Extortion, do you mean?" Mrs. Kean's face lit as she pondered the idea. "That could explain why Harrowby tolerated Sir Walter when it was clear he had no pleasure in his company. I thought it might be because he'd furnished Harrowby with a mistress, but I had no idea how great an obligation that would impose . . . not having experience in that regard, you understand."

Gideon tried not to laugh, but his lips were twitching. Perceiving this, she gave her first genuine smile, but it was quickly smothered.

Turning serious again, she sighed. "I thought you should be told of this, my lord. Harrowby has forbidden me to investigate Sir Walter's death, so there is little more I can do. It is your family's affair, and your family's name."

A grim idea came to him. "Could my cousin have murdered Sir Walter?"

She hesitated, then shook her head. "I have asked myself that question, but still I cannot believe him capable of it, even in a fit of anger."

"Then I shall have to ask Mistlethwait." He thought for a minute then asked, "Do you think Mistlethwait has ever met Sir John?"

"I doubt if he has. He did not attend Sir Walter's funeral. And when he paid the visit to Sir Walter's corpse, Sir John was not yet in town."

An idea inspired him with a sense of mischief. "Describe Sir John for me. Would he be roughly my age?"

"Yes." She eyed him quizzically, but complied in a few succinct phrases.

He repeated her description. "A young gentleman, my age or thereabouts, wearing a shoulder-length wig of light auburn hair and a pleasant expression—sounds a bit like me, don't you think?"

At last he had provoked her. She gave him a threatening look. "What are you thinking, my lord?"

"Simply this—that if my cousin was thrown into a panic by a visit from Sir John, then perhaps Mr. Mistlethwait will be, too. And if he has never met Sir John, he will have no reason to doubt I am he."

"But what if he has met him?"

"Then I shall bolt for a window. No, seriously," he said, when she started to protest, "I doubt if he has. Did you not say that Harrowby had never seen Sir John till he came to pay his respects? And, if Mistlethwait was not invited to Sir Walter's obsequies, and Lady Tatham showed no desire for his acquaintance, why should they ever have met?"

She mused just long enough for him to add, "Come now, Mrs. Hester. You know my reasoning is sound."

A reluctant smile teased the corners of her mouth. "Very well, my lord. You have nearly convinced me. But what would you hope to accomplish?"

"Perhaps I can get Mistlethwait to drop a hint about the mischief he and Harrowby are involved in. If it's the same sort of mischief, at least. If not . . . well then, we shall know that, too."

She still looked worried. "But are you quite certain you have the time for this, my lord? What about your plan for Mr. Breed?"

"That is out of my hands at the moment. Tom is taking care of it, so this visit to Mistlethwait will give me something to do while I wait for the next stage to unfold."

Her curious look encouraged him to continue, so he told her of his plan to disguise Breed as a woman, telling her what parts Nancy Cole and Katy would play. He did not tell her how beautiful or how seductive Nancy was—although he was tempted to, to see if it would spur any jealousy. But her coolness this morning had warned him that she was in no frame of mind to be teased.

"And Mrs. Cole is someone you can trust? I could have helped you with this, my lord." Even, as she said it, he saw her shudder at the thought.

He gave a firm shake of his head. "I do not wish to subject you to the unpleasantness of Newgate. Besides, the whole plan depends on the turnkeys' and guards' becoming used to seeing the women. You can barely escape Hawkhurst House as it is. You could not arrange to be absent every night, or even every other night, to visit Breed."

She acknowledged this with a reluctant nod. "I cannot deny it, and I'm reminded that Will is waiting for me at the wax chandler's, so I had best be on my way."

She avoided his gaze when they parted, though he took her hand and kissed it, saying, "I'll report to you as soon as I've seen Mistlethwait, shall I?"

Her eyes had already turned towards Cheapside, but she nodded. "Thank you, my lord. Just promise me you will not endanger yourself." Then, without waiting for a reply, she withdrew her hand from his clasp, and hastened away.

As Gideon watched her go, he felt a frown pull at his face. There was something wrong with Mrs. Kean, and he wished he knew what it was. It could be that her aunt was abusing her even more than usual or something about her family that she was not telling him. Loyalty was one of her many good qualities. He had learned not to make unfair criticisms of Isabella, for as little as he thought she deserved it, Isabella did hold a place in Mrs. Kean's affections, and in fairness, Mrs. Kean was dependent upon her cousin's goodwill and should not risk offending her.

Well, the sooner he got to the bottom of Harrowby's predicament, perhaps the sooner she would get some relief. At least, there was one thing he could do for her.

The next day, dressed in a light brown periwig and the kind of modest suit a country gentleman might wear, he presented himself at the door of Mistlethwait's house and sent in the name, Sir John Tatham. After the servant disappeared, a murmur of voices, some raised then hushed, gave Gideon the impression that the announcement of his visit had caused something of stir.

He was kept waiting a quarter of an hour, which gave him a chance to look about. Taking a turn about the antechamber, he paused at a window in time to see a gentleman emerging from what must be a servants' door. Gideon could not see who the man was, for he had taken care to cover the lower portion of his face with a neckcloth and to tilt his hat in a way so as not to be espied from the house. But the man who had left was clearly no servant. His clothes bespoke a person of consequence.

It was reasonable to assume that "Sir John's" arrival had caused the surreptitious departure. Now Gideon had only to worry that Mistlethwait had seen Sir John before, in which case his ruse would soon be discovered.

The man who eventually joined him, however, gave no sign of ever having met Sir Walter's son. Mr. Mistlethwait was a withered specimen, who did his best to conceal a meagre physique under a quantity of jewels, an expensive wig, and copious padding to his coat. He greeted "Sir John" with a baring of his teeth, which Gideon saw was a nervous attempt at a smile. The muscles in the JP's face twitched, and his eyes were wide.

Taking his cue from these signs, Gideon regarded him with a steely eye. He swept his gaze over his host as if to say he had expected a worthier opponent.

"I assume you've been expecting me," he said.

Mistlethwait uttered a gasp, but he said, "Not at all, Sir John. I've no idea why you've paid me this honour."

"Come, come now, Mistlethwait. It's a waste of time to dissimulate. I know you've been trying to discover who would inherit my father's business."

There was no mistaking Mistlethwait's reaction now. He snarled, "At least, your father had the grace to pretend it was a gift."

Interpreting this instantly, Gideon knew he was on the right path. "But I'm a much younger man, and I have less patience for games." He paused. "I am willing to negotiate, however, if you make a strong case for it. It's impossible to squeeze blood from a turnip."

If Mistlethwait thought this metaphor in any way insulting, he made no complaint, but seized on the chance to improve his position. "There, now. That sounds more like your old pa. He had a light hand, he did."

"Really?" Gideon drawled. "You shall have to tell me something of his technique. If I'm going to assume control of his affairs, I shouldn't like to offend his . . . shall we say, his friends?"

Hatred burned in Mistlethwait's eyes. "Oh, I misdoubt you've got your hooks into more fish than just me. I heard you've even got my Lord Hawkhurst on your line."

Gideon gave a smug look. "Yes, Lord Hawkhurst has been a very useful connection. You say you know about that business?"

"No. And even if you've a mind to tell me, I don't wish to know it. Just heard he was pokin' his nose around, sniffin' the air so to speak. But, now, don't you go spillin' my business to him neither, or our deal is off. It's your silence I'm buyin', so don't you forget. And if you squeek beef on me, you'll lose your share."

Gideon thoughtfully inclined his head. "Then, why don't we begin with a discussion of my father's arrangement, and see how fair it seems to me?"

"But that's just it!" Mistletwait snatched at the bait. "When your pa whiddled the scrap, business was good, y' see. Now, with the Pretender on the run, people are bein' more careful. They're afraid they'll get caught. Why, that fellow was just in here afore you was the only customer I've had this week."

Gideon was left at a complete loss, but he tried not to let it show. He frowned, as if displeased, and rubbed his chin, all the while trying to imagine what Mistlethwait was doing. If the Pretender was a factor, it was something treasonous—that was certain. But what could a justice of the peace have to sell to Jacobites?

He was wondering what to say to trick more information from Mistlethwait without giving his ignorance away, when, evidently, thinking he'd been caught in a lie, the JP blurted, "Now, I'm not sayin' business won't pick up. Once they give up on the rebellion, if they really mean to stick by the Pretender, they'll have no choice but to come to me. The word's out, y' see. They know they can come here, and get their certificates and still keep hold of their immortal souls." A rude laugh invited Gideon to join him in the joke on such fools.

Now Gideon knew what the game was about. It was the justices of the peace who certified that people had taken the oaths of allegiance, abjuration, and renunciation. The oaths were required by all persons holding civil or military office, members of foundations at the universities, schoolmasters, preachers and teachers of separate congregations, and legal practitioners. This included seats in Parliament. The penalties for members of Parliament not taking the oaths were particularly severe. In addition to a fine of five hundred pounds, they included the disability to sue in any court, to take a legacy, to hold any office, to vote at parliamentary elections, or to be an executor. Any gentleman wishing to hold a government or Church office, any lady wishing to have a position at Court, must take them, and not to do so would expose them as Roman Catholics or Jacobites.

The oaths had been rewritten on the death of James II to exclude his Catholic son James from the succession to the throne. Jurors had to abjure all his rights to the Crown, as well as reject the doctrine of transubstantiation of the soul.

No faithful follower of the Pope would take the oaths. Neither would a Jacobite who believed in James's divine right to the throne of Great Britain.

It appeared Mr. Mistlethwait was signing certificates for people who did not wish to take them and exacting money illegally for his service. And, somehow, Sir Walter had found out and demanded a share of the business.

Had he demanded so much of it that Mistlethwait had killed him? Gideon stared at the little man before him.

His suspicious gaze seemed to throw the JP for a loss. His confusion appeared genuine. There was no hint of guilt on his face.

"My father was killed because of something he knew," Gideon said.

A look of anger mixed with terror came over Mistlethwait. "You don't think it was me what did it! I swear to God, Sir John, I had naught to do with it! Why would I run a risk like murder?"

"You gamble your neck every day with treason. Why wouldn't you risk hanging for another crime?"

Mistlethwait's eyes bugged even larger. "But your pa and me, we had a good business together. We were partners! Haven't I offered to bring you in, same as him?"

"If I asked for more than you wished to give me, would you poison me, too?"

Mistlethwait frantically shook his head. "Why do you think that was me? Look at me," he said, glancing down at his frail body. "Do I look big enough to carry a corpse down onto the ice and dress it up in coronation robes?"

He did not appear to know that someone else had moved and dressed the corpse. He could be using ignorance as a ruse to distract Gideon from what he had done, of course. But, besides his demeanour, which was convincing, there were circumstances which made him an unlikely suspect. Mr. Gayet had discovered the body somewhere in the vicinity of Covent Garden, and Mistlethwait's house was in the parish of St. Andrew's Holborn, a significant distance away. For Mistlethwait to be the murderer, he would have had to meet Sir Walter in a tavern or a coffee-house and slip poison nut into his drink. It could have been done, but he would have run the risk that Sir Walter would collapse while they were still together. Poison nut killed quickly.

These thoughts flew through Gideon's mind in seconds, reinforcing an impression he had registered instinctively. Something in Mistlethwait's eyes had revealed how much it had cost his pride to draw attention to his frailty. Using it as an excuse was clearly not something he did. Acknowledging the meagreness of his frame caused him shame. It put him at a disadvantage, and he was the type of man who enjoyed exercising power over others.

"For the moment," Gideon said, "I shall accept what you say, but if ever I hear that you were seen with my father on the day of his death, I will return with a constable."

Mistlethwait's fright receded. "You never will. Your father 'adn't called here for at least three weeks when I heard his body'd been found. He had much bigger game in mind than me. If y' want to know who killed him, I'd take a good look at Hawkhurst."

The certainty in his voice sent a chill down Gideon's spine. He asked, "What do you know?"

Mistlethwait shrugged. "Nothin'. But it stands to reason, don't it? The more they have to lose, the more desperate they can be."

"You speak from experience." Gideon reached out a hand and grabbed the JP by his neckcloth. "Then explain this to me if you can. What more could one lose than to be accused of treason when the penalty is a painful death?"

The JP's countenance went pale. Gideon did not wait to hear his response, but released him roughly and left, saying, "I shall return."

He had taken no pleasure in bullying a smaller man, even so loathsome a creature as Mistlethwait. His hands felt dirty, and he had a strong urge to wipe them clean, but he was not convinced that the JP had murdered Sir Walter. And, until he uncovered Harrowby's dealings with his extortioner, he could not eliminate his cousin from suspicion.

With nothing at the moment he could do to pursue the matter further, Gideon took advantage of being in town to go to Newgate to check on Nathan Breed. As he strode up Holborn Hill, past the inns of chancery, and onto the bridge over the New Canal, he pondered what he had learned from his visit to the JP.

At least he had discovered that whatever Harrowby's business with Sir Walter was, it was not the same as Mistlethwait's. He had also confirmed that Sir Walter was an extortioner. That information alone could explain Harrowby's peculiar behaviour. He had tolerated Sir Walter's claim of friendship because he'd had no choice. Then, when Sir Walter was killed, Harrowby feared he might have left something in writing about his crime or passed the knowledge to someone else. He had sent Mrs. Kean to discover who might inherit the information. But, as time passed and nothing happened, he began to believe himself safe . . . until, that was, Sir John appeared at Hawkhurst House and requested an audience. Then, when Sir Walter's son made no demands upon him and even left town, Harrowby became convinced that all danger was past.

Gideon recalled that Tom had seen Sir Walter at Hawkhurst House and that his father had refused to see him. Perhaps Sir Walter had tried his tricks on the former earl, who had been too sharp to fall under the power of an extortioner.

As Gideon finished this train of thought, he found himself outside an ordinary, and the aroma of cooked beef made his stomach growl. It would be late when he reached his house, so he stopped to see what was being served for dinner.

Satisfied by the fare the host offered, which included oyster soup and a baked rump of beef, he sat down at a table and awaited his food. The small place was filled with law students, a rowdy group, released for a short time from their copying and studying. Against the background of their cheerful banter, the last thing Mistlethwait had said teased Gideon back to his reflections on his cousin.

He wished he could present himself to Harrowby as an extortioner, as he had to Mistlethwait, and see what confession he could extract, but as well as his disguises usually worked, he knew that a face-to-face confrontation with a relative would be impossible. Still, he toyed with the idea. From what Mrs. Kean had said, it appeared that Harrowby had never seen Sir John, and the temptation to scare his cousin was almost more than Gideon could resist.

It would not do, however. He had to keep himself safe to free Nathan Breed. Still, it was hard to imagine what Harrowby could have done that having it revealed would ruin him. He had always been prone to exaggeration, but the fear Mrs. Kean described seemed too profound for that. Gideon was frustrated by the inability to question Harrowby himself. For an account, he had to rely solely on Mrs. Kean.

A serving maid brought him his fare, and he started to dig in. Before he did, however, a thought provoked a rueful smile. What more reliable witness could he have than Mrs. Kean? Had she not proved again and again that her judgements were never made lightly and were almost always correct? He ought to review what she had said and see if his new information could shed light on any obscure spots.

He took his own spoon from his pocket and used it to sip the oyster soup, which was hot. The beef that followed had lain in salt, then been soaked in red wine and vinegar before roasting. Its gravy was flavoured with oysters and butter. Gideon ate the whole meal with gusto, thanked his host for an enjoyable repast, paid his account, and left.

As he walked, his thoughts seemed clearer as he reviewed his conversations with Mrs. Kean. What struck him most was that as long as Sir Walter had been alive, Harrowby had appeared out of spirits, but nothing worse. His terror had only begun after learning of Sir Walter's death.

If Gideon was correct, and it was the fear of not knowing who might take up Sir Walter's extortion, and whether that person would reveal his secret—or else that he might be more demanding as an extortioner—then it seemed Harrowby had no motive to murder Sir Walter.

The realization gave Gideon a measurable sense of relief. He had no particular fondness for his cousin, but neither did he bear him any hatred. It was not Harrowby's fault that Parliament had branded Gideon a murderer and given the succession to him instead.

He could not be perfectly certain of his cousin's innocence, of course, but if Harrowby had murdered his extortioner, Gideon doubted he would have sent Mrs. Kean to ask questions.

Gideon breathed a deep sigh, feeling a lightening in his chest. He had dealt with more than one killer whose end had not been pleasant. He would not have enjoyed bringing his cousin Harrowby to an ugly justice.

When he arrived in Nathan Breed's cell, he found the room was crowded with people, some prisoners lingering at the board set up for their meal, some with visitors, including a few children.

Breed was lying on his bed in the far corner, staring up at the ceiling. He glanced listlessly at the door to see who had entered, then sprang to his feet the second he recognized Gideon.

Waving him over to his bed, Breed invited Gideon to sit beside him. The sheets were rumpled and smelled well-used, but so much money had been spent on freeing Breed from his fetters, paying for his room, and buying drinks for the guards, Gideon was not surprised to find him practicing small economies.

The mood in the room was subdued, but the steady hum of voices was loud enough to cover their conversation.

"How long before we can try another escape?" Breed asked eagerly. "I don't know how much longer I can stomach this place."

Gideon gave a quick glance about. No one was listening, but still he cautioned, "I know how impatient you must be, but try not to show it. No one must suspect we have a new plan."

Breed lowered his head and rested his elbows on his knees. "Is this better?" he said, gazing down at the floor.

"Yes. You look despondent. Maintain that attitude while we speak."

"I'm concerned. Since Lord Nithsdale's escape from the Tower, the gaolers have watched us more."

"I'm not surprised, but the good news is that several of the trials have been postponed. That should give us a bit more time to do this right." Gideon paused, then said, "I understand Nancy has been here twice. How is it working?"

Breed hunched his shoulders. "Well enough, I suppose."

"Is she attracting much attention?"

Breed glanced up and gave a snort. "What do you think? I had to remind her to keep her head covered. Once she did, the guards stopped staring. But it's hard to keep the other prisoners from being curious. I've had to give them a few brotherly, threatening glares."

Gideon could not restrain a grin. "That was my only reservation about the plan. We shall both have to remind her that this is not a stage performance. I trust Katy is keeping her hood on, as well? She's the one who will have to slip out unnoticed. Do you think you can make yourself look shorter?"

"I can stoop and bend my knees a bit. The cloak and skirt should hide my posture."

"Good. You should also watch Katy for any characteristic movements she makes, see if you can imitate her posture. Unfortunately, you will not be able to rehearse."

"When can we make the attempt?" Breed asked again. "You still haven't said." His hands were tightly clasped. Clearly, his patience was running thin.

"No more than another week or two. Try to be patient. It depends on how quickly the turnkeys get used to seeing the women come. You and they will be the best judges of that. Katy has a good head on her shoulders, and she is not unobservant. She can tell me when they no longer draw any lingering glances. But it must take place on a dark night."

"I trust everyone is enjoying drink at your expense?" he asked.

Breed took a deep breath as if trying to ease the tension in his shoulders. "No problem there. By eleven o'clock they're all staggering drunk. I doubt if they would recognize their own mothers."

"Perfect. Keep it up." Gideon gave the young man a gentle clap on the shoulder and stood, ready to leave.

Breed leapt nervously to his feet again. He was coiled as tightly as a spring, but Gideon suspected he was also reluctant to be left alone.

"Almost forgot." Gideon peered round again to make sure no one was listening. "You may not be told in advance. The night we choose depends on Nancy and when she is free of her protector."

"She told me. She said she couldn't come every night or he would grow suspicious. Said she would have to fob him off."

"Do you know who he is?"

"No, but you know, she did seem vexed when I teased her. I asked her how she was able to get away from him already two nights this week."

Gideon raised his brows. "Is she afraid he's losing interest?"

Breed snorted. "Nancy—afraid? Never. I'd say rather, 'woe unto him who tries to thwart her.' She'll find a way to latch hold of him until she's ready to let him go."

Gideon was puzzled by Breed's meaning, but a question to which he had wanted an answer popped into his mind. He found it easy to believe that any gentleman would be reluctant to abandon Nancy. Even though he had discovered a reason for resisting her charms, he still found her extraordinarily alluring. "Do you know who Nancy is? Or where she comes from? There's nothing very common about her, I'd say."

Breed shook his head. "There isn't. Our Nancy is the daughter of a well-respected clergyman in Hampshire. He had no money—or at least not enough to suit her—so she came to London, determined to make her fortune precisely the way she is doing it. She's always been sure of her beauty, you see."

Gideon experienced a rare feeling of shock. The harlots he had encountered had always started life poor, or else they'd been women who had lost their virtue and been turned out to fend for themselves. He doubted many of them had had a choice if they did not want to starve. For Nancy to choose a dangerous route to a courtesan's life, when she could have made a respectable marriage, was something he could not understand, especially when doing so meant sacrificing any possibility of family and hearth. But perhaps her life before coming to London had been more wretched than Breed knew, and she did not believe that it would ever improve? With her beauty and allure, she could easily have won the heart of a local gentleman, even without a dowry.

As he left the prison to go home, bothered by what he'd learned from Breed, he thought about what a tragic waste it was. But Nancy's fate was not something he could allow himself to worry about. She would help him to free Nathan Breed, and that would be the end of their association.

The Heav'ns are all a-blaze, the Face of Night
Is cover'd with a sanguine dreadful Light;
'Twas such a Light involv'd thy Tow'rs, O Rome,
The dire Passage of mighty Caesar's Doom,
When the Sun veil'd in Rust his mourning Head,
And frightful Prodigies the Skies o'erspread.

CHAPTER XVI

On Thursday, the first of March, the Court had celebrated the birthday of the Princess of Wales, and of course, everyone had gone to the Palace where a large and splendid company of nobility attended the ball. The ladies had purchased new gowns to mark the occasion. Hester had been obliged to make a trip into the City to get a suit of gold ribbons for Isabella's new gown, but she had not stopped to see her brother. Nor had she tried to see St. Mars.

The day before, Madame Schultz had called on Isabella and asked to borrow her emerald necklace for the occasion. Mrs. Mayfield had grown livid, and even Isabella had felt insulted, in spite of Madame Schultz's assurances that she would not need to wear jewels, as she showed to better advantage without them.

During the following week, Hester had scarcely been given a moment to think. First, she'd had to sit down with Isabella and her mother to plan how many tickets to issue to the ball. A certain number would be given directly to their friends, with the remainder offered to the Prince and Princess of Wales to invite whomever they pleased. As large as Hawkhurst House was, it could accommodate almost as many revelers as Montague House, but the expense of an assembly so large would be immense. With a number finally settled upon, then the tickets must be printed, and it was on that errand that she had seen St. Mars.

Afterwards, she could congratulate herself on the friendly tone she had set. If she was to accept James Henry's offer, then she mustn't encourage St. Mars to flirt. Just being his friend would be a betrayal to her husband, without any more to her feelings. Though she had not yet decided to become James Henry's wife, until she knew what answer she would give, she believed she should behave in accordance with the honour he had done her. Besides, hadn't she convinced herself that St. Mars's sentiments would never be as strong as her own?

But it had been difficult to resist his teasing and his smiles. It would be impossible to resist them entirely, but if she could contain her responses, perhaps he would stop trying to solicit smiles from her.

She knew she should accept James Henry. It was the only logical step to take. As busy as she was, night after night, she lay awake in bed, making mental lists of the advantages of such a marriage.

To be free of her aunt—but then, she wondered what revenge Mrs. Mayfield would take upon James Henry for daring to marry her niece, especially when he robbed her of an inexpensive servant.

To have an establishment of her own—but his house was near Rotherham Abbey where she would always think of St. Mars and wonder where he was.

She would have no regrets about leaving Court, or maybe even London, except that if she married James Henry, would she ever see St. Mars again? Might she not lose his friendship entirely?

To have children—that was a blessing she had always desired. And, if she did not marry James Henry, the likelihood that she would ever have children was slim indeed. The thought of lying with James Henry to produce them was something she preferred not to think too much about. She could only hope she would not mind it. Ladies learned to accommodate their husbands. Over time, she might even grow to want James Henry as much as she wanted St. Mars.

She was almost grateful that Mrs. Mayfield gave her no time during the day to agonize over the choice she had to make. Every minute was filled with a task. Messages flowed back and forth to Rotherham Abbey over the meat and other victuals that must be supplied from its

farms for the guests' supper. Merchants had to be consulted about the
candles and the wine. Harrowby's hot houses must be ready with the
fruit to be served and the flowers to be arranged.

Isabella's and Mrs. Mayfield's costumes needed to be made, and
even this they seemed unable to oversee without Hester's help. Mrs.
Mayfield's excuse, if she had ever felt compelled to make one, would
have been that their days were too filled with engagements at Court to
make time for anything else.

The rest of the week had its usual collection of drawing rooms, card
parties, and assemblies. And at all of these, it was important to toast
the defeat of the Pretender and to give no sign that the recent executions at the Tower—and other executions in Liverpool, Manchester,
and Wigan, intended to frighten the local people into submission—
had caused anyone distress.

On the Tuesday following, his Majesty King George gave the royal
assent to an act for the speedy and easy trial of the rebels still awaiting
their fate.

That same evening, Hester found herself alone at Hawkhurst
House. Isabella and her mother had both gone to Court. Harrowby
was sitting in Parliament, but had promised to join them later, after
visiting "a friend in town."

Hester tried very hard to keep her mind on the preparations for
the ball, but so many restless and sleepless nights had taken their toll
that she could not concentrate well enough to check a simple column
of figures in a tradesman's bill. The fact was that Harrowby's clerk of
the kitchen should be making these calculations, but there was no time
to wait for Robert Shaw, who had been taken with the flux and—as
James Henry had written—could not travel as he might communicate
the disease to the family.

As the figures swam before her eyes, Hester laid down her pen to
rub them. Images of St. Mars appeared in the privacy of her mind, but
she shoved them away. Trying not to think about her conundrum, she
forced her thoughts onto a safer subject and wondered if St. Mars had
called on Mr. Mistlethwait and what he might have discovered. She
had no idea what she would do with the knowledge, as Harrowby was

acting as if he had never even known a Sir Walter. At least, she would be able to do nothing until the ball was behind her. And her aunt had started dropping hints that soon it would be time for Georgie to be conveyed to Rotherham Abbey, and that Hester should accompany him to make sure all the arrangements for his care were carried out.

Hester knew her aunt was eager for Isabella to get with child again—this time by her husband. As reconciled as Harrowby seemed to be to Georgie, Mrs. Mayfield would not feel secure in her daughter's influence until he and Isabella had children of their own. And, clearly, she believed the presence of an infant was not conducive to romantic activities.

With a final rub of her eyes, Hester was about to take up her pen when she heard raised voices outside the door of the room. It sounded as if two footmen were up to mischief. Ignoring them, she went back to her work, but in a few seconds the door flew open and Will burst inside.

"Sorry to bother you, Mrs. Kean, but you must see this!" he said, running to the window and pointing up at the sky. "I don't know what it is, but Rufus said it started a quarter of an hour ago!"

His tone was so insistent—such a strange mixture of excitement and awe—that Hester got up immediately and joined him. Not knowing what to expect, she noticed nothing at first. Then, he pointed to a light in the western sky and blurted, "There! See them? Those flames? What do you think it is, Mrs. Kean? Is the country on fire?"

The light, which at first looked like a pale blaze, started moving then, rolling up and down the sky as if an engine were manipulating the scenery at a play. A sense of foreboding filled Hester. She had never seen anything like it before. ""I have no idea what it is," she said, wondering aloud.

Then, suddenly, the flames appeared to burst, shooting out rays all the colours of the rainbow. Hester gasped and, next to her, Will swore. She didn't know if they should seek greater cover, but, when Will said, "Let's go outdoors so we can see better," she did not hesitate but hurried with him down the stairs and out into the courtyard of Hawkhurst House.

The word had spread quickly through the household. All the servants were standing outside, tilting their faces up to the lights, and crying and exclaiming with fright.

Within a few minutes, the rays of colour receded and bands of elemental fire leapt up from the horizon, like pillars of flame. They issued from all sides, but gathered mostly in the northern and western skies. Their movement was rapid, as if God with all His swiftness was throwing fire into the celestial dark.

All at once, one of the pillars flew across the breadth of the sky to the southeast, where it undulated and vibrated. A continual fulguration appeared, interspersed with green and red, blue and yellow. Cries of terror sprang from the people clustered in the courtyard. Grooms, footmen, and maids huddled close together, covering gaping mouths. Voices muttered prayers for mercy. Once, Hester heard Pierre's gasped words, *"Sacré bleu!"*

As she stood watching the heavens, it seemed they were all waiting for God to explain the signs. Was it the end of the world as promised in Scriptures? Would they all be struck by lightning or raised to heaven by a mighty wind?

The spectacle raged on for hours. No one among them even thought of going indoors. As tired as she was, Hester could not have turned her gaze from the sight. At some time during the evening, Will brought out a cloak and placed it around her shoulders. Until that moment, she had not even known she was shivering.

She kept repeating to herself that she did not believe in signs, that there had to be an explanation for what they were seeing. Perhaps a fire was somewhere on the ground, and the light from it was reflecting off the Thames? Or a military battle was raging downwind, so they could not hear the cannons exploding as they launched their fire?

As the clocks in Hawkhurst House struck one, the light was so intense she could distinguish other figures outside the gates in Piccadilly, all gazing up at the sky. The whole of Westminster seemed to be out in the streets, asking what the sign from heaven meant.

Finally, although they did not stop, the lights settled once again in the North. Hester's eyelids had grown intolerably heavy, so at last she decided to seek her bed.

In the hall, several servants were standing about, still clothed for work. As if she'd been elected to speak for them, Mrs. Dixon, the housekeeper, approached Hester and asked, "What does it mean, Mrs. Kean? Is it the Pretender? Is God angry at King George?"

Hester supposed they asked her because her father had been a clergyman, but she knew no more about the phenomenon they had witnessed than the scullery maid did. It would be unwise to alarm them, though. If ever there were a time to reject superstitious speculation, it would be now.

"I do not understand what we saw, but I am certain it had nothing to do with the Pretender. And I do not believe God would express his anger that way."

"He'd send locusts or boils!" a footman volunteered, and a general murmur of agreement arose, but still the servants waited to see if Hester would confirm his opinion.

She was touched by their confidence, but she was also very tired. "We shall just have to see what our men of science say about it—Mr. Newton and Mr. Halley. They are sure to have a better understanding of it than we do, as much as they study the skies."

More murmuring followed. Hester was unable to tell if she had comforted them or made things worse. As she turned to go upstairs, noises in the courtyard announced the return of Harrowby's carriage. If she had not been so exhausted, she might have stayed down until he came in, to see what he had heard about the lights, but the last thing she wanted now was to be kept awake.

The return of their master put everyone to flight. As she ascended the marble steps, Hester heard the servants scurrying back to their rooms or their posts. She reached the first floor landing just as Harrowby entered the house. The bend in the staircase concealed her from view, but her progress was arrested by Philippe's cries of distress and his calls for help.

A scurry of footsteps told her there were footmen near to aid him. She listened intently, as several voices responded to Philippe's orders. Before she could decide whether she should go downstairs, a struggling group came into view, consisting of Philippe, three footmen, and Harrowby, whose prostrate form they were carrying up the stairs.

Harrowby's cheeks were pale. His face was bathed in perspiration.

He had closed his eyes, and held a handkerchief and a hartshorn in his hands.

"My goodness, Philippe!" Hester said. "What has happened to your master?"

At the sound of her voice, Harrowby opened one eye and groaned. "The sign, Mrs. Kean—did you see it? It's over. It's just as I feared . . . I'm ruined!"

The footmen's eyes went round with fear. One let slip his hold on Harrowby's leg, and the procession halted for him to recover his grasp. Philippe scolded, *"Imbecile!"* then scurried ahead of the others to ready his lordship's bed.

As the entourage moved past Hester on the landing, she detected a strong smell of brandy coming from Harrowby's breath, and the worry that had built in her stomach relaxed. She should have known that he would be undone by the phenomenon. He was scarcely better than a child.

Certain there was nothing more serious to his collapse than his usual cowardice, she gave the footmen a firm, reassuring look. "Carry his lordship to his bed, and then go to your own. I daresay, everything will seem more cheerful to him in the morning."

They must have sensed his drunkenness, but the strange lights in the sky had unnerved everyone. "We all could use some rest," Hester said, turning her back and refusing to turn around when Harrowby muttered, "Ruined . . . it's a judgement. Oh, what can I do?"

She was in her chamber before the possibility dawned on her that he might have lost St. Mars's entire fortune on cards.

In the morning, over her cup of chocolate Isabella exclaimed over the spectacle, a part of which she had witnessed from a courtyard at the Palace. "I could hardly make my chairmen carry me home," she complained. "They were that frighted. I was forced to let down my glass and beg them to keep going. The streets were so full of people, we could hardly pass. And all of them frighted to death! If you had heard half the dialogue in the street, Hester, I vow you would have laughed yourself sick. Such a collection of nonsense as I heard! I don't give a fig for what they're saying. For all we know, it was just a joke played on us by the Duke of Montagu, and the next time I see him, I shall rally him on it!"

At dinner, Hester was alarmed to hear that Harrowby had not left his bed. When she tried to discover the nature of his indisposition, a footman told her that Pierre had not dared leave his side. Their master was refusing to see any visitors, even members of his family. But the moment he had awakened, he had sent a messenger to Rotherham Abbey to fetch James Henry at once.

Hester had to ask herself whether the scenario she had briefly considered in the night could be true. Could Harrowby have lost all his fortune? Why else would he have this urgency to recall James Henry, who had only just left? She calmed herself with the recollection that Harrowby had panicked over nothing several times before, and that this was likely to be a case of the same.

In spite of the many tasks awaiting her, she accompanied Isabella to St. James's to learn what was said about the spectacle they had witnessed, and found the whole Court abuzz with fearsome speculation over what the sign in the heavens had signified.

The newssheets that morning had reported that the Earl of Mar was at Paris and that the French were making war-like preparations, but their design had not yet been declared. The Government let it be known that it was ready to prevent any potentate from disturbing Great Britain. Still, the news about the French added fuel to the speculation and the disquiet, as both parties turned the mysterious lights on their enemies. The Tories said it was God's judgement on the Whigs for executing the two lords, and the Whigs said it was a judgement on the Tories for the horrid rebellion. From what Hester observed, the first explanation came from the same people already rumoured to support the Stuart cause, while those like Harrowby who had never entertained the Pretender's claims espoused the latter. She knew from experience how much it took to alter an entrenched opinion, and how strong the tendency was to interpret every phenomenon as a confirmation of one's own beliefs.

Maybe Harrowby had succumbed to the notion that he had taken the wrong side, but her knowledge of human nature told her it was improbable that whatever ailed him was of a political nature.

Whatever had caused him to take to his bed, she thought she could count on James Henry to ferret it out.

But she had counted on not seeing James Henry for a month. Would he expect her answer now? And if he did, would she have one to give him?

✐

Gideon had witnessed the streaking coloured lights from his house on the bank of the Thames. Though he was no more inclined than Hester Kean to assign superstitious meanings to natural phenomena, the fact that neither he nor anyone else had ever witnessed anything of its kind gave him a sense of unease. The amazing spectacle had awed both him and his servants, and he had spent a great deal of time reassuring Tom and Katy that they had nothing to fear. His preference was to enjoy it and leave the speculation to others, and he roundly dismissed any suggestion that God had taken a stance on the Pretender's claim. But some beliefs were rooted since birth, and no amount of reason or even experience could entirely erase them from the bones on which they had been imprinted. His father's insistence on the divine right of succession had been unyielding. How sincere his belief truly was, Gideon had never discovered; but however strong it had been, his father had died because of it, so Gideon would always be beset by guilt for abandoning the cause.

Rather than nurse his guilt, since for the moment he had nothing to do to prepare for Nathan Breed's escape, he sent a note round to Mrs. Kean to advise her that he had carried out her task. She replied that she could speak to him through the fence at the rear of Hawkhurst House, at the spot where he had left her before, and appointed a time on the following morning before the others were likely to be out of bed.

Again, Gideon sensed that something was wrong. To meet where he could not even see her? What the devil was amiss?

All the same, the next morning, he took himself round to Glasshouse Street, to the back corner of the garden to Hawkhurst House. Today, instead of dressing in fop's clothes, he wore the breeches, shoes, and smock of a stable servant, the only things concealing his identity—a cheap horsehair wig and a felt hat with a large, soft brim. He stopped outside the fence and waited until he heard Mrs. Kean's voice calling softly to him from between the planks.

"I am here," he answered, peering over his shoulder to see if anyone was observing him.

Directly across the street was a vacant piece of property, where Mr. Sandys, the night soil collector for the Parishes of St. Martin's and St. Giles's, had deposited his filth. He had entered into an agreement with the Glass Sellers' Company to supply them with saltpetre, which was used to make glass. The Earl of Burlington and Gideon's father had complained repeatedly to the vestry of St. James's about the stench coming from the yard where the waste was boiled for its production, and finally the business had been abandoned. The yard was still empty, but houses of the meaner sort backed onto it, and a few of the residents were out in the streets.

As soon their backs were turned, Gideon turned and spoke to Mrs. Kean through the planks, "Are you alone?"

"Yes, of course."

Casting a furtive glance over his shoulder, he gave a leap, caught hold of the top of the fence, and pulled himself up and over it. "Then," he said, jumping down to land beside her within the shelter of the hedge, "we can speak to each other face to face."

They were standing within the thicket formed by the ancient espalier, which blocked most of the view from the house. Mrs. Kean was dressed in her usual neat style in a simple grey gown, but her eyes were round as saucers, as she exclaimed in a strained whisper, "My lord, are you mad! What if someone sees you?"

"Perhaps that is something you should have thought of before appointing such a ridiculous spot for our rendezvous. What possessed you to do it?"

"I did not think it ridiculous. Indeed, I thought we would be able to hear each other quite well, as we did on the night of the ball."

"There is more to communication than hearing, my dear. Besides, I refuse to be caught in the daylight, addressing whispers to a fence. Someone would order me locked in Bedlam, where everyone would presume me to be mad." He added teasingly, "Why on earth would you ask me to meet you like this? I almost think you're avoiding me."

A furtive movement of her eyes suggested there might be some truth to his accusation. His heart sank, as she gave an unconvincing laugh and shook her head. "Now, who is being absurd? I've told you how busy I've been."

Short of charging her with a lie, he did not know what to do other than to ask her outright what the trouble was. She did not look happy, and dark circles showed under her eyes as if she had not been getting enough sleep.

Instead of accusing her, he asked gently, "My dear, are our cousins causing you so much distress?"

A suspicious sheen collected in her eyes, but she gave another short laugh. "No, but I thank you, my lord, for asking. It has been rather a trying time."

She recovered her composure and told him of Harrowby's latest start. "I cannot get in to see him. He's spent the past two days in bed, though I did hear from Philippe that he went to visit his mistress last night. Have you any notion what could make him act so strangely, my lord?"

A weight descended on Gideon's chest, and he attempted to relieve it with a huge sigh. "No, none whatsoever. Could it have anything to do with this business of Sir Walter?"

She shook her head helplessly. "I cannot tell." There was something else troubling her, and at last she ventured, "Is it possible he could have gambled your fortune away, my lord? He did send for Mr. Henry."

An instant's worry pricked him, but he quickly dismissed it. "That is most unlikely. Even if he played very deeply and lost, it's impossible to imagine he could have lost so much. I can see him wagering one of the properties, but not all six of them at once. And if my cousin ever did have a virtue, it was that he was not addicted to gambling. At least, he wasn't when I knew him."

She looked relieved. "No, I've observed that myself. When it comes to wagering, my aunt is the person who concerns me." She rolled her eyes with mortification.

"Just see what you can get out of James Henry when he comes. Perhaps, if you ask enough questions, he'll reveal the substance of the matter."

Her eyelids flickered again before her gaze moved to the ground. "Yes . . . I'm certain he will tell me." She spoke in a hollow tone. "But you wished to say something about Mr. Mistlethwait, my lord."

He did not like the look Mrs. Kean had given when James Henry's name was mentioned, but he said, "I went to see Mistlethwait as planned."

He told her about the strange interview and of learning that Mistlethwait received money from non-jurors in exchange for certificates saying they had taken the oaths. This spurred her to excitement. Clearly she believed the corrupt justice of the peace might have murdered Sir Walter to keep him silent.

Gideon told her why he had doubts—how Sir Walter's death had frightened both Mistlethwait and his cousin, when they did not know who might inherit the information Sir Walter had used against them, and how both men seemed to fear that a new extortioner could be worse.

This gave her pause, and she pondered his information. While she did, he watched the ideas playing across her face. It was seldom he had the chance to study her face in broad daylight, yet he found he knew every line of her countenance, and could read her every expression. He could almost hear the thoughts churning inside her brain, and before she uttered a syllable, he knew the instant when she'd come to agree with him.

There was nothing romantic in the subject they were discussing, yet at that moment he wanted her as much as he had ever wanted any woman—even more. If she had given him the faintest sign that she reciprocated his feelings, he would have taken her into his arms, but even now, she would scarcely meet his gaze. He had to clear the huskiness from his throat before he said, "Tell me what else I can do for you, my dear."

She took a sudden step backwards, as if burned by his tone. She glanced nervously towards the house, then down at the roots of a shrub. "You are much too kind, my lord. I doubt there is anything either of us can do about this matter. All our leads seem to have vanished. You have enough to concern you with Mr. Breed's escape, but if I learn anything that explains your cousin's behaviour, I shall report it to you, of course."

"Are you abandoning the search for Sir Walter's killer?"

She sighed and gave a rueful look. "I mustn't fool myself, my lord. Just because you and I have managed to resolve a few puzzles doesn't mean we will always succeed."

"Is that reason enough to give up? We've hardly started. Besides, if we do not discover who did it, then will we not always wonder if Harrowby is a murderer?"

That made her reconsider. He could almost see the struggle taking place inside her head. This was not the Hester Kean he knew, who had always been eager for justice. She had a strong sense of fairness that was offended by any unsolved crime, as well as an attachment to her family that, he thought, should make her wish to clear Harrowby of all suspicion.

Besides, on the night of the ball, hadn't she commented on how well they worked together? There had been a spring her step and joy in her face. Now, all of that was gone. Something had occurred to rob her of any pleasure in his company.

"Very well," she said finally. "I shall keep investigating, but at the moment, there's nowhere to start." She paused. "I assume it will mean speaking to Lady Tatham again, and I shall have to do it before she leaves town. Otherwise, without your cousin's cooperation I don't see how I can discover what other connections Sir Walter had who might have killed him. And, surely, if Lady Tatham had suspected anyone, she would have told us."

"Unless," Gideon said, "she killed him herself."

Mrs. Kean quickly raised her eyes to his face. She frowned, considering. "I had not thought of suspecting his wife, my lord."

"No, but perhaps that is because we knew only a man could have carried his body onto the Thames. But now we know the murderer didn't place him there. Poisoning requires no physical strength."

"That's true. A woman can do it as easily as a man."

"Perhaps even more easily, if it is a woman who prepares his food."

She was pulling nervously on her fingers. "But Lady Tatham was here at Hawkhurst House the night Sir Walter was killed."

"Are you certain? I thought it was days before his corpse was identified."

"That is true. I do not remember the exact day that he was found. I shall have to ask." She gave a helpless shrug. "But I do not see how I can involve myself in this again until the ball is past. I simply do not have the freedom or the time."

"Very well. I shall excuse you till then. But as soon as it is done, I shall expect you to do your part. You know, I cannot solve mysteries without you."

Instead of the pleased look he had hoped for, he thought he saw a hint of wistfulness, as if she did not believe him. The sound of dogs barking, growing nearer, made her glance away. She said hastily, "You must get away, my lord! The dogs are out."

"Let them come. When they see me here with you, they'll know me for a friend."

In barely a few seconds, the barks had turned to delighted whimpers as close to a dozen dogs of all sizes and shapes burrowed their way through the espalier to circle and sniff him, pushing him and Mrs. Kean apart. Most of the dogs were ones he knew, and they leapt against him, ecstatic. Gideon laughed, succumbing to the pleasure of their greetings. The few who were new to him wriggled back and forth between him and Mrs. Kean, eventually coming near to sniff at his ankles and wag their tails.

"See," he said, looking up, "now they will know me when I visit you here again."

Her expression warned him not to make a practice of it. "They are very happy to see you, my lord," she conceded.

"And I them." With a final rough rub of a terrier's ears, he straightened and sighed. "But what about you, Mrs. Kean? Are you happy I came?"

She was visibly taken aback, but his direct stare compelled her to answer. Her voice shook when she said, "Of course, I am always glad to see you, my lord."

She seemed to be on the verge of tears, but a wall had risen between them, preventing him from reading the reason behind them. He did not wish to distress her, but unless she told him what the trouble was, how could he do anything to help?

He took both her hands in his, and she stiffened, averting her face as if she could not bear to peer up at him.

"Something is wrong—I can tell. You and I have been too good friends for me not to notice when you're unhappy. Is there anything I can do, my dear?"

She hung her head and shook it, but at least she did not deny the existence of a problem. "Thank you, my lord, but no. 'Tis a private matter, which only concerns me. And it is nothing for my friends to worry themselves about."

She spoke as if she had other friends as important as he. How could she, after all they had been through together? Didn't she know how vital she was to him? She was the only true friend he had—and if his feelings for her included those of a lover, too, hadn't he often seen glimmers that she might feel the same way about him?

A sense that he'd missed something important assailed him. He wanted to hit something and curse. Instead, he released her hands, which she used to hug herself, as he said, "I hope you know that I am ready to assist you if ever you need me."

She gave a small smile. "Indeed, my lord, this is a matter I shall have to deal with myself. But I am grateful for the steadfastness of your friendship. I shall always value it—" A thickening in her voice cut off whatever she had intended to say.

Seeing that his presence was bringing her no comfort—indeed, it appeared to distress her even more—and not knowing what else to say, he repeated that she had only to send for him and he would slay any dragons in her path.

The only answer she could manage was a nod. It seemed she held onto herself by a thread.

"I bid you good day, then." He turned to the fence, found a toe-hold, and grasping the tops of two planks, launched himself up and over.

A few new observers were out in the street. They were startled to

see a strange man leaving the gardens of Hawkhurst House in so furtive a manner. Gideon suppressed a strong urge to run, and instead,
turned back to examine the fence as if looking for places along it that
needed mending. He ran a hand up and down the planks, occasionally
squatting to examine the bottoms for rot. When he showed no sign of
being afraid, the pedestrians resumed their progress. He waited until
the last of those who had seen him climb over the fence passed out of
view, before straightening and moving off towards the livery where he
had stabled Looby, Looby being the only horse he had that would not
be recognized by everyone at Hawkhurst House.

As he walked along Brewer Street, it was all he could do not to kick
a hitching post for lack of anything he could beat with his hands. Why
would Mrs. Kean not confide in him? Was there anything he had ever
kept from her? But there was more to his anger than that, and it was
something that felt remarkably like fear. She was slipping away from
him. She had turned her face away, shutting him out. And he didn't
know why.

Desperation threatened to send him into a panic. The feeling was
nearly as strong as the one he had experienced on being arrested for
his father's murder, a feeling of helplessness and loss, when he had no
way of saving himself.

All he could do now was to wait until after the ball. Then, if she
still acted as if she had forgotten the intimacy they had reached, he
would do everything in his power to make her remember.

Drawn by a fraudful Nymph, he gaz'd, he sigh'd;
Unmindful of his Home, and distant Bride,
She leads the willing Victim to his Doom,
Through winding Alleys to her Cobweb Room.
Thence thro' the Street he reels, from Post to Post,
Valiant with Wine, nor knows his Treasure Lost.

CHAPTER XVII

Hester stayed in the garden until she knew she could face her aunt without revealing how upset she had been by St. Mars's visit. When she had composed herself, she returned to her duties in the house. The musicians she had hired for the ball were coming to discuss the arrangements for their instruments and the list of music they should play.

Later that day, James Henry arrived from Rotherham Abbey and went immediately to see his lord. The knowledge that he was in the house and that he would surely come to find her made it hard for Hester to concentrate on her work.

No matter how many days and nights she had pondered James Henry's offer of marriage, her heart still fought against the logic in her head. She knew that for most gentlemen the only reasons for marrying were to increase their fortune through a prudent choice of bride and to produce an heir to carry on their name. Most would never consider wedding a penniless woman, if they contemplated matrimony at all. Marriage as an institution was broadly feared and ridiculed. One had only to see the most popular plays to know how it was regarded by many gentlemen. That it was most women's only chance to avoid penury was not an argument they believed important enough to rob them of the freedom to waste their time and money on vices.

Hester knew she was blessed to receive an offer from such an honourable gentleman. Another chance to secure her future would likely never come along. At the end, what her dilemma boiled down to was this: if she accepted James Henry's offer, she must lose her friendship with St. Mars.

She thought she could marry a man she respected, but did not love. If she had never met St. Mars, she would have leapt at the opportunity to escape her aunt and an uncertain future, dependent entirely on the goodwill of Isabella and her husband. If St. Mars stated that he intended to flee to his French estate and never return, she believed she could find solace in his half-brother's company and in the possibility of having children.

It was still the fear that she might never have the opportunity to bear children that tore at her heart. Why some women who had no interest in them should be burdened with so many, when women like herself who had always wanted babies would not have the chance to have them, was a cruelty she hesitated to attribute to God. But she knew herself and how much she had yearned for them since she was old enough to bear one. Was her yearning strong enough to turn her back on St. Mars?

As long as he remained in England, even if he did not love her the way she loved him, she was still important to him. That much she knew. As an outlaw, as far as she knew, he had no other friends, no one else to believe in his innocence, no one remotely from his former life who could keep him apprised of the developments in his household. No one to try to prove his innocence, as she had pledged herself to do. She had not forgotten the piece of paper once in her possession, which might have convinced a judge that someone else had a stronger motive to kill the former Lord Hawkhurst. It had been taken by Mrs. Mayfield, who would never admit to its existence as long as her daughter was Countess of Hawkhurst. Hester did not know for certain that it had been destroyed, but she knew her aunt and her potential for extortion. If Mrs. Mayfield had seen anything in the letter to hold over her son-in-law, she would have kept it.

And who would ever find it if Hester married James Henry and moved out of this house?

She had searched through her aunt's belongings at every opportunity and not discovered it. Perhaps it was time she gave up. But was it right for her to give up before St. Mars bade farewell to England and his connections here?

James Henry did not remain long with Harrowby. Then, as Hester expected, he came in search of her. She had purposely surrounded herself with servants to avoid a private tête-a-tête, so when he found her, she was in the kitchen office with the cook and the caterer going over the menu for the supper to be served at the ball.

James Henry did not interrupt their meeting. Instead, he nodded to her and waited, standing at a window and looking out at the kitchen gardens with a troubled frown on his face.

The ball would take place in Lent. As Whigs, however, Harrowby and Isabella did not fast, so the usual selection of cold meats could be served. Hester reviewed the caterer's list of dishes and approved a large selection of dried fruits and candied flowers, potato and turbot pies, spinach tarts, oysters and Cheddar cheese, spiced balls with eggs and white bread, puff pastries and cheesecakes, apple pasties, wigs and cakes of all kinds, some with almonds and plums, marzipan, lemon puffs, jellies and creams.

When the cook took the caterer to view the kitchens, Hester turned and begged James Henry's pardon for keeping him waiting.

He waved her apology away with an absentminded smile. "I shall not keep you from your duties, but I wished to ask if you had any notion of the cause behind my lord's change of heart."

Hester was puzzled. "What change is that? I have not been in his confidence. Indeed, I have not been near him for the past two days. I understood he was ill."

James Henry's frown deepened. "He did not say anything to me about being sick. When I spoke to him, he was dressing to go out. He had just one reason for calling me back, which was that he wishes me to proceed with the purchase of the carriage for his mistress."

Hester stared at him in astonishment. Of all the things he could have said, none would have surprised her more. Finally, she said, "I assure you I have no idea as to the meaning of this. In truth I expected it would be for something much more serious." She told him about the eerie lights in the sky and Harrowby's return in the wee hours of the morning, describing how overcome he had been.

"He spoke of being ruined—said it was a judgement of some kind. I did not take him seriously at first, as it was plain he had been drinking heavily and the lights had frightened everyone. Then, the thought occurred to me that he might have wagered a big sum and lost, but he has refused all visits from the family since that evening."

"He may not have lost a vast sum at cards, but purchases like this—if there are many more of them—will have the same effect. This time he would not listen to my urgings to be prudent. But I did not get the impression that the gift would give him any pleasure. It was as if he had no choice."

Hester thought she might fairly be considered a patient person, but Harrowby's fits and starts were beginning to try her. The trouble was that he could be so idiotic, she had no way of judging whether his actions were taken for valid reasons. In the current instance, how could she discover what was bothering him if he would not even agree to see her? She did not even know whether she should inform St. Mars.

"Did he say anything else? Anything that could explain his strange behaviour of late?"

"Nothing that I could discover, but I got the impression Pierre might know a bit more."

Hester thoughts were so absorbed by this turn of Harrowby's, she had forgotten to be shy with James Henry. So, she was startled when he said, "Have you decided to accept the proposition I put forward on our last meeting?"

For a moment she could not speak. The struggle between reason and emotion held her paralyzed.

He read the indecision in her eyes, and said, "Forgive me. I said I would give you a month to consider, and you are unprepared." There was a slight stiffness in his manner, as if he had expected a positive response.

Flustered, she said, "Please . . . believe me when I say how grateful I am for your proposal. I am mindful of the honour you have done me and of the great generosity of your offer. I promise I shall give you my answer soon, but there are . . . several things I must consider . . ."

His smile, though small and a bit confused, told her he was not very angry. "Until I return next time, then."

"Yes."

He made a solemn bow, and she responded with a formal curtsy. Then, he went off, presumably to purchase the carriage his master had ordered.

Hester took a deep breath, just now realizing how constricted her chest had been while they had spoken. It pained her to offend James Henry, who had always been such a good friend to her. It was due to his offices that she received an allowance from Harrowby. And she could never forget his kindness to her brother.

He would be a good husband—much better no doubt than she deserved.

But she could not make such an important decision when she had so many things to do. The right decision would require deep reflection and prayer.

⌀

Every night of the following week, Tom rode with Katy to visit Nathan Breed. First they called at Nancy's house and sent a message up to see if she was free to accompany them to the gaol. On the first three nights, her servant informed them that she was entertaining company and could not go out. On the fourth night, she did go with them to Newgate, but still Gideon fretted. For his plan to work, the guards must become so accustomed to seeing the two women that they would not examine them closely when Nathan Breed left the gaol disguised as Nancy's servant.

On Wednesday, the guards foiled another escape in which a group of prisoners tried to break through a wall. Fortunately, Breed was not involved, so his fetters were not applied again, but Gideon feared the turnkeys' vigilance would increase.

Two days later, the Earl of Winton was tried. Generals Will and Carpenter testified that they had made no promises of mercy upon his surrender. Winton was found guilty and received a sentence of death.

Gideon told Katy it was time for the next stage in his plan. On every visit, he wanted her to exit the prison alone and return in time to leave with Nancy, to accustom the turnkeys to her slipping out, in the hope they would not notice her leaving alone on the night of the escape. But when, on the next night, Nancy again failed to make the trip to Newgate, Gideon grew angry. He decided to have a word with her.

The next morning, he got Nate to row him to York Stairs in time to reach Nancy's house by ten o'clock, the hour she had said would be safe for him to call. The river was once again teeming with small boats in spite of the March winds, which created waves in the water.

Nate was in a grumbling mood, for he had hoped for the morning off to visit an apothecary's shop.

"Me mate Jeremiah was relieved of a worm by this feller Moore," he explained. "They say as how it was more'n four yards long! They've got it in a jar at the Pestle and Mortar over in Abchurch Lane, and I wants ter go see it. Mebbe ye'd like to go wif me and see it fer yerself. We could take a little jaunt over there on the way back."

"Abchurch Lane is not remotely on the way. It is as far as London Bridge. So, no, thank you. You will be free to go as soon as you have rowed me home."

"That means I've got ter cross the river three times and cover the same route to boot. Are ye sure ye don't want ter go see it?"

Gideon gave him a quelling look. "Perhaps you are dissatisfied with our arrangement. Would you rather go back to earning your living? If my demands are too onerous, I'm sure I am the last person to begrudge you your independence."

Since Nate had asked to become his retainer precisely to avoid the uncertainty of employment as a Thames waterman, and had obtained his position largely through threats, Gideon could only give an inward grin. Indeed, it was his pay alone that had supported Nate throughout the frost which had left other watermen with no income.

"No, I s'pose we can keep on the way we're goin'. It ain't all that bad."

Gideon turned his back on Nate so he could not see his smile. It would not be wise to let the old scoundrel know that he found his impertinence amusing. Gideon missed his valet Pierre's antics, so it was a comfort to know he could occasionally count on Nate for entertainment.

When Gideon knocked on Nancy's door in James Street, Alfred admitted him wordlessly and, with a gesture indicating that Gideon should follow, led him upstairs. In her parlour, he waited the usual interval before Nancy made her entrance. When she did appear, it was clear she expected the same tribute to her charms he had paid on his previous visits, but today he was in no mood to cater to her vanity.

Apparently, his greeting was curter than she liked, for she revealed her displeasure with a twist of her shoulders and a delicate lift of her brow. With a sweep of skirts, she assumed a chair, but she did not invite Gideon to sit. She stared while, again, he explained the necessity for frequent trips to Newgate and demanded to know whether she intended to uphold their agreement.

She did not respond immediately, and when at last she spoke it was to say languidly, "I am not in the habit of being lectured by my visitors, Robert. Perhaps you would like to reconsider your tone and return when you are in a more pleasant humour."

Gideon swallowed an angry retort. He had no patience for posturing when a man's life was at stake, but if Breed's escape depended on this woman, he would have to try to appease her.

Feigning a smile, he said, "The condition of my humour seems irrelevant, but I am sorry if I have appeared offensive. My only concern is for Nathan Breed, and I thought we had an agreement."

She gave a graceful shrug. "And I thought I had made it clear that I could not afford to raise the suspicions of my protector. If he desires my company in the evenings, it is impossible for me to go out."

He was forced to acknowledge the fairness of this. Nevertheless, he had hoped the possibility of currying favour with a duke would inspire her to dissemble.

"I understand his Grace of Bournemouth called upon you?"

"Yes, his Grace was most . . . kind." She gave him a look that was both smug and coy "But he did not offer to take me under his wing, if that is what you are asking."

Gideon shook his head with a helpless smile. Nancy was awake to every nuance.

"Very well, then. What can we do to make it possible for you to visit Breed more often? And do not suggest daylight visits, as the pattern we set must be at night."

She mused, while eyeing him with a speculative look. "You could ask his Grace if he would undertake to support me, but I should require several years' commitment in advance. You could call it a retainer."

Incredulity made Gideon bluster, "Why the devil should he agree to such a thing?"

"I have already told you. My protector is extremely devoted. He refuses me nothing. I cannot risk offending him unless I know I'll be cared for in the same style. And if Nathan's uncle wishes me to help free him, he should be willing to make me a promise."

"Breed thought we could trust you. He thought you were his friend."

"I am." Her expression softened, and her eyes implored him. "But I have to think of my future, too. I do not expect you to understand what it is like for us women, but men leave us no choice. Someday I shall not possess the powers of attraction I do now, and then the world will turn cruel. You should not begrudge me the opportunity to secure my future while I have it."

If Breed had not just informed him of her origins, Gideon might have been taken in, and even now, he wondered if there was not a bit of justice in what she said. The fate of such women could be very hard, but surely she had realized this when she had chosen this life. Or had she been so naive as to believe that one of her lovers would care for her until her death?

Regardless, he would not let himself be taken for a fool. It was plain that Nancy knew how to get what she wanted from men. She was mistaken, however, if she believed she could use his dependency on her to milk as much from him—or more properly from the Duke of Bournemouth—as she possibly could.

"I thought we had an agreement," he repeated with no heat. "If your arrangement with your lover makes it unfeasible now, perhaps I should find someone else to help me. There must be other women—an actress, perhaps—who would be happy to earn a smaller sum for the same performance."

She stiffened. With alarm at the thought of losing his business?

She quickly recovered, though, smiling at him coyly. "Come now, Robert . . . if that is truly your name. You know you cannot ask another woman to pose as Nathan's sister now. The turnkeys have all seen me. What would they think if someone else suddenly appeared with Katy as her servant? Besides, as you said, I do care about Nathan, and I have pledged my discretion. You cannot be certain that anyone else will not sell him out to the authorities."

Something in her look warned him that she was not speaking of any actress he might hire, but issuing a threat. If he did hire a replacement for her, their agreement would be at an end. What was to stop her, then, from selling information about his plan to the authorities? Nothing but her supposed affection for Breed, and already she had shown that money was more important than any trust they had once shared.

He had to walk a tightrope if he wanted to salvage this plan. And, as no better idea had sprung to mind, for the moment he had no choice but to employ her.

He gave her what he hoped was an appreciative smile. "I confess, it would be a hardship to start over, and we cannot be certain of having enough time. It cannot be long before Breed is brought to trial, and if he's convicted, an execution will quickly follow."

If he had hoped to remind her of her affection for Breed, she gave no sign of it. "What shall it be, then? Will you speak to his Grace?"

He shook his head. "He is away from London, and by the time we could negotiate, Breed's trial could have been set. We shall simply have to—"

The door opened suddenly. Gideon reached for his sword, but saw it was only Alfred.

In a growling whisper, Nancy's servant warned her, "Yer rum cully is 'ere!"

Nancy turned quickly back to Gideon. "You must go now!" She pointed behind her. "Go through that door. There's another set of stairs in the back. I'll keep him waiting here long enough for you to escape."

Gideon instantly obeyed, taking a few quick strides into her bed-chamber. He had no sooner closed its door quietly behind him than he heard her greeting a visitor. Her voice came to him much more clearly than it should through a shut door, leading him to suspect there was a spy hole somewhere in the wall between the rooms.

He listened for footsteps and, hearing none, took a few moments before making his way through the door at the back of her chamber, which supposedly led to the second set of stairs. The room was luxuriously appointed with velvet curtains on the windows and silk coverlets on the bed. Behind a screen he spied her dressing table, complete with a large gilt looking glass and a handsome set of silver-backed brushes. Boxes for powder and patches, pots for pomatum and unguents, silver flasks for perfumes, orange and myrtle waters vied for place with a lace pin cushion, two loo masks, a few handkerchiefs, and a japanned coffin he supposed was filled with jewels, undoubtedly gifts from her lover.

It was then that he realized the voice he had heard in response to her greeting sounded familiar. Gideon raised his head and listened intently. It took only a few seconds for him to be certain that the man on the other side of the wall was none other than his cousin Harrowby.

A tangle of emotions hit him—chagrin that his cousin should be the dupe of such a grasping female; anger to think of the fortune Harrowby had wasted on a mistress, when supposedly he had a willing and beautiful wife; and—yes—even envy for the pleasure Nancy must give him. All of these feelings, and at the same time, nervousness, for he must not be discovered in her bedchamber. Not only would his discovery jeopardize Nathan Breed's chance of escape, but it might lead to an exposure of his own identity, in which case he did not know who he would have most to fear, Harrowby, Nancy or Alfred, any of whom might turn him in for the reward.

He listened for one minute more and was astonished to hear Harrowby making excuses for disturbing Nancy so early, and begging her forgiveness since he would not be able to attend her this evening. Though Nancy accepted his apology in a cooing voice, there was a note in Harrowby's implying he was not at all certain she would receive it with such grace.

Then, from the other room, Gideon heard the rustle of feet, alerting him that he must not linger. He moved on tiptoes to the back of the room, opened the door quietly, and finding a narrow, spiral staircase took it to the bottom, where another door opened onto an alley. Once outside, he saw that the alley ran between Long Acre and Hart Street. Before going any farther, he took a moment to slow his pulse, which had started to race, before walking to Hart Street and peering round the corner to make certain that no servant from Hawkhurst House was standing within view. Seeing no one he recognized, he started walking down to the river.

As he strode briskly, he honestly did not know what to feel. On the one hand, it was lucky that he had not run into Harrowby sooner. He found it almost unbelievable that Nancy, as clever and alluring as she was, would take up with his foolish cousin, but he was forced to acknowledge that the Hawkhurst fortune made Harrowby a worthy prize for anyone as ambitious as she clearly was. He could better understand that she would be willing to trade Harrowby for the patronage of a duke, but he could not help feeling annoyed that the man who held his father's position could be such a namby-pamby as to be entirely under the thumb of his mistress.

There had been nothing masterful, or even confident in the tone that had floated through that wall. Harrowby had subjected himself to a stronger character. No wonder Nancy had said that her protector refused her nothing. The galling thing was, he was using Gideon's money to appease her appetite for luxurious things.

But one important piece of information had come from his eavesdropping. Harrowby would not be with Nancy tonight. She would be free to visit Nathan Breed. Gideon wondered if he might find out from Mrs. Kean what other nights Harrowby would be occupied. There would be the night of the ball, at least, and as long as the moon was on the wane, it could be the perfect night to appoint for Breed's escape. They would have no fear that Nancy's protector might interfere.

Gideon was in Half Moon Street, almost at the New Exchange, when abruptly crossing the street, he glanced to the right. As he did, he was certain he saw Alfred dart back into Maiden Lane. If Alfred was following him, there was nowhere else for him to hide to avoid being spied, for there were no alleys off this street. His movement was certainly suspicious. Gideon wondered if Nancy had set Alfred to track him. If she had, the question of her motive was disturbing.

Gideon recalled a phrase she had used, but he had not questioned at the time: "Robert . . . if that is truly your name . . . ." It seemed she had developed an unhealthy curiosity about him, a desire to know who he really was. And since that knowledge had no bearing on her agreement to help Breed escape, as Tom paid her promptly each time she accompanied Katy to Newgate, Nancy must want the information for some other purpose.

For the first time, Gideon felt threatened by his part in this scheme. Breed had made it clear how ambitious Nancy was. Her own actions had made Gideon question how mercenary she was prepared to be. Would she betray him to the authorities if she learned who he was? He had no doubt that she would betray him to Harrowby.

He must not allow her to come by any information about him. Even his disguise as Mr. Mavors would be at risk if she decided to inform on the person who had helped Nathan Breed escape. They had no history of intimacy or trust. Nothing in their agreement could be interpreted as a requirement to shield him, even if she did honour her word, which Gideon had begun to fear it would be foolish to assume.

He purposely slowed his steps to give Alfred a chance to catch up to him. Then, just outside the entrance to the New Exchange he gave a quick glance behind him.

Yes, there Alfred was. He checked his pace and bent over, as if to pick up something he had dropped. But now, Gideon had no doubt that either Alfred or Nancy meant him harm.

Evasion was required. Gideon entered the New Exchange at a stroll, then turned immediately into the shop on his right. A shop assistant came quickly forward to solicit his trade, but Gideon gestured that he wished to be left alone. The girl retreated with a pout, while Gideon hid in the shadow of the door until Alfred hurried past. Certain he had not been spotted through the window, he waited for a moment, then peered after Alfred, who had paused in the middle of the

Exchange. As Alfred searched left and right, Gideon pulled his head back into the shop.

He took a moment to look about him and, with a grin, realized that he had taken refuge in a staymaker's shop. It was a good choice, as there was less reason to fear Alfred would search for him here. Gideon waited for another few seconds, then peered out again in time to see Alfred resuming his walk, moving slowly away from Gideon as he looked into the shops on both sides.

Gideon hastily left the staymaker's shop and retraced his steps, exiting from the New Exchange by the entrance he had used. In a fast stride, he rounded the corner into George Street and walked down to the top of York Stairs, where he turned again to assure himself he was not being followed. Alfred was nowhere in sight, so he ran briskly down the steps. With a command to Nate to start rowing, he pushed off from the dock and leapt into the boat.

As Nate pulled steadily on the oars, Gideon looked furtively behind him. This latest manoeuvre of Nancy's had unsettled him. He should never have trusted her. What did he know of her, after all, except that she made her living going from one man's bed to another, calculating the moves that would result to her advantage. He wished he had asked Breed earlier about her origins, though he doubted it would have made much difference. There had not been anyone else they could trust with their plan.

Still, he might have been more careful in his dealings with her. And now that he knew she meant to get information about him, undoubtedly to benefit herself, he must do his best to avoid giving her any opportunity to use it.

He would contact Mrs. Kean immediately to find out the date of the ball, and to see if she could devise an excuse to occupy Harrowby in the evenings leading up to it. The sooner Nathan Breed was sprung from Newgate gaol, the sooner Gideon could sever his ties with this troublesome woman.

§

Perhaps because he had embarrassed her over her choice of meeting place, or else because she wished to keep him from climbing into the garden of Hawkhurst House again, Hester agreed to meet him at St. Martin in the Fields.

They were to look for each other on Monday morning, after the service, which was attended by only a few parishioners. With the weather warming up, the prostitutes who had huddled inside the church all winter no longer needed its shelter.

Hester reached the church in time for Morning Prayer, hoping to find the inspiration she needed to make her decision. When the service ended, she stayed in the communion pew and soon St. Mars joined her.

He was wearing the olive green coat she had first seen on him outside the stationer's shop along with the black wig and face paint that hid his identity so well. She had placed a copy of the prayer book on the seat next to her, so after a moment's pause, he sat on the bench across the communion table.

His hesitant expression told her that he was remembering the last time they had sat together in this pew, snuggling together for warmth. She tried not to recall it herself, for it was just the kind of memory that made it harder for her to take a reasoned step.

"You have something urgent to tell me, my lord?" she asked to divert their minds.

His manner towards her was strained. "Yes, if your offer of assistance still holds."

She sat up straighter, intrigued. "Of course. You'd like my assistance in freeing Mr. Breed?"

He nodded. "I do not think it will cost you much effort. But first, I must ask, what is the date you have planned for the ball?"

Hester started. She prayed he was not planning to attend, for besides the fear that he might be exposed, if he tried to dance with her, all her fortitude would be undone. "I do not understand how that will help you."

He grinned. "Just tell me, and I shall tell you how."

She sighed. It would do no good to lecture him about safety or thwart him in any scheme he had in mind. He would have his way. "The ball is to be on the twenty-eighth March. Since Parliament doesn't sit on Wednesdays, we won't run the risk the gentlemen will be detained."

He made a face. "That's more than a week away. I had hoped it would be sooner. But, still, the moon is right. It may be possible."

"For what?"

"For Breed's escape. We need an evening when Harrowby will be occupied."

Hester frowned in surprise. "Why? What does he have to do with it?"

His grin was wicked. "That is why I wished to see you so urgently. I told you of Breed's friend who has agreed to play the part of his sister in the scheme? Well, on Saturday I learned that she is Harrowby's mistress."

Hester's mouth flew open. "How did you discover it?"

"I heard him myself when I hid in her bedchamber."

A pang of jealousy took her by the throat. For a moment she could not speak. But, then, his face revealed that this was precisely the reaction he had wished to provoke. Hester hardened her heart. It was on the tip of her tongue to inform him that she had received an offer of marriage from his brother, but something besides the sheer absurdity of such a remark kept her from it. She was so annoyed, she did not know what had stopped her, but it was one thing to joke about hurtful things and entirely another to use the truth to wound. Even if St. Mars never intended to marry her, she knew he would be hurt by the thought of her desertion.

His smile faded. His manner turned gentle. "I went to her lodgings to complain when she repeatedly failed to accompany Katy to see Breed. While we were talking, Harrowby arrived, and I barely escaped before he came in. Until I heard his voice, I had no idea who her protector was. She had justified her failures by saying she could not afford to be absent when he visited her. I hoped you would be able to tell me what nights he will be otherwise employed, but the night of the ball is an obvious one."

"Yes, of course. I see now. Let me think. There must be other nights." She racked her brain, but her thinking was all muddled. It was not just because of her personal dilemma, but something about knowing who Harrowby's mistress was that disturbed her. Perhaps it was because she had thought of her only in one context, and not as someone who would be involved with St. Mars. Hester blamed her uneasiness on jealousy and tried to put it out of her mind.

"I know he plans to go to Newmarket for the races, but that will be after the ball. I'm sorry, my lord, but I cannot think of any engagements he has before then, except for his attendance in Parliament, of course."

He looked sideways at her, a speculative gleam in his eye. "Is there anything you could do to occupy him? Something that might keep him home for a night or two?"

"Such as what, my lord?"

"Well . . . what about slipping an emetic into his drink? Nothing strong enough to kill him, of course."

"And turn myself into a poisoner? I should think not!"

His look was so crestfallen, she realized he must have been joking and glared at him in reproof.

"Very well," he said, with an exaggerated sigh. "If you refuse to do that, is there anything you can do to detain him? If we knew he would arrive at Nancy's at a later hour, perhaps she could make a brief visit to Newgate and return before he arrives."

"I will try. It will not be easy. I've scarcely seen him in days."

This reminded her that she had not seen St. Mars since her conversation with James Henry. To repay him for his teasing, in a dire tone of voice, she said, "I should be careful in your dealings with that woman, my lord. She has managed to persuade your cousin to buy her an expensive carriage."

His stunned expression reminded her it was really St. Mars's fortune that would pay for the coach.

She started to apologize, "I am sorry, my lord. It was insensitive of me to tell you in that fashion. I—"

"No," he interrupted. "Never mind that. What was that about a carriage?"

Self-conscious now, Hester stammered everything she knew about Harrowby's asking James Henry to purchase a coach for his mistress, and how James Henry had managed to talk him out of making such an expensive gift. "Then, after the mysterious lights were seen in the sky, he called Mr. Henry back from Rotherham Abbey, as I told you, and the only thing he ordered him to do was to execute the purchase, after all."

St. Mars frowned intently, but Hester could tell it was not the exorbitant gift that disturbed him—or at least, not the money.

"I do not like the sound of this," he said, staring unconsciously and worrying his lip.

"Neither does Mr. Henry. His fear is that too many gifts of this size will put a severe strain on the estate, which is why he tried so hard to dissuade him."

St. Mars shook his head impatiently. He moved his gaze to her face. "No, there's something else. Did you not say that Sir Walter had found Harrowby's mistress for him?"

For a moment, Hester said nothing. Then, something clicked inside her brain. She gave a start. "Yes, is it possible . . . ?"

"Let's think." He spoke rapidly, his mien excited and grim. "What if Nancy knew of the threat Sir Walter held over Harrowby?"

"You think they may have been in league?"

"It's entirely possible. If Sir Walter was a procurer, he would want a portion of anything Nancy earned. But she's a clever girl, much too clever to be anyone's tool. It's likely that they were conspirators."

"That still doesn't tell us what the information was."

"No . . . but what if she was the person it came to, and not Sir Walter's son?"

Worry filled Hester's breast. "You have met her," she said. "Does she seem capable of extortion?"

He grimaced. "Most harlots wouldn't scruple to pick their customers' pockets, and extortion is just a sophisticated form of thievery. It's easy to forgive a prostitute for taking advantage of the men who use them—almost like trading one insult for another. But there is something colder about Nancy."

"I thought Mr. Breed was fond of her."

"He was, but even he recognizes how little room her ambition leaves for friendship. She would not be helping him now if his uncle could not pay her handsomely to do it."

"I didn't know that. Do you mean they . . . they were intimate, and still she has not enough affection for him to save him from death?"

Her incredulity made St. Mars smile. He looked at her so warmly that heat rose up inside her. When she thought of Nancy again, however, she shivered. "I do not think I should like this woman."

He said wryly, "I hope you never encounter her. But I have learned that she is not to be trusted." He told her that he believed Nancy had set her servant to following him.

"Thank goodness you spotted him before he discovered where you live!"

He sighed, "Yes, I should regret having Mr. Mavors exposed. And Nancy is so quick-witted, I would not put it past her to uncover my real identity—but enough about that. I'll take care not to be followed again. The real question is if I can still trust her with Breed."

He spoke half in jest, but Hester was not so sanguine. "My lord, I doubt you should have anything at all to do with her! If she is capable of watching a former lover go to the scaffold, when she might have done something to save him, she is capable of anything."

Their gazes met. His expression showed that he had followed her thoughts.

"Murder?" he said.

"Is it not a strong possibility? It's at least as strong as the notion that Lady Tatham killed her husband. If Nancy was in league with Sir Walter, they could have had a falling out. What if he tried to take more of her earnings than she considered fair?"

"It is rare that a harlot turns against her procurer. As despicable as it sounds, procurers are needed to bring them customers. Sir Walter was in a position to bring Nancy aristocratic clients she might not otherwise have met."

"Like your cousin . . . who is now entirely in her power."

"And . . . as long as he stays there," St. Mars mused, "she has no more need for Sir Walter's help. Harrowby's wealth would be a temptation for any woman, and if she could be certain he would never dare leave her, she could live well all the rest of her life."

"Perhaps she is certain. Whatever threat she holds over him, she obviously can get anything she wants."

"And without Sir Walter taking his pound of flesh, there is more for her."

Hester thought about Harrowby's behaviour and how it had recently changed. "It's possible that when Harrowby denied her the carriage, she decided it was time to use her leverage against him. He had begun spending time with Isabella again, so Nancy may have feared she would lose him."

Hester stared at St. Mars across the table, convinced that the scenario they had imagined could be true. She grew aware of the rustlings and creaks of the old church around them, hinting at the presence of ghosts. Sir Walter's perhaps?

"But how can we ever prove it, my lord?" Hester asked, feeling gooseflesh on her neck.

"Indeed . . . and dare we? If we alert the authorities that Nancy might have murdered Sir Walter, she could try to save herself by betraying Breed—or even Harrowby, if his secret would be of interest to them."

Hester was silent while she pondered the problem. "Breed will be safe if we do nothing about the murder until after he is free. But do you dare trust her with your scheme?"

"She will not get the remainder of her money until his escape is successful. As grasping as she is, that should keep her committed until the Duke pays her, and by that time, we shall have spirited him across the river. If she found out where I live, I assume both of us would be in peril the instant Bournemouth paid her."

She shuddered. "I really do not like this, my lord. I'm almost afraid she's followed us here."

He grinned. "I'll take care never to tell her where our meetings will be. I doubt she frequents churches."

She reproved him with a frown. "I was only half-joking. I'm convinced you should not use her in your scheme."

He sobered. "I have no choice. But it's only nine days more, and I'll stay away from her until then. I'll have to alert Tom and Katy to watch out for her servant, too."

She spoke earnestly, "My lord, please let me do it in Nancy's stead. You could tell her the plan is too dangerous, and that you will not be needing her help."

"If I do that, she may well tip the authorities now. For her to keep silent, she must believe there is money in it for her. If I were to cancel our arrangement, I don't doubt she would threaten to betray us unless we paid her even more than the price we agreed upon."

Hester had to concede he had valid point. "But if anything further worries you, I hope you will reconsider."

He promised he would keep her offer in mind.

"I suppose I shall have to be content with that. But this does not solve your cousin's problem, my lord."

Where frequent Murders wake the Night with Groans,
And Blood in purple Torrents dies the Stones . . .

CHAPTER XVIII

For a while longer, they puzzled over what Harrowby's misdeed could be, but in the end agreed there was nothing that could be done to extract him from his predicament until Nathan Breed was safely out of London. Gideon would like to have lingered in St. Martin's, but Mrs. Kean insisted she had to get back to her work.

After a cool farewell, he watched her go, wondering again what had occurred to make her distance herself from him. Then he met Nate's boat at Hungerford Stairs and brooded while Nate rowed him home.

As the oars dipped rhythmically, he mused upon the change in her manner. He doubted it was caused by the work she had to do for the ball. He tried to think if he had done anything to hurt her feelings or to betray her trust, but try as he would, he could think of nothing he had done wrong. One day they had been as close as two friends could be, and the next, it was as if something, or someone, had drawn a curtain between them. He could still see her on the other side, but her expressions came to him through a haze, and her emotions were filtered before her voice reached his ears. If she did not tell him soon what the cause of the change in her was, he would seize her and not let go until she did.

The ill-ease between them was costing him sleep. Last night he had dreamed that James Henry had caged her and refused to let him free her. There was something in her manner when James was mentioned that had provoked his suspicions—but suspicions of what he could not say.

He had seen them together and noted how attentive his half-brother was to her. It was James who had first seen she was paid an allowance, not him. James who had taken care of her brother Jeremy in prison, and James who had brought her back to Hawkhurst House when Mrs. Mayfield had banished her out of fear of the smallpox. Gideon wondered what other services he had done her, and whether they were things he should have done for her himself. But Mrs. Kean had always been reluctant to receive his gifts. On the few occasions he had presented her with anything, she had been adamant that he must never do it again.

No, it was something much more serious, something which would not allow her to confide in him. For the moment, at least until Breed was safe, he could do nothing but hope that whatever it was would simply go away.

The next day, Gideon received a letter from Mrs. Kean saying that she expected Harrowby would remain in the House of Lords every evening that week until the last peer left the building. She did not say how she had got him to act so dutifully, but Gideon suspected she had made a casual remark that King George had spies monitoring every peer's attendance to gauge his degree of loyalty.

The newssheets reported that now that the Pretender's forces had been routed, King George intended to spend the summer in Hanover. Gideon hoped that meant Parliament would be sitting late every night in order to accomplish all the King's business before he left.

Over the next week, Nancy managed to visit Breed's cell another three times. Katy reported that on all three occasions she had slipped out of prison with her hood covering her face and had returned for Nancy without being pestered by the guards. They had left Nancy's lodgings after dark and had returned to her house long before eleven o'clock, by which time the turnkeys were always well on their way to drunkenness.

Even the moon seemed ready to cooperate. It would be very thin on the night of the ball. Gideon had not informed Nancy that the escape was to take place on Wednesday night, but he anticipated she would be ready when he, Tom, and Katy came for her.

Today was Monday. They were two long days away from the event. It was difficult to remain at home with nothing to pass the time, so Gideon took Penny out for a ride.

As he rode through the gate into the lane, he saw a boy he had never noticed before leaning against a fence post. The boy straightened as if startled. Gideon nodded, not wishing to frighten the lad, who had the bedraggled appearance of a street urchin.

He held Penny to a canter, making a circle through Clapham, Wandesworth, Streetham, Dulwich, and Camberwell before returning by way of Lambeth Marsh. There he found a few signs of spring to come—green grass growing beside the shallow water, a few early terns among the geese and waders preparing to fly north. In the Weald, buttercups and anemones would soon be blooming beneath the trees. He took a few deep, cautious breaths of the still-cold air, which was purer here, but still tainted by the smoke of burning coal blown across the river by the spring winds.

He would be glad when this mission was over and he could head into the country. He would take Nathan Breed to the coast and put him aboard a smuggler's vessel bound for France.

With the Pretender vanquished, it should soon be safer to cross the Channel. Gideon thought he should consider visiting France again himself. The impediments to his freedom and the loneliness had grown almost intolerable. He had counted on Mrs. Kean to break up the monotony, to amuse and challenge him, but of late even she had seemed to shut him out.

The ride on which he had embarked to ease his tension turned sour. He turned Penny homeward by way of Newington Butts and Kennington Lane.

He was almost upon his gate when he caught a glimpse of the boy again, no longer alone, but standing with a man who was peering into his yard. Their bodies were turned away but Gideon could see the boy spoke eagerly as he pointed towards Gideon's house.

With a start, Gideon realized that the man was Alfred.

Abruptly, he turned his horse back the way they had come—not easy since the ride had been long and Penny was eager for her feed. It took all his strength to force her away from the river into a short lane that led to the Vauxhall Spring Gardens. At this hour with the weather still cool, the lane was deserted. Gideon dismounted and led her on foot back to the road that fronted his yard.

Alfred was still peering through his gate, skulking behind a hedge to avoid being seen by anyone in the house. It took Gideon no more than a few seconds to reason out how Alfred had found him, and he cursed himself for underestimating the man's wiles.

Instead of following Katy and Tom, he had employed a street urchin to do it. Then the boy had guided him here.

Gideon waited to leave his own hiding place until the two tired of spying and vanished up the lane on their way back to London. There was nothing he could do now in broad daylight to stop Alfred from reporting the location of his house to Nancy. In truth, the only way to stop him would be to kill him, and Gideon would not commit murder to guard his secret.

As soon as he reached the house, Tom emerged to take Penny from him. Gideon said, "Stable her. Then bring Katy upstairs. We need to talk."

In the kitchen Katy had his dinner cooking over the fire. She started to tell him it would be ready in a few minutes, when he forestalled her, telling her to wait for Tom before joining him in his chamber.

Waiting for them, Gideon paced his room, cursing under his breath. *What a damnable thing to have happened! And what wretched timing!* In just two days, Breed could have been safely brought here. Now Gideon did not dare bring him to this house unless he could find a way to eliminate the danger Nancy posed. But they couldn't wait any longer. Some of the rebels in Newgate were down with gaol fever. The escape must not be postponed.

He had barely started to think of an alternative plan when Tom and Katy appeared in the doorway, worry written large across their features. Gideon bade them enter. Then without preamble he told them about the boy and the man he had seen in the lane.

Tom turned grim. He stammered, "I—I'm sorry, my lord. We didn't—"

Gideon waved away his apology. "It's not your fault. Nancy outsmarted us, you and me both. If the boy had followed me, I should not have noticed."

"What can we do? Do we need to leave this house?" It was Katy's turn to be upset. This was the first decent home she had had since being released from gaol. She did not protest aloud, but the helplessness in her eyes was eloquent enough.

"Let's not be hasty." Gideon pinched his brow in thought. "She may know where we live, but I assume that is all she knows. She has no cause to suspect I'm an outlaw."

"Not yet. But what if she does find out?"

"We'll deal with that when it comes. Meanwhile, we must find another way to free Nathan Breed."

Tom and Katy exchanged anxious glances. Tom said, "You can't mean to go through with it, my lord!"

"Indeed, we will . . . but Nancy will no longer take part in the scheme."

"How can we do it without her?" A new concern appeared on Tom's face. "You wouldn't send Katy in there alone?"

"No, of course not. The escape will take place as planned, but someone else will play Nancy's role."

As they stared at him in confusion, the outline of a new scheme took shape inside his head.

☙

On the morning of the ball, amidst a flurry of preparations, a footman brought Hester a note left supposedly by a tradesman at the gate. She had received so many messages concerning the arrangements for the ball, her first reaction was to pray that nothing else had gone wrong. The morning had already been filled with last-minute problems—flowers refusing to open, a late shipment of the wine, Isabella's sudden distaste for the costume her seamstress had laboured over the past two weeks. Hester had dealt with the seamstress's hysterics, and persuaded her cousin that she looked ravishing in the milkmaid costume, which naturally she did.

The possibility of another catastrophe made Hester want to scream, but something in the script addressing her name caught her eye. The sender had taken pains to disguise his hand, but there was a flourish in the final letters she thought she knew.

She found a solitary spot in which to open the note. Inside, St. Mars had written, "My dear friend, I fear I must impose upon you, after all. Meet me tomorrow night at eleven o'clock at the door of St. James's Church."

Excitement and fear raised a gasp in her throat. Something had happened to change St. Mars's mind. She could not believe he would ask her to assist in his dangerous scheme—unless, of course, someone's life was at stake, which indeed it was. But what had caused this alteration in his thinking? And could she manage to slip out unseen in the middle of the ball?

The courtyard would be a scene of flurry and bustle, but a single lady departing through the gate could attract a certain degree of attention.

Throughout the day, as she moved through the house, giving final instructions, examining the table linen, and overseeing the placement of candles and chairs, she thought about how she would make her exit from the house. It was a much less alarming occupation for her mind than wondering what St. Mars would want her to do, whether he would ask her to enter Newgate prison—and, if he did, whether or not she would ever leave it again.

At last, all the rooms were ready, bedecked with flowers and lit by hundreds of candles. Isabella and her mother had been coaxed into their costumes with the aid of tight corseting. Georgie had long since been packed off to bed with his nurse, but Hester had been gratified to see that neither Isabella nor her husband had forgotten him in the excitement of preparing for the evening. Both had visited the nursery to kiss him good night.

Fortunately for St. Mars's plans, Hester had been too occupied with other arrangements to prepare a costume for herself. She wore a mantua of pale blue satin, embroidered with leaves and flowers down the front. Its cuffs ended in lace, but of a modest length, nothing to compete with the splendour of Isabella's gown, but enough to show her kinship to the lady of the house.

At eight o'clock the guests started to arrive, and by half past ten, every room was filled with chatter and laughter, the clink of glasses, and the occasional scrape of a chair leg, while music wafted from the saloon. In spite of several last minute adjustments, everything was running smoothly. The servants were performing at their best. Mrs. Mayfield had even stopped finding fault with Hester's preparations as she immersed herself in cards in the room set aside for players. Isabella had played at hostess just long enough to escape censure before dancing off to enjoy the flattery of her swains. She would never notice anyone's absence as long as there were enough young gallants to keep her entertained, and the guest list had been heavily skewed in that direction.

Harrowby, who had spent a good half-hour in the nursery earlier, bidding a maudlin goodnight to his heir as if he fully expected to be drawn and quartered on the morrow, had now imbibed enough wine to make him forget whatever threat loomed over him. He stood surrounded by his more foolish friends, giggling, and ogling the riper beauties among his guests. Such unbecoming behaviour was licensed by a masquerade.

The only person Hester truly feared might notice her absence was James Henry, who had arrived that evening in time to dress for the ball. He had stationed himself in the corner of the saloon, from which angle he could see that everything was running smoothly and be ready to help in case anything should go amiss. He looked very handsome in a sober suit of brown satin, which perfectly conveyed his status in the household. It was neither as fancy as a guest's nor like the livery that defined the lower servants. Hester had avoided meeting his gaze, giving, she hoped, the impression that her mind was absorbed by the duties concerning a hostess.

Excusing herself from a conversation with Madame Schultz—who had come to advise her that she would be pleased to receive a gift of the China bowl she had discovered in the small parlour—Hester left the saloon and wove her way through the noisy crowd in the hall. James Henry would assume she had gone to attend to the arriving guests. What he would think when she did not reappear, she could not imagine, but the rooms were now so filled, she hoped he would assume she was merely out of sight among the crowd.

Earlier that evening, when the guests were first arriving, Hester had secreted one of Isabella's riding hoods amongst the ladies' cloaks. After giving some final instructions to a butler, concerning the serving of supper, she made her way to the antechamber where the wraps had been stored and told the waiting maid she needed the cloak because the owner had suffered a fainting spell and would soon have to leave. With the cloak draped across her arm, she crossed to the opposite side of the hall, stole into a darkened office, and donned the hood, as well as a half-mask she had concealed in her pocket. Now, with her hair, face, and gown partially covered, she could blend with the masked guests moving in and out the door without being recognized.

The hall was a scene of lively confusion with maids and footmen rushing about to relieve the guests of their cloaks. Gentlemen, already the worse for drink, greeted their friends with good-humoured oaths, while the ladies arranged their skirts and waited for their pages to brush off any flecks of mud before entering the saloon. One of the older ladies was accompanied by her black page, carrying a pet monkey on his shoulder. Something offended the animal, and it shrieked, climbing on the young boy's head. The child's howls, when his hair was pulled, attracted the stares and laughter of the guests.

Hester took advantage of the commotion to slip past the footman manning the door. The gate to the forecourt was standing wide to admit the guests' carriages. She walked through it, dodging the wheels of a coach emblazoned with a duke's coat of arms, without pausing to see whether Rufus the gatekeeper had noticed her. He would not interfere with a strange lady's passage, even if he had.

Out in Piccadilly, she gave a sigh and tried not to think about the tricks she would have to employ to regain entrance. The street was clattering with horses hooves and wooden wheels as more guests arrived, but she felt safer away from the lanterns illuminating the gate.

From here it was no more than a few dozen yards across Piccadilly to St. James's Church, their parish church. St. Mars would never have chosen this place in broad daylight for fear of being seen by his family or nearest neighbours.

At this late hour,, however, the church was cloaked in darkness, its spire a ghostly black needle pointing up to an overcast sky. Hester cautiously made her way round the familiar path to the main entrance on the south side of the nave. Although she had expected to find St. Mars somewhere near, still she jumped when a man stepped suddenly out of the shadows.

"Sorry to startle you," he said in a whisper, "but there's no point in going inside. We must make haste."

"Do you need me to—"

"—to bring Nathan Breed out of Newgate? Yes. Are you still willing to risk it? I would not ask if there were any other way."

"Of course. But what caused the change in your plans?"

"I'll explain on the way." He took her elbow and steered her out into Jermyn Street, then past St. James's Market into the Haymarket, where he found them a hackney. As soon as he had closed the door of the coach behind them and joined her on the seat, he drew her hand through his arm. He held it there, while relating the events, leading up to the note that had summoned her from the ball.

On the way to Newgate, whenever they passed a lamp or a link-boy's torch, Hester glanced over at him. She could tell he was not wearing his daytime disguise. His yellow hair was tied back in a queue, his head covered by a tricorn hat. His cloak was fur-lined with many capes.

In a few short minutes, she had gone from the bright, crowded, perfumed rooms of Hawkhurst House to this snug, quiet space, with St. Mars's warm, firm body pressed against her side. Smelling of buckskin and wood smoke, he cushioned her from the hackney's worst jolts, while telling her of the boy who had followed Tom and Katy home.

His voice was low and confiding in the dark. "Now that Nancy knows where I live, I cannot keep Breed at my house. And I dare not let her know he's escaped until he is safely out of London."

"But what if she discovers who you are!"

"I will think of something to keep that from happening, but first we must free Breed." He did not ask if she had experienced any trouble stealing away, but focused instead on what she must do.

"Katy will carry a basket with the clothes Breed will wear. The guards should not bother to search it, but if they do give you trouble, she has money to bribe them with. By this hour, they should be quite drunk—Breed will have seen to that. I doubt they will do more than glance your way.

"I hope your cloak has a good hood . . . ?" He raised a hand and felt the side of her head. "Yes, that will do. You must keep it down, so they will take you for Nancy—or rather for Breed's 'sister'—who supposedly has been visiting him often these past few weeks. Once you are safely past them, Katy will guide you to the room where Breed is kept. He will have to don the woman's clothes without arousing the interest of the other prisoners in his ward. Then, he must carry the basket and walk out with you as if he is your servant."

"What about Katy?"

"She will slip out before. You must give her a few minutes before you and Breed follow. Our gamble is that the guards will be too drunk to recall that she has already left."

Hester posed the few questions that came to her, while trying to still the hammering in her heart. St. Mars answered her briefly, but she could barely think well enough to attend to his words.

"Where will you be?" Unconsciously, she tightened her clasp on his arm.

He returned it with a comforting squeeze. "Tom and I shall wait for you in an alley off the Old Bailey, about half the distance to Fleet Lane. Take this hackney to the gate and tell the driver to wait. Then, when you leave, tell him to convey you to Blackfriars Stairs. We'll keep a sharp lookout. As soon as we see you leaving the gaol, we'll follow. Nate will be at the bottom of the stairs with his boat. If we have not arrived within five minutes, tell him to row Breed to my house and you take the hackney home."

She started to protest, but he hushed her by saying, "We will arrive, but it's wise to plan for contingencies."

Their hackney slowed. Hester glanced out the window and saw that they were approaching Temple Bar. Since she had last passed this way, two traitors' heads had been hung there. The grotesque masks, hardly human now that the crows had been at work, made her shrink back against St. Mars, who wrapped a bracing arm about her shoulders. She understood, then, why he had to ask her to undertake this night's adventure. No one should be subjected to such a punishment.

In a few moments the coach turned left into the Old Bailey. Before they arrived at Newgate, St. Mars called out to the driver to stop. Then, he turned and took both Hester's hands in his.

"Are you certain you're willing to do this?"

She had to clear her throat before saying, "Yes."

"Brave girl!" He kissed the backs of both of her hands, giving them a final squeeze, before opening the door to jump out.

While he paid the driver and gave him further instructions, someone moved in to take his place. Out of the night, Katy's voice greeted her with nervous breathlessness. "It's me, Mrs. Kean. Don't be afeared, now. Just let me do the talking with the guards."

As if in a dream, Hester clung to Katy, while the hackney took off again and rolled the last few yards to the prison gate.

"C'mon, mistress. We're here."

Katy jumped out first and raised her hand to help Hester down. Light from the torches on the massive gate revealed that, indeed, Katy was carrying a large basket over her arm. A cloth, such as one might use to cover bread or cheese in the larder, was tucked over its contents. Katy herself was wearing a riding hood of simple woolen cloth. Hester supposed there would be another like it in the basket.

Taking Katy's arm as if for support, Hester accompanied her to the gate where she rang the bell before she readjusted Hester's hood to hide her face. The last time Hester had been to Newgate, it had been to find her brother. The same nightmare-like feeling filled her now, except that on that occasion she had come during the day and had been refused admittance to the gaol. This time, after a short delay the gate opened unceremoniously, releasing the sound of many voices, which issued from the barred windows lining the street to their right.

Calls and jeers in slurred, drunken voices floated out towards them. St. Mars was correct about the guards, however, for as soon as Katy slipped some coins into the turnkey's open palm, without even asking to know their business, he led them unsteadily to the door of the lodge. This he opened after fumbling a good while over the lock.

Already the stench Hester recalled from her first visit to the street warned her of worse to come. As the door creaked open, the full force of it hit her in the face, and she gagged, grateful she had been too busy that evening with preparations for the ball to eat. Holding a handkerchief to cover her nose and squinting from the acrid fumes of urine, she followed Katy across the threshold.

Inside was a scene out of a brothel—or so Hester imagined. Men and women caroused on the scant furniture of the lodge, while to her left a constant flow of prisoners and their guards staggered through the door from the cellar with mugs of spirits in their hands. One guard stood in that doorway, exacting the fees it cost prisoners to enter. Others staggered in and out of the door leading to the wards, some accompanied by visitors on their way out. The guards paid them little mind, engaged as they were in drinking themselves senseless.

Hester had no more than a few seconds to take in the scene full of people making a din before she followed Katy's steps through a door, then along a corridor which lined a ward with a low gallery layered with prisoners' cots, and onto a set of stairs. Some prisoners, probably those who could not afford to rent a cot, lay huddled on the cold, stone floor.

Everywhere about her, the sights and smells of abject misery met her eyes. The odour of feces and vomit bespoke the sickness rife in the gaol, where more prisoners died from gaol fever than from the hangman's noose. More men had been forced into these tight quarters than even the number she imagined a ship's berth would hold. In the first ward scarcely a candle was lit. The gaolers were said to make an excellent living off the exorbitant prices they charged for such luxuries.

With no wish to witness anything else, Hester fixed her gaze on Katy's back as they ascended two flights of stairs. The hood of her cloak helped block the disturbing sights, but could not hide the sounds and smells, as they passed by a series of smaller rooms. On their left, groaning came from an enclosed room. To their right, muffled pants and grunts issued from the beds.

Suddenly aware of what these noises meant, Hester was shocked to think that men and their wives would be coupling in the presence of so many others. Then, she realized that these were not married couples, but prisoners mating—no doubt, so the women could plead their bellies to escape a sentence of death. That exclusion had turned London's prisons into brothels. The ploy, of course, would work only until a baby was delivered or nine months had passed, but the women could hold out hope that something would occur in the meantime to spare them from death.

A few furtive looks from beneath her hood told her that the prisoners barely bothered to remark their passage. That part of St. Mars's plan had worked, in that by now Katy and Mr. Breed's "sister" had become common sights.

This thought had just crossed her mind when Katy halted in front of a door, where a turnkey sat dozing against the wall. When she roused him, he stumbled to his feet, cursing and fumbling with his keys. The problem was not only with the weak light in the passage, but with the man's drunken condition. When he finally opened the door, and Hester followed Katy inside, a strong odour of spirits wafted from him. Muttering, he closed the heavy door after them, but did not bother to lock it, presumably so the visitors could leave without troubling his sleep. He would be counting on the guards downstairs to stop anyone trying to escape.

The air of the ward they had just entered was thick with fire and pipe smoke, but mercifully less of the stench that made her sick. Fewer prisoners were crowded into a larger space. The men she could see in the dim candlelight were better dressed. Nevertheless, an air of despair still prevailed. As the two women entered, some prisoners did look up from their beds or cast a glance from the table where a few sat playing at cards. These last made gestures of greeting to the women, but their efforts were lackluster at best. When two called out in Hester's direction, saluting her with an unfamiliar name, she was afraid they might come close enough to see that she was not the lady who had visited Breed as his sister. She inclined her hooded head in a manner to discourage further conversation, but evidently the game occupied them intensely for none chose to leave it.

A few candles flickered around the ward, illuminating the table and two or three spots where men were trying to write or read. She could only suppose their eyes had grown accustomed to what seemed like the darkness of a cave, for she could barely see well enough to keep from tripping against one of the few pieces of furniture.

One gentleman rose from his bed. She followed Katy across the room towards him. This was the moment in which she might be exposed if Breed reacted visibly to the substitution.

Katy curtsied and bid him, "Good evening, sir," giving Hester a few seconds to think what she must do. As Katy moved aside, she stepped forward and embraced the stranger long enough to whisper in his ear, "We have come to take you out of here tonight."

At the sound of her voice, he jerked beneath her hands then stilled before whispering, "Who are you—where is Nancy?"

"She was unable to come, but the plan remains the same."

She drew back then, doing her best to look steadily at Breed while he peered down into her face. His visage was pale, no doubt from months of incarceration, but she could see that the surprise had unnerved him. His hands, still gripping her shoulders, started trembling. She noted how young he was, perhaps no older than herself, and she shuddered to think how close to execution he was, for this would undoubtedly be his last chance to escape. It did not take a memory of the heads hanging on Temple Bar to make her pulse race furiously with the danger he faced.

Or perhaps, the danger they all faced. She did not know what the penalty would be for helping a traitor to escape. Her throat constricted at the thought, as Katy emptied the basket upon Breed's bed.

Her skirts blocked the other prisoners' view of the woman's clothes she piled atop the covers, but truly no screen was needed for this part. The light in the ward was too low for anyone to distinguish a woman's dress from a gentleman's long coat on a prisoner's bed.

"Put these on over your shirt," Katy whispered. "Then master said to pack your waistcoat and coat in the basket, and be sure to cover them with this cloth."

She pulled Hester next to her, making a screen of their bodies, while Breed fumbled with the unfamiliar garments, his trembling hands making him clumsy with the task. Before he could find the opening in the loosely made gown, a rusty squeak alerted them to the fact that the door to the ward had opened again. Breed quickly stuffed the gown back into the basket next to him on the bed, as the sound of booted feet drew nearer and nearer behind Hester's back.

"I see ye got vis'ters there, Mr. Breed," a wheedling voice said over her shoulder. "And a fine good evenin' to ye, too, mistresses." The slurred words caused a chill to run down Hester's spine, but she turned her head just enough to give a regal nod in acknowledgement. Katy turned more fully and curtsied to the man, whom Hester had recognized as Pitt, the Keeper of Newgate prison, with whom she had spoken only a few months previously. It was possible he would remember her, too, if he could see her face. And if he had seen Nancy's before, he would surely notice the substitution.

"What can I do for you now, Pitt?" Breed asked impatiently. Hester wished she could congratulate him on the steadiness of his voice. She knew the effort it must have cost him.

"Some o' the lads and me, we're runnin' a bit low, ye see. I thort ye might like to stand us anovver glass." He coughed—a phlegmy sound—then spit on the floor beside Breed's bed.

Hester pulled her skirt closer, a natural instinct, whether or not Nancy would have done it.

"Ye gods, Pitt!" Breed complained, as he dug into his pocket. "Haven't I already treated you enough?"

"We saw as'ow yer sister'd come again, so's we thort she mighta brung ye som'fing to tide ye over, like. Would'n want ye ter waste it now, would we, or lose it afore yer trial?" He gave a coarse laugh, which, plus the joke she assumed, was to frighten her into paying him more.

She spoke in a voice too low to be recognized, "Give Mr. Pitt another guinea for his troubles, Katy."

"Now that's wot I likes ta 'ear, mistress." He took the gold coin Katy pulled from her pocket and bit it to test its genuineness. "It's got 'is new Majesty's face on it, too. Very pretty that is." He contemplated the coin in a drunken haze, before recollecting himself enough to tuck

it into his vest pocket. "I guess that oughter do us fer now. We won'
be botherin' ye fer anovver littl' bit. Good evenin' to ye, mistress," he
said again.

They waited with held breath while Pitt stumbled out again, leaving the door as he'd found it. Hester took a deep breath to stop the
fluttering of her heart. "Does he often do that?" she asked Breed in a
low voice.

"Only recently. I think he noticed the extra bribes I was giving the
guards and wanted to make sure he was getting his share."

Katy was fidgeting at Hester's side, and now she uttered an anxious, "Mistress . . . ?"

"We had better hurry while he's content," Hester whispered.

With steadier hands Breed found the opening to Katy's gown and
pulled it over his head. Then he fumbled with the sleeves, and Hester
fretted with the temptation to help him dress. When he had smoothed
the gown to his waist, the riding hood followed. Breed had left the
gown unfastened at the back. It would not have closed completely
over his broader shoulders, but the cloak concealed the gap. Now Katy
could do her subtle best to straighten the garments on him. She did
not dare ask him to stand for fear the increased activity would draw
the other prisoners' attention. She pulled down the sleeves of his shirt
as far as possible to cover his masculine hands and folded the lace of
his cuffs under the sleeves to hide it.

As soon as she was satisfied with his appearance—as best as she
could see in the gloom—she whispered a caution for him to keep his
hands out of sight, to bend slightly at the knees and to take smaller
steps than was his custom.

Hester heard her take a deep breath before she asked, "Can you
find your way out of this place, mistress?"

This made Hester start, but Breed said, "Between us we can. Let's
make haste."

"You'll have to stay till I've been gone awhile. A quarter hour
should be enough. If the turnkey outside wakes when I open the door,
I'll have to come back." To Hester she held out a small purse of coins
and said, "Sit here with Mr. Breed, and play like he's me, and you're
waiting for him to come back from using the bucket."

She gave them a curtsy and turned towards the door, her head bowed and her motions quiet. Her cloak and hood were made of dark brown cloth, which meant that in a few seconds her figure nearly vanished in the dark.

Hester did what she had said and sat down upon Breed's bed. The two sat quietly, stiff with apprehension, listening hard for any noise that could alert them to trouble. The rusty hinges on the door gave a long, low groan, but it was almost lost in the din that continually issued from the other wards. By now, Hester's eyes had grown accustomed enough to the dark that could make out Katy's hooded shape as she slipped silently through the cracked door. The heavy iron hinges gave a squeak, but as she and Breed waited, no other sounds came from the turnkey. The only noise raised near them was the murmur of the players as they wagered and grumbled about their cards.

Hester wondered how long it would be before someone noticed Breed's disappearance, and with this thought, started gathering the sheets behind them into a lump to make it appear, at least until dawn, that he was lying in the bed. After a few seconds, Breed guessed what she was doing and helped by rolling a few of his belongings inside the covers.

Now they had to wait. Next to her, Breed started to fidget. He seemed to be waiting for her to determine when to move. He could not know how unprepared she was for this escapade, but it was safer to let him think she knew what she was about. Assuming more confidence than she felt, she covered his hand with hers in a plea for patience.

"Surely it's been long enough!" he whispered.

With her heart in her throat, she answered him as calmly as she could, "Just a few minutes more."

She waited until a ruckus erupted over the card table, when two gentlemen started to quarrel over whose turn it was to deal, before whispering, "Now."

Together they rose and stepped quietly across the room, arriving at the door without any of the players seeming to notice their movement. If they did look up, Hester hoped the dark and their own befuddled state would make them overlook Breed's absence as two women ostensibly disappeared through the door.

Katy had left it more ajar than it had been. The turnkey was still snoring outside in what seemed a deep, drunken coma, the lantern on the floor at his side emitting a low beam. After only a second's pause, Breed widened the opening a bit further while she winced at the rusty noise; then he courteously signaled for her to lead.

On their trip into the ward, Hester had kept her eyes on Katy's back in front of her, but she knew from which direction they had come. The corridor they needed to traverse faced them, but now that the turnkey's lantern was behind them, the width of their skirts blocking its glow. Ahead the darkness was so deep it seemed like a well or a chasm. Hester hesitated and nearly lost her balance. Breed grasped her elbow and propelled her forward into the inky blackness, which still echoed with the cries and moans of Newgate gaol.

They had nearly reached the stairs when a door to their right opened, and a guard carrying a lantern issued from it. Hester squinted from the onslaught of light, raising a hand to shield her eyes. As she did, she caught a glimpse of two large cauldrons inside the room, and a memory of something she had heard made her recoil in horror. It was said that a kitchen in Newgate held cauldrons for boiling the limbs and heads of prisoners who'd been quartered.

She must have gasped, for Breed tightened his grip. Hester hurried past the room, careful to hide her face from the guard, who looked as if he might ask a question—perhaps for a bribe—if they hesitated. The stairs descended for two floors with the noise of drunken revelry growing louder with every step. They landed on the ground floor, where Hester paused just a second before following the overhead gallery back to the lodge.

Little had changed in the short time since their entry, though perhaps the guards and debtor prisoners employed to carry spirits from the drinking cellar to the wards were moving in more of a trance. They paid no attention to the two departing visitors until Hester and Breed made their way towards the door to the lodge, when one of the men called out, "Now don't ye wanna join us, pretties? I've got a pair o' sturdy knees ye could sit yer arses on!"

Who can the various City Frauds recite,
With all the petty Rapines of the Night?
Who now the Guinea-Dropper's Bait regards,
Trick'd by the Sharper's Dice, or Juggler's Cards?
Why shou'd I warn thee ne'er to join the Fray,
Where the Sham-Quarrel interrupts the Way?
Lives there in these Days so soft a Clown,
Brav'd by the Bully's Oaths, or threat'ning Frown?
I need not strict enjoyn the Pocket's Care,
When from the crouded Play thou lead'st the Fair;
Who has not here, or Watch, or Snuff-Box lost,
Or Handkerchiefs that India's Shuttle boast?

O! may thy Virtue guard thee through the Roads
Of Drury's mazy Courts, and dark Abodes . . .

CHAPTER XIX

As laughter filled the lodge, Hester froze, a thrill of panic skipping down her spine. At her side, Breed started to turn as if to confront the man, but Hester quickly put out a hand to prevent him. In a low voice she said, "Do not pay him any mind, Katy. Remember why we are here."

She held onto Breed until she felt the muscles in his arm relax. Giving a sharp nod, he lowered his gaze as if in affronted modesty, and meekly accompanied her to the door, which a guard, still chuckling from his friend's jest, unlocked to admit them to the street.

From here Breed would have taken off at a brisk trot, had Hester not restrained him to a lady's pace. In what seemed like forever, but could only have been a half-minute, they passed through the immense gate and instantly filled their lungs with gulps of cleaner air, not pausing in their stride until they reached the waiting hackney coach. Then, after Hester told the driver to take them to Blackfriars Stairs, Breed handed her into the carriage and awkwardly lifted his skirts to follow.

The horses started immediately, as he fell into the seat with a shaky sigh. "My God, we did it!" he rasped. "You did it! May I please know the name of my deliveress?"

Hester saw no reason to keep her name a secret, so she answered in a voice trembling with relief, "I am Hester Kean, sir, though that name will mean nothing to you."

"It shall from here on, I assure you! What brought you to my rescue? And what happened to Nancy?"

Hester did not know what he had been told about Nancy's affairs, but she knew St. Mars would wish him to be warned not to trust her. Quickly, Hester told him why she'd been asked to take Nancy's place, and of Nancy's successful attempt to find out where they would be taking Breed.

"We fear she means to use the information to extract more money from you or, perhaps, from our friend, who could be charged with treason for helping you to escape. Perhaps even to claim a reward for finding you—after your uncle pays her for saving you, of course."

He listened to her in stunned silence. "You believe she murdered Sir Walter Tatham? But why? I thought they were friends."

"Did you know him?"

"Yes. He often called at her lodgings. It was he who introduced us. He . . . that is . . . they had an arrangement."

"What sort of arrangement?"

"Oh . . . introducing her about, don't you know."

"You mean he procured patrons for her?"

She could feel his embarrassment, even in the dark. "Er . . . yes."

"That much we know, but we still don't know why she killed him. Can you think of any reason why they might have fallen out?"

For a moment he was quiet. The clop of the horse's hooves and the creak of the wooden carriage filled the silence. It would not be long before they covered the short distance to their destination, and Hester wanted to learn whatever Breed could tell them.

Then, he said, "I suppose, if Sir Walter got too greedy . . . if he took a greater share of her money than she was willing to part with, they could have fallen out."

"Did you know he was an extortionist, too? He learned people's secrets and threatened to reveal them, unless they paid him to keep quiet?"

"No, but it wouldn't surprise me. Even when I knew him, he used people's secrets to weasel his way into their society. Sir Walter was a cagey man. I've often thought it was he who prodded Nancy to end our affair. I could not bring them enough money, and he must have found someone who could."

He paused. "I guess I should feel lucky. Otherwise, I could have been bled dry, but I never shared my political sentiments with him —or with Nancy."

"Could he have held a secret over Nancy? Could that have been her motive?"

He huffed. "What secret could a courtesan at Nancy's level possibly have? She was never at Court, and her sins were public knowledge."

"What if she had stolen? Or killed someone else?"

His voice held a shrug. "It's possible, I suppose, but I don't see what need she would ever have to steal, as long as she had a protector to milk. And she is not the passionate type who would murder someone in anger. No. From what I know of Nancy, money is the only thing that truly matters to her."

A smell of river mud and the sound of lapping water alerted Hester to their arrival at Blackfriars Stairs before the carriage came to a halt. Breed opened the door and jumped down, not bothering to move like a woman. He assisted Hester down. Throughout their coach ride here, Hester's ears had been alert for any sound of pursuit, but the streets behind them were still quiet. She paid the driver, telling him to wait, and in a few minutes they were joined by St. Mars, Tom, and Katy, who arrived on foot.

When Breed started to greet them with cheer, St. Mars forestalled him with, "Not here—not yet." Turning to Hester, he clasped her hands and whispered, "Good girl!" Then, after calling to the driver that they would be no more than a minute, he rushed everyone down the stairs to the Thames.

There was a different feeling among their party now, a sense of re-strained jubilation. It was too soon to celebrate though. Breed would not be out of harm's way until he was safely across the Thames.

At the riverbank, they found a boat bobbing up and down in wait. As soon as he saw them coming, Nate leapt out and pulled the boat up in the mud. Gesturing its way, St. Mars told Breed to go with Tom and Katy, saying he would be taken to a place where he could rest, but that he should be ready to ride before dawn.

"You're not coming with us?"

"No, but I'll follow you soon. I'll escort Mrs. Kean home first. Tom, tell Nate to meet me at Salisbury Stairs. He may have to wait."

At the mention of Salisbury Stairs, Tom, who was holding the bow of the boat for Katy to climb in, started up with an anxious tone. "My lord—"

"No. You go on with Breed. Make sure he's had food and rest, and is ready to ride when it's time to leave. If anything should detain me, you know where to take him."

Tom reluctantly obeyed, his elation clearly gone. St. Mars did not bother to wave them off. Instead, he took Hester by the hand again and led her rapidly back up the stairs and to the waiting coach.

No sooner were they settled, than Hester said, "Salisbury Stairs, my lord? Those are not the stairs nearest to Hawkhurst House."

"No. I must deal with Nancy tonight. There is no other option. Tomorrow she will hear of Breed's escape, if not sooner, and there is no telling what she will do when she discovers she's been cheated."

"How do you mean to stop her?"

"I'll think of a way. But she must be confronted."

"About Sir Walter's murder? But how can you deal with her when you cannot call a constable?"

She sensed his shrug in the dark. She did not like to think of him confronting a murderer on his own, especially not a female one, not when his sense of chivalry could put him in a vulnerable position.

"Let me come with you," she said. "Then once she's confessed, you can raise the cry for a constable, and I can stay there until he comes. Someone will have to explain what she's done."

St. Mars was silent for a moment. "There could be problems. Perhaps I should have worn my disguise, but there was no time to plan. We have to gain entry, and her servant will put up a good fight. I don't want to let her see my face in case anything goes wrong."

"Did you bring your mask?"

"Yes, and my cape. I had thought of overpowering her servant."

Hester thought, then said, "Why not let me knock at the door? If her servant opens it, you can follow me in and subdue him. I'll say I've come with a message from your cousin."

By the time they reached Covent Garden, St. Mars had agreed to her suggestions. He told the hackney driver to set them down at the bottom of James Street to avoid the more crowded areas of the piazza. Not knowing the location of Nancy's house, Hester stayed tightly by his side as they entered the part where James Street narrowed, and he halted between two doorways.

St. Mars took a long look around and waited for the few pedestrians in this quieter street to disappear into the gloom, before saying, "It is here. We'll have to move fast, or we'll have more witnesses than just her servant to worry us."

There, in the darkness between the circles of light cast by the lamps over the two doorways, he removed his cloak and donned the black half-mask and blue satin cape he'd withdrawn from his deep coat pocket. He rolled the heavy cloak into a dark bundle and stowed it in the shadows, where it was barely visible and should be safe for a while.

"When the door opens, stand back and give me space to push my way in." Then, giving Hester leave to knock, he drew his sword and pressed himself against the side of the building.

It was a few moments before her knock was answered, long enough for Hester's palms to become damp. When the door opened, she was startled to see a woman—a very beautiful woman—standing in the doorway and haughtily looking her up and down.

If Hester had not been dressed so finely, she had the feeling the woman would have slammed the door in her face without even bothering to ask her business. As it was, a faint trace of alarm showed in the delicate lifting of her brow, as she said, "Yes?"

Still a bit shaken by the surprise, on top of her earlier adventure at Newgate, Hester gave an involuntary glance at St. Mars's masked face, before turning her eyes back to the woman and stammering, "I am come on the part of Lord Hawkhurst. I am searching for a woman named Nancy."

"I am Nancy," she said, opening the door wider and taking a step aside. "You had better come in."

The words were no sooner out of her mouth than St. Mars swept in front of Hester and pushed his way into the house, leaving Nancy no time to react. She gasped when he placed a gloved hand over her mouth, his sword raised near enough to her face for her to see.

"Is your manservant here?" he asked quietly. "Nod, if he is."

Nancy gave a slow shake of her head. *No.*

"Good." With a jerk he indicated the stairs. "We will follow you up."

As soon as Nancy put a foot on the first step, he signaled for Hester to close and lock the door. She secured it before joining them on the stairs. Hester could not help admiring the poise with which Nancy had greeted this assault on her house, but perhaps she believed they were indeed sent by Harrowby and that all would be explained.

They entered a sumptuous parlour on the first floor, a room she realized St. Mars must have entered many times. There was something about it that made Hester uncomfortable, beyond the natural dismay she should have in the presence of a killer. Then, she realized it was the seductive atmosphere of the parlour that offended her, as if the furnishings had been designed to stimulate every sense towards sex, and every piece of f upholstery had been planned to highlight Nancy's beauty.

Instead of facing them in fright, Nancy lowered her elegant figure onto a settee and struck a pose, Hester could only imagine she had learned it for the sensual effect it would have on her clients.

"Well, well," she began, languidly. "Will you not be seated? I suppose I should be honoured by a visit from the notorious Blue Satan. But if you wished to see me, I do not understand why you brought your strumpet with you."

They ignored her invitation to sit, and her implied invitation to Blue Satan. St. Mars took a looming stance in front of her, while Hester stood two steps back. She could not be offended by an insult from a courtesan and murderess, but St. Mars took umbrage on her behalf. "This lady is no one's whore. She is exactly who she pretends to be, a relation of Lady Hawkhurst."

Hester saw that, in spite of herself, Nancy was intrigued. She could not know where this encounter was going or even what it was about. She tilted her head and studied Hester more thoroughly before stating, "Then, you must be Mrs. Kean. Lord Hawkhurst has spoken of you. I make it a practice to know everything about my protector." She smiled, revealing a hint of a sneer. "Has Lady Hawkhurst sent you to frighten me off? If she has, you may tell her that it will not work. Lord Hawkhurst does not take his orders from her. Perhaps I should have asked you what business you have with an outlaw?"

St. Mars said impatiently, "We are not here to answer your questions. Tell me first, where is your servant, and when do you expect him to return?"

When it seemed she would not answer him, he brought the tip of his sword to within inches of her faces. "You will want to tell me." His voice was so low and so soft, Hester could barely hear it, but the threat gave her a chill.

Nancy's clipped response conveyed her resentment. "He is on an errand. I do not know when he will get back."

"Then, we should get on with our business. It concerns Sir Walter Tatham."

Hester, who had been watching Nancy very intently, noted a flicker in her gaze. It was as if the sun had cast a fleeting shadow across the face of a stone statue. Betraying no emotion whatsoever, however she feigned a mild interest. "Sir Walter? What business can we have concerning him?" Suddenly she widened her eyes as if a thought had just occurred to her. "Was it you who placed his body on the Thames?"

Of course, that would have tormented her. She must have wondered how the corpse had ended up in a peer's coronation robes.

"No," St. Mars said, "that was done by a despicable creature by the name of Gayet. But . . . you do not ask if I murdered Sir Walter. Why is that?"

"Didn't I?" She pretended to be startled. If Hester had not been convinced of Nancy's guilt, she might have believed her. She was a very good liar.

Nancy continued the pretence. "Then, did you? Did you murder Sir Walter?" Her expression changed to reflect righteous anger.

"No . . . but you knew that already."

Nancy's arm had been resting along the back of her settee. Now, her manicured fingers played with the seam in its upholstery. "You are mistaken. I have no notion how he was carried onto the ice or how he came to be in those clothes."

"I concede, you do not. Shall we tell you? It seems that Mr. Gayet and his fellow Mohocks found Sir Walter's body somewhere here, near Covent Garden, and thought it would it be amusing to dress him up in a coronation robe and set him up to frighten people attending the Frost Fair."

"Terrible!" Nancy gave a delicate shudder. "How did you ever discover the perpetrators of this travesty?"

When he answered, St. Mars's voice made Hester shiver. "I have a talent for discovering people's secrets . . . and so does Mrs. Kean."

Nancy licked her lips. "I daresay Mrs. Kean does. Lord Hawkhurst has made reference to her intelligence." She gave a little start, accompanied by a musical laugh. "But I forgot my manners! You've a message for me from Lord Hawkhurst." Rising gracefully from her seat, she said, "You must let me offer you a dish of tea."

Hester would have stopped her, but with a small shake of his head, St. Mars held her back while Nancy walked to a table near the hearth on which a tea caddy stood. She unlocked the caddy and measured a quantity of tea into a pot. Then before fetching the kettle from the fire, she opened a smaller box, the contents of which they could not see.

She turned to smile at Blue Satan. "I shall have to ask you to pour the water into the pot. The kettle is too heavy, and my servant would do it, were he here."

"Then, should I be pouring my own poison?"

Nancy paused, the teapot in her hand. Her expression revealed nothing but polite offense. "I beg your pardon? Do you accuse me of wishing to poison you?"

"No, I accuse you of murdering Sir Walter Tatham."

She gave a trill of laughter, before reaching for the kettle and turning to pour the water into the pot herself. "It wanted only this to complete this extraordinary visit. If you do not wish for a cup of tea, I shall not force you, but there are ways of refusing a dish without insulting one's hostess. You will not be offended if I take a dish myself?"

When neither of them spoke, she poured herself a cup, then after adding more leaves and more water to the pot, placed it on a brazier near the settee, and resumed her seat. She took a careful sip from the cup she had poured. Then glancing at the clock on the mantelpiece, she said, "You see? The tea is not poisoned. It will not be too late if you change your mind."

St. Mars, too, glanced at the clock, then back at Nancy. "You are wondering how soon your servant will return. But it's a long way to Lambeth, is it not? And if you instructed him to wait, there's really no way to know how long he will take."

This was a guess on St. Mars's part, Hester knew, but an angry flush on Nancy's cheeks confirmed that his guess was correct. She must have wondered why Katy and Tom had not come for her this evening and had sent Alfred to see what he could discover at St. Mars's house. And if that were the case, Alfred would see Nathan Breed arrive and would undoubtedly make haste to tell his mistress what he had seen. They had no time to waste.

St. Mars betrayed no concern on this score, but he must have been aware of the risk, for he said, "We can drop this foolish pretense. We know how you murdered Sir Walter. You have nothing to do but tell us why before we hand you over to a constable."

She curled her lip. "And, pray, how do you intend to do that? The last I read there was a considerable price on your head. In fact, were I to scream out my window that Blue Satan had broke into my house, the constable would arrest you before you had a chance to accuse me."

"That is why Mrs. Kean is here. By the time the constable arrives, you will be bound, and I shall be gone. The constable is sure to believe her word over the word of a courtesan."

She darted a nervous look Hester's way. Hester realized that Nancy had forgotten her presense, but she was so accustomed to ignoring women in favour of men that focusing on St. Mars had come as naturally to her as breathing.

"Lord Hawkhurst will not be pleased with you for accusing me," she said, threatening Hester with a glare. "I can easily persuade him to throw you out. Then, where will you go? You're more dependent upon him than I am."

"Perhaps you can," Hester said, "but you mistake if you think that will deter me."

At her steady look, Nancy paled.

St. Mars unwound the long scarf from about his neck with the clear intention of tying her hands.

Her expression altered. Tears came into her eyes. "I beg you to wait. At least until I've finished my tea."

St. Mars took a few steps towards her, then paused, uncertain. Nancy hastened to pour another cup. As she raised the dish to her lips, her hands shook, but she drank it completely. She poured another and sipped. "Besides, I should like to know how you discovered my guilt."

St. Mars turned to Hester with a question in his eyes.

It was true they had no time to waste, but Hester wanted to know what hold Nancy had over Harrowby. She must know something that could harm him. Else, how could she be so certain that Harrowby would take her side?

"We know Sir Walter was an extortioner," Hester began. "That is how he worked his way into my cousin's graces. I assume you know what information he was using to force him to tolerate his companionship?"

A bitter expression crossed Nancy's face. "Yes. Sir Walter's 'friends' paid him dearly for his friendship—too dearly. He presented me to his lordship. He said we would share his fortune equally. But soon he wanted most of your cousin's fortune for himself, when it was I who had to entertain him. I did not work that hard to captivate an earl, only to have his money stolen from me."

"So you killed Sir Walter?"

Nancy's smile was so cold with hatred, it made Hester shiver. "Yes. But how did you uncover Sir Walter's business?"

"It wasn't difficult. My cousin is easily read. It was plain he did not care for Sir Walter, but still he allowed him to treat Hawkhurst House as if it were his own. Then, when Sir Walter died, he was terrified that someone would inherit Sir Walter's 'business,' but according to Lady Tatham, her husband had no business. My lord asked me to discover who else might know about Sir Walter's affairs, but when the weeks passed and no one seemed to know anything about them, he started to relax. He cared nothing for Sir Walter's murder, but the thought that someone might know the business that existed between him and Sir Walter frightened him considerably. There were other people with the same fear, too.

"That was when you started asking him for more and more expensive gifts," Hester said, realizing that this would account for Harrowby's despair. If his mistress had the secret, whatever it was, he would never be free of her powers of extortion.

Nancy endeavoured to look smug, but a sour twist to her lips gave Hester another insight.

"He refused to buy you a carriage, did he not? That was when you must have told him that you knew his secret, so he would never dare refuse you anything again."

A spark, like a memory of triumph, lit Nancy's eyes. Then pain contorted her features. She dropped her tea cup to the floor and pressed a hand to her midriff. Her cheeks turned ashen, and she gasped.

Hester took an involuntary step towards her but stopped. Nancy might be feigning illness with the intention of overwhelming her. She could not be trusted.

A knock sounded at the door. Nancy moaned, and an angry flush filled her face as she clutched at her stomach. She looked weaker and as if she might become ill or faint.

As the knocking repeated, more loudly, Hester turned to St. Mars, who said, "That will be Alfred."

When Nancy heard him name her servant, she raised her head with apparent pain and seemed to search the room for his voice, which St. Mars had failed to disguise. "Is that you, my dear Robert?" She gasped for breath, as if a weight were crushing her chest. ""I might have had the reward . . ." her voice sounded hazy, confused . . . "had I known . . ."

He glanced at her briefly then focused his gaze on the door, not believing in her distress. "I doubt it would have been enough to satisfy your avarice."

The pounding below suddenly ceased. As St. Mars moved to the window to peer down into the street, Hester said, "I fear she truly is ill, my lord."

Without looking at Nancy, he said, "Good. That will make it easier for you to guard her, while I take care of Alfred."

No sooner had the words left his mouth, than from the next room came the sounds of a door crashing open and heavy footsteps moving their way.

"Tie her hands with this," St. Mars said quickly, throwing his scarf to Hester. He drew his sword as Alfred rushed into the room.

With scarcely a glance at his mistress, who had fallen back helplessly on the settee, he ran at St. Mars, ignoring his blade. The sudden onslaught caught St. Mars off guard—his mind must have balked at the prospect of stabbing an unarmed man. Alfred grasped both of St. Mars's wrists, rendering his weapon useless, and the two grappled, with St. Mars striving to release his hands as they crashed into the gate-leg table, sending the tea canister flying onto the floor.

Hester did not want to take her eyes off the fight, but knowing what she must do, she hurried to Nancy's side. When she reached her, she saw there was no need to tie her hands. Nancy's eyelids squeezed tightly shut with pain. Her gasps were more desperate, as if she could hardly breathe. Angry red hives were spreading up her neck.

Sitting down beside her, Hester set to work on Nancy's bodice, ripping it open to get at the stays underneath. She loosened them quickly, asking, "What ails you? How can I help?"

Through sneering lips, Nancy whispered, "You cannot . . . foxglove . . ."

Hester's fingers faltered with the laces. They trembled as she stared into the face that steadily turned grey even beneath the spreading hives. Nancy had poisoned herself rather than face the hangman—or worse, the flames.

Behind her, the fight continued, as the men staggered back and forth in their deathly grip. Throwing a look over her shoulder, she saw St. Mars was still grasping his sword, despite Alfred's heavier build. Both were breathing loudly. Alfred's face was crumpled in an angry red mask. St. Mars's gaze, focused and intense, directed an invisible beam between the other man's brows.

Nancy no longer posed a danger. Not even an actress could counterfeit these symptoms. Hester looked frantically about her for something with which to help St. Mars. Her gaze landed on the poker standing near the hearth. With a wary eye on the two combatants, she crossed the room for it and raised it over her head.

The sound, when she brought it down on the top of Alfred's head, made her cry out with revulsion, but when she opened her eyes she saw that she had not killed him. Her blow had stunned him, long enough for St. Mars to land one of his own in Alfred's face. The big servant went crashing to the floor and lay still.

Wiping his mouth on the back of his sleeve and breathing hard, St. Mars said, "Thank you, my dear. I wasn't certain I could handle him without your help."

These were the perfect words to restore her equilibrium. She heaved a great sigh and the worst of her trembling abated.

"Now, if you would be so kind as to return my scarf, I'll truss him up."

Recalled abruptly to their purpose, Hester hurried to the settee and sat beside Nancy again. "She's poisoned herself, my lord. Foxglove she said."

He moved to join her and peered over her shoulder while she patted Nancy's hands then her face. Nancy's eyes flickered open.

"Is there nothing we can give you?" Hester asked insistently.

When Nancy did not answer, St. Mars laid a hand on Hester's shoulder and said softly, "There is nothing we can do. It has gone to her heart. We should leave—no reason to call a constable now. I'll leave Alfred untied, so he can attend to her when he regains consciousness."

He started to pull her gently away, but Nancy's eyes were still open. She tried to speak.

"Just another second, my lord," Hester said quickly. She bent over the other woman. "What is Lord Hawkhurst's secret? What has he done?"

Confusion clouded Nancy's gaze. "Done?" she whispered, then moaned. A shudder ran through her and she retched, but she was too weak to vomit.

"Yes, what secret would do him harm if it were known?"

Amusement crossed Nancy's face, but weakness slurred her words. "'S nothing he's done."

Hester felt her wrist for a pulse. It was so slow and weak, she could hardly find it. Part of her cringed from trying to extract information from a dying woman, but she felt compelled to discover the secret. What if it was something that truly could ruin Harrowby?

Before she could press Nancy again, she spoke in halting phrases, as if to herself. "Not him. His cousin . . . St. Mars . . . innocent . . ." She started to laugh, but her laughter ended in a gasp. Then before either Hester or St. Mars could speak, her chin fell onto her breast.

Hester raised her eyes to St. Mars, who had leapt forward on hearing his name. He took Nancy by the shoulders and gave her a shake, willing her to speak again. "How do you know?" When she didn't raise her face, he yelled, "How do you know that St. Mars is innocent?"

Nancy's eyes flew open, but there was no life in their depths. St. Mars shook her one more time, before Hester grasped his arm.

"She is dead, my lord! Shaking will not bring her back." Pushing him aside, Hester felt for a pulse, but there was no trace. Nancy's graceful body lay slumped on the settee. Hester closed the beautiful eyes and eased her corpse until it lay on its side with her head resting on the cushioned arm.

Behind Hester, St. Mars's furious curses singed the air.

Here Rows of Drummers stand in martial File,
And with their Vellom-Thunder shake the Pile,
To greet the new-made Bride. Are Sounds like these,
The proper Prelude to a State of Peace?

CHAPTER XX

O nce he had gained control of his anger, they did not linger. St. Mars made certain Alfred was still unconscious, saying roughly that he should live. Then he removed his cape and mask, and they left the house, St. Mars retrieving his heavy cloak outside. They walked to Covent Garden, found another hackney cab, and remained silent as it covered the short distance to Glasshouse Lane.

Hester tried once to comfort him. "My lord—" she began in a gentle voice, reaching for his hand in the dark.

But he cut her off. "No—don't. There is nothing to say." He did not repulse her entirely, though, returning her clasp and going so far as to press a kiss on the back of her hand, before turning to stare out at the houses they passed. She sensed that fury was still driving his pulse, but words could not erase the feelings of betrayal he must be suffering, so she held her peace.

When the coach pulled up behind Hawkhurst House, he told the driver to wait. Taking her by the hand, he led her again to the corner of the fence. There, he said, with an attempt at lightness, "I'm afraid your landing will be rougher in the dark."

"It doesn't matter. This way is preferable to the questions I would incur by trying to sneak through the gate."

She wanted so badly to comfort him, to pull his face against her breast and to tell him she understood his disappointment, but he did not want that from her now. The wound was too fresh, his anger too profound. It was all the comfort he desired. She only hoped he would not cling to it until it burned him permanently inside.

With no more speech, he grasped her waist and waited stiffly for her to ready herself. After gathering as much of her skirts as she could in one hand, she rested the other on his shoulder and said, "Now, my lord." Then, drawing on his pent-up fury he tossed her up until her foot found the post. He held her hand until she had a secure grip on the fence with which to lower herself to the ground. Perhaps, because she had done it once before, this time she found her footing without a fall and with only a small tear in her skirt.

Peering warily through the hedge, she saw the house brightly lit by candles. Lanterns had been hung in the garden near the house, so the guests could refresh themselves with a walk around the parterre, but the corner where she stood was all in shadow. No one had seen her arrival. Now, she had only to smooth her hair and her skirts, put on her mask again, and pretend to be a guest returning after a stroll.

St. Mars called softly through the fence to ask whether she had landed without incident. She answered him that she had and waited, holding her breath, to see if he had anything else to say. But no more came to her through the palings. She listened to the wheels of his coach receding until there was not another sound.

A little more than a week later, Hester made her way through the streets to Hungerford Stairs. It was market day, and the shops in Hungerford Inn were bustling with shoppers with baskets hooked over their arms. As Hester neared the steps leading down to the Thames, she saw that the river was humming again with life. The clunks and splashes of oars and the snaps and creaks of sails floated up to her from the water, and the bankside bustled with cheerful wherrymen, relieved to have work again.

She had not spoken to St. Mars since the night of Nathan Breed's escape, but a message had arrived, inviting her to witness Tom and Katy's wedding. She had begged leave to visit her brother Jeremy in the City, and it was grudgingly given by her aunt. Mrs. Mayfield and Isabella had been so delighted with the ball, that for most of that week, Hester had basked, if not in their gratitude or approval, at least in their inattention. But now that the first glow of self-congratulations had worn off, things had returned to normal, and once again, Mrs. Mayfield resented any hint of indulgence towards her on the part of Isabella.

No one in her family had noticed her absense from the ball. If James Henry had, he had kept it to himself. The night's adventures had been so fraught with emotion, she had fallen into a deep sleep and had not risen until late the next morning. That evening, when Harrowby had returned to the house, it was clear that something had stunned him. Hester supposed he had paid a visit to Nancy's house to make up for his neglect on the night of the ball and had learned of his mistress's death.

She had observed him over the next few days as a range of emotions had altered his mood, beginning with shock, then relief as if a tremendous weight had been lifted from his shoulders, followed by elation as if he had been freed from a trap. She had searched for any sign of guilt in his demeanour, not for the relief he felt over Nancy's death, but for the lengths to which he had gone to conceal the truth—that his cousin St. Mars was innocent and should be Earl of Hawkhurst in his place. But little, if any, guilt had shadowed his relief.

Hester had considered confronting him with what she knew, but to do so would be to risk St. Mars's life. Harrowby could claim ignorance. He could deny that Nancy or Sir Walter had ever mentioned St. Mars's innocence to him, and it would be his word against Hester's, when the fact that she had consorted with an outlaw would condemn her in everyone's eyes. The thought of how deviously Mrs. Mayfield would work to keep her daughter's position was enough to deter her from trying to shame Harrowby into making the ethical choice and espousing his cousin's cause.

She dreaded the moment when St. Mars would ask her how Harrowby had reacted to the news of Nancy's death. She dreaded the disappointment she would surely see on his face.

At the top of Hungerford Stairs, she was hailed by the same gnome-like man who had brought her St. Mars's invitation to the Frost Fair. He beckoned her with a wave of his hand, and when she reached him, informed her that his master awaited her below in the boat. Giving his name again as Nate, he took her by the elbow and helped her down the steps, teeming with workers unloading barks, to the river where the boats were moored. In one of the wherries, she spied St. Mars, who stood up to hand her in.

For the occasion, he had dressed in his knee-length scarlet coat, to which Katy had added fresh gold braid, and the long black wig that concealed his yellow hair. His face was painted and patched until none but the most discerning eye would ever know him, but paint could not hide his strong, slender build or his striking sapphire eyes.

"We had best be quick," he said, as he helped Hester down on the bench and placed a blanket about her shoulders, "or they might be married before we arrive." While Nate unmoored the boat and jumped in, St. Mars joined her on the forward bench.

"I am sorry to arrive so late," Hester said. "I came as quickly as I dared, but my aunt gave me a last-minute task."

"I did not mean to scold you. The parson will wait, but Tom will be impatient. He has been waiting months for this."

On the seat across from them, Nate snorted. "The great noddy! He could've 'ad 'er to bed any time these two months past, if 'e weren't such a dunderhead."

St. Mars glanced at Hester with twinkling eyes. She was at pains to stifle a grin. "You think so, do you?" St. Mars said, turning back to Nate. Beneath the blanket, his hand found Hester's and gave it a squeeze, telling her he meant to egg his oarsman on.

Nate pulled with long, sullen strokes, "Aye. And it's a dog's business 'e's made of this weddin', too. Nobbut two witnesses! No noise and no drums. What kind o' weddin' is that, I arsk ye?"

"Perhaps Tom believes he is past the age of such tomfoolery."

"Pah! His bride's not, and so I told 'im. I told 'im, 'e could be married at the Bear Tavern, and a right time we'd all 'ave 'ad." Nate looked put out at the thought of missing a feast.

"It won't be quite as flat as you expect. You will just have to wait and see."

"And we mustn't abuse Tom," Hester said. "Not on his wedding day."

Nate scowled, but he swallowed further comments, reserving his energy for the row across the river. The morning air was still cold and Hester was grateful for the blankets St. Mars had supplied, as well as for the heat from his body, but there was so much she wanted to talk to him about and now was not the time. There was one thing she could ask him, though.

"Mr. Breed, my lord?" she said, glancing up at him.

"Safe," he answered, nodding. "Tom took him down into Kent, where no one will find him. As soon as the furor has died down, I will take him myself to the coast and help him to find a boat for France."

Hester wondered if he meant to take that boat himself and vowed to ask him before this morning was over. Tomorrow James Henry would return to Hawkhurst House, and she would have to reply to his offer of marriage. Somehow, between today and then, she would have to make her decision, but everything depended on St. Mars.

As if reading her mind, he suddenly released her hand and threw his arm about her shoulders to gather her close. "Tom will be grateful you came to witness his marriage, but we mustn't let you catch cold. You are trembling."

He felt as if he was trembling, too, but Hester did not point this out, just enjoyed the wonderful feel of his warmth. She was anxious to speak to him, but she would just have to wait.

Nate's strokes were long, powerful, and even, and before she thought to ask exactly where they were going, he had rowed them up on the opposite bank, where a strong smell of rotting plants and fish met her nostrils. Before reaching their mooring point, they had rowed past a row of respectable-looking houses, the kind that could belong to a farmer or merchant. Beyond them, however, the buildings were more squalid, with a tavern or two set among them.

Hester stayed seated until Nate had leapt out onto the bank and pulled the wherry farther out of the water. Then, St. Mars stepped out first, and, seeing how deep the mud was, decided to carry her up to higher ground. At his insistence, she put her arms about his neck and he scooped her up into his arms.

The bank was so slippery he had to keep his eyes on the ground before him. Hester did not dare breathe until he set her down on an earthen wall raised to prevent the river from flooding the boatmen's and sailors' houses which lined this part of the river. Children were skipping stones across the water and women carried baskets of fish. They stopped to stare at the finely-dressed couple landing in front of their houses. A pile of torn sails that needed mending stood outside one door.

Hester did not linger to see more, for St. Mars had no sooner put her down, than he pulled her to one of the wherryman's houses, where a horse was tied to a post, and a toothless old man, who had minded it for him, waited with a grin. The horse was not his beauty Penny, but a taller, long-necked bay, which she thought she recognized.

"Is this—?" she started to ask, as St. Mars tossed the man a coin and reached to untie the horse.

"Yes, it's Looby. Tom retrieved him from the coast." Choosing not to elaborate on an episode they both would prefer to forget, he avoided her gaze. With the same fast pace he had set, he led Hester to an over-turned boat and lifted her up onto it. "Use this for a mounting block." Then, with one leap he threw himself into the saddle. He brought the horse close beside the boat and, gathering her with one strong arm, pulled her up behind him to ride pillion on Looby's blanket.

Hester did not need to be told to hold on, for she had already grasped him about the waist.

"Good girl," St. Mars said, as she clung to his back. "If you are ready . . ." Feeling her nod, without another second's hesitation, he put his heels to Looby's flanks, and the horse started forward.

St. Mars kept his horse to a walk, for which Hester was grateful. She did not want to arrive at the church unkempt. Looby was steady on his feet, and his back was both flat and broad. In a short while, she felt secure enough to ease her desperate grip and to ask where they were going.

"To St. George the Martyr," St. Mars said. He spurred Looby across a ditch and up onto a raised lane. "There are only a few churches within reasonable distance of my house, and St. Mary Lambeth is too elegant for Tom. Besides, the Reverend Mr. Gibson has been there for

many years and might recognize me. I would not like to finish this day
in the Clink."

"No, indeed!" Hester said, giving an involuntary shiver.

St. Mars must have felt it, for he laughed. "St. George's will be fine
for all of us. We have only to steer a way through this mud and avoid
the Mint, and we'll be there in a little while."

"Where exactly are we?" she asked. Hester had never seen any of
the area between the horse ferry and London Bridge. The reputation of
the Bankside was unsavoury. For centuries it had housed all the vices
and dirty industries the City of London did not wish to deal with, but
at the moment all she saw were muddy fields that must be the market
gardens, attached to the respectable houses they had passed.

"We are just east of Cupid Gardens, there where the trees are,"
he said, pointing to his left. "The bowling green is that flat area this
side of them. This lane will take us round to the north of St. George's
Fields. That steeple you see over there is Christ Church."

The ground here was so low, she was surprised to see a church
built upon it. St. Mars explained that this was part of Lambeth Marsh.
The road was pitted and sunken and its holes were full of mud, but he
guided Looby around the worst of them. Soon Hester spied vineyards,
and gardens with leafless trees set out in rows, but in places the ground
was still low and spongy. Across the fields she could see more raised
earthen walls, and water from the melted snow collected in ponds.

The road bent left, and beyond them lay St. George's Fields, an immense open area, the commons of Southwark. Though no beasts were
grazing yet at this time of year, people still stood out in the fields and
in the lane. The road joined with another beside a vinegar yard. Here
they bore right and soon some cottages appeared, lining the north side
of the street.

"Hang on tightly," St. Mars said. "This would not be a good place
to fall off. We're not far from the Mint, and these people are not to be
trusted. No honest person would choose to walk here."

The Mint was still considered a sanctuary, inhabited by a mixture of desperate persons—prisoners of the King's Bench who had
purchased the liberty to live within its Rules, a group of debtors and
felons, sheltering from arrest, and a free population of former prison-

ers who chose to remain within its precinct. Hester held on, clasping her hands together about St. Mars's waist as he wove a path through narrow lanes filled with almshouses and brought them suddenly out into a much broader street, lined with respectable-looking inns. St. George's, with its square bell tower, stood just up the street. St. Mars guided Looby to the door, where a boy stood holding the reins of another horse, which Hester recognized as Tom's.

After Gideon lowered Mrs. Kean to the ground, he dismounted himself. He handed the boy his reins and promised him another penny, then ushered her inside.

Tom and Katy were waiting nervously near the altar. As Gideon and Mrs. Kean made their way up the aisle, a look of profound relief washed over Tom's broad face.

"Sorry to keep you waiting," Gideon said, "but now we're here. It's time to fetch the vicar."

He watched as Mrs. Kean greeted Katy and offered her best wishes for their happiness. He appreciated the courtesy and kindness with which she always treated his servants, greeting Katy with as much grace as duchess.

For her wedding, Katy had dressed in a simple gown. After tonight, though, according to custom, she would put on the new, finer gown he had bought her to alert everyone to the change in her status, but she could not look lovelier than she did right now with happiness radiating from her eyes. As they waited for Tom to return with the parson, Gideon glanced about him at the church, which he had never visited before. St. George the Martyr was an old church, large and spacious, with pillars, arches, and Gothic windows. Tombs and stones with Latin inscriptions lined the aisles. The floor had been repaved, and the paint and pews were new, but the foundation was bad and the floor had sunk in places, due to the marshy ground.

The vicar came then. As everything was in order—the license absolving Tom and Katy from the reading of banns having been obtained—in as short a time as anything could be accomplished, Tom and Katy were pronounced man and wife.

The vicar produced the parish registry and entered the bride's and groom's names. First Mrs. Kean signed as witness. Then she peered over Gideon's shoulder, he supposed, to see what name he would use. He signed it legally, Gideon Fitzsimmons, but in such a scrawl, he thought the vicar would find it impossible to read. Then, finished with the official business, Gideon gave Katy a hearty kiss upon both cheeks and offered Tom his hand to shake. When Tom hesitated, visibly moved and gratified by this condescension from his lord—the boy he had raised as much as anyone had—Gideon had to clear a sudden lump in his throat.

Tom finally shook his hand amidst the laughter, congratulations, and thanks that flew all around. Then he led Katy, Gideon, and Mrs. Kean outside into a glorious spring day.

As Tom went to fetch his horse, Gideon held Mrs. Kean back, and said quietly, "I don't suppose you could come to my house? I've engaged a surprise for the newly-weds."

A little gasp escaped her as her gaze flew to his face. Disappointment and regret softened her eyes.

"I dare not," she said. "If my aunt ever discovered how many times I've used Jeremy as an excuse to leave the house, when I have not visited him in months, she would have my head. And she would ask a multitude of questions, I should never be able to answer. I've used that excuse so often these past few months, my real concern is that Jeremy will come searching for me, wondering why I have not been round to see him and Sally. I absolutely must go see them today."

A wave of melancholy swept through Gideon, but he smiled in understanding. She had risked so much censure in his behalf, he should not press her. But he dreaded the rest of the day without her, when his house would be filled with neighbours, celebrating Tom's and Katy's nuptials. Wedding festivities could easily last into the night, and there would be nowhere he could go to escape them.

"Then, I shall see you to a boat," he said, as lightly as he could. "But before I do, would you have a few moments to take a turn here in the churchyard?"

When she agreed to that, he called out for Tom and Katy to ride on. "I will join you as soon as I've escorted Mrs. Kean to the river."

They waved the newly-wedded pair away and then Gideon offered her his arm. They strolled slowly among the few graves in the churchyard. Since the trees had not yet put out their leaves, most of the yard still looked lifeless except for the hawthorn bushes growing in bunches. The only thing blooming was a Jack-run-along-the-hedge, with its white, star-shaped, fragrant flowers.

A rabbit, startled by their passage, scurried beneath a bush, and a small flock of sparrows took wing.

"What is the surprise you have planned for Tom?" Mrs. Kean asked, breaking their silence.

"Oh, the usual . . . I told the farmer's wife who occasionally comes in to give Katy a hand that the wedding would take place this morning. I expect she'll have the neighbours there all ready to beleaguer the couple with hoots and drums, and will have a posset cooking over the fire. The only thing for me to do will be to pay the drummers."

"Will Tom not mind? He seems such a quiet sort of fellow."

Gideon grinned. "I'm quite certain he will mind. He'll fume and fuss, but in the end, all the nonsense will make him forget how nervous he is about tonight's activities. I know him, you see."

She dimpled at him, trying to hide a smile. "I can see you do. And what about Katy?"

He replied more seriously, "I believe Katy will feel more honoured if her marriage is celebrated in the traditional way. She has not had an easy life, you know."

The approving expression on her face gave him the answer he'd been looking for. "That was very wise of you, my lord."

Their stroll had taken them once around the yard, and now they found themselves at the base of the steeple. When Mrs. Kean paused as if to suggest she must be going, Gideon hastened to speak about his reason for asking her to delay her return.

"I never thanked you for your assistance the other night," he said. "And I must beg your forgiveness for my behaviour, but I was taken by surprise."

She did not pretend to misunderstand him. Her hand tightened on his arm. "My lord, I wish you will not apologize. Of course you were shocked, as I was myself. I have tried to think of a way to reveal Nancy's confession to the authorities, but every idea I have seems too risky, when your cousin . . . ."

He waited for her to finish, but when she did not, he ended her sentence himself, "When my cousin is likely to deny it. I know. Do not blame yourself, my dear. I, too, realize that Harrowby was willing to pay a fortune to hold onto the title that was taken from me. I only wish to know whether he's been aware of my innocence all along." He was sorry that some of the bitterness he felt had entered his voice. He had promised himself he would not display the feelings that had seized him on the night of Nancy's death, even though they had kept him awake for hours every night since.

"Oh no, my lord!" Mrs. Kean said, turning to him with an earnest gaze. "I cannot believe that he knew. As much as I deplore your cousin's selfishness and his moral corruption, I believe the knowledge that you were innocent came to him as a shock. There was never the slightest hint of guilt in his demeanour until Sir Walter came into his life. I can almost give you the hour he must first have threatened your cousin with losing the title, the change in his manner towards Sir Walter was so sudden."

Gideon heaved an inward sigh. "Well, that is something at least. It is easier to forgive Harrowby for not wishing to give up a powerful position than for scheming against me to get it." He forced a rueful smile. "Thank you, my dear. As usual, you have managed to make things better."

He turned to face her and reached to draw her into his arms, but with a slight gasp, she pulled away from him. She turned to stroll again, withdrawing as if behind a screen. The coolness she had demonstrated towards him, which had seemed resolved on the night of Breed's escape, was once again between them.

Feeling a pain in his chest, he tried to cover up his hurt, by changing the subject, but found he had to clear his throat first. "I returned to Nancy's house. It occurred to me that she might have had something in writing that proves my innocence, but the place was locked, and there were too many people about. When I went back again, all her things had been removed, but I've seen nothing about Nancy's death in the newssheets."

"Neither have I. I can only assume that Alfred carried her body from the house, as he must have done with Sir Walter's. He might have been afraid to be accused of her death. If she was found, it's possible that the death of a courtesan did not merit the attention of our newspaper writers."

"You must be correct. I half-expected him to come to my house to find me, but then he doesn't know that the man he followed there is Blue Satan." Thinking of Nancy, and how she had used so many to her own ends, he suppressed a shiver. "What a ghastly, cold woman she was!"

She peered at him sideways from beneath her lashes, a touch of the old teasing in her smile. "Ghastly . . . but beautiful, too. You must have found her so, my lord."

He chuckled and would have raised her hand to kiss it, if he had not been afraid she might withdraw from him again. "Very well. I admit I thought her beautiful at first, but it was not long before her avarice and her callousness made her repugnant to me. Didn't Shakespeare say, '. . . beauty lives with kindness'?"

"If he did, I much prefer him to Mr. Farquhar, who, as I recall, said, 'No woman can be a beauty without a fortune.'"

He laughed, grateful that whatever had made her reject him, they were still friends. He could not understand her. There were times he'd been sure that she would welcome his kisses. She never seemed to mind his closeness, but for whatever reason she was unwilling to let him take it any farther. It might simply be her sense of virtue, and yet he knew there was something more. Whatever it was, it was driving him slowly and painfully mad. He did not know how much longer he could continue to be patient, especially when no other woman appealed to him now. Did she not feel as he did that they were meant to be lovers?

They had made their second tour of the yard, this time without the company of rabbits or sparrows. The sun was moving higher in the sky, and by the time she reached Sally's bookstall, where her brother Jeremy was certain to be, the morning would be nearly gone.

He could tell that the same thought was in her head as she turned her nervous gaze his way, so with a nod, he directed their steps towards the boy who was still holding onto Looby.

Once they were both mounted again, he did not retrace the way they had come, but instead took her up St. Margaret's Hill and the borough High Street, until they came to London Bridge. At the foot of the bridge, he set her down and dismounted to escort her to the bottom of Pepper Alley Stairs. Neither had spoken during the brief ride. Gideon had tried not to focus on the hands gently looped around his waist. If he let himself imagine them stroking the rest of his body, he would lose his sanity, and the loneliness that faced him until they met again was hard enough to bear.

She would have walked down the slippery stairs alone, if he had not insisted on accompanying her, but he was in no hurry to release her. He paid the wherryman in advance to take her to Temple Stairs, the nearest disembarking point to St. Dunstan's Church, against which Sally's bookstall stood.

Mrs. Kean gave him her hand to bid him goodbye, but before she did, she smiled at him and said in a friendly voice, "May I ask what you intend to do now, my lord?"

He cocked his head, momentarily puzzled. "I shall return to my house, in time, I suppose, for the stockings to be thrown."

She gave an embarrassed laugh, and her voice trembled, as if it were difficult for her to ask the question. "I did not mean today, but in the days or weeks to come. I wondered if you had given any thought to what you might do or where you might go."

She waited for him to answer, and she seemed to swallow. Now that he understood her question, though, he knew that her thoughts, as usual, had paralleled his own.

"I see," he said. "Yes, I have thought of going to France. With the Pretender defeated, the Channel should be relatively safe, and if I do not go within the next few months, I could be trapped here by the weather again."

The pink that had coloured her cheeks seemed to drain from her face, but she smiled politely. Her voice shook, as she offered him her hand and said, "Then I shall wish you a successful voyage, my lord."

Thinking she feared for his safety again, he grinned at her and said, "Aren't you going to try to stop me? No words of caution?"

She pulled back her hand, looking as if he had slapped her. Then, not meeting his gaze, she shook her head and said with an uncomfortable laugh, "No, indeed, my lord. You must do whatever pleases you," and turning to go, raised her skirt with one hand and, taking the boatman's hand with the other, stepped into the boat.

This all transpired so fast that Gideon did not know what had happened. He knew that his teasing had somehow gone awry, that something he had said had upset her. But as her boat floated away, she raised a hand and waved, as if nothing had disturbed her. He returned the wave and stood watching her boat growing smaller in the distance.

He no longer understood Mrs. Kean, he thought miserably, as he climbed the stairs and untied Looby. Hoisting himself into the saddle, he wondered again if something could be going on at Hawkhurst House, something she could not tell him about. If there were, and that was what had come between them, he would get to the bottom of it. He would not lose Mrs. Kean.

As Hester was rowed away from him, she felt that her heart would break. He was leaving again, and she did not know if he ever meant to return. Why should he, when he could live openly in France, and this last experience must have convinced him he would never regain his freedom in England? Every time she saw him, she was struck by his increasing loneliness and boredom. There was no life for him here, no justice. She could only imagine the hurt he had felt on learning that his cousin Harrowby would pay an extortioner and lie to keep his title from him. No, St. Mars would be much happier in France, and she should not wish to keep him here.

Now she knew what her answer to James Henry must be. She would be a fool not to accept him. It was what she must do to stop this pointless hoping that St. Mars would fall in love with her, for she could not waste what was left of her youth, perhaps even her life if she was taken by a fever, as so many were. St. Mars had not invited her to go to France with him. He enjoyed flirting with her. He would be happy to kiss her. But he did not love her.

She would do the rational thing. She just wished she had not revealed her hurt feelings so blatantly to St. Mars just now. She knew he had just been teasing, but still his words had stung. He would never hurt her on purpose, nor could he know what was in her head. It was only because she wanted him to say something else to her that she had taken his teasing amiss.

James Henry would be with her tomorrow afternoon and she would thank him for his generous offer, and by the time St. Mars returned to England—if he did, and truly, she saw no reason why he should—she should be married and living in Kent.

In the afternoon of the following day, Hester stood to greet James Henry where she had awaited him in the small parlour behind the saloon. With trembling knees and a knot lodged stubbornly in her gullet, she answered his sober bow with a curtsy, before inviting him to sit in the chair next to her.

She asked if his journey had been pleasant, and for a few minutes they exchanged polite conversation, while her heart fluttered in her ribs like a wild bird in a cage. Throughout a sleepless night, she had reviewed her circumstances again and again, but had always reached the same conclusion. The only sensible course for her was to marry this sober, kind, generous man, who was watching her intently for any sign that might reveal her thoughts.

Finally, after a moment of uneasy silence, he said, "Mrs. Kean, it has been a month or more since I asked for your hand in marriage. Did you come to a decision?"

Hester opened her mouth to speak, but emotion clogged her throat. When she managed to clear it, her voice was shaking. "I did," she said. "Your offer is far more generous than I can ever deserve, and nothing would do me greater honour than to be your wife. I respect you more than anyone I know, and I believe we could deal together. For these reasons, as well as for a multitude of very selfish ones, I decided to accept your proposal today."

She paused. He was frowning in concentration, attending to her every word, but there was no joy, no spark—not even a sign of relief—on his face. She swallowed a lump so painful that her eyes misted over.

"It would be very wrong of me to accept your offer, however. You are an inestimable man, Mr. Henry, and you deserve to have a wife you truly love and who truly loves you. I am aware that a major reason for your offering for me is the pity you feel for me in my circumstances. We are both alone, and—yes, lonely, perhaps, and since your fancy has not lit upon any other lady, you have settled for me with the very best of motives. But I would be doing you too great a wrong to rob you of the prospect of real joy when you someday meet a lady to whom you can give your heart instead of merely your goodwill."

He listened to her without a word, his frown deepening. Now, as she finished, his gaze fell on the hands clasped tightly in his lap.

Hester's lips trembled and her eyes filled. The last thing she had wanted to do was to hurt him. She hoped he would still be her friend, for she had come to rely on his support in the household, and without it, her life would be even more dismal than it was. But she knew she had made the right choice. Already, the weight that had oppressed her breast for weeks was lifting. There was sadness, especially when she thought of the children she would never have, but how could she have contemplated accepting James Henry when she knew he did not love her as a man should love his wife? It would not be fair to him, and only now had she realized how much a burden that unfairness had been to her unconscious mind.

He looked up, and a reluctant smile eased his face. "I was looking forward to your companionship," he said, "but I see that what I offered is not enough."

She quickly reached over to grasp his hands. "It is not enough for you either. It should not be. At least, if you do end up marrying just for companionship, you might marry a woman with some property. There is nothing I could bring to you but my friendship, and you already have that."

His smile broadened, and he patted her hand. "I doubt I shall meet another lady who merits the respect I have for you."

"Perhaps not," she said, lightening her voice, "but I do not know that respect is the first feeling a gentleman wishes to have for his wife, as much as she might desire it. For women for their husbands, it may be, but I have yet to hear a poet or a gallant extolling the respect he has for the object of his desire."

His cheeks took on a more vivid hue. He looked down at her hand in his lap, and released it, too shy to meet her gaze. He sighed and looked about as if ready to leave. "Well . . . that is that, then, I suppose."

"Yes, and if I were you, I should make my escape before anything occurs to change my mind. I did not refuse you without many regrets, I promise you."

A faint look of alarm crossed his features, and Hester had to laugh, though he quickly hid it. He stood and bowed to her, taking the hand she extended and kissing it. "If you ever do change your mind, or if I can be of any assistance, you must tell me."

"No to the first—you must not leave such a generous offer open-ended—but a hearty yes to the second. I do not know what I would do without your friendship in this house. And as unlikely as it seems that I could be of any help to you, I hope you will consider me, if ever the situation arises."

That seemed to recall something to his mind, and after apologizing for changing the subject, he said, "Before joining you here, I was with my lord, and I was very happy to hear that he wishes me to cancel the order for the carriage you and I discussed." James Henry looked quiz-zically at her, clearly asking what she knew about this development.

Hester could not think of Nancy's death without a shudder. Sober-ly, she said, "There should not be any more expenses in that quarter."

"Indeed?"

His expression invited her to elaborate, but she did not want to talk about Nancy. Let him think she was too demure to discuss their lord's mistress.

She said merely, "I understand there has been a breach."

He looked gratified. "Then let us hope he does not find another distraction anytime soon."

As James Henry took his leave, Hester thought she would be very surprised if Harrowby took another mistress, at least before a very long time had passed. If anyone had ever been punished for the sin of lust, Harrowby had.

Now, he was positively jubilant, making plans for summer. As soon as the King left for Hanover, they would be travelling, maybe to

Tunbridge Wells, maybe farther—he had not decided.

At least for Hester, it would be a much-needed change of scenery while she grieved for the opportunity she had just thrown away and the possibility that she would never see St. Mars again.

THE END

AUTHOR'S NOTE

The advantage of doing extensive research is that so many ideas come from it, including suggestions for characters. As I have noted in previous books, the dearth of diaries and letters for the years 1715–1716 was due to fears that the government would seize them and use them to prove malfeasance or treason. One of the only diaries in existence is that of Mary, Lady Cowper, who was Lady of the Bedchamber to the Princess of Wales, and I am grateful to her for the Court gossip, the comings and goings of the royal family, and character sketches of the persons at Court. She seems more reliable in this regard than Lady Mary Wortley Montagu, who by the time of this book, had left to accompany her husband on a diplomatic assignment to the Ottoman Empire.

My character, Madame Schultz, was modeled on Mademoiselle Schutz, the niece of Baron Bernstorff, the Hanoverian minister who accompanied George I to England. Perhaps because of the enmity between the King and the Prince of Wales, Lady Cowper did not trust either Baron Bernstorff or his niece. In November, 1715, Mademoiselle Schutz brought Lady Cowper an offer from the baron that if she wished, he would let her kinsman Tom Forster escape upon the road to London after his capture. Lady Cowper did not know how to interpret the offer, so she did not take advantage of it. Later, Tom Forster did escape from Newgate just a few days before the date appointed for his trial, possibly with the baron's assistance, but to my knowledge there is no proof of this. In any case, Mademoiselle Schutz's impertinent attempts to gain bribes for her connection to the King, recounted in Lady Cowper's diary, struck me as comic.

The escape of Nathan Breed from Newgate was modeled on Lord Nithsdale's escape from the Tower. His wife smuggled in women's clothes, and together they left with Lord Nithsdale—a member of the Maxwell clan—disguised as his wife's maid. On hearing of her husband's capture, Lady Nithsdale had ridden on horseback through the brutal cold all the way from Scotland to plead her husband's case. When George I refused to pardon him, she grasped hold of his coat tails and was dragged across the room before he managed to break her hold. After their escape, they eventually made their way to the Pretender's court in Rome, where they lived and died in poverty, faithful Jacobites to the last.

The Frost Fairs of London were scattered over several centuries, the first recorded in the year 1150 A.D. Queen Elizabeth attended the Frost Fair of 1564–65, but the first great fair was in the winter of 1683–84. It held every entertainment that Bartholomew Fair promised, from bull-baiting and bear-baiting to gambling dens and bawdy houses. The ice supported coaches with as many as six horses under harness. Charles II took a large party to enjoy the treat. I could find no evidence that King George or the Prince and Princess of Wales attended the 1715–16 Frost Fair, but by this time fairs in general had fallen into disfavor because of their rowdy natures. Other Frost Fairs occurred in the winters of 1739–40, 1788–89, and the last and greatest in 1813–14, the last time the Thames froze hard enough to hold one. The new London Bridge, constructed when the old one was torn down in 1825, allowed the current of the Thames to increase, making it far more unlikely to freeze. This also coincided with the end of what is called the Little Ice Age, a period of cooling that lasted roughly three centuries.

After the failure of the "Fifteen" as it is known, James Stuart made other attempts to gain the throne of England, including a failed invasion in 1719, backed by Spain, but never again would so many Englishmen take up arms in his name. He was banished to Rome, where his plots became more difficult and even more ineffectual. This did not stop a large percentage of the English from bemoaning his loss, and the Jacobite spy wars continued up until his son, Bonnie Prince Charlie, took over the cause as the New Pretender, his story playing out in the rebellion of 1745.

After making an example of Lords Derwentwater and Kenmure, King George became more merciful, understanding that the public execution of Englishmen would not endear him to the English people. He opposed Robert Walpole and his own Hanoverian ministers who advised punishing the rebels to the extent of the law. In 1717, he signed an Act of Grace, releasing the Jacobite lords remaining in the Tower, and he decided that income from the rebels' forfeited estates should be used to provide schools in the Highlands and to reduce the public debt of Britain. He ignored a great deal of the Jacobite unrest in London until looting and burning terrorized law-abiding citizens. After five looters were hanged in 1716, for the attack on Read's Mughouse, the violent protests came to an end.

The challenge with this book was to make the two historical elements I wanted to include come together in a plot. These were the Frost Fair and the rebels in prison, awaiting their sentence of death. I hope I have succeeded.